Janus

ANDRE NORTON

JANUS

This is a work of fiction. All the characters and events portrayed in this book are fictional, and any resemblance to real people or incidents is purely coincidental.

A Baen Books Original

Baen Publishing Enterprises
P.O. Box 1403
Riverdale, NY 10471
www.baen.com

ISBN: 0-7434-7180-6

Cover art by Larry Elmore

First paperback printing, January 2004

Library of Congress Catalog Number 2002023223

Distributed by Simon & Schuster
1230 Avenue of the Americas
New York, NY 10020

Produced by Windhaven Press, Auburn, NH
Printed in the United States of America

"The *Grand Dame* of science fiction."
—*Time*

How far away was the river? Naill tried to place landmarks about him. And then he heard the hounds again—faint, to be sure, but with an exultant note in their cry. They had picked up the fugitives' trail, knew the scent was fresh. He hoped they were still leashed.

Ashla huddled down, her eyes wide and wild as she watched his every move. But she no longer tried to scream. If he could only bring Illylle memory to the surface of her mind again!

"Illylle!" Naill did not try to touch her, made no move toward the shaking girl. "You are Illylle of the Iftin," he said slowly.

Her head shook from side to side, denying that.

"You are Illylle—I am Ayyar," he continued doggedly. "They hunt us—we must go—to the forest—to Iftcan."

She made a small choking sound and her tongue swept across her lips. Then she lunged past him, to the side of the pool, hanging over the water and staring down at her reflection there. From mirror to man she glanced up, down, up. Apparently she was satisfying herself that there was a resemblance between what she saw in the water and Naill.

"I—am—not—" She choked again, her wailing appeal breaking through her hostility.

"You are Illylle," he responded. "You have been ill, with the fever, and you have had ill dreams."

"This is a dream!" She caught him up.

Naill shook his head. "This is real. That"—he waved a hand southward—"is the dream. Now—listen!"

The baying reached their ears.

"Hounds!" She identified that sound correctly, glanced apprehensively over her shoulder. "But why?"

"Because we are of the Iftin, of the forest. We must go!"

BAEN BOOKS by ANDRE NORTON

Time Traders
Time Traders II
Star Soldiers
Warlock
Janus
Darkness & Dawn

Contents

Judgment on Janus

ONE

THE STUFF OF DREAMS

Here even the sun was cold. Its light hurt the eyes as it glittered on the square, sullen blocks of the Dipple. Naill Renfro leaned his forehead against the chill surface of the window, trying not to think—not to remember—to beat down those frightening waves of rage and frustration that brought a choking sensation into his throat these past few days, a stone heaviness to his chest.

This was the Dipple on the planet of Korwar—the last refuge, or rather prison, for the planetless flotsam of a space war. Forced from their home worlds by battle plans none of them had had a voice in framing, they had been herded here years ago. Then, when that war was over, they discovered there was no return. The homes they could remember were gone—either blasted into uninhabitable cinders through direct action,

3

or signed away at conference tables so that other settlers now had "sole rights" there. The Dipple was a
place to rot, another kind of death for those planted
arbitrarily within its walls. A whole generation of spir-
itless children was growing up in it, to which this was
the only known way of life.

But for those who could remember . . .

Naill closed his eyes. Limited space, curved walls,
the endless throb of vibrating engines driving a Free
Trader along uncharted "roads" of space, exciting
glimpses of strange worlds, weird creatures, new
peoples—some alien of mind and body, some resembling the small boy who lurked in the background,
drinking in avidly all the wonders of a trade
meeting . . . these he could remember. Then
confusion—fear, which formed a cold lump in a small
stomach, a sour taste in throat and mouth—lying in
the cramped berth space of an escape boat with warm
arms about him—the shock of the thrust-away from
the ship that had always been his home—the period
of drift while a mechanical signal broadcast their
plight—the coming of the cruiser to pick them up as
the only survivors. Afterwards—the Dipple—for years
and years and years—always the Dipple!

But there had been hope that the war would end
soon, that when he was big enough, old enough, strong
enough, he could sign on a Free Trader, or that they
would somehow find credit deposits owed to Duan
Renfro and buy passage back to Mehetia. Wild dreams
both those hopes had been. The dull, dusty years had
wasted them, shown them to be flimsy shadows. There
was only the Dipple, and that would go on forever—
from it there was no escape. Or, if there was for him,
not for her—now.

Naill wanted to cover his ears as well as close his
eyes. He could shut out the grayness of the Dipple;

he could not shut out now that weary little plaint, half croon, half moan, sounding monotonously from the bed against the far wall. He swung away from the window and came to stand at the side of the bed, forcing himself to look at the woman who lay there.

She—she was nothing but a frail wraith of skin and bones, not Malani.

Naill wanted to beat his fists against the gray wall, to cry out his hurt and rage—yes, and fear—as might a small child. It was choking him. If he could only gather her up, run away from this place of unending harsh light, cold grayness. It had killed Malani, as much as Duan Renfro's death. The ugliness and the hopelessness of the Dipple had withered her.

But instead of giving way to the storm within him, Naill knelt beside the bed, caught those restless, ever-weaving hands in his own, bringing their chill flesh against his thin cheeks.

"Malani—" He called her name softly, hoping against all hope that this time she would respond, know him. Or was it far more kind not to draw her back? Draw her back—Naill sucked in his breath—there was a way for Malani to escape! If he were just sure, overwhelmingly sure that no other road existed . . .

Gently he put down her hands, pulled the covering up about her shoulders. Once sure . . . He nodded sharply, though Malani could not see that gesture of sudden decision. Then he went swiftly to the door. Three strides down the corridor and he was rapping on another door.

"Oh—it's you, boy!" The impatient frown on the woman's broad face smoothed. "She's worse?"

"I don't know. She won't eat, and the medico . . ."

The woman's lips shaped a word she did not say. "He's said she ain't got a chance?"

"Yes."

"For once he's right. She don't want any chance—you gotta face that, boy."

What else had he been doing for the past weeks! Naill's hands were fists against his sides as he fought down a hot response to that roughly kind truth.

"Yes," he returned flatly. "I want to know—how soon . . . ?"

The woman swept back a loose lock of hair, her eyes grew suddenly bright and hard, locking fast to his in an unasked question. Her tongue showed between her lips, moistened them.

"All right." She closed the door of her own quarters firmly behind her. "All right," she repeated as if assuring herself in some way.

But when she stood beside Malani, she was concerned, her hands careful, even tender. Then she once more drew up the covers, looked to Naill.

"Two days—maybe a little more. If you do it—where's the credits coming from?"

"I'll get them!"

"She—she wouldn't want it that way, boy."

"She'll have it!" He caught up his over-tunic. "You'll stay until I come back?"

The woman nodded. "Stowar is the best. He deals fair—never cuts . . ."

"I know!" Naill's impatience made that answer almost explosive.

He hurried down the corridor, the four flights of stairs, out into the open. It was close to midday, there were few here. Those who had been lucky enough to find casual labor for the day were long since gone; the others were in the communal dining hall for the noon meal. But there were still those who had business in certain rooms, furtive business.

Korwar was, except for the Dipple, a pleasure planet. Its native population lived by serving the great and the wealthy of half a hundred solar systems. And in addition to the usual luxuries and pleasures, there were the fashionable vices, forbidden joys fed by smuggled and outlawed merchandise. A man could, if he were able to raise the necessary credits, buy into the Thieves' Guild and become a member of one of those supply lines. But there was also a fringe of small dealers who grabbed at the crumbs the Thieves' captains did not bother to touch.

They lived dangerously and they were recruited from the hopelessly reckless—from the Dipple dregs, such as Stowar. What he sold were pleasures of a kind. Pleasure—or a way of easy dying for a beaten and helpless woman.

Naill faced the pale boy lounging beside a certain doorway, met squarely the narrow eyes in that ratlike face. He said only a name: "Stowar."

"Business, boot?"

"Business."

The boy jerked a thumb over his shoulders, rapped twice on the door.

"Take it, boot."

Naill pushed open the door. He felt like coughing; the smoke of a hebel stick was thick and cloying. There were four men sitting on cushions about a bros table playing star-and-comet, the click of their counters broken now and then by a grunt of dissatisfaction as some player failed to complete his star.

"What is it?" Stowar's head lifted perhaps two inches. He glanced at Naill, acknowledging his presence with that demand. "Go on—say something—we're all mates here."

One of the players giggled; the other two made no sign they heard, their attention glued to the table.

"You have haluce—how much?" Naill came to the point at once.

"How much do you want?"

Naill had made his calculation on the way over. If Mara Disa could be relied upon, one pack . . . no, better two, to be safe.

"Two packs."

"Two packs—two hundred credits," Stowar returned. "Stuff's uncut—I give full measure."

Naill nodded. Stowar was honest in his fashion, and you paid for that honesty. Two hundred credits. Well, he hardly expected to have it for less. The stuff was smuggled, of course, brought in from off-world by some crewman who wanted to pick up extra funds and was willing to run the risk of port inspection.

"I'll have it—in an hour."

Stowar nodded. "You do that, and the stuff's yours . . . My deal, Gram."

Naill breathed deeply in the open, driving the stink from his lungs. There was no use going back to their own room, turning over their miserable collection of belongings to raise twenty credits—let alone two hundred. He had long ago sold everything worthwhile to bring in the specialist from the upper city. No, there was only one thing left worth two hundred credits—himself. He began to walk, his pace increasing as he went, as if he must do this swiftly, before his courage failed. He was trotting when he reached that other building set so conveniently and threateningly near the main gate of the Dipple—the Off-Planet Labor Recruiting Station.

There were still worlds, plenty of them, where cheap labor was human labor, not imported machines which required expert maintenance and for which parts had to be imported at ruinous shipping rates. And such places as the Dipple were forcing beds for that labor. A man or woman could sign up, receive "settlement pay," be shipped out in frozen sleep, and then work for freedom—in five years, ten, twenty. On the surface that was a way of escape out of the rot of the Dipple. Only—frozen sleep was chancy: there were those who never awoke on those other worlds. And what awaited those who did was also chancy—arctic worlds, tropical worlds, worlds where men toiled under the lash of nature run wild. To sign was a gamble in which no one but the agency ever won.

Naill came to the selector, closed his eyes for a long moment, and then opened them. When he put his hand to that lever, pulled it down, he would take a step from which there would be no returning—ever.

An hour later he was once more at Stowar's. The star-and-comet game had broken up; he found the smuggler alone. And he was glad that was so as he put down the credit slip.

"Two fifty," Stowar read. From beneath the table he brought a small package. "Two here—and you get fifty credits back. Signed up for off-world?"

"Yes." Naill scooped up the packet, the other credit slip.

"You coulda done different," Stowar observed.

Naill shook his head.

"No? Maybe you're right at that. There're two kinds. All right, you got what you wanted—and it's all prime."

Naill's pace was almost a run as he came back to the home barracks. He hurried up the stairs, down the corridor. Mara Disa looked up as he breathlessly entered.

"The medico was here again—Director sent him."

"What did he say?"

"The same—two days—maybe three . . ."

Naill dropped down on the stool by the table. He had believed Mara earlier; this confirmation should not have made that much difference. Now he unrolled the package from Stowar—two small metal tubes. They were worth it—worth selling himself into slavery on an unknown world, worth everything that might come to him in the future . . . because of what they held for the dying woman who was his mother.

Haluce—the powder contained in one of those tubes—was given in a cup of hot water. Then Malani Renfro would not lie here in the Dipple; she would be reliving for a precious space of time the happiest day of her life. And if the thin thread that held her to this world had not broken by the time she roused from that sleep, there was the second draught to be sure. She had had to live in terror, defeat, and pain. She would die in happiness.

He looked up to meet Mara's gaze. "I'll give her this." He touched the nearer tube. "If—if there is need—you'll do the other?"

"You won't be here?"

That was the worst—to go and not to know, not to be sure. He tried to answer and it came out of him in a choked cry. Then he mastered himself to say slowly, "I—I ship out tonight . . . They've given me two hours . . . You—you'll swear to me that you'll be with her . . . ? See"—he unrolled the slip for fifty credits—"this—take this and swear it!"

"Naill!" There was a spark of heat in her eyes. "All right, boy, I'll swear it. Though we don't have much to do with any of the old gods or spirits here, do we? I'll swear—though you need not ask that. And I'll take this, too—because of Wace. Wace, he's got to get out of here . . . not by your road, either!" Her hands tightened convulsively on the credit slip. Naill could almost feel the fierce determination radiating from her. Wace Disa would be free of the Dipple if his mother could fight for him.

"Where did you sign for?" she asked as she went to heat the water container.

"Some world called Janus," he answered. Not that it mattered—it would be a harsh frontier planet very far removed from the Dipple or Korwar, and he did not want to think of the future.

"Janus," Mara repeated. "Never heard of that one. Listen, boy, you ain't ate anything this morning. I got some patter-cakes, made 'em for Wace. He musta got labor today, he ain't come back. Let me—"

"No—I'm shipping out, remember." Naill managed a shadow smile. "Listen, Mara, you see to things—afterwards—won't you?" He looked about the room. Nothing to be taken with him; you didn't carry baggage in a freeze cabin. Again he paused to master his voice. "Anything here you can use—it's yours. Not much left—except . . ." He went directly to the box where they had kept their papers, their few valuables.

His mother's name bracelets and the girdle Duan had traded for on Sargol were long since gone. Naill sorted through the papers quickly. Those claim sheets they had never been able to use—might as well destroy them; their identity disks . . .

"These go to the Director—afterwards. But there's this." Naill balanced in his hand Duan Renfro's master's ring. "Sell it—and see . . . she has flowers . . . she loves flowers . . . trees . . . the growing things . . ."

"I'll do it, boy."

Somehow he was certain Mara would. The water was steaming now. Naill measured a portion into a cup, added the powder from the tube. Together they lifted Malani's head, coaxed her to swallow.

Naill again nestled one of the wasted hands against his cheek, but his eyes were for the faint curve of smile on those blue lips. A tinge of happiness spread like a gossamer veil over the jutting of the cheekbones, the sharp angles of chin and jaw. No more moaning—just now and then a whisper of a word or a name. Some he knew, some were strange, out of a past he had not shared. Malani was a girl again, back on her home world of shallow seas beaded with rings and circles of islands, where tall trees rustled in the soft breeze that always came in late spring. Willingly she had traded that for life on a ship, following Duan Renfro out into the reaches of space, marrying a man who had called no world, but a ship, home.

"Be happy." Naill put down her hand. He had given her all he had left to give, this last retracing—past care, sorrow, and the unforgivable present—into her treasured past.

"You there—you Naill Renfro?"

The man in the doorway wore the badged tunic of the Labor Agency, a stunner swung well to the fore at his belt. He was a typical hustler—one of the guards prepared to see the catch on board the waiting transport.

"I'm coming." Naill gently adjusted the blanket, got to his feet. He had to go fast, not looking back, never looking back now. But he halted to rap on Mara's door.

"I'm going," he told her. "You will watch?"

"I'll watch. And I'll do all the rest—just like you'd want it. Good luck, boy!" But it was plain that she thought that last a wasted wish.

Naill walked for the last time down the hall, trying to make his mind a blank, or at least hold to the thought that Malani was out of the Dipple in another way, a far better way. The guard gathered up two more charges and delivered them all at the processing section of the port. Naill submitted without question to the procedure that would turn him from a living, breathing man into a helpless piece of cargo, valuable enough once it was delivered intact and revived. But what he carried with him into the sleep of the frozen was the memory of that shadowy smile he had seen on his mother's face.

How long that voyage lasted, what path it took among the stars, and for what purpose, Naill was never to know, or really care. Janus must be a frontier world, or else human labor would not be necessary there. But that was the sum total of his knowledge concerning it. And he was not awake to see the huge dark green ball grow on the pilot's vision plate, develop wide continents and narrow seas—the land choked with the dense green of forests, vast virgin forests that more civilized planets had long since forgotten existed.

The spaceport on which the cargo vessel landed was a stretch of bare rockland, scarred and darkened by the years of fiery lashing from arriving and departing ships. And extending irregularly from that center were the clearings made by the settlers.

Garths had been hacked out of the forest, bare spots in the dark green. The green carried a hint of gray, as if some of the wide leaves of those giant trees had been powdered with a film of silver. Men cleared fields, setting disciplined rows of their own plants criss-crossing those holdings, with the logs of the forest hollowed, split, and otherwise forced into serving as shelters for the men who had downed them.

This was a war between man and tree, with here a runner of vine, there a thrust of bush, or a sprout of sapling tonguing out to threaten a painfully cleared space. Always the forest waited . . . and so did that which was within the forest . . .

The men who fought that battle were grim, silent, as iron-tough as the trees, and stubborn as space-scoured metal. Their war had begun a hundred years earlier, when the first Survey Scout had marked Janus for human settlement. An earlier attempt to conquer the world for man had failed. Then these off-worlders had come and stayed. But still the forest had been cleared only a little—a very little.

Settlers were moving portward from the scattered garths, gathering at the town they hated but which they had to endure as their link off-world. These were hard men, bound together by a stern, joyless, religious belief and unshakable self-confidence. These were men who labored steadily through the daylight hours, who mistrusted beauty and ease as part of deadly sin, who forced themselves and their children, their labor slaves, into a dull pattern of work and worship. Such came now to buy fresh labor in order to fight the forest and all it held.

TWO

FRINGE OF FOREST

"This is the lot, garthmaster. Why should I hold back my wares?" The cargomaster of the space freighter balanced lightly, his fists resting on his hips, a contemptuous light in his eyes. Beside the would-be customer he was wire-slim and boyish in appearance.

"For forest biting, for fieldwork, you bring such as these?" His contempt was as great, but divided between the spaceman and his wares.

"Men who still have something to bargain with do not sign on as labor, as you well know, garthmaster. That we bring here any at all is something to marvel at."

The settler himself was quite different from the miserable company he now fronted. In an age when most males of Terran descent, no matter how remote from the home planet that strain might be, eradicated facial and body hair at its first appearance, this hulking giant was a reversion to primitive times. A fan of dense black beard sprayed across his barrel chest masking his face well up on the cheekbones. More hair matted the backs of his wide hands. As for the rest of him, he was gray—his coarse fabric clothing, his hide boots, the cap pulled down over more bushy hair.

His basic speech was guttural, with new intonations, and he walked heavily, as if to crush down some invisible resistance. Tall, massive, he resembled one of the trees against which he and all his kind had turned their sullen hatred, while the men before him seemed pygmies of a weaker species.

There were ten of those, still shaken by the process of revival, and none of them had ever been the garthmaster's match physically. Men without hope, as the cargomaster had pointed out, were labor-signers. And by the time they had reached that bottom in any port, they were almost finished already, both physically and mentally.

The settler glowered at each, his eyes seeming to strip the unfortunate they rested upon in turn, measuring every defect of each underfed body.

"I am Callu Kosburg—from the Fringe. I have forty vistas to clear before the first snow. And these—these are what you offer me! To get an hour's full labor out of any would be a gift from the Sky!" He made a sign in the air. "To ask a load of bark for such . . . it is a sin!"

The cargomaster's expression was serious. "A sin, garthmaster? Do you wish to accuse me of such before a Speaker? Here—now? If so, I shall bring forward my proof—so many credits paid for sign-on fees, cost of transportation, freeze fees. I think you will find the price well within allowed bounds. Do you still say 'sin,' Garthmaster Kosburg?"

Kosburg shrugged. "A manner of speaking only. No,

I make no charge. I do not doubt that you could bring your proof if I did. But a man must have hands to help him clear—even if they are these puny crawlers. I will take this one—and this—and this." His finger indicated three in the labor line. "Also—you." For the first time he spoke directly to one of the laborers on view. "Yes, you—third man from the end. What age have you?"

Naill Renfro realized that demand was barked in his direction. His head was still light, his stomach upset by the concoction they had poured into him. He struggled to make a sensible answer.

"I don't know—"

"You don't know?" Kosburg echoed. "What sort of an empty head is this one, that he does not even know how many years he has? I have heard much foolishness spoken here by off-worlders, but this is above all."

"He speaks the truth. According to the records, garthmaster, he was space-born—planet years do not govern such."

Kosburg's beard rippled as if he chewed his words before spitting them out. "Space-born—so . . . Well, he looks young enough to learn how to work with his hands. Him I will take, also. These are all full-time men?"

The cargomaster grinned. "For such a run—to Janus—would we waste space on less? You have the bark ready for loading, garthmaster?"

"I have the bark. We shall put it in the loading area. To be on the road quickly, that is necessary when one travels to the Fringe. You—before me—march! There is unloading to be done—though by the looks of you, not much will pass by your muscles this day."

The spaceport of Janus was a cluster of prefabs about the scorched apron of the landing field, having the strangely temporary look of a rootless place, ugly with the sterile starkness of the Dipple. Urged by a

continuous rumble of orders, the laborers hurried to
a line of carts. Their cargoes, unwieldy bundles of silvery bark, were being transferred by hand to growing
stacks carefully inspected by a ship's tally-man.

"This—goes there." Kosburg's simple instructions
were made with waves of his hand indicating certain
carts and the bark piles. Naill looked up at the man
standing in the nearest wagon, balancing a roll of bark
to hand down.

He was a younger edition of Kosburg. There was
no mistaking they were father and son. The beard
sprouting on his square thrust of chin was still silky,
and the lips visible above it pouted. Like his father,
he was dressed in heavy, ill-fitting gray clothing. In fact
all the men working along that line of rapidly emptying wagons presented a uniformity of drabness that was
like some army or service garb.

But Naill had little chance to note that, for the
bundle of bark slid toward him and he had just time
to catch it. The stuff was lighter than it looked, though
the size of the roll made it awkward to manage. He
got it to the stack safely in spite of the unsteadiness
of his feet.

Three such journeys brought him back to an empty
cart. And he stood still, with a chance to look about
him.

Two heavy-shouldered, snorting beasts were harnessed to each of the wagons. Broad flat hind feet and
haunches were out of proportion to their slim front
legs, which ended in paws not unlike his own hands.
They sat back on those haunches while, with the hand
paws, they industriously scratched in the hairy fur on
their bellies. In color they were a slaty blue with manes
of black—a dusty black—beginning on their rounded,
rodentlike skulls, and running down to the point end
of their spines. They had no vestige of tail. Wide collars

about their shoulders were fastened in turn to the
tongue of the cart by a web of harness, but Naill could
see no control reins.

"In!" Kosburg's hairy hand swept past his nose. And
Naill climbed into the now empty wagon.

He settled down on a pile of rough sacking, which
still gave forth the not unpleasant odor of the bark.
Two of his fellow immigrants followed him, and the
back of the cart was locked into place by the
garthmaster.

The son, who had not uttered a word during the
unloading, occupied the single raised seat at the front
of the wagon. Now he raised a pole to rap smartly in
turn the two harnessed scratchers. They complained
in loud snorts, but moved away from the port strip,
their pace between a hop and a walk, which made the
cart progress unevenly in a fashion not comfortable for
passengers. One of the men was promptly and thor-
oughly sick, only managing to hang over the tailboard
in time.

Naill studied his companions dispassionately. One
was big, even if he was only a bony skeleton of the
man he must once have been. He had the greenish-
brown skin of a former space crewman and the flat,
empty eyes of one who had been on more than one
happy-dust spree. Now he simply sat with his shoulders planted against the side of the cart, his twitching hands hanging between his knees, a burned-out
hulk.

The one who had been sick still leaned against the
tailboard, clawed fingers anchoring him to that prudent position. Fair hair grew sparsely on a round skull;
his skin was dough-white. Naill had seen his like before,
too. Some skulker from the port who had signed on
for fear of the law—or because he had chanced to cross
a powerful Veep of the underworld.

"You—kid—" The man Naill watched turned his head. "Know anything about this place?"

Naill shook his head. "Labor recruiter said Janus— agriculture." In spite of the jiggling process of the cart, he ventured to pull himself up, wanting a chance to see the countryside.

They were following a road of beaten bare earth, running between fenced fields. Naill's first impression was of somberness. In its way this landscape was as devoid of color and life as the blocks of the Dipple.

The plants in the fields were low bushes set in crisscross lines, while the fences which protected them were stakes of peeled wood set upright, a weaving of vines between them. Mile after planet mile of such fields—but, in the far distance, a dark smudge that might mark either hills or woodland.

"What's all that?" The man had moved away from the tailboard, edging around to join Naill.

Naill shrugged. "I don't know." They might be companions in exile here, but he felt no liking for the other.

Small but very bright and knowing eyes surveyed him. "From the Dipple, ain't you, mate? Me—I'm Sim Tylos."

"Naill Renfro. Yes, I'm from the Dipple."

Tylos snickered. "Thought you was gonna get yourself a new start off-world, boot? The counters don't never run that way 'cross the table. You just picked yourself another hole to drop into."

"Maybe," Naill replied. He watched that smudge at the meeting of the drab, unhappy land with a sky that carried a faint tinge of green. Suddenly he wanted to know more about that dark line, approach it closer.

The hop-shuffle of the animals drawing the wagon was swift. And the group of five wagons, their own the leading one, was covering ground at a steady and distance-eating pace. Sim Tylos with a lifted finger indicated the driver of their own cart. "Suppose he'll talk a bit?"

"Ask him."

Naill let Tylos pass him but did not follow when the other took his stand behind the driver's seat.

"Gentlehomo—" Tylos's voice was now a placating whine. "Gentlehomo, will you—"

"Whatcha want, fieldman?" The younger Kosburg's basic was even more gutturally accented than his father's.

"Just some information, gentlehomo—" Tylos began. The other cut in: "Like where you're goin' and what you'll be doin' there, fieldman? You're going right on to the end of the fields—to the Fringe, where like as not the monsters'll get you. And what you'll be doin' there is good hard work—'less you want the Speaker to set your sins hard on you! See them there?" He flicked the end of his encouragement pole at the bushes in the fields. "Them's our cash crop—lattamus. You can't set out lattamus till you have a bare field—no shoots, no runners, nothin' but bare field. And on the Fringe getting' a bare field takes some doin'—a mighty lot of axin', and grubbin', and cuttin'. We aim to get us some good lattamus fields 'fore you all go to account for your sinnin'.

"'Course"—young Kosburg leaned over to stare straight into Tylos's eyes—"there're some sinners as don't want to aid the Clear Sky work—no, they don't. And them has to be lessoned—lessoned good. My sire back there—he's a good lessoner. Speaker puts the Word on him to reckon with real sinners. We're Sky People—don't hold with killin' or such-like off-world sinnin'. But sometimes lessonin' sits heavy on hard-hearted sinner!"

Though his words might be obscure, his meaning was not. There was a threat there, one that young

Kosburg took pleasure in delivering. Tylos shrank back, sidled away from the driver's seat. Kosburg laughed again and turned his back on the laborer. But Tylos now stood as still as the jolting of the wagon would let him, staring out over the countryside. When he spoke again, it was in a half whisper to Naill.

"Nasty lot—not by half, they ain't. Work a man— work him to death, more'n likely. This here's a frontier planet—probably only got one spaceport."

Naill decided the little man was thinking aloud rather than taking him into his confidence.

"Got to play this nice and easy—no pushing a star till you're sure you got a line on the comet's tail—no fast movin'. This lessonin' talk—that ain't good hearin'. Think they has us all right and tight, does they? Let 'em think it—just let 'em!"

Naill's head was aching, and the lurching of the cart was beginning to make him queasy. He sat down, across from the still-staring ex-spaceman, and tried to think. The agreement he had signed in the labor office—it had been quite detailed. So much advance—Naill's memory shied away violently from the thought of how that advance had been spent—so much for expenses, for shipment to this world. He had no idea of the value of the bark that Kosburg had paid for him, but that could be learned. By the agreement he should be able to repay that—be a free man. But how soon? Best settle down and learn what he could, keep eyes and ears open. The Dipple had been a static kind of death; this was a chance at something . . . what he had no idea, but he was hoping again.

Duan Renfro had been a Free Trader, born of a line of such explorers and reckless space rovers. Though Naill could hardly remember his father, some of the abilities of that unsettled and restless type were inherited qualities. Malani Renfro was of a frontier world, though one as far different from Janus as sere autumn was from spring. She had been third generation from First Ship there, and her people had still been exploring rather than settling. To observe, to learn, to experiment with the new, were desires which had lain dormant in Naill growing up in the vise of the Dipple. Now those needs awoke and stirred.

When they stopped for a meal of gritty bread and dried berries, Naill watched the beasts munching their fodder. The driver of the second cart was small and thin, a seamed scar of an old blaster burn puckering the side of his head, plainly another off-world laborer.

"What do you call them?" Naill asked him.

"Phas." His answer came in one word.

"Native here?" Naill persisted.

"No. They brought 'em—First Ship." He pointed with chin rather than hand to the Kosburgs.

"First Ship!" Naill was startled. He tried to remember the scant information on Janus. Surely the settlers had been established here longer than one generation.

"Came in twenty years ago. These Sky Lovers bought settlement rights from the Karbon Combine and moved in. Only the port's free land now."

"Free land . . . ?"

"Free for off-worlders. Rest's all Sky Lovers' holdings—family garths—pushing out a little more each year." Again his chin pointed, this time to that dusky line on the horizon. "Gotta watch yourself 'round these phas. Look peaceful but they ain't always—not with strangers. They can use them teeth to crack up more'n a borlag nut, do they want to."

The teeth were long and white, startlingly so against the dark body fur of the animals, and very much on display. But the phas themselves appeared to be completely absorbed in eating and paid no attention to the men.

"Holla!" Kosburg, the elder, bellowed enough to excite even the phas. "Get them animals ready to move out. You"—his wave put Naill in motion back to his own wagon—"climb up."

As the afternoon wore on, the supply of lattamus bushes dwindled in the roadside fields. Here and there were patches of grain or vegetables, the fences about them of a lighter shade, as if they had weathered for only a short space of time.

And always that dusky shadow crept toward them . . . or that was the way Naill felt it moved—a shadow advancing toward the men and carts, not men and carts creeping up to it. Now it was clearly a dark wall of trees, and here were evidences that it had not been dispossessed easily. Vast stumps stood in the fields, some of them smoking as if eaten by fires kept burning to utterly destroy them. Naill had a vision of the labor needed to win such a field from virgin forest, and he drew a deep breath of wonder.

He tried to put together what he knew or could guess about the garths and the men who worked them. Clothing, carts, the allusions in the speech of both Kosburgs and that of the laborer-driver led Naill to believe that this was a sect settlement. There had been many of those through the centuries after the first Terrans ventured into deep space and began their colonization of other worlds. Groups knit together by some strong belief sought out empty worlds on which to plant their private utopias undisturbed by "worldly" invaders. Some had become so eccentric as to warp life on them into a civilization totally alien to the past of the first settlers. Others liberalized, or dwindled forgotten, leaving only ruins and graves to mark vanished dreams.

Naill was uneasy. Farm labor would be backbreakingly hard. He had expected that. A fanatical belief was something else, a menace which was, to his mind,

worse than any natural danger on a strange planet. The
Free Traders were also free believers, their cosmopoli-
tan descents and occupations making for wide toler-
ance of men and ideas. The guiding spirit of Malani's
kindly home world had been recognized by the wor-
shipers there as a gentle and benevolent Power. The
narrow and rigid molds that some men cast their belief
in a Force above and beyond themselves were as much
a peril to a stranger in their midst as a blaster in the
hands of an avowed enemy. And now that sinister talk
of "lessoning," which young Kosburg had used earlier,
struck home to Naill.

He longed passionately for a chance to ask questions.
But again such inquiries as he wanted to make might
well bring down upon him the very attention he wished
least to attract. Those questions—concerning religion
and purpose—were oftentimes forbidden, even to the
followers within the mold of a fanatical community.
No—better to watch, listen, try to put the pieces
together for himself now.

The wagon turned from the road into a narrower
lane and then passed the gate in a stake wall higher
than any field partition, one that might have been
erected as a defense rather than to mark a division
between one section of land and the next. And their
arrival was greeted by baying.

Hounds—enough like the Terran animals that had
borne that designation to be named so—a half dozen
of them, running and leaping behind another and
lower fence, were slavering out their challenge to the
newcomers. Naill watched that display. What menace,
living in the shadow of the now plainly visible forest, moved the garth dwellers to keep such a pack?
Or—there was a chill between his shoulder blades,
creeping down his spine—were those guards to keep
workers like himself in line?

The carts pulled on into a hollow square, surrounded by buildings, and Naill forgot the hounds momentarily to gape at the main house of the garth. That—that—thing—was fully as tall as two stories of the Korwar Dipple, but it was a single tree trunk laid on its side, with windows cut in two rows, and a wide door of still-scaled bark. Why—the stumps he marveled at in the fields were but the remains of saplings compared to this monstrosity! What kind of trees *did* make up the forests of Janus?

THREE

TREASURE TROVE

Naill leaned against the supporting haft of the big stripping ax. On his body, bare to the waist, silver dust was
puddled into patches by sweat. Overhead the sun,
which had seemed so pale on that first day of his
arrival, proved its force with waves of heat. His head
turned, as it so often had these past weeks, toward the
cool green of the woods they were attacking. The dim
reaches of dark green were as promising as a pool into
which a man could plunge his sweating, heat-seared
body—to relax, to dream.

Kosburg had lost no time, after their arrival at this
Fringe garth, in outlining to his new hands all the dire
dangers of that woodland which beckoned so enticingly.
And not the least of those perils was marked by the
solitary, ruined hut he had shown them, well within
one strip of forest that licked out into his painfully

27

freed acres. It was now cursed land, which no man
would dare to trouble. That hut—they viewed it from
a safe distance—had been, and still was, the tomb of
a sinner, one who had offended so greatly against the
Sky as to be struck down by the Green Sick.

The Believers did not kill—no, they simply abandoned to the chill loneliness of the forest those who
contracted that incurable disease, which was sent to
them as a punishment. And what sufferer raving in the
high fever of the first stages could survive alone and
untended in the wild? Also—who knew what other
dangers lurked under the shadow of the great trees?
There were the monsters, seen from time to time,
always viewed in the early morning before the sun's
rising, or in the twilight.

Naill wondered about those "monsters." The stories
Kosburg's household related with a relish were wild
enough, but the creature or creatures described were
surely born from over-vivid imaginations. The tales
agreed only upon the fact that the unknown was nearly
the same color as the vegetation wherein it sheltered
and that it had four limbs. As to whether it walked
erect on two, or ran on four, the information appeared
to be divided. And against it the hounds of the garths
had an abiding hate.

Curiosity was not one of the character traits the
settlers either possessed or encouraged. Naill's first fears
concerning the society on Janus had been fully sub-
stantiated. The belief of the Sky Lovers was a narrow,
fiercely reactionary one. Those living on the garths
might well have stepped back a thousand years or more
into the past history of their kind.

There was no desire to learn anything of the native
Janus, only dogged, day-in, day-out efforts to tame the
land, make it conform to their own off-world pattern
of life. Where another type of settler would have gone

exploring into the vastness of the forest lands, the Sky Lovers shunned the woods, except when armed with ax, lopping knife, shovel, and the thirst for breaking, chopping, digging.

"You—Renfro—bend to it!"

That was Lasja tramping into the half-hacked clearing, his own ax across his shoulder. He had been the longest in Kosburg's labor service and so took upon himself the hustling of the latest comers. Behind him came Tylos carrying a slopping water bucket, his face puckered in an attempt to act out the pain such a vast effort cost him.

The ex-crook from Korwar was striving to use every wile and trick he had learned in his spotted past to make life for himself as easy as he could. His first day at clearing had brought him back early to the garthstead with a swollen ankle from what Naill thought was a carefully calculated misstroke of a grubbing hook. Hobbling about the buildings, he then strove to ingratiate himself in the kitchen and weaving house, his quick, sly tongue as busy as his hands were slow, until the womenfolk of Kosburg's establishment accepted him as part of their aids to labor. So he escaped the fields, though Naill, having heard the flaying tongue of the mistress of the household in full flap, doubted whether Tylos had won the better part.

Now he leaned against the bole of a fallen tree and smirked behind Lasja's broad back, winking at Naill as the latter began to shape up one of the waiting logs.

"Seen any of them monsters?" he asked as Naill paused and came over for a drink. "Reckon their hides might bring a good price down to the port, was anyone smart enough to take him out a pair of hounds and do a little huntin'."

His half suggestion only pointed up the thought that was at the back of all newcomers' minds—the driving hope of somehow managing to get some trade goods independently, to build up credits at the port and some day—no matter how far away—to earn one's freedom.

Lasja scowled. "You stow that! Ain't never goin' to get any trade goods—you know that, scuttle-bug. Anything you get—or find—belongs to the garth-master—and don't you go to forget that! Want to be judged a first-degree sinner and have the Speaker reckon with you?"

Naill glanced over the rim of the wooden dipper. "What could a man get—or find—around here, Lasja, that's worth bringing in a Speaker?"

Lasja's scowl blackened. "Sinful things," he muttered.

Naill allowed the dipper to splash back into the bucket. He was aware of Sim Tylos's sudden start, stilling instantly into watchful waiting. When the big man did not continue, it was Tylos who asked the question in both their minds.

"Sinful things, eh? And what're them, Lasja? We don't want to get no Speaker on our backs—better tell us what we ain't to pick up, if we are findin' of 'em. Or else, do we get into trouble, we can say as how we was never told no different. This Kosburg, he's a terror on two legs, all right, only he might listen to us sayin' somethin' like that."

Tylos was right. Stern and narrow as was the garth-dwellers' creed, their sense of justice still worked—justice, not mercy, of course. Lasja paused, his ax still upraised. His lower lip pushed out so that he had the side profile of some awkward, off-world bird thing—round head, outthrust bill.

"All right—all right!" He brought down the ax mightily and then let the haft slip through his hand until the head rested on the chip-littered ground. "Sometimes, men workin' out to clear the forest—they find things . . ."

"What kind of things?" Naill took up the questioning.

But Lasja's discomfort was growing. "Things—well, you might say as how they was like treasures."

"Treasures!" Tylos broke out and then clamped his pale lips tightly together, though his avid interest blazed in his narrowed eyes.

"What kind of treasures?" Naill asked.

"I don't know—just things—rich-lookin'."

"What happens to 'em?" Tylos's tongue stopped its passage across his lips long enough for him to ask.

"The Speaker comes and they break 'em all to bits—burn 'em."

"Why?" Naill demanded.

"'Cause they're cursed, that's why! Anybody as touches 'em is cursed too."

Tylos laughed. "That's rich, that is. 'Course they're cursed, do we find 'em. We might just take 'em down to the port and buy ourselves free. But why smash 'em up? They could use some treasure here—import some machines so we don't have to go on breakin' our backs cuttin' down trees and grubbin' out stuff."

Lasja shot him a hard glance. "You ain't breakin' your back none, Tylos. And the Sky Lovers don't use no machines. Anyway—does a man try to hold out on treasure and they learn it, he gets put out there"—he jerked a thumb at the forest—"alone—no grub, no tools, nothin' but his bare hands. And you ain't sellin' nothin' at the port. You don't get to the port less'n they make sure they's nothin' a man's got on him but his clothes over his bare skin. No—they's right—that treasure's not for the takin'. When it's found, the finder sings out, and loud, too."

"Where does it come from? I thought this was an empty world, no native race," Naill said.

"Sure—never found no people here. Funny thing—

I've heard a lotta talk. This here planet's been known
for about a hundred years, planet time. The Karbon
Combine bid it in at the first Survey auction—just on
spec. That was before the war—long before. But they
didn't do much more than just hold it on their books—
sent in a couple of explorin' parties who didn't see
more'n trees, messes of trees all over the place. There's
a couple of narrow little seas—all the rest forest. No
minerals has registered high enough to pay for
exportin'—nothin' but a lotta wood.

"Then, when it looked like the Combines were
stretchin' too far, mosta them started unloadin' worlds
what didn't pay—gettin' rid of 'em to settlers. These Sky
Lovers—they were over on some hard-soiled scrap of
an overbaked world which gave 'em a hardscrabble livin'.
Somehow they got the down payment for Karbon and
jumped the gulf to here. Then—when the war broke—
well, then they had it made. Karbon holdin's were all
enemy then—they cracked wide open and nobody came
around here askin' for what was still owin'. Far's I know,
the Sky Lovers have Janus free and clear all to their
selves. They get out lattamus and bark enough to keep
the port open and themselves on the trade map.

"That's all the history we know. And there's never
been no sign of natives, just these treasures turnin' up
every once in a while. No pattern to that neither, no
ruins—nothin' to say as how there was ever anythin'
here but trees. And those've been growin'—some of
'em—nigh onto two thousand planet years! Might just
be that this was some sort of a hideout for raiders or
such once. But they ain't never found no marks of a
ship landin' neither. The Sky Lovers, they have it that
the treasures are planted by the Dark One just to make
a man sin, and so far they ain't found nothin' to prove
that wrong."

Tylos laughed scornfully. "Silly way of thinkin'!"

"Maybe—but it's theirs and they've got the say here," Lasja warned.

"Did you ever really see any such treasure?" Naill went back to his stripping job.

"Once—over on Morheim's Garth. He's to the south, next holding. That was last fall, just when we was doin' the season burnin'. Was his son as found it. They had the Speaker in right away—rounded us all up for the prayin' and the breakin'. Didn't do 'em much good, though—only kinda proved their point about it bein' sinful."

"How?"

"'Cause just about a week of days later, that same son as found it—he came down with the Green Sick. They carted him off to the forest then. I was one of the guards they set for the watchin'."

"The watching?"

"Yeah. With the Green Sick they go plumb outta their heads—sometimes they run wild. Can't let 'em get back where there's people. They touch you and you get it too. So if they try to break back, you rope 'em— pull 'em in and tie 'em to some tree."

"Leave sick people that way to die!" Naill stared at Lasja.

"There ain't nothin' as can be done for 'em—no cure at all. And the port medico says as how they could infect the whole lot of us. Sometimes their folks give 'em a sleep drink so they just die that way. But that ain't right, accordin' to the Speakers. They ought to be made known as how they's sinned. And, lissen here, boy, the Green Sick ain't nothin' to want—nor to look at neither. You ain't human no more, once it begins on you." Lasja chopped at the tree. "They say as how it never touches no one 'less he's broken some sorta rule of theirs—been different somehow. That Morheim boy—he was lessoned once or twice by his father, right out before the whole garth—for doin' wrong. So when he took sick, it was a judgment, like."

"You believe that?" Naill asked.

Lasja shrugged. "Seen it work that way—or heard as how it does. Them what takes the Green Sick, they's all had some trouble with the Rule. Once it was a girl as was kinda queer in the head—used to want to go into the forest, said as how she liked the trees. She got lessoned good for wanderin' off. Just a little thing she was, not full growed yet. They found her burnin' up in her bed place one night—took her right off to the woods. It weren't pretty—she cried a lot. And her mother—she was Kosburg's second woman—she took on somethin' awful. Old man had her locked up for a couple weeks—till he was sure it was all over."

Naill chopped savagely. "Why didn't they just kill her? Would have been kinder!"

Lasja grunted. "They don't figure so. Bein' kind to her body wouldn't save her spirit. She had to die hard in order to get rid of her sin. They think as if a man don't die in the Clear—as they calls it—he'll be in the Shadow always. If you sin big, you have to pay for it. Makes for a lot of hard dealin' one way or another sometimes. You can't change their way of thinkin' and it's best not to meddle. They hold that lessonin's good for everyone, not just those that believe. Now—we've had enough jawin'! You, Tylos, make tracks with that bucket to the splittin' ground. Tell the garthmaster as how we have a load 'bout ready. And don't you linger none on the way, neither."

Tylos, his bucket slopping, hurried as long as he was in Lasja's sight. Probably that scuttle would drop to a crawl as soon as he put a screen of brush between them. Since the usually taciturn Lasja seemed in an open-jawed mood, Naill determined to make the most of the opportunity to learn what he could.

"Lasja, has anyone ever bought free here?"

"Bought free?" The axman appeared to jerk out of some private path of thought. He grinned. "You needn't wear yourself out, boy, thinkin' 'bout that. Iffen you can shoulder a phas and trot him twice 'round the garth—then you can think of buyin' free. This is a dirt-poor world—and Kosburg's in an outer-Fringe holdin'. He ain't goin' to let loose of any pair of hands he gets. Not while they can still work, that is. You're right puny, but you ain't no shirk like Tylos. You do a day's work right enough. Me—I was prisoner of war on Avalon. They came 'round to the camp and made labor offers. I took that—better than stayin' in and goin' mad with bein' cooped up. When I came here—sure, I had big ideas about doin' my time and buyin' free. Only—this is the way of it—all the land, every stinkin' wood-rotten bit of it, belongs to the Sky, accordin' to their reckonin'. And only a true Believer can get rights to take up a garth. And—this is the trick star in their game—you can't be no true Believer 'less you was born so. They made them a pact, when they took off from that mistake of a world where they was roostin' before, that they wouldn't let in no disturbin' outsiders with different ideas. So you gotta be born a Believer, you can't up and say as how you'd like to join 'em now.

"Once here, they've got you tighter'n an air-lock door. You can go up against 'em and get yourself lessoned—or maybe thrown out in the woods—but they've got you just where it suits 'em! Now, you do that there smoothin' down. We'd better have a fair load for the old man when he comes sniffin' 'round."

How far were they from the port? A good day's travel in one of the phas-drawn carts—maybe longer on foot. And how could anyone work out an escape even if he were able to reach that single tie with space? To hire passage on a spacer would cost indeed a "treasure"; to try to work some deal with any ship's commander to be taken on as crew would be useless. The sympathies of the officers would all be with the master one was trying to escape. And if there was no system of legal buyfree . . . Naill dug savagely with the point of his ax against the hard wood. He hated to believe that Lasja's gloomy report was the truth, but it sounded likely.

"You take that rope." Lasja broke into his assistant's train of discouraging thought. "And drag out another of them logs. You can plunk it 'bout here."

Naill put down the ax and went back into where the trees had been felled during the past two days. He was still out of the coverage of the full forest, but the mass of greenery, just beginning to wilt, was somehow refreshing. There was a different feel here to the land, smells that were aromatic, free from the taint of human living. On impulse he stripped off handfuls of silver-green leaves, their touch fur-soft against his damp skin as he held them close to his nose and drank in a spicy fragrance.

He was filled with a sudden desire to keep on going into the domain of the trees. What if a man did take to the woods? That would mean becoming an outlaw in unknown country. But was that state so much worse than garth life? His mind nibbled at that as he hunched down to knot the rope about a tree trunk. The twist of cordage cut cruelly into his shoulder on the first pull. There was resistance, too much. Naill knelt again, saw a branch had cut into a soft place in the ground and pinned the tree fast there.

With his lopping knife he set to work digging that free. Sunlight lay in ragged patches. And something blazed with leaping light where he dug. Naill clawed out loose handfuls of moist loam and uncovered what lay beneath.

He blinked. Lasja's stories had not prepared him for this. And truly—what was it? A figure of—was it a tree?—a ball, a box, a rod the length of his palm and perhaps two inches thick, a necklace spilling a circlet of green-fire droplets on the gray soil.

Naill's hand closed upon the rod, brought it into full sight.

He drew a deep breath of pure wonder. There had been so many years of drabness, of ugliness. And now he could not give name to what he held in his hand. The substance was cold, with the pleasant coolness of springwater cupped in a sweaty hand to be brought to a thirsty mouth. It was all light—green, gold, opaline—jeweled light. It was a form—in traceries of patterns—to entrance, to enchant the eyes. It was a fabulous wonder that was his! His!

Moved by some instinctive fear, Naill sat half crouched, looking about him. Smashed, burned—that was what Lasja said was done to such things! Sure—that was part of their narrow world. Break beauty, destroy it, as they broke and destroyed the beauty of the Forest. He had not the slightest hope of keeping the entire treasure: he had no desire to. But this rod—this tube with all its imprisoned, magic splendor—that was not going to be broken!

Lasja would be along any moment, and Naill had no doubt about the other's reaction. He'd call Kosburg at once. Where—where was a hiding place?

He balled his fist tightly about his treasure. The woods—perhaps he could find a place of concealment there. Naill got to his feet, stole into the shadow of the trees, and saw there on the bole of one a dark hole. He thrust the tube into that hollow just as Lasja called from close at hand.

Naill leaped, kicked soil back, took up the rope to pull as the other came into view. He dared not turn his head to see how much dirt his kicks had replaced, whether he had again concealed the rest of the treasure.

"You empty-skulled lackwit!" Lasja bore down upon him. "Whatta you doin', pullin' out your guts that way? You got a limb caught under that thing!"

The older man went down on one knee to dig with his lopping knife, just as Naill had done before him. Then that busy arm paused. Lasja tumbled away as if he had just laid hand on a lurking jacata worm. He scrambled to his feet and grabbed Naill, propelling him away from the tree. And at the same time he gave a carrying call that would summon Kosburg. It was plain Lasja was obeying the Rule.

FOUR

SINNER

Tylos stood against the wall bunk, his hands opening and closing as if he wanted to grab and hold what was not there. He leaned toward Naill, his pale tongue sliding back and forth across his lips.

"You musta seen somethin'—you musta! Treasure—what kinda treasure, man?"

They were all herded in the bunkhouse, the dozen off-world laborers Kosburg had. And all eleven pairs of eyes were on Naill. Only Lasja was missing, kept behind as a guide. Naill hedged.

"Lasja dug it out—the tree branch was caught. I was on the rope drag and he dug. Then he pushed me out of there and called Kosburg. I saw something shining in the dirt—that's all."

"Why—why call Kosburg?" Tylos demanded of the company at large. "Treasure—get that down to the port,

39

and any trader'd take it off your hands for enough to buy your passage out."

"No." Hannosa, never a talkative man and one of the older laborers, shook his head. "That's where you're off course, Tylos. No trader landing on Janus would deal with one of us—he'd lose port license if he tried."

"Not the master, maybe," Tylos conceded. "But don't tell me the whole crew of every ship is gonna turn blind eye to a profitable little deal on the side. Lissen, dirt grubber, I come from Korwar—I know how much can be made outta treasure. Alien things—they bring big prices—big enough to make the cut worthwhile all along the line from a crewman up to the final seller in some fancy Veep place."

Hannosa continued to shake his head. "This is a matter of belief. And you know—or ought to know— that means a complete clampdown at any port. There've been five treasures found in the past three years—that we've heard about—in this district alone. Every one of them finished the same way—destroyed under careful supervision."

"Why?" Naill was the one to ask now. "Don't they realize that these finds are important?"

"To whom?" Hannosa retorted. "To the Sky Lovers their own creed and way of life is all-important. If news of such finds brings in strangers, archeologists, treasure seekers, then they would open the door to what these people came to Janus to escape: contact with other beliefs and customs. That mustn't happen, they think. As they see it, there is evil inherent in these objects— so they are destroyed."

"It ain't right!" Tylos pounded a small fist against the side of the bunk. "It purely ain't right to smash up stuff like that!"

"Go tell Kosburg that," one of the other men suggested. "Me—as long as we have to stay outta the fields till the Ceremony, I'm gonna get some rest." He stretched out on his bunk, setting an example most of the rest were quick to follow.

Tylos went to the window, though what he might be able to see from there Naill did not know. He himself lay flat and closed his eyes. But through his whole body there was a quiver of excitement so intense that he feared everyone in the room could sense it. Had he really done the impossible, kept for himself a fraction of that find? Had luck favored him that far?

When he closed his eyes, he could see vividly again that tube with its patterns, its color. And in his palm he could feel the sleekness of its substance. What was it? For what purpose had it been fashioned? Who had left it there and why? A burial hoard—loot hastily concealed? There were questions he longed to ask those about him concerning the other finds. Dared he try, without revealing to the curious that he knew more about this one than he had admitted?

If he was successful in keeping his find—then was Tylos right? Could a deal be made with some crewman? Only—how could he account for the funds afterward? Well, there would be time, plenty of time, to think that out later. It all depended on how well he had hidden the tube, whether the tree hollow would be safe.

Green and gold, red, blue—even colors he could not put name to, shades melting into one another, whirling, forming this design and that. Naill longed to have it in his grasp again, just to hold and watch for longer than the few moments he had had it after freeing it from the ground. It was beauty in itself—more than beauty: warmth. If he could take it in his two hands, bring it to Malani . . . Naill rolled over on the hard and narrow bunk, his face to the unpeeled bark on the log wall.

"Out!" That was Kosburg's order as he banged open the door. The tone of that bellow brought instant obedience from his laborers.

Naill followed Hannosa into the open, to discover the entire population of the garth was assembled in the yard. A baby or two cried protestingly in a mother's arms. Small children stood sober-faced and wondering. Kosburg himself, cap in hand, was at the head of the family line of Believers, facing a man wearing a long gray cloak over the usual dull apparel of the settlers.

The stranger was bareheaded, and his shock of uncovered hair and chest-spread of beard were as gray as his cloak, so it was difficult to see where fabric ended and hair began. Out of that forest of beard a sharp beak of nose stuck, and curiously pale red-rimmed eyes, one of which watered constantly so that those involuntary tears dribbled into the waste of hair below, shone brightly.

"Sinners!" The cracked voice was, in its way, as authoritative as Kosburg's.

A visible shiver ran along the line of Believers at that accusation.

"The Dark One has chosen to set the snare of his devising on this garth. Dark is only drawn to dark. Your Sky has been clouded."

A moan came from some of the women and two of the children began to whimper. The cloaked man lifted his head, turned his face to a sky which was indeed cloudier than it had been that morning. He began to chant words unintelligible to Naill, the whole a croaking like the rasp of an ill-set saw.

Still looking skyward, the stranger pivoted his body toward the woodlands. And then, without watching his footing, he marched in heavy strides in that direction. The Believers fell in behind him, men to the fore, and Naill joined the laborers who brought up the rear.

It was only coincidence, of course, but the clouds continued to thicken overhead, the heat of the sun was shut off, and from somewhere a chill breeze had arisen. It wrapped about them as they came into the clearing where lay the treasure cache.

Three times the Speaker marched about the glittering heap on the ground. Then he took up the ax that Lasja had earlier wielded and passed it to Kosburg. The garthmaster reversed the tool, bringing its heavy head rather than the cutting blade down on the objects there, battering and breaking them into an undistinguishable mass of crushed material, while the Speaker continued to chant. As Kosburg moved aside, the old man brought from beneath his cloak an old-model blaster.

Now he did look down as he aimed at the broken bits Kosburg had battered into shapelessness. The dazzling beam of the ray shot at that target, and the spectators pushed away from the heat of the blast. When the Speaker was done, there was only blackened earth in a pit. Whatever residue of metal had remained after that fiery attack had seeped into the ground itself. The Speaker turned to Kosburg.

"You will cleanse, you will atone, you will wait."

The garthmaster nodded his shaggy head. "We will cleanse, we will atone, we will wait."

They re-formed the procession and passed back across the fields to the homestead.

Tylos was the first to ask of the old hands, "Whatta they gonna do now?"

"One thing," Brinhold, another of the veteran laborers, told him. "We go to bed with flat bellies tonight. Lasja," he asked, "why didn't you just let that mess rot there? Why get the old man started on all this cleansin' business?"

"Yes!" There was a sullen chorus from his fellows.

"Now we're gonna have to fast while they try to appease the Sky."

Lasja shrugged. "You know the Rule. Better go hungry a couple of days than have a full lessonin'."

"He's right, you know," Hannosa pointed out. "It's just our bad luck we found it here. It's been about two years since Kosburg himself stumbled on that other one."

Naill looked up. "There was another found here, then?"

"Yes. Kosburg was out hunting his daughter. She was the strange one who used to go running off into the woods whenever she got free of the house. They said she wasn't right in the head." Hannosa's quiet face was shadowed by an expression Naill could not read. "Me, I'd say she was a reversion to what these people might have been before they became Believers. They used to have strange old tales on my world—a legend that there was an earlier race who had fled into the hills, gone into hiding, when invaders took over their land. And now and then the survivors of that earlier people would visit a house in which there was a newborn child and steal it away, leaving one of their own kind in its place."

"Why?" Naill asked. There was an odd feeling in him, another surge of that weird excitement that had tensed his body when he thought of the hidden tube.

"Who knows? Perhaps the blood was wearing thin and they had to have some of the new breed to mate with their own dying line. Anyway, the changeling— that was the name given to the child who was left— was alien and usually died young. Aillie was like that, unlike the rest of Kosburg's get—odd enough in her ways to be of a different race."

"Yeah, she sure was different," Lasja agreed. "Didn't have no luck neither."

"What happened to her?" Naill wanted to know.

"I told you about her—she took the Green Sick and they put her out in the forest like they always do. Only they needn't have made so big a to-do about her being a sinner! She never did no one no harm—only wanted to go her own way."

"But that is a sin here. In other places, too. No one must leave the herd—to be different is the complete and damning sin." Hannosa lay back on his bunk and closed his eyes. "Might as well relax and take it easy, boy. We don't work and we don't eat until the period of cleansing is past."

"How long?"

Hannosa smiled quietly. "That depends on how Kosburg intends to fee the Speaker. Old Hysander has quite a shrewd bargaining sense, and he knows that our worthy master wants to get those western fields cleared before the winter burning. There'll be some smart trading going on over that little matter just about now."

They had not found the tube; Naill hugged that thought to him as he lay through the hours of early evening. He had not seen it in that pile of objects destroyed. How soon dared he return to take it out of hiding? Good sense dictated a long wait for that. And yet his hands itched and twitched; he had a hunger for it as sharp as his hunger of body. Far back in his mind a small wonder stirred at this preoccupation with the alien artifact—why did it pull him so? Did it represent his chance of freedom, always providing he was able to get it to the port and make a deal with it? Or was it for itself that he wanted it so? And his wonder was tinged with a cat leap of fear.

Somehow Naill fought down that strong pull. He was physically tired, yet his mind was not lulled into any drowsiness. Instead he thought intently of small things—the leaves of the trees, the depths of the forest past the scars of the clearing, the aromatic smells, the way the wind lifted and rippled branch and bush.

He must have been asleep, for, when his eyes opened once again, it was dark. Naill stared into that dark. Overhead was the top bunk. He could hear the creak of wood, a sigh, a mumble where one of his roommates stirred unhappily. He was here, in Kosburg's garth—on a holding ripped out of Janus's forest covering by human will, hands, and stubborn determination.

But where had he been? Someplace else— someplace—right. Startled, Naill turned that impression over in his mind, tried to understand meaning through emotion. He had been elsewhere . . . that place had been right. He was here now—and it was wrong, wrong as a piece of machinery someone was trying to fit into a place where it did not belong, to do a job it could not manage.

It was hot. He was shut in, boxed, trapped. Naill moved softly, with sly pauses to listen, as an animal deep in the territory of a natural enemy might move. He wanted out—into the dark cool of the open. Then across the fields—to his tree—to what lay hidden there. His hands were shaking so much that he pressed them tight against his chest, and under them his heart beat wildly. Out—free—in the night!

His caution held until he was past the door of the bunkhouse. Then that wild exultation swept through him completely and he ran, seeming to skim across the rough surface of the field as if he were being drawn along by a tie uniting him to the waiting tree hollow. Dark here, but not the same kind of dark that had held back in the bunkhouse. Again that small part of his brain which could still wonder, was still unabsorbed by the desire that heated the rest of him, noted that he could *see* in this dark, that only the hearts of the deepest shadows were veiled to him.

And as he pushed into the roughly cleared land where they had been working, the wind wrapped around him softly, welcomingly. The leaves were not just set rustling by its fingers now; they sang—sang! And Naill wanted to sing, too. Only a last dying spark of caution choked that mutely in his throat.

Stench of burning . . . He skirted the spot where the Speaker had used the blaster, not realizing that his lips were set in a snarl, that his eyes blazed, that he tasted anger, an anger out of all proportion to what had happened there only a few hours ago. Then he was through the veil of bushes, reaching up. His fingers on bark, smooth, welcoming bark . . .

Why welcoming? asked the now almost quiescent questioner in him, the questioner that vanished as his fingers passed from bark to tube. Naill held that out and gave a cry of pure delight. Color—swimming color—shades combining, dancing—color from elsewhere, from the place where he was meant to be. A key . . . for the gate he must find—his own!

"Well, so that's it, boy. You did it—just like I kinda thought you did all along."

Naill spun around in a half crouch, the tube cupped in a hand tight against him. Tylos! Tylos standing there, grinning.

"Held out on 'em, Renfro? That was a right smart trick. Gonna pay off too—pay off for both of us."

"No!" Naill was only partly out of the spell that had held him since his awakening in the bunkhouse. The only decision he was certain of was that Tylos had no part, and would never have any part, of the thing he held.

"Now, you ain't gonna push me out, Renfro. All I gotta do is yell out nice and clear and you won't have no treasure left. You saw what they did to the rest of that today, didn't you?"

"If I don't have it, then you don't either." A portion of reasoning returned to Naill.

"True enough. Only I ain't gonna let you walk off with it neither. The boys back there, they said as how this is the second cache of this stuff found around here. Could be three, you know. And Sim Tylos, he's never been pushed outta no deal yet—not never by any Dipple creeper, he ain't. Give us a look."

The bole of the tree was hard at Naill's back. "No!"

"No?" Tylos's voice still held to the pitch of ordinary conversation, but his hand moved. The light of the blue-green Janusan moon picked up the sheen of the knife blade, point up and out. "These here garthmen, they don't hold with blood-lettin'—not out and open—or so the boys say. Only I ain't no Believer—nor you neither. You give me that!" The knife sliced air. Tylos, armed with naked metal, avid for what Naill held, was not the same scrounging, sly, work-dodging weakling he had been.

"So!" Shadows out of shadow: Kosburg, his son, two more of his kinsmen, coming in a hunter's circle. "So— the evil still is—the sinning is yet! Well that we watched this night. Andon, you take the small one."

A loop of rope snapped out to pin Tylos's arms to his side, effectively halting before it began any struggle he might have made.

Kosburg regarded the small laborer. "He has not touched it. Intent but not yet the full sin. Put him in keeping. He shall be lessoned—well."

Another vicious jerk took Tylos off his feet, brought a hardly coherent stream of pleas and attempted self-justification out of him, until a kick from Andon impressed upon him the wisdom of silence.

"You—" Kosburg had turned to face Naill. "You are the complete sinner, infidel! You found—you concealed. You brought down upon us Sky wrath!"

His hand shot out and up with a speed Naill had not realized him capable of, and the club he held struck numbingly on Naill's forearm with force enough to bring a choked scream out of the younger man and throw him to his knees. Yet, in spite of his pain, he watched the tube, free of his grasp, roll to the open and lie there, warm, beautiful, glowing, in the moonlight. Only for an instant was it so. Then Kosburg leaped upon it, stamping with his heavy boots, grinding it into a powder that could not be told from the silvery wood dust—all that warmth and life.

Naill cried out, threw himself at the dancing hulk of the man treading in a frenzied shuffle up and down in the mass of withered leaves and churned earth. He did not see the blow that laid him limp and helpless a moment later.

Dark again, pain in his head and dark—a musty dark, the very taste of which made a sickness come into his throat. Dark . . . Why should a fire be dark? And surely he lay in the heart of a fire from which he could not escape. The fire was in him, outside him—filled the world.

There was a long time when he awoke to the dark and the fire, to moan for water, to roll across an earth floor, tearing at his already tattered clothing, then to lapse once more into that other place, which he could never remember but which was so much more important than the dark and the fire.

Light struck in. It seared his eyes and made him cower and hold his hands before his face. He shrank away from the light, which mixed with the pain in his head and the fire that consumed him. But the light filled the world—there was no place to hide or shelter from it.

"Look at him!" Revulsion, fear—those emotions

reached him even in that place where he crouched trembling.

"Green Sick! Get him out of here—he has the Green Sick!"

Then the harsh croak of another voice. "The sinner is condemned by the Sky. Let him be dealt with after the custom, garthmaster."

Ropes coming at him, all around him, fastening to drag him out into the light, which was torture to his eyes. He was prodded, pulled, hustled along, sometimes wavering on his feet, sometimes falling to be dragged across the earth. This was a nightmare he could not understand, only endure. He was like an animal on its way to the slaughter pen, hoping that it would not last long, that he could return once more to the dark.

FIVE

CHANGELING

Water—water running over rocks, downstream under an open sky—water to drink, to pour over his burning body. To lie in the midst of flowing water . . .

Naill crawled on hands and knees, his eyes narrowed slits against the terrible pain of light. But there were spaces of cool shadows where the light was muted, screened away, and those grew larger and larger.

Iftcan . . . The Larsh forces had attacked at moonrise, and some weakling had let them seep through the First Ring. So Iftcan had fallen, and the Larsh now hunted fugitives from the Towers.

Naill crouched in the greenish shadow, his hands covering his face. Iftcan . . . Larsh . . . Dreams? Reality? Water—he must have water! Shivering he crawled on between trees, his hand groping, his legs sinking into a muck of decaying leaves and earth. Over him leaves whispered until he could almost understand a slurring, alien speech.

Now he could hear it, the murmur of water, and it grew to a roaring in his ears. He half fell, half rolled, down a slope to the side of a pool into which water was fed by a miniature falls he could have spanned with his two hands. A gasping rush plunged him into that water, where he laved hands, head, the whole upper part of his feverish body. He gulped from his cupped palms, felt the liquid run down his parched throat, wash about him, until at last he squirmed back—to lie limply, staring up into a lace of leaf and branch overhead, a round circle of open sky far above.

Naill ran his hands across his face, up over his head. There was a mat of stuff left between his fingers when he brought them unsteadily down to eye level again. Hair . . . loose, wet hair!

It took him a long moment to realize what he held, to raise his hand again for a more thorough examination of his head. The soaking at the pool had driven some of the bewilderment from his mind. He was Naill Renfro, off-world laborer on Janus. He had been sick . . . was sick.

Now he sat up abruptly, a cold shiver shaking him. Those searching fingers had encountered only bare skin, save one more small patch of hair, which had fallen from his scalp at first touch.

What—what had happened to him? Once more his hands went to his head, slipped across skin bare of hair, touched at the sides, stiffened at what they found there. He crouched, knees pulled to his chest, half bent over, breathing hard. Then his eyes, still squinted against the pain of light, saw a second pool, smaller, fed by the larger, but still of surface, a mirror in which the drooping foliage about it was reflected.

He crawled to that, leaned over so his head and shoulders would be reflected there.

"No!" That denial was torn out of him in a word half a moan. Naill drove his fist at the surface of the pool, to break that lying mirror, to blot out the thing it reported. But the ripples died away, and again he saw—not clearly, but enough.

Naill's hands went to his head for a second touch—exploration, to verify the reflection. Hairless head—ears larger than human, with the upper tips sharply pointed and rising well above the top line of his skull. And—he held his shaking hands out before him, forcing his eyes wide open for that study—his skin, which should have been an even brown, was now green! That was no fault of the tree shade, no trick of Janusan sunlight. It was true—he was green!

The tatters of his shirt were long since gone, and his bare chest, shoulders, ribs—all were green. He did not need to pull away the ragged breeches still belted about him, or kick off his scuffed and battered boots, to know that hue was universal. What looked back at him from the pond mirror, what he could see with his eyes when he surveyed himself, was no longer human. He was Naill Renfro . . .

He was Ayyar . . .

Hands twisted, wrung, though he was unconscious of that despairing gesture. Ayyar of Iftcan, Lord of—of—Ky-Kyc. The Larsh had broken the First Ring—they were into the Inner Planting. This was the time of the Gray Leaf and there would be no other seeding.

Naill swayed back and forth. He made no sound, but in him there was a wailing he could not voice. An ending—an ending—the time foretold had come upon them—the ending. For the barbarian Larsh had not the secret. They could destroy but they could not re-seed.

When Iftcan fell, so did the Older Race die and the light of life and knowledge go out of the world.

But he was Naill Renfro! Iftcan—Ayyar—Ky-Kyc— the Larsh. He shook his head, inched away from that mirror pool, tried to push out of his mind what he had seen there. He had a fever; he was simply delirious—that was it! His eyes—they hurt in the light, didn't they? They were playing tricks on him. That was it! It had to be!

Only now he no longer felt the burning heat consuming him. And he was hungry, very hungry. Slowly Naill got to his feet, found he could stand erect, walk. He stumbled along, scrambling up the small embankment down which splashed the miniature falls. There was a bush there, hung with puff-pods as big as his little finger. Mechanically he gathered them, popped them open with a snap, and eagerly stuffed the seeds they contained into his mouth. He had dealt with a full dozen of them before he began to wonder. How had he known they were edible? Also—when he opened them, why did he think he had done this many times before?

But of course he had. They were fussan, the hunters' friend, always to be counted upon at this time of the year, and he *had* feasted on them many times before. Naill paused, hurled that last pod from him as if its touch burned. He did not know about such things—he could not!

He collapsed on the ground again, quivering, his arms folded across his bent knees, his head forward on them, his body balled as if he wanted to pull back into nothingness, forgetfulness. Maybe if he slept once more, he would wake—truly wake. He slipped into the state he longed for. But when he lifted his head again, he was alert, his nostrils expanded, savoring, identifying scents, his ears picking up and naming the sources of sounds.

The hurtful sunlight was gone, the mist of twilight was balm to his eyes, and the soft shadows were no bar to seeing. Seeing! Naill could make out every rib of leaf, the network of veins across their surfaces—this was seeing such as he had never experienced before! Naill moved alertly, coming to his feet with a lithe readiness in what was almost one supple movement of muscles.

A borfund with cubs was feeding downstream. He did not need to see through the masking brush; his nose told him, and his ears picked up the crunch of double-toothed jaws moving greedily. And—aloft—there was a peecfren lying flat, belly to tree limb, watching him curiously. *Borfund—peecfren.* He repeated the names wonderingly in a low whisper. And his mind answered with mental pictures of living things he was sure he had never seen.

Then panic caught at him hard and heavy—as might the ray of a blaster. Blaster, that other part of him questioned—blaster? His hands flew to his head, clamping hard over those monstrous ears. *Borfund— blaster* . . . memories alien to each other warring in his mind.

He was Naill Renfro—he was the son of a Free Trader, born in space . . . Malani . . . the Dipple . . . Janus . . . sale to Kosburg. Kosburg . . . the garth: there was sanity. He must get away from here—back to where there were men . . . men.

Naill broke away from the streamside, began to trot, weaving a way between the trunks of trees, trees that grew larger and larger as he moved away from the open glade of the stream. He went without path guidance but with purpose. Somewhere—somewhere there was an end to trees. It was open and in the open were men—men of his own kind. This was a fever dream and he must prove it so!

Yet as he went, nose, ears, eyes reported to his brain, and his brain produced answers to scent, hearing, sight, which were not a part of Naill Renfro at all. His headlong flight slackened as he leaned panting against a tree bole. As his panicky breathing began to slow, his head came up again and he battled shakiness, fear. The soft whisper of breeze in the leaves, the warmth— the caress of that same wind against his bare chest and arms. . . . And now that feeling of content, that this was right, the way life should be. As if he, too, reached down roots into the earth underfoot, raised swaying branch arms to the sky—a kinship with the forest world.

But he went on, though at a soberer pace, schooling his unease. He stopped once to strip long, narrow leaves from a low-hanging branch, crushed them between his palms, and then inhaled deeply of the scent from their bruised surfaces. He felt clear headed, alert, tireless, and eager.

However, that eagerness was replaced by another emotion as he came into the hacked trace of the settlers' war against the wild. Wilting leaves, broken branches—Naill's nostrils twitched in a spasm of distaste. He was scowling and unaware of it. The smell of death, decay, where it did not belong, and with it another stink—of an alien life form, defiling yet familiar.

He traced that smell out of the clearing, through the thinning of brush racked and torn by the logs pulled through it. Then he was on the edge of a field, a field where the butts of forest giants still stood as raw and ugly monuments to the death dealt them weeks ago. Naill snarled at the spoilation, and within him grew the disinclination to advance any farther into the open.

Pinpoints of light pricked beyond. His gaze centered there, narrowed. That was a garth—Kosburg's? Dared he chance moving closer? Yet he must. He was a man . . . there were men. If he could see them, speak with them, then he would know that his eyes had deceived him back at the pool, that he was not—not that thing!

Though that need drove him forward, Naill did not go openly, nor did he realize that the action he took, seemingly by instinct, would have been totally foreign to Naill Renfro. His noiseless step—with a foot planted with infinite care, his crouching run from one bit of cover to the next—was that of a scout deep on a spying trip within the holdings of the enemy.

Always that stink was heavy in his nostrils, clogging up the air to sicken him, growing heavier the closer he drew to the farmstead. He was still a field away when the clamor broke out—the hounds! Their baying was a war cry. Somehow he knew—as well as if they had human speech and shouted—that he was the quarry. So he had been right in that long-ago guess: the garths kept those four-footed hunters as a threat to laborer runaways.

But Naill also remembered the custom at Kosburg's. The animals had not been loosed in the fields at night. There was too much chance of their disappearing on some game hunt into the forest and not returning. No, they patrolled inside the wall of the garth yard.

And this was Kosburg's right enough. Naill recognized the set of the big main house against the night sky. There was a place where an active man could climb the outer wall, look in at the top floor window of that building, avoiding a descent into the yard. Why he had this pressing need to do just that he could not have explained, but do it he must.

Though he flinched as the hounds bayed, he ran in a zigzag from shadow to shadow until his hands were on the stake wall near the house. He leaped, again not

aware that his effort was far more powerful than any
Naill Renfro could have made.

Killing trees to make shelters. Why did these people
not know that trees could live and yet welcome
indwellers? No—always this kind must kill, use dead
things to pile about them until their lairs smelled—
reeked of foul decay as did the pit of a hunting kalcrok!

The stench was almost more than he could bear,
making his stomach protest. Yet he crouched before
the incut which held an open window and looked into
the lighted room beyond. He jerked and nearly lost his
balance. That—that *thing*—two of them! They were
monsters—as horrible as the smell of these dead lairs
of theirs!

"Men" hammered one small part of his brain—or
rather one man—the younger Kosburg—and a woman.

Monsters! The revulsion was sharp. Hairy as
beasts—alien, not only in body but in mind. Looking
at them now, Naill could in a way he could not
understand savor their crooked thoughts, look into the
narrowness of them. There was a wrongness every part
of his own spirit rejected without pity.

The woman turned her head; her eyes by chance
were on the window. Her mouth shaped into a distorted square. She screamed tearingly, and continued
to scream with sharp, mindless cries.

Naill leaped outward, landing lightly on his feet. Just
as he had been revolted, had rejected kinship with this
species, so had the woman felt about him. He ran, away
from the stench of the dead wood and the creatures
who laired in it, heading for the forest with its clean
shelter.

But his repudiation of the garth was not the end.
An hour later he lay with heaving shoulders and
laboring lungs, hearing still the belling of the hounds.
They had brought them out, those garthdwellers, to

pick up his trail across the fields. Only the fact that they had kept the dogs leashed had saved him. But, judging from the sounds, they had not ventured yet beyond the roughly cleared land. Were they waiting there for daylight?

Then would the settlers overcome their dislike of the forest and again put the hounds on his trail? Or would he be safe if he retreated farther into the deep woods? To go deeper, he would be lost to his own kind—alone . . . His own kind?

Spirit of Space—who were his kind now? Naill shivered. His revulsion for the garth was a real thing, as real as the heat of fever, the pain in his head. He could not go to those people and claim kinship—never again.

And that fact, standing stark and black in a chaotic world, had to be faced. Something terrible had happened to him—outside, inside. He was no longer Naill Renfro. Though he was not now looking at a strange reflection in a pool, he was looking inside him at what had taken over his mind as well as his body.

Ayyar . . . who was Ayyar? If he were not Naill Renfro, then he was Ayyar. And he had to know who—what—was Ayyar, to whom the forest was truly home, to whom there came strange memories in ragged tatters. He must find Ayyar.

To do that . . . where did one search for such a weird trail? Physically, in the aisles of the forest; mentally, where? Because Naill did not know, he got to his feet and started in the only direction of which he was sure—back to the pool where he had first seen the mirrored face of someone who was no longer Naill Renfro.

Now that he had admitted that much, more and more of the new person took over. He stopped, pulled at the fastenings on the heavy boots that weighed down his feet. Footgear should be so different—made of borfund hide, fitting snugly, reaching from sole of foot to just below the knee—hunters' boots, through which one could feel any inequality of footing, not these clumsy coverings that locked the foot in prison, away from the good earth.

He pulled in irritation at his breeches. These, too—formless, coarse—were wrong. Green-gray silky stuff which caressed the body—spider thread wound and woven, packed in stass buds and the whole pressed firm to dry and age—that made proper clothing for the wood. Iftcan . . . But the Larsh were there. Naill stumbled against a tree, stood rubbing his head. Never a clear memory, just bits and patches . . . tiny fearsome scenes of men like himself, a desperate, driven handful, fighting among trees, trees in which they dwelt, going down one by one before a rabble horde of wild men . . . scattered, broken. Somehow he knew that had been the end of his kind.

His kind? What *was* his kind? Who was Ayyar? He blundered on, though he knew where he was going, that he would come out at the pool side.

And he did, falling down by that quiet pocket, drinking again from his cupped hands, slapping the pool's bounty over his sweating body. The rill ribboning from the smaller mirror pool, that should drain into the river—and beyond the river. He drew a ragged breath. Beyond the river stood Iftcan, tall and beautiful, silver leaves and singing leaves—the tower trees of Iftcan!

But he was tired, so very tired. As he relaxed beside the water, that tiredness caught at him. His feet hurt; perhaps he should not have thrown away those imprisoning coverings—only he could no longer stand their touch. Water rippled about his feet as he lowered them into the pool, soothing away smart and burn. He rubbed them dry with handfuls of grass and curled up drowsily.

The sound brought Naill out of sleep so deep dreams did not reach it. He lay where he was for a moment wrenched out of ordinary time, every part of him questioning by senses far more specialized than any off-worlder's. He rolled under a bush and brought his head around to look skyward.

No sun yet—but the lighter sky of dawn. Against it that blot—man-made. A flyer from the port—small, two-man job—and coasting low. Naill Renfro's memory supplied that much. But why—how—?

Had Kosburg appealed for such help in his hunting? Why? Trying to answer that was folly. Soon it would be full day—and while Naill could travel in the gloom of the forest, he dared not try to face the open under the sun. Best move now: the river—with Iftcan across it. Were the wild ones still there? No, there was a dimness, a feeling that what had happened in Iftcan was long past. But that place drew Ayyar, and to its pull Naill Renfro made no discouraging answer.

He started downstream, keeping under the roof of the trees. Overhead he could follow the circling of the flyer by the waxing and waning of the engine purr. The pilot was hunting something right enough, swinging the machine in a steady pattern of rings over the forest. What he could see below, save a carpet of tree crowns, puzzled Naill. But the circling was too regular to doubt that the port pilot did have a definite purpose, which could only be a search.

The rill that was Naill's guide joined another stream, widened, developed a visible current. Water things swam, or popped into the flood from along the verge as he passed. He found another fussan bush, stripped its pods and munched the seeds as he went.

Then his nose warned danger—not the man smell,

no, this was vile in another way. His mind supplied a murky picture of a danger that ran on many legs, lurked, hid, pounced on anything venturing into the forest strip it had appropriated as hunting territory. Naill leaped to catch at a low-hanging bough. Its elasticity helped to whip him up into the mass of the tree. And so he passed over that path with its evil smell, staying above and traveling from one tree limb to the next until the last taint of that odor was lost.

The day was on him, but the full dazzle of the sun did not reach here. Then he saw it blindingly bright before him, reflected from water, a sheet of swiftly running water. He shielded his eyes with his hands and tried to make out what lay on the opposite shore. Was there an Iftcan still?

SIX

IFTCAN THE DEAD

Dark green, but only in patches. Elsewhere stands of white—stark white pillars, dead trees around which only small brush crept, a few stunted saplings grew. Yet in his mind it was alive! Silver-green, tall and beautiful, the tree towers of Iftcan! If he could only remember clearly—and more.

Naill cupped hands over his eyes, peering through finger slits to shut out the light as much as he could. The river was wide, but there were rocks jutting above its shrunken summer surface. One could cross by aid of those. Only—it was open sky there and he could hear the hum of the flyer.

Suppose—suppose a man could slip down into the flood a little to the east, let the current carry him in an angle downstream to where a point of tumbled rocks speared into the water? A mat of old storm flotsam

63

clung and banked there to form cover. Beyond it was brush into which one could duck.

Naill tensed, listening to the sound of the overhead menace, trying to gauge just how far away it was, speculating as to how much of the riverbank its pilot could observe. He dared not look aloft into the sky; his eyes protested even this amount of sunlight and he feared blindness.

He dropped his hands and eased off his breeches. Green body against the earth might have a better chance. Now . . . ! As well as Naill could judge, the flyer was on the farthest edge of the loop it was traveling. He began his crawl down-slope to the water, keeping to all the cover there was. The flyer was headed back!

Naill froze, hugging the earth, feeling the despair of an insect overhung by a giant boot ready to stamp it flat. He found himself furiously willing blindness on the pilot, invisibility for himself.

The motor beat loudly in his ears. Was the machine hovering right over him? By a gigantic effort of will he lay quiet, made himself wait and listen.

No, not a hover—it was passing! Passing south. When it reached the far point of the swing, he could make a run that should slip him into the water. He listened—then moved.

The water was cold; it chilled his bare body as he tried to enter without betraying splashes. Then he let the current pull him along. Above the sound of the water he caught the hum of the flyer on its backsweep.

Naill's nails grated on a rock as he clung in its shadow, trying to make himself small. Luck was with him—the machine was passing over. He loosened that frantic hold, allowed himself to drift downstream. When he caught against the rock point, he could control himself no longer but scrambled out of the water, scuttled over the rocks, and dived into brush cover at the foot of one of those bleached bones—the dead tree towers of Iftcan.

For several long moments he merely lay there, listening, fearing that he had betrayed himself in that small burst of panic. Only the hum was fading again; the flyer was going north. He had made the crossing undetected.

Now to find a hiding place in which to wait out the day, to favor his smarting eyes. Naill put out a hand, drew it down the dry bark of the dead tree against which he had taken refuge. It was huge, this tall trunk. Was this not Iftcan, whose trees had known a thousand planet years of carefully tended growth?

His hand fell away as he drew back from the dead. In its way he knew a little of the same revulsion he had known at the garth. Living things did not shelter among the dead.

Naill moved on from the verge of the river, keeping prudently under cover. Always about him were the leafless trees, long since finished, yet standing as monuments to their own ends.

They were quiet, those forest aisles of Iftcan. His passing alerted no bird or small living thing; no insect sped away. And here no breeze sang a song he could almost but not quite put words to. At least the flyer had not followed; it still circled above the river.

Naill was through the First Ring now. Here was a belt of denser green, and in it lifted the crowns of two saplings, untended, unshaped—yet the species was not dead, then! Naill pushed his way to one, regardless of scratches and the stinging whip of small branches, to stand and run his hand along its trunk. It seemed that the bark pulsed under his palm as if he stroked a pet animal that responded by arching its body to fit closer into his hand.

"Far, far, and first the seed,
    Then the seedling,
    From the rooting, to the growing.
    Breath of body, stir of leaf,
    Ift to tree, tree to Ift!"

He crooned the words hardly above a whisper. What did they mean, demanded Naill Renfro. Growing words, power words, words of recognition, replied Ayyar. The death was not wholly death! The triumph of the Larsh was not complete. And these saplings had seeded aright—somewhere one or more of the Great Crowns was yet alive!

Weaving a path between the dead, he cut deeper into the unknown. Another living sapling! And then . . .

He stared in wonder. Old, very old . . . huge. . . . This—his tangled memory sought, found—this was Iftsiga! The ancient citadel of the south. And it lived!

No ladder hung from the great forelimb stretching high above his head. There was no way to reach the hollow he could sight where that mighty limb joined the parent trunk. And he had no wings to whisk him aloft. Naill's head turned slowly as he caught, on the breeze ruffling the tree leaves, the slight hint of another scent.

Tracing it, he found what otherwise he might have overlooked—the sapling ladder carefully hidden in the leaf mat on the ground. To off-worlder or settler it would have been nothing more than a dead tree with stumps of branches still sprouting jaggedly from its trunk. Ayyar of the Iftin knew it instantly, swung it up against the bulk of Iftsiga, and climbed it nimbly to a limb that was wide enough to accommodate four of his kind walking abreast.

He traveled along it and paused for only a moment

at the hollow of the doorway before stepping into the past—the far, far past.

The walls of that circular room were very thick, as they should be when the sap and life of Iftsiga were housed within them, a living shell to encase the hollowed center. The odor that had guided him to the ladder was stronger here. Yet the upper room was empty.

Light pulsed on the ceiling over his head—lorgas, the larvae that clustered in the tree cores, attracting to them by that phosphorescence of their bodies the minute flying creatures on which they fed. They made a ring about the opening that held the stair pole reaching up—and down—in the middle of the tree. And Naill's present interest was downward.

He fitted his hands and feet into the old slots in the pole and descended nimbly. The odor of occupation was still here, but it had been three or four days since those others had left.

Another room—but not an empty one. Naill swung away from the stair well to look about him. The subdued light given off by a second cluster of lorgas was satisfactory. Carven stools—several. A neatly piled collection of sleep mats. And—against the far wall . . .

He made for that, his hands reaching out eagerly to lift the inlaid cover of a chest that was a masterpiece of construction, an intricate combination of many kinds of wood. Naill went down on one knee to roll back the protecting bark cloth. Then his breath expelled in a hiss of pleasure and content as he picked one of the exposed weapons from its oily nest of floosedown.

It caught the soft light, glinting green-silver. And it might have been forged for him alone, that sword with the leaf-shaped blade and the perfect balance, so well did its gemmed hilt fit to his hand as he swung it experimentally. To Naill Renfro it was a strange, if beautiful, weapon; to Ayyar it was comfort, an answer to his desires for defense.

A sword, even completed with scabbard and shoulder belt, as this was when he explored the contents of the arms chest further, was not all he needed. Clothing, food, shelter . . . He began to examine the other furnishings of the tree room.

Clothing—packed carefully in a long basket of woven splints with dried, aromatic leaves to be shaken from the folds as he pulled it forth to measure against his own lank body. He stood up minutes later, the soft green-silver-brown fabric stretching and accommodating itself to every movement of his frame, in tight breeches, a tunic laced over the chest with a silver cord, the supple boots he had longed for earlier. Also he wore a cloak with a hood, and a gemmed buckle to fasten at the throat—all strange and yet very familiar.

Naill smoothed the fabric across his thighs. He had given up wondering why he knew what he knew . . . all the bits about this other life. He welcomed Ayyar and Ayyar's broken memories, his alien knowledge, instead of striving to thrust that odd intruder out of his mind. This was Ayyar's world—now his. Wisdom dictated that he accept that fact and build what future he could upon it.

He sat down on the pile of mats, munching a crumbling cake of stuff Ayyar had welcomed eagerly, and tried to put his thoughts in order, to reach back to the beginning of all this. Naill Renfro had found a cache of the mysterious treasure that turned up without reason here and there on the holdings of the Believers. And from that had come all the rest.

The Green Sick—he could remember that dimly— of being dragged out of Kosburg's prison room and hearing his fate pronounced: exile and death alone in the forest. But Naill Renfro had not died—not wholly;

he had instead become Ayyar of the Iftin, who also could remember—a battle through a city of towering trees and the bitterness of an overwhelming and complete defeat.

And physically he was no longer Naill Renfro either. He was a green-skinned, big-eared forest dweller who apparently could frighten garthmen into panic . . . a monster.

Green Sick—change—monster. . . . The procession of events made sense of a kind. But there had been others who had fallen ill in the past—had they all been changed? His hands paused with the bread stuff. If so, then they could be out here, too. They could be the ones who had left their scent, their signs of occupation, here—right where he was! He would not be alone in his exile!

They had been here, and left their possessions laid up carefully against a future return. To wait here for them—that might well be his brightest move. At any rate he needed rest, and he wanted to do nothing to provoke any investigation from those who rode the flyer. He would wait until night . . . for the night was his!

Naill finished the bread, flicked the crumbs from his fingers and lay back on the mats, pulling the cloak over him, his unsheathed sword beside him where hand could reach and curl about its hilt in an instant. He blinked drowsily at the ring of lorgas. Some had spun threads beaded with sticky dots to better entrap their lawful prey, and those drifted lazily in the air. The quiet held him and then it seemed as if the living tree that encased this chamber exerted its own soothing spell, and he slept, this time with no dreams at all.

How long he slept Naill could not have told, but he awoke quickly, with every faculty alert. The chamber was as it had been; he could hear no sound. Sitting up, he stretched, got to his feet, and went to the pole ladder. On impulse he descended another level in Iftsiga.

Here was a third circular chamber, slighter larger. There were chests against the walls, one pulled away from the rest. Naill went over, lifted the lid. He ruffled aside more bark cloth packing, only to be startled into an exclamation.

Green-stoned necklace, box, tube of glowing colors—piece by piece he beheld an exact duplicate of the treasure he had uncovered in the clearing! Naill lifted out the color tube. It was the same as the one Kosburg had stamped into the dust, in every flit of color, change of pattern, along its surface! But why? Slowly he took out each object and studied it carefully before putting it aside for the next. The chest was still far from empty; there was a second layer of cloth—and then another treasure set!

With the same care as he had brought them out, Naill repacked the objects. He sat on the floor, his hands still resting on the lid of the chest as he thought this through. Two sets of treasure, perfect reproductions of each other—and both like the set he had seen destroyed at Kosburg's. He wished he knew if all the other treasure caches the settlers had blasted had also been as these. If so—why?

Ritual objects placed as offerings or to mark graves? Naill tried to find the answer in Ayyar-memory, but there was no response from his new alter ego. Either Ayyar had known nothing of such things, or else there was a block between his memory and Naill Renfro. But there had to be a purpose for the caches—in the forest and in storage here. This chest had been moved out of line. Why? To better abstract part of its contents recently?

Why? Naill could have screamed that aloud in his frustration.

Perhaps somewhere else in Iftsiga he could find his answers. But when he went back to the pole ladder, he discovered that the opening to the chambers below was sealed. And for all his exasperated pounding, that round of wood did not give way. Baffled, he climbed once more into the room where he had slept and then decided to go up.

The dim light of twilight came in through the limb door as he reached the entrance chamber. There was no sound from without, save the rustle of leaves. After a moment or two he climbed to the level above. Here were no lorgas on the ceiling, only gray outer light admitted through window holes. The chamber was empty save for powdery dust and the ghostly remnants of long-shed leaves. Perhaps every upper level was the same, but he decided to try one or two more.

Naill was still on the pole ladder when he heard it—a furious snapping, ending in a hooting call, low pitched, yet with an urgency in it that could not be denied. And the Ayyar part of him responded to that with a burst of speed. He scrambled through the ladder well to face fluttering, beating wings, to look into a feathered face where great eyes were ringed darkly to seem the larger. And when that set gaze met his own, Naill was startled again.

Speech? No—the hoots and clicks of the big curved bill did not add up to human speech. Yet this flying thing recognized him, welcomed his aid, traded on an alliance between them! Not an alliance such as existed between man and animal as he had known, but between one species of intelligent life form and another of equal if different mentality. It was as shocking in that first moment of realization as if the tree holding them both had broken into intelligible words.

The bird thing was hurt. It had been blasted by—by men! Naill had an oddly distorted mental picture of hunters, which must have flashed from the other's mind to his. Someone from the port, trying to relieve the tedium of a planet-side stay, had gone hunting.

A wing trailed for his inspection, showing singed feathers, the raw bite of a blaster burn. It was big, this Janusan bird—with a wing spread of close to five Terran feet, its body, puffed in fluffy white-gray feathers, standing on huge talons intended for hunting. Now its demand for aid and attention grew sharper in his head.

It allowed him to inspect the burn. The wound was not bad enough to incapacitate it entirely. Naill received another blurred mental impression of the victim fluttering from tree to tree, working its way farther into the forest and away from the off-world invaders. But he had not the slightest idea in the world of what to do for the injury.

The bird squatted down before him as he sat crosslegged. Its folded its good wing to the body, kept the other outspread. And Naill winced as that strange mind deliberately invaded his own. It was as if one had two recordings, similar in most major features, differing in smaller details, which must be fitted one upon the other for a matching of patterns. That could not be done entirely—but on the major points where the match could be made . . .

"Yes!" Naill said as if the bird could understand. "Yes!"

He swung down the pole ladder to the room that had been inhabited. The same woven wicker basket that had held the clothing had what he sought, a pouch he had overlooked. With its cord hooked over his arm, Naill reclimbed to where the bird waited.

Awkwardly he mixed powdered leaves from one small box into a paste held by another, then spread that dressing with all the care he knew onto the raw burn.

When he had done, the bird hooted again and walked about in a circle as if testing its ability to do that, though it did not try its wing.

"Who—what—are you?" Naill asked suddenly. But Ayyar was answering that for him.

A quarrin, the tree dwellers who far in the past had made a pact and alliance with the Iftin, who were also tree dwellers and lovers of the forest world. Hunter on two legs, hunter on two wings, warrior armed with sword, warrior armed with talons and sundering hooked bill, they had hunted, they had fought side by side when need arose, because by some trick of nature they had been able to communicate after a fashion. It was not an alliance between thinking man and instinct-ruled animal or bird, but a partnership between two species of equal if different prowess. Hurt, the quarrin had returned to the place where it could expect aid, and it claimed that from Naill as a right.

Now, moved by something he could not understand, Naill held out his right hand. The round head, with its upstanding ear tufts of feathers—not too unlike his own pointed ears—leaned forward a little.

The big eyes, with the yellow-red fires deep in them, studied his outheld hand with odd intentness. Then the head bent more, the cruelly hooked bill opened and closed on his flesh, not to rend or tear, but in firm pressure, as a man's hand might clasp his fellow's hand in a signal of greeting and friendship—a quick grasp, over almost at once. But Naill smiled slowly. Naill-Ayyar was no longer alone in Iftcan the Dead.

SEVEN

DOUBLED TRAIL

"Hoorurr,"—Naill had made of the bird's call a name—
"I don't think they *are* coming again—soon." He sat in
the upper door to Iftsiga, a perch he had made his own
for hours at a time while he waited for the
unknown to return.

Three days—or rather nights, for the nights were
now his time of action—and no sign that any Ift had
climbed that ladder or made camp within the tree bole
for years. Yet Naill's nose had told him that he had
arrived there only hours after them that first day.

In spite of patient mental probing and attempts to
communicate with the quarrin, he could not learn
whether the bird had been left behind by any of his
kind, or if the relation between the winged tree dweller
and the footed ones had been more than a casual one
of simple acquaintance. With no speech in common,

the mental contact could convey only imperative ideas and needs.

But Hoorurr was company and Naill fell into the habit of talking to the bird. There was no reason to remain in Iftsiga if it was now deserted. And who had been those temporary indwellers? Other changelings such as himself—or remnants of the true Iftin who had survived, broken shadows of what they had once been?

The trouble was that Ayyar's knowledge still reached Naill only in bits and pieces, and most often widely separated and disconnected bits and pieces. Matters pertaining to the daily round of maintaining life—that information came to Naill easily. He had known just where to go within the tree to tap the water supply; he knew food supplies and how to seek them out. But all the rest—those strange memories were hazy, impossible to fit together.

Once on Janus there had been two peoples—the Iftin dwelling in trees, possessing knowledge that allowed them to shape and tend growing things so that they had a kinship of feeling, if not of blood and body, with the forest; and the Larsh, more primitive, not resembling the forest men either mentally or physically, fearing the "magic" of the tree peoples, dreading it enough to want to kill—to stamp it out—as the garthmen fought to eradicate the forest nowadays.

The Larsh were not off-world settlers, though. And the war between Iftin and Larsh had been centuries ago. Iftin had been dead a long, long time. Then why did Ayyar remember? And how had Ayyar become in part Naill Renfro—or Renfro Ayyar?

Whenever his thoughts poured into that familiar path, Naill was uneasy, sometimes treading around the tree chambers while Hoorurr clicked his bill impatiently.

"No," Naill repeated now, "they are not returning.

All was stored here for a period of waiting. Those swords were in oiled covering, the rest was put away. They have gone—so I go after!"

If he could pick up the trail of those who had been here, find them, then he would know the truth! And there had been no sign that either settlers or port flyer had ventured this side of the river. He had never heard of Iftcan at the garth. Yet such a forest space with the trees already dead would have been seized upon by the settlers had they known of it. But was he too late in trying to trace the unknowns?

"Hoorurr,"—he looked straight into the bird's big eyes—"this I must do—go after them." With his mind as well as his lips, Naill strove to make his need plain, experiencing once more that weird mix-match of thought patterns.

The bird stretched wide wings, moved the injured one experimentally, and then sounded its haunting call. Hoorurr would manage, but Naill must walk this path alone; the quarrin did not intend to leave Iftcan and its chosen hunting grounds.

It was one thing to come to such a decision, another to carry it out. Naill, down from Iftsiga, the sapling ladder once more concealed as he had first found it, stood in the shadows, the difficulty of his quest brought forcibly home to him as he looked around. He did not believe that he would find those he sought still within the bounds of Iftcan, even if others of the tree towers still lived.

But now—north, south, west—which way? South were the spreading garths. He thought he could safely rule out that direction. And to the northeast was the spaceport, eastward more garths. Somehow he believed he would not discover those he sought too near any off-world place. West, where the maps said one of the narrow fingers of sea lay?

In the end he decided to let his path be set by chance—and the wind. For the wind sighing through the leaves was oddly company of a sort, a comforting voice overhead—and the wind pushed him west. He had made his first mistake in lingering so long at Iftsiga; the trace of scent which might have guided him must now be lost. Yet he still depended upon his nose to pick up hints of life in the dead forest.

Life there was—Ayyar memory identified most of it—animals, flying things, in the patches of vegetation that straggled among the bone-bare boles of the dead tree towers—more as he came to the First Ring.

Here the trees were scorched with ancient fire, eaten away as they lay toppled to the ground. And the spreading wasteland was dreary but already half covered once again by a ragged growth of rank things, things that the Iftin would neither encourage nor allow to root near their city in the old days. Naill's half knowledge took him on detours to avoid certain plants from which came a stench to twist the nostrils. And there were thorn-studded vines running lines to entrap unwary feet.

In that unwholesome mass lurked other life inimical to his species. This was a waste where Larsh destruction had begun a work of defilement, and the evil that had always waited for a chance to break the defense wall had entered in greedily, to take possession of the once clean city. The inner part of Iftcan had become a sad place; this was a filthy charnel house, and Naill hesitated to force a path in that direction. As he stood there, Ayyar memory stirred, supplied a strange emotion. He felt more than disgust . . . danger . . . a barely understood warning that something old and perilous lay there.

There remained the river. To travel along its bank should eventually bring him to the sea. Why the sea?

The forest was Iftin country—not that restless water to the west. Yet . . . the wind blew him seaward.

Naill cut away from the edge of the waste to the running water, reaching the river, he believed, not far from the point where he had swum to safety. The moon made a silver ribbon, waved and broken by the current, to serve as his trail marker.

When dawn showed gray, he made himself a nest in a thicket well shaded from the sun, and lay there, lulled by the water's murmur. In that half-drowsing state, another scrap of Ayyar memory made for him a vivid picture of a boat—oared by men who wore the Iftin dress, watched shadows with Iftin eyes, bore Iftin swords—steered down between threatening rocks where water boiled, a boat, bearing Iftin warriors to the sea. This was an old trail, then, this water one.

Naill was on the trail again in the late evening when he found the camp site, coming down into a rock-enclosed hollow to stand, nostrils expanding, picking up that lingering trace of scent that the wind had not yet pushed away. He went down on his knees, studying the floor of the hollow, trying to pick out some track that would prove his guess correct.

River sand filled that stone-walled cup, and he sifted the coarse stuff through his fingers, until he uncovered a fussan pod, split open, seed gone. A pod here with no bush nearby to shed it naturally—he was right! This was the path of those he sought. As had the boatmen of his memory, they were heading seaward!

His pace became a trot when he left that camp; he was ridden by an increasing feeling of urgency, that he must catch up with the strangers, reach them soon, or it would be too late. Too late? Why? Just another of the many mysteries that had been his portion on Janus.

But Naill could not throw off that feeling, and it became so strong that he did not pause with the dawn, but kept on, trying to travel under cover. By mid-morning he was forced to admit he could not go any farther. For the forest was dwindling. Since early light the larger trees, standing fewer and farther apart, had vanished altogether. Now smaller growth and bush were common, with wide strips of grass open between them.

Naill found shelter in a shade that was neither constant nor thick enough to make him truly comfortable. His head pillowed on his arm, his body and legs aching with fatigue, he tried to rest. But that need for speed ate at him, so this time was only one of impatient waiting for the dusk.

In the twilight he went on into the open, to top a hill there and walk into a change of wind. Now the breeze was chill, salt-laden. Beyond lay ridges of smaller hills, some half sand masses. And ahead of those were curling feathers of white marking waves along a strand.

Immediately before Naill was a low scoop of land where the river emptied into the ocean. Cliffs raised walls on either hand. Naill looked to them and his hand came to his mouth.

Light! A spark of light! He could not have been mistaken—surely he could not! And why such a beacon there? A signal? Or some off-world explorers' encampment? Prudence dictated caution to temper his first wild desire to run toward that light. He waited in suspense, but there was no second spark there. Had he been mistaken, seeing what he had hoped to see?

Best go there and be sure. Naill started down the rise, slipping and sliding through the loose earth, heading for the northern cliff point. Distances must have been deceiving, or else the tricky footing in the sand hills slowed his progress. He had no way of measuring time, but he thought that at least an hour had passed and he had yet to reach the foot of the cliff where the spark had blazed. He could smell the sea in the wind, hear the pound of the waves along the shore. Otherwise he might be plodding through an empty and deserted world.

Here was the cliff. Surveying its rugged wall, Naill sighted nothing except the rock. But that offered hand holds and toe openings, and he could climb, reach the crown, make sure.

Naill pulled himself up and over, sprawled panting. He had been right! They had been here, those from Iftcan, or some like them, and a very short time ago. He rolled over on his side, too spent for the moment to rise, and saw a hollow in a pinnacle of rock that made a pointed, easily detected finger in the night sky. And in that hollow . . . !

On hands and knees he came to it, thrust his hand out to explore a plate of stone. On it were ashes yet warm enough to make him jerk back his fingers. A signal surely. . . . Set why? For whom?

The reason must lie still beyond. Naill clung to the rock and wriggled out to the very edge of the northern drop. Again he looked down into a sea basin. The cliff on which he was had a twin perhaps half a mile away, and between them the waves washed well inland, making a natural and protected harbor. A harbor which now sheltered . . .

A ship?

But that object was unlike any ship Naill had ever seen. He would rather have thought it a log, one of the gigantic logs from the old forest, bobbing up and down in the hold of the waves. There were no oars, no sails, no break in the rounded surface lying above the waterline. And this time Ayyar memory did not supply him with an explanation.

Yet he knew that that huge log did not ride in the waves without purpose. Did it hold men, men such as himself, as the tree houses of Iftcan had

held and sheltered? And if so, where would it carry
them now?

There was no sign of any movement, except the slow
swing of the log in the waves. That signal. . . . Naill
studied the drop below him, seeking a path to the
water's edge. But he was forced to retreat some distance inland before he found a ledge leading to a zigzag
cutting, which revealed the fact that visits to the signal post on the cliff must be regularly made. He
rounded a last outshoot pinnacle and met a faint path
leading to the beach.

That log, which had apparently floated without
control or direction when he had watched from the
cliff, was now turned end on toward the sea and was
traveling out, against the toss of the waves, as if
below the water surface some propelling agent moved.

"No!" Naill cried that aloud, ran stumbling through
the sand to the water's edge, where a wave foamed
about his ankles. There was nothing to be seen save
the log. And that was moving with a purpose, under
command, he did not doubt. It was already passing
between the outer hooks of the cliffs, fast turning into
only a black blot on the water.

Too late—he had come too late!

Slowly he retreated out of the wash of the foam, and
it was then that he saw those other marks, indentations
one could not truly call footprints, a cluster of them
where the sand had been widely distributed . . . the
embarkation point?

Since the tracks were all that remained, he studied
them. They marked, he believed, the end of a fairly well-
defined trail leading back into the interior of the continent. One source of answer to his collection of
mysteries, the log—which was more than a log—was
now beyond his pursuit. But this trail, did it lead from
Iftcan? Or from some other and more enlightening

beginning? It was recent, made within hours, and it was the only trace the strangers had left him.

Naill turned his back on the sea, where the log was now only a black point, and began to walk along the trail of those who had manned that peculiar vessel.

Much later he lay on a mat of leaves against the trunk of a tree, peering through a screen of brush at what he had least expected to discover. At the end of the trail he had traced, through two nights, well away from the seashore, across the river again, and southward he had found more settlers' Fringe lands. During the past hour he had been skirting the ragged edges of a garth—not Kosburg's, too far west for that, and it was smaller, a newer beginning for some less well-established settler.

The strangers he scouted after had come here from the northeast—perhaps straight from Iftcan. And they had spent some time slipping in and around the outer edges of the clearing to the south and west, as if they were on the hunt for something—or someone. He had discovered one place where at least two encamped for some time—perhaps through a day or more. Had they been spying on the activity about the garth? Planning a raid? They had certainly taken every precaution to keep their presence a secret.

Now he had come to the focal point of their explorations. They had scouted, they had spied, and then they had finished here—finished what? Naill only knew that from this place led the return trail to the seashore. So here their mission had been either accomplished or abandoned.

It was early morning, leaving him very little time to make his own search before having to retire to the tree hollow where those others had waited out the sunlight hours before him. He could hear the sounds of awakening life at the garth several fields' lengths away—the howl of a hound, the chittering complaint of a phas disturbed against its will. If the garthmaster was a pusher, his field laborers might be hurried out before dawn to start their day's work here.

There was one glimmering of an idea that had ridden Naill for the past half hour. He had begun to believe that what he sought here was buried: a cache set skillfully and with cunning to be discovered by someone from the garth, treasure trove—not remaining hidden from vanished years in the past, but from days earlier. And if his guess was the truth, he believed he knew now where to look for its confirmation.

He scrambled around a log, began a careful search of the ground. But what he sought was not located near the fallen trees waiting to be branch-stripped and hauled away. It had been placed in the midst of a tangle of wild berry bushes. The swollen, yellow fruited brambles had been carefully rearranged to hide turned earth, but there was a gleam of metal artfully exposed to catch the eye.

And the berries—Naill recognized those, too. They were sweet, entrancing to anyone who was thirsty. The bait was excellently planned. Any man working here would be drawn to strip a handful of the fruit during a rest period, perhaps to pick more to share with his fellows, pick enough to uncover that piece of metal, and then . . .

Naill twitched the bramble back into place. A call from the garth moved him to haste in his withdrawal. He had been right; they were already heading for clearing work, early as it was. And if they brought hounds with them . . . !

He slipped among the bushes and ran, hoping that the workers were not accompanied by dogs, believing he could outwit any settler who tried heavy-footedly to follow his trail. Minutes later he was at the hiding place the trappers had established, listening intently to the growing noise of a phas-drawn roller bumping over the fields in the direction of the clearing, near which the bramble hung.

Trappers—he was certain of that now—trappers who had left a baited trap! He had been caught in such a trap. Now he was able to fit one more piece into his broken picture. The tube he had hidden, held, wanted for his own—and the Green Sick. Was one born of the other? That could be. Those who sinned by concealing or handling the treasure were punished speedily for that sin—cause and effect, which was closer to the truth than the settlers knew for sure.

But the purpose of this elaborate scheme still eluded him. By some alien means—and Naill was now certain his illness was no natural ailment, unless it could be a Janusan disease induced and controlled by will—he had become a different person, strange to his former self, not only physically but mentally, too.

Traps—trappers—the log ship—Iftcan—Ayyar. . . . Naill's head ached dully. It was as if inside his skull there was a stirring, a battering against some tightly bolted door . . . some hidden part of him fighting for freedom. He caught the reek of man scent, of animal odor. But there was no tonguing from a hound. For the period of the day he must keep under cover.

As much as his senses flinched from the alien activities of the garth, Naill knew that he would remain—if not in this special hideout, then nearby—until he witnessed the springing of the trap, learned what did follow its discovery.

EIGHT

THE TRAPPED

His hiding place, Naill speedily discovered, had been carefully chosen by those who had first used it as an observation post. It gave him a good view of the clearing. The working party that came there now was smaller than those Kosburg had mustered. There were only two slave laborers, and three bearded Believers, one of those hardly more than a boy, his beard a few silky straggles on his chin.

They began to work well away from the brambles that masked the trap, and the garthmaster kept them busy with a vigor and concentration that suggested that he, like Kosburg, ruled the holding with an iron-rooted will. The labor of clearing was the same Naill had sweated over, but inside him now a new anger coiled and raised. This destruction of what was right and good to make more ugly bareness! He realized his fingers had curved about the hilt of that leaf-bladed sword, that he was eyeing hotly the leader of that work gang.

To remain where he was could be the rankest folly, and yet he was held there by that curiosity, the need for knowing what would happen if and when the treasure was found. Would one of those laborers uncover the cache out of sight of his master and seek to conceal part of it for his own?

Naill was so intent upon watching the workers that he missed the arrival of a second small group at the edge of the clearing. And he was startled to see suddenly the flap of a skirt.

His first impression of the womenfolk of the Believers had been that they courted dour plainness with the diligence with which off-world women strove to develop the current ideal of beauty. Their sacklike clothing, fashioned of the same dull browns, shabby grays, and sullen black-greens the men also wore, carefully concealed any hint of form, while their hair was screwed back into tightly netted knots. Away from their own hearthsides they followed the dictates of the Rule and went masked, a strip of cloth with holes for eyes, nose, and mouth rendering them both anonymous and safely hideous.

Not that they ever ventured very far from the buildings of the garth. In all the time Naill had been at Kosburg's, he had never seen any of the women farther afield than the stableyard, except driving, fully masked and covered with additional muffling cloaks and hoods, to the weekly Sky Stand of the elect.

But here a woman escorted three smaller figures, all masked. Baskets on arm, they were heading toward the berry-hung bushes.

"Ho!" The garthmaster upped his ax for a swing, to drop it without delivering the full blow. He was no giant to match Kosburg, but a thin, active man, and the forward-thrusting beard he displayed was fair and lank.

The woman stopped, turned to face him, her smaller companions retreating a little behind her as if cowed by such public notice of their being. They remained so while the garthmaster climbed a fallen tree trunk and came to them.

"What do you do here, girl?" he demanded.

One work-reddened hand gestured at the heavy harvest of berries.

"These will be uprooted soon." Her voice was low, without expression. "There is no need to waste this present crop."

The garthmaster considered that point, approached the berry bushes closer as if to estimate the value of their wild abundance. Then he nodded.

"Keep to your work, girl," he ordered. "And make haste—we want to clear here before night."

The children scuttled to the picking as he strode away. But for a moment the woman stood where she was, her head now turned to the forest, her eyes, Naill thought, not on the berries at all but on the woodland behind them. Then he saw her do an odd thing—put out her hand and draw one finger down the graceful bend of a stem from which hung a cluster of small white flowers. Her head turned sharply right and left, and then she bent to smell that flowering spray before she went on to strip the berries into her basket in quick, efficient motions.

Whether by chance or design, she pushed her way, picking as she went, until the patch of bramble was a screen between her and the other working party. Then, having added a last handful of fruit to her basket, she set it carefully on the ground and straightened to her full height, once again facing the depths of the forest. Her hands went to the back of her hood, fumbled with the cords, and she jerked off her mask with an impatient gesture. Her head was up, her chin raised, with a movement into which Naill read defiance.

She had the pallid skin of all garthside women, and her features held no hint of beauty. But she was young, no more than a girl. A high-bridged nose centered above a small mouth, one with thin, pale pink lips. Her eyes were well set, but above them were thick brushes of brows, giving them a harsh and forbidding half frame. No—she was not even remotely pretty by off-world standards, and that alien which was within Naill now found her pale skin repulsively ugly.

Raising her hands, she pressed her palms against her cheeks in a gesture he could not understand. And then, as if some pull beyond control moved her, she walked forward, her clumsy skirts catching and holding on the branches, into the shadow of the trees. Once well hidden by their overhanging branches, she paused once more, standing very still, her head raised. She did not appear to be looking, only waiting, listening. For what Naill could not guess.

Timidly, shyly, her hand came up again to pluck a spray of flowers. She cupped the blossoms in her fingers, bending her head as if she studied some treasure. With a glance over her shoulder, furtive and guilty, she tucked the flowered stem into the front of her robe. Her head up again, her eyes sought now along the green-silver curtain of the woods.

"Ashla?"

The girl's whole body jerked in answer to that call. Her hand went swiftly to the flowers, pulled them loose, and threw them away in what was a single motion of repudiation. Then she was busy adjusting her mask. When she turned to face the child, that covering was safely in place. She beckoned the little girl to her, looked into the other's basket.

"You have done well, Samera," she approved, with a warmth in her tone that had been lacking when she answered the garthmaster. "Tell Illsa and Arma that you may all eat a handful yourselves."

The child's masked face was raised. "Is it allowed?" she asked doubtfully.

"It is allowed, Samera. I shall answer for it."

When the child left, Ashla went back to her picking, moving closer to the laden branch that dipped above the trap. Naill's eyes smarted; the sun broke through here and there—dazzling, too dazzling for his altered sight. Yet he must witness what might happen now. Would she find it? Or would the cache be left for the discovery of a laborer who came to grub up the brush?

The bramble moved closer to her as she tugged it and stripped berries in double handfuls. Then her hands gave a harder tug, bringing up all of the long branch. She stood very still, masked face bent groundward. Her head turned; she glanced in the direction of the children. But they were half hidden, their dull dresses only patches between the bushes. She stooped and caught up a dead branch, dug into the earth with short, quick jabs.

Green fire flashed in so bright a spark that Naill winced, hand to eyes. When he was able to see again, she was holding the necklace before her. No expression could be read behind the enveloping mask, but she had made no sound, given no call to summon the men. Instead she spread out the necklace so its lace of gem drops hung smoothly in graduated rows. Naill, who had given that part of the treasure only passing attention before, could now observe and appreciate its full beauty. If the jewels were real, that garth girl now held a kingdom's ransom, such a necklace as an Empress would wear to her crowning. And he had no reason to believe that they were not stones of price.

Almost as if she had no control over her own

desires, Ashla drew the lovely thing to her so those connected rivers of rich green fire now lay on the sacking stuff of her robe, making the coarse material twice as ugly in contrast. Maybe she thought that too, for she quickly held the stones away again. Then, to Naill's surprise, she balled the necklace and wrapped it in a big leaf culled from a nearby plant, tying it into a packet with a twist of grass.

One more glance at the children to make sure of their continued inattention and she pulled her skirts free from the clutch of the bushes to walk on into the woods. A sandaled foot came out from under her voluminous clothing as she dug with heel and toe in the leaf mold, dropped in her prize, and then pulled a stone over the hiding place. It was so speedily and deftly done that Naill might have been witnessing an action performed many times before.

Ashla gave a last searching inspection, then hurried back to the bramble. With her digging branch she recovered the rest of the treasure and was stripping the remainder of the berries when the children came straggling by with their own baskets.

"Ashla!" The call came from the garthmaster, and one of the children caught at the girl's skirt. She nodded a brisk reassurance in that direction and started out of the glade, the children in her wake, heading toward the open fields.

So—even the Believers were not immune to the temptations of the treasure traps! Naill remembered the story of the girl at Kosburg's who had kept running away to the forest until the Green Sick put an end to her "sinning" forever. Had she also secreted some part of a treasure, kept it hidden as he had tried to do, as this Ashla was attempting?

The ring of axes, the loud voices of the workers marked a change of direction. They would soon reach

the bramble patch, too near his own lurking place. He
must slip farther back into the wood.

Naill found shelter where the ring of axes was only
a very distant sound and slept out the rest of the day,
rousing after dusk to find a stream and drink. He still
had a supply of bread from Iftsiga's supplies and he
ate that slowly, savoring its flavor. There was no moon
tonight; the wind was soft, moisture laden. Rain coming
soon . . .

It might be wise to hole up again and wait out any
storm. Yet he wanted to know—had the cache been
discovered by those in the clearing? Would they have
a guard there now? Or could their fear of the forest
by night be determent enough?

Naill approached the clearing with stalker's caution,
testing the air with his nose, listening to every sound,
as well as using his eyes. The stone Ashla had left to
mark the necklace was undisturbed. But beyond, the
brambles had been grubbed away and . . .

He caught the enemy scent. Luckily the wind blew
in his direction and not away. Ready for trouble, he
dodged back in the forest and an instant later heard
the coughing bay of a hound, followed by excited shouts
from at least two men!

A guard right enough, reinforced by one of the
watchdogs. But Naill did not believe they would dare
to track him far; their superstitious fear of the thickly
treed lands would be doubled at night, and he was
certain they had not actually sighted him. The settlers
at Kosburg's, at least, had been active in populating the
inner woods with unseen enemies. The hound's uproar
might be attributed to the prowling of an animal. No
hunt would draw them this far.

But guards at the clearing meant that the cache had
been discovered, that tomorrow or the next day or the
next—whenever the garthmaster could summon a

Speaker—the sinful objects would be ceremoniously destroyed and the "sin" of the whole small community purged by fasting and ritual. It would be best to lie low until that was over.

Yet—he had to know if his guess concerning the treasure trap was correct. Would Ashla follow the pattern—fall victim to the Green Sick, be exiled as a contamination, finally become what he was? He must know!

Why? Who? The questions still rode him. But more important—what was he to do now? Return to Iftcan to wait? Or . . .

In that moment Naill learned that one should never forget the forest was not all friend.

He plunged forward in a sprawl in the same instant that his nose was assaulted by a most stupefying charnel reek. Rolling, kicking, unable to free his right foot from a loop of dark ropy stuff, he hung at last head down and feet up against the wall of a pit, the stench from which turned him sick.

Kalcrok! Ayyar memory identified the enemy, the method of its attack. Naill twisted, trying to bring up his head and shoulders, the sword now free in his hand. He gained purchase with his elbow against the wall, enough to wrench his shoulders partly around. But he had only a second to bring out the sword point before the phosphorescent bulk on the other side of the hole moved.

The thing came in a flying leap meant to plaster it against the earth of the wall with the dangling body of its prey flattened under it. The very force of that spring brought its belly down upon the sword Naill held.

He cried out as claws scissored at his legs, as the terrible odor of that body, the disgusting weight of its mass struck against him. Then, as he hung gasping and choking, there came a thin screech, so high in the scale of sound as to cause a sharp pain in his head, and the kalcrok fell away, kicking and scrambling in the noisome depths of its trap, taking his sword, still in the deep belly wound, with it.

Naill, very close to unconsciousness, dangled head down once more. Then Ayyar memory prodded him to weak effort. To hang so was to die, even if the kalcrok had also suffered a death blow. He must try to move.

There was a bleeding rake across one arm; his legs were torn, too. But he must get free—he must! He twisted and turned, rubbing his body against the wall.

Perhaps the force of the kalcrok's spring had already weakened the web cord that held him, or perhaps his own feeble efforts fretted it thin against the rough wall. But it gave and he slid down into the debris at the pit bottom.

The gleaming lump that was the terror of that trap lay on its back, its clawed legs still jerking, the sword hilt projecting from its underparts. Naill retched, somehow got to his feet, and stumbled over to drag his defiled blade free. He ran it into the soil of the pit wall to clean it and looked about him half dazed.

To climb those walls was, he believed, close to impossible. They had been most skillfully fashioned to prevent the escape of the trapped. But kalcroks had back doors—they did not depend altogether on their pit traps to supply their food needs.

Only—such an exit would lead past the kalcrok's nest, and past any nestlings such a shelter might contain. Ayyar memory was clear enough to make Naill shudder. Move now—at once—before there was any stir there . . . if there were any to stir! He edged around the confines of the hole, supporting himself with a hand against the wall. The pain of his leg wounds was beginning to bite now. He must go, before those wounds could stiffen and keep him from moving at all.

This was it—a hole into blackness, from which issued a fetid odor to make him sick again. Forcing down his fear and repulsion, Naill went to his hands and knees, his sword ready, and crawled into that passage.

The walls were slick with slime, well polished by the kalcrok's constant use. This was an old, well-established den; all the more reason to fear a nest! And here the dark was such that his night sight, good as it was, could not help him. Scent? How could one separate any one evil odor from the general stench of this devil run? Hearing? He must depend now upon his ears for any warning.

And to do that he must go slowly.

So he crept onward, sweeping the sword back and forth ahead, to assure himself that there was no opening on either side of the run, pausing to listen. A scrape of leg against earth, the moving of a body—would he be able to recognize that for what it was, the warning of a nearby and occupied nest?

Sword point met nothingness to his left. Naill stiffened, listening. Nothing—nothing at all. Were the infant monsters alert and waiting to make their pounce? Or were there any nestlings now? Naill dared not linger too long.

It was the hardest test he had ever placed upon his courage and will, that slow forward creep. His only defense against attack, the sword, he kept point out, aimed at the opening he could not see, behind which lay death, not sudden, but very terrible.

The sword point bit at wall again—he had reached the other side of that opening. Now—now he must go forward with his back to that, never knowing when attack might come. This was an endless nightmare such as he had once awakened from in the past, shaking, wet with terror sweat.

On—on—no sounds . . . no, no sounds from behind. An empty nest—but he still could not be sure of that or count on such fortune. Relief could make one careless. Be ready, listen—creep—though how he could turn to fight in this narrow passage Naill did not know.

Then, abruptly, the surface under him angled sharply upward and he drew a breath deeper than a gasp. This was the exit! Up—up and out! He dug the sword into the earth, used it to lever himself out . . . to be met with rain full in his face, cold and slashing on his body. And not too far away he heard the torrent of the river. The river—and beyond: Iftcan!

Did Ayyar take over wholly then? Naill afterward thought so. It was as it had been when the fever held him—small broken snatches of dream action wrapping him round. Or were they real, those times when he clung to river-washed rocks while a swollen stream rose about him, when he staggered on through gusts of beating rain with lightning flashes showing him the towering dead of the tree city?

There was one crash of thunder, blast of lightning bolt so great, so dazzling, that together they blacked out the world. And from then on he had no memories at all.

Trees—Iftsiga! He lay looking up into the might of the ancient citadel, its silver-green crown so far above him that the leaves were only a haze of color against the sky—as high as the stars almost.

The Larsh! Naill sat up, reaching for his sword, looking about him for some sign of the enemy. His body hurt—battle wounds. He had survived, then, the overrun at the Second Ring.

"Jagna! Midar!" His call issued from his lips a weak whisper.

A swish of displaced air overhead. He held his sword

ready. Wide white wings, which clapped to body as talons touched earth—a quarrin came to him, a pouch dangling from its beak. "Hoorurr!" Naill loosened his grip on the weapon hilt. Once more he blinked awake from a dream Ayyar had known. "Hoorurr!"

The bird dropped the pouch by his hand, snapped and chittered a reply. Then the quarrin walked slowly down the length of the man's body as if inspecting his clotted wounds. Naill *was* back—in the safety of Iftcan—though he did not remember anything since he had crawled out of the kalcrok's den.

NINE

MONSTER

The storm that had raged in the forest as Naill won
free from the kalcrok pit did not quickly blow itself out.
His wounds tended with the same salve that he had
used on Hoorurr's seared wing, he managed the climb
into Iftsiga and lay there on the mats as the living wood
of the chamber walls about him throbbed and sang with
the fury of the gale.

Once there was a crash, heavier than the roll of
thunder, and the whole of Iftsiga quivered in sympathy until Naill feared that an earthquake shock had
threatened the rooting of the citadel. He guessed that
one of the long-dead tree towers had been struck by
lightning and wind-toppled.

There was no way to mark the passing of time, no
period of sun alternating with the welcome cool of
night. Hoorurr shifted from chamber to chamber,

closing his wings to clamber down or up through the ladder hole, visiting Naill, or withdrawing restlessly again. The quarrin was unhappy, resenting the imprisonment forced upon him by the storm.

Then Naill awoke to silence, aware as he tentatively stretched his legs that the healing wounds no longer smarted, that he could move with a measure of comfort. And the pound of the wind was stilled, the tree silent, no longer pressed or battered.

He replaced his torn and soiled clothing with fresh from the stores; swung up and out on the entrance branch to look out over the forest in the fading, pale, watery sunlight. The storm had indeed wrought changes. Those trees that had shown bone-gray among the shorter green of new growth had been shattered. Smoke curled from charred and smoldering trunks. To the west where that wasteland of evil stretched, there was a drifting murk, as if fire burned thereabouts.

From this perch Naill could see across the river through the storm-torn gaps of foliage. There was a new chill in the air. He had landed on Janus—how many weeks ago? Now as he tried to count that tale of planet-spent days, first in his head, and then childishly on his fingers, he found too many discrepancies. But he had been brought to Kosburg's in late mid-summer. The days were now chilling into the fall season. And he knew from what he had heard at the garth that when winter gripped this land, it could be sere and bitter.

Yet—Ayyar memories again—there had been other winters long ago when men had not been bound to shelter against storm blasts and leaves lingered, if more heavily silvered, until new opening buds pushed them free in the spring. But that had been before the death of Iftcan.

Now the garths must be preparing for the cold season. And this past gale had brought with it the first whispers of the autumn change. Naill was glad for the cloak about him when the wind reached exploring fingers to the branch on which he sat. Winter—the leaves gone, the forest naked . . . then if there was a hunt, any fugitive would have far less of a chance. Had it been approaching winter that had sent the strangers from Iftcan to the sea?

He bit on that, savored what it might mean, as he might bite doubtfully on a newly discovered fruit—to find it sour. One could remain here in Iftsiga. But winter was the season in which the garths burned off the Fringe. Fire so set was never controlled as far as its spreading in the forest was concerned. The farther the flames ate into the woodlands, the better the settlers like it. And the dead trees about here would make one great torch of the whole dead city.

Somewhere to the west, nearer the sea . . . Naill considered that move thoughtfully. And in so going west, he could swing by the frontier garth—see what had happened there to Ashla. Tonight—no, perhaps a day's more rest . . . then with his wounds less sore, he could move fast and quietly.

That night he hunted with Hoorurr, the bird dropping noiselessly to buffet a borfund with beating wings and slashing talons until Naill's sword brought an end to the bewildered animal's life. The man kindled a small fire among stones, toasted lean flavorsome meat over the flames on sharpened sticks, and found the taste good after his long diet of bread from the strangers' stores, the berries and seed pods of the forest. This had been done many times, Ayyar memory told him— this was the old free life of the Iftinkind.

The third night after the end of the storm, Naill sorted carefully through the supplies in the tree chamber and made up a journey pack, which must serve him if he did not or could not return over a period that might run into weeks. Another change of clothing, including skin boots, the bread stuff, a pouch of healing ointment, a knife he found. During that search for supplies, he opened and investigated every box and chest in the upper chamber—but he did not touch those of the treasure room below.

There was a reluctance in him now to have anything to do with those objects. Almost he could believe the settlers' conviction that danger clung to the caches, and he had no desire to test that theory further. As he stood at the foot of Iftsiga before setting out, Naill was struck by a sudden feeling of peril, so intense only determined effort of will set him moving.

As he went, Hoorurr winged down the forest aisle over his head, uttering a querulous, complaining cry. From quarrin to man a distorted message sped . . . danger! Naill paused, alert, looking up to the bird now perched over head.

"Where?" His lips shaped the same word his mind formed.

But the concept that answered him was too fragmentary, too alien, to provide any real answer. Only that the danger was not immediate, only that it was old, old maybe as Iftcan itself.

"Fire? Settlers?" Naill pushed his demand for knowledge.

Neither. No, this was something else. Then he got an answer that was sharper, clearer. From the west came the threat—out of the splotch of the wastes. Keep away, well out of that. Old ills dwelt there, which might spread again were they to awake. Awake? How? What? But Hoorurr provided no understandable reply.

"All right!" Naill agreed. "I go this way." He tried to mind-picture a southwestern route, back along the river, to the garth where he had seen Ashla.

Hoorurr's orb eyes regarded him measuringly. Now

there was no flicker of thought from the bird. He might be considering Naill's reply, turning it over in his mind to compare with a conclusion of his own.

"Do you go, too?" Naill asked. To have the keen-eyed, winged hunter with him would mean doubled security. He had no doubt the quarrin's senses were far keener than his own.

Hoorurr's feather-tufted head turned on round shoulders. The quarrin faced west—that west against which he had just warned. Now his wings mantled as if he were about to launch at some prey—or some enemy—and he hissed, not cried aloud. That hiss was filled with cold venom and rage. He was a figure of pure defiance.

For it was defiance! Hoorurr was posturing against something to be feared. Again Naill tried desperately to reach the quarrin's mind, to learn, to share in what information was locked in that feather-topped skull.

With his wings folded neatly against body again, talons scraped along the branch as Hoorurr sidled to a point directly above Naill's head. The quarrin gave voice once more, this time with no hiss, but a clacking of beak the man had come to learn was a signal of assent.

They found the river high, the rocks necklaced with foam. Debris loosened by the storm rafted down with the current. To Hoorurr the crossing was no problem. He flapped over to a tree on the opposite bank. Naill moved along the shore, studying the lie of the rocks and calculating the possibility of using them as stepping stones.

Once there had been a bridge there, its arches long since tumbled and riven apart by numerous floods. Perhaps only Ayyar memory could have moved Naill's eyes now to pick up those points, align them, and see what way to take. A chancy path with the rocks wet, the water awash over at least two.

Settling his pack to balance evenly, he took a running leap. Somehow he made it—though he was shaking with more than the chill of water spray when he reached the far bank and sank to his knees, a little weak and a great deal amazed at the success of his efforts. On this side of the river the storm rack was as evident. And, not having Hoorurr's advantage, Naill had to make wide detours to avoid the tangles where trees—not as huge as those of Iftcan, but still large enough to amaze off-worlders—had gone down, taking their lesser brethren with them. There was a wide path of such wreckage cutting across the shortest route to the garth, and the hour was past dawn before Naill worked his way through that to take shelter for the day.

When did he become conscious of that thin, wailing plaint? The sun was no longer watery. Its rays beat into the opening left by the storm winds' fury, prisoning him in a half cave beneath upturned roots. And the sounds of the daytime dwellers of the woods were all about him. Small creatures had come into the new open space to root about in the disturbed soil.

But this sound . . . Naill lay with his head on his pack listening, giving it the same attention that he had afforded Hoorurr's warning. No, this was no animal cry—no bird call! Low, continuous, wearing on the ears—and coming from some distance.

How long before he was able to associate that in his mind with pain? Some creature trapped in the snarl of wind-tossed wood, pinned between trunk and earth, or mangled and left to suffer? Naill sat up, hunched together, his head turning southward as hearing traced that sound. Sometimes it sank until it was scarcely audible; again its keening wail rose, broke, until he was sure he could almost distinguish words! A lost settler?

Naill crawled to the outer opening of his burrow, tried to shade his eyes well enough to see through the shattering brightness of the sun. He could just make out a mass of green several hundred yards away that the destructive path of the whirlwind had spared rather than flattened.

From there . . . or from beyond? Out in the open he would be as good as blind. But if he could work his way on to that other strip of standing wood, he might be able to make some progress. And the call—if call it was—pulled him, would not let him settle back into his hole.

Naill pursed his lips, imitated Hoorurr's hoot as he had learned to do in summons. The answering beak snap came from where the quarrin roosted in the upturned root mass over Naill's head.

"See—what—calls." The man thought that out, aimed the order at the bird. "See what calls."

Hoorurr snapped angrily, protesting. But he gave a hop to the next tree trunk and walked along it. His gray-white feathers made a blinding dazzle in the sun as he took off with a flap of wings. The quarrin preferred the night, but he could move better than Naill by day.

Naill tried to mark the shortest distance across that open space to the trees beyond. And always came that crying.

He shouldered his pack and moved out, squinting as he tried to avoid pitfalls underfoot. With one twist of his ankle that wrenched a half-healed wound the kalcrok had dealt and that left him limping, he made it across the open.

That crying—it did hold words, slurred together, undistinguishable, but words. And it came from a point that could not be too far from the garth fields. What had happened? Had the holding been swept by one of the devastating winds, its people driven into the forest they dreaded?

"One . . . alone . . . not right . . ."

Hoorurr's message came from up ahead. One

alone—but what "not right" meant was a puzzle. Hurt—trapped? Naill plunged on. He came to the edge of a glade—and understood.

The broken and forsaken hut Kosburg had shown the newcomers as a warning, its moldering ruins shunned by everyone on the garth—here was another such, hardly more than a lean-to of brush. Hoorurr perched on the highest point of its flimsy roof.

Naill made a second rush across the open and stooped to enter the place. The voice had fallen to a muttering. He smelled the fetid odor of sickness, and his foot struck against an earthen water jar, which rolled away empty.

She had no mask, no hood now, and her sack robe was torn so that her restlessly moving hands and her arms were bare. The pallid skin was splotched with great blotches of green, and masses of loose hair had fallen away from her ever-turning head. Her eyes were open, fixed on the brush of the roof covering, but they did not see that—or anything about her, Naill judged.

He slipped his arm under her, raising her rolling head, steadying it against his own shoulder while he moistened her cracked lips from the water bottle he had filled at the river.

She licked her lips and made a faint sucking sound, so he let her drink more. Under his touch her skin was fire-hot, and she was plainly deep in the fever of the Green Sick. He settled her down once more and looked about the hut. The girl lay on a pile of torn and earth-stained bags, which must have been used for the storing of grain earlier. A plate was by the door, with some crusts on it and a mash of bruised fruit over which insects now crawled. Naill sent that spinning out with a grim ejaculation. Food—water—a bed of sorts! But what more could a sinner hope for?

In spite of the changes of the sickness, he knew her

for Ashla. And Ashla must be a proven sinner by the rules of her own people.

Naill's expression was a half snarl as he glanced momentarily in the direction of the garth from which she must have been expelled as soon as they recognized the illness that had struck her down. But he had survived and, he suspected, so had others—perhaps many of them. There was no reason to believe it would be different for Ashla.

"Water—" Her hands groped out as if searching for the container she had long since emptied.

Naill helped her drink for the second time, and then wiped her face and hands with moistened grass. She sighed.

"Green—green fire . . ."

At first he thought she spoke of her illness, remembering his own delirium. Then Naill saw her hands were spanning apart, and he recalled how she had stood that day holding the beauty of the alien necklace before her in just the same fashion.

"Cool green of Iftcan . . ."

He caught those words eagerly. Iftcan! Did Ashla, deep in the clutch of the fever, now also house a changeling memory, know what had never been a part of the garth or of her own settler history?

On impulse Naill took her two hot hands into his, holding them tightly against her small attempts to pull free.

"Iftcan," he repeated softly. "In the forest—cool forest. . . . Iftcan stands—in the forest."

The restless turning of Ashla's head slowed. Her eyes were closed, and suddenly from beneath those lids tears gathered, made silken tracks down her sunken, splotched cheeks.

"Iftcan is dead!" Her voice was firmer, held an authority that surprised him.

"It is not—not all of it," he assured her softly. "Iftsiga stands, living still. Cool—green—the forest lives. Think of the forest, Ashla!"

Frown lines appeared over her closed eyes. The heavy brows that had given her face harshness were gone now, as was most of her hair. Naill wondered how close she was to the complete change. Her ears—yes, they were definitely pointed, larger than natural for the human kind.

Now her hands tightened on his, rather than trying to pull free.

"The forest—but I am not Ashla." Again that note of firmness, of decision. "I am Illylle—Illylle!" Some of that confidence trailed away.

"Illylle," Naill repeated. "And I am Ayyar—of the Iftin."

But if she could still hear his voice, his words meant nothing to her now. More of the tears ran down her cheeks from beneath her lowered eyelids. And her lips shaped a small, soft moaning, not unlike the crying that had drawn him there.

Water—he needed more water. But to return to the river . . . the journey was too long to be made in daylight. Naill shaped a thought for Hoorurr, hoping the bird might guide him to some forest spring.

"In the leaves—above," came an answer Naill did not understand until he freed himself from Ashla's hold and crawled into the glade about the hut. The quarrin fluttered from the roof, reached a tree branch well overhead, and moved along it toward a cluster of differently shaped leaves the man had not noticed before— some form of parasite growing there.

The center portion of those drifting stem-branches was a large rounded growth, not unlike a bowl fastened levelly on the branch of the supporting tree. Naill climbed, worked his way out, and did indeed find a source of water—two full cups or more held in that tough fiber basin—and he filled his water bottle from its bounty.

He was in the hut again sponging Ashla's face, when a sharp gasp brought him half around to see a figure in the doorway. Masked and hooded, but small—small as one of the girl children who had accompanied Ashla to pick berries days earlier. The newcomer held a basket before her, and now she backed away—raising that as if to use it as a frail barrier against some expected attack.

"No—no—please!" It was a shrill, frightened wail, rising fast to a scream that held no words at all. "Go—go away!"

She flung the basket at him, a water bottle spinning from it to strike against his arm. Then she stooped and caught up a clod of earth, letting fly without aim.

"Let Ashla be—let her be!" Once more she screamed.

Behind Naill, Ashla herself stirred. A hand caught at his shoulder, as, without apparently seeing him, she dragged herself up on the bed of sacking.

"Samera—" Her voice was a hoarse croak, but in it was recognition, a sane awareness.

The child froze, the eyes frantic where they were framed by the mask holes. Then she screamed again, this time touching a terror that was beyond words.

She fell, twisted about, and scrambled away on all fours, still screaming, the terror in those cries so great that Naill was kept from any move after her.

"Samera! Samera!" Ashla swayed forward, tried to crawl after the little girl. Naill caught her shoulders, drew her back against him in spite of her weak struggles. Now he partially understood Samera's horror. The change in Ashla was almost complete; he steadied a woman who was now as much a changeling as himself. Ashla had truly become Illylle of the Iftin and a monster in the sight of those of her own kind.

TEN

ILLYLLE

Ashla's eyes closed; her head lolled forward as Naill lowered her on the bed place. Samera's cries still sounded, fainter now. That clamor—would it draw others from the garth? He sat back on his heels. The girl was changed enough to arouse fear and aversion, as was seen in the child's actions. The Believers did not kill—that was their creed. But he had been hunted away from Kosburg's garth by hounds that knew no law. And Samera could touch off such a hunt here and now.

He could leave, could easily be away before the hunt was up. But Ashla—to the settlers he owed nothing. However, she was no longer a garth woman; she was one of his own kind. Could he rouse her enough to get her away?

"Illylle!" Once more Naill caught her hands, moved by some hope as he called to the Iftin part

109

of her. "Illylle—the Larsh come! We must home to Iftcan!"

Slowly and emphatically he repeated those words, close to her ear. Her eyes half opened; from under the droop of those swollen lids she looked up, appeared to see him. There was no fear nor repulsion in her gaze, only recognition of a sort, as if he were what she had expected.

"Iftcan?" Her lips shaped the word rather than repeated it aloud.

"Iftcan!" Naill promised. "Come!"

To his surprise and relief, when he tried to raise her, she was more than able to get to her feet. If Illylle possessed Ashla's half-alien body now, she had the power they needed. But Naill kept his arm about her shoulders, steering her out of the hut, catching up his pack as he went.

She cried out and covered her eyes with her hands when they came into the open.

"Aiiiii—there is pain!" Her voice had a different intonation.

"Do not look," he cautioned, "but come!" Naill half led, half supported her across the glade of the hut and into the forest beyond. At the same time he aimed a thought at Hoorurr.

"Watch—see if those come after!" He heard the whirr of wings as the quarrin took off.

Whatever spirit or determination supported Ashla, it continued to hold, kept her tottering on. In fact her steps grew firmer as she seemed to recover balance and energy. How long did they have? Would Samera's outburst bring hunters behind them? Naill clung to the memory that Kosburg's people had told stories of "monsters" but never of capturing one—they were never followed far into the fastness of the forest they were reputed to haunt.

If he could get Ashla to the river, and beyond that barrier, he did not believe that anyone would follow them into Iftcan. The woodland they were now traversing was speedily pierced, even at their wavering pace, and now they had before them the opening the wind had slashed. To guide and pull the tranced girl through that under the sun . . . Naill doubted he could do it.

Though he listened, he had not yet heard any hound yap. And Samera's cries had been ended for long precious moments. Perhaps the child had been visiting the glade hut in secret, against the orders of the garthmaster. If so, perhaps her terror would not override the other and longer-held fear of household punishment.

"Close your eyes, Illylle," Naill ordered. "Here the sun is bright."

He had slung the pack thongs over his left shoulder; his right arm was about her fever-hot body in support. Now he squinted his own eyes into narrowed slits as he tried to steer them a course in and out among the tumble of storm-scythed growth. Here and there some broken canopy of withering leaves provided temporary sanctuary where they could halt and drink. And Naill could ease his eyes by swabbing a dampened cloth across the closed lids. He feared to pause too long, to allow his companion to slip to the ground, lest he could not urge her up and on again. But she walked more strongly, caught up in another world from which she seemed to draw energy. Her muttered words told him that she was now matching those dreams that had haunted his own fevered flight to Iftcan—now she was Illylle.

The sacking robe, hanging in tatters about her thighs and knees, continued to catch on broken branch stubs or in tangles of vine. She jerked out of Naill's hold, when he tried to pull her free from the third such noosing, and unfastened the belt and the lacings at the throat, dropping it to lie in a dingy circle about her scratched and dusty feet.

"Bad!" She kicked at the roll of cloth. "Ahh. . . ." She stretched her arms up and out. A short, thin under-garment clung to her body.

Their struggles through the rough brush had rid her of the last straggling locks of hair, and under the sun the green pigmentation of her skin was complete. Before, judged by off-world standards, she had had no beauty, nothing but youth. Now, once you accepted the skin tint, the bare skull, the tall, pointed ears—why, she was fair!

Naill blinked from more than the excess of light. How deeply was Illylle now rooted in Ashla? Would she be horrified, frightened, when she learned what had happened to her—as he had been when he had first seen Ayyar's reflection in the pool?

A hound gave tongue and was answered by a leash fellow. Naill caught at her hand.

"Come!"

Her eyes flickered at him without any true aware-ness. She tried to pull free from his hold, shaking her head.

"The Larsh!" Naill traded on those alien memories. And it worked. She ran, heading straight for the next patch of woods, while he limped after past the tree roots where he had sheltered earlier. His twisted ankle hurt, and the half-healed wound in his calf throbbed as if a band of fire had been linked there. But the cool of the wood now cloaked them.

Perhaps Naill was a little lightheaded, too, or the Ayyar memory grew stronger, for he felt that behind them snuffed and ran . . . not the hounds from the garth . . . but things that were not yet men, only held the rough outward seeming of men. He felt that he must reach Iftcan before the Larsh gathered for the final test of strength against strength, life against life.

There was a flurry of wings overhead. Hoorurr had come, and the thought that reached from quarrin to Iftin was a drawing cord. Naill stumbled into the green world as if he plunged from a fire-haunted desert into the body of the sea.

"Throbyn . . . Throbyn . . . !"

Naill's head turned as the cry acted like a sharp slap across his sweating face to arouse him. Ashla was backed against a tree trunk, her nostrils expanded as she drew deep breaths. In these shadows her eyes had a luminescence. But once more there were tears on her cheeks, and she smeared the back of her hand across them with the gesture of a small child who has whimpered out her hurt to meet no comfort.

"Throbyn?"

"Illylle!" Naill took a step toward her.

"You are not Throbyn!" Her accusation was sharp. Then, before he could reach her, she was gone, flitting down the tree aisles.

Kalcrok pit, faintness born of her fever, a fall—all the dangers she could meet there alone sent him limping on. Would the same homing memory that had led him to Iftcan guide her north? The river . . . it was in flood! If she dared a crossing there unheedingly . . . !

"Hoorurr!" He appealed to the quarrin and watched, with only a very small lightening of his concern, the white wings beat after the vanished girl, leaving him to hobble after.

His pack, caught in the undergrowth, was a delaying irritant, but he dared not, or could not, bring himself to abandon it and the supplies. So, juggling it into a better position on his shoulder, Naill struck a crooked lope, which did not favor his injured leg as much as it needed. Whenever he drew a deeper breath than a gasp, there was a stab of pain beneath his lower ribs, and he thought longingly of the river as a spent swimmer might watch the nearest shore.

"Here!" Hoorurr's call—came from the west.

Trouble of some kind. Naill risked further hurt to leap a fallen tree, and struck left. The kalcrok trap— where did it lie? Even with its dreadful maker dead, the pit itself was a threat to the unwary. Had Ashla fallen there?

But Naill found her lying in a small dell by a spring, where drooping branches cut off the direct rays of the sun. She was crouched together, her arms about her knees, her head down upon them, her body shaken by shudders.

"Illylle?" Naill halted, called softly, not wanting to send her into another headlong flight.

At the sound of his voice her body stiffened, the line of her bent shoulders went rigid. But she did not lift her head or move.

"Illylle?" He took a step and then a second into the dell, not quite sure whether he could keep on his feet.

Now her head did come up—slowly. He could see her face. Her eyes were closed so tight that her features seemed twisted. Her mouth worked as if she screamed, yet she made no sound save the rasp of breath whistling in and out of her distended nostrils.

The pool! Now he knew what had shocked her into this almost mindless state of fear. As he had met Ayyar, so had she in this place seen Illylle's countenance for her own. Going down on his knees, Naill cupped his hands together and caught up a scoop of water, cold on his heated flesh. This he threw straight into her convulsed face.

Her eyes opened. First they held in a rigid stare as if she saw nothing but what had frozen her into

close-locked fear—then that broke as she looked at
him. And the increase of terror in her eyes, in her
face, was frightening to watch. She squirmed away
from Naill, her mouth still writhing out soundless
screams. There could be no reasoning with her at this
moment; she was beyond the wall shock had erected,
deep in a place where sane speech could not reach her.

Naill threw himself forward, locked his hands around
her thin wrists. She thrashed about under his weight,
but he pinned her fast. The quickest and best way to
deal with her might be to knock her out completely—
but he doubted if he could. She was almost as tall as
he, and her body had been hardened and strengthened
by labor. Thin as she was, he could not carry her the
rest of the way to the river.

Somehow he got a lashing of vine about her wrists
and leaned away, panting, to consider the next move.
How far was the river? Naill tried to place landmarks
about him. And then he heard the hounds again—faint,
to be sure, but with an exultant note in their cry. They
had picked up the fugitives' trail, knew the scent was
fresh. He hoped they were still leashed.

There was no heading directly for Iftcan. Even if
Ashla came out of her present state of shock, and was
eager and willing to make that journey with him, he
doubted if they could recross the stream there. And
if she must remain a desperate prisoner, it was worse
than useless to try.

Westward there was a portion of the river he had
passed on his way to the sea. Where the bed widened,
the waters, even when storm-fed, would run more shallow. But—that fronted the waste that Hoorurr had
warned against.

They could cross there, keep close to the
riverbank, and so avoid all but the fringe of that
waste—or turn completely west to the sea and

abandon the seeking of Iftcan. That, Naill decided, was the wisest course.

Ashla huddled down, her bound hands pressed tightly against her, her eyes wide and wild as she watched his every move. But she no longer tried to scream. If he could only bring Illylle memory to the surface of her mind again!

"Illylle!" Naill did not try to touch her, made no move toward the shaking girl. "You are Illylle of the Iftin," he said slowly.

Her head shook from side to side, denying that.

"You are Illylle—I am Ayyar," he continued doggedly. "They hunt us—we must go—to the forest—to Iftcan."

Now her mouth worked spasmodically. But he did not believe it was a scream that could not win free. She made a small choking sound, and her tongue swept across her lips. Then she lunged, past him, to the side of the pool, hanging over the water and staring down at her reflection there. From mirror to man she glanced up, down, up. Apparently she was satisfying herself that there was a resemblance between what she saw in the water and Naill.

"I—am—not—" She choked again, her wailing appeal breaking through her hostility.

"You are Illylle," he responded. "You have been ill, with the fever, and you have had ill dreams."

"This is a dream!" she caught him up.

Naill shook his head. "This is real. That"—he waved a hand southward—"is the dream. Now—listen!"

The baying reached their ears.

"Hounds!" She identified that sound correctly, glanced apprehensively over her shoulder. "But why?"

"Because we are of the Iftin, of the forest. We must go!"

Naill shouldered the pack, caught up the end of vine

dangling from the binding on her wrists. Briefly he wondered why it was so important that he take her with him, away from her kin. Only they weren't her kin any longer, that hunting party coursing "monsters" with their hounds. They were changelings together, he and she, their loneliness so halved. He had known loneliness in the Dipple when Malani had fallen ill and strayed so often into her chosen dream escape. But the loneliness he had known when Ayyar claimed him had been the worst of all.

"Come!" That was an order. When he saw that she could not easily rise, he drew her up to him. She shrank in his hold, her face a little averted as if to escape looking directly at him. What if she never accepted the change?

Naill started on, pulling at the vine tie. She came with him, her eyes half closed, her mouth set. But she held to his pace; she did not drag back.

"You are hurt—there is blood . . ."

Naill was startled at her first words. He had stains above the boot top on his bad leg, but they were already stiff and drying.

"I was caught in a kalcrok pit." He answered with the truth, wondering if Illylle memory could supply the rest.

"That is an evil creature, living partly underground," he added. "The wound was healing. I fell and opened it again."

"This kalcrok—you killed it?" Her question was simple, such as a child might ask. "With the big knife?" Her bound hands gestured toward the sword in the sheath of his sword belt.

"With the sword," Naill corrected absently. "Yes, I killed it—because I was lucky."

"You have lived here always—in the forest?"

"No." Naill took the chance to drive home the idea

of the fate they shared. "I was a laborer—on a garth—
and I found a treasure."

"A treasure," she interrupted, still in that childish
tone. "Green and pretty—so very pretty!" She had her
hands up, trying to pull them apart as if holding the
necklace once more. "I had one too—green—like the
woods."

"Yes," Naill conceded, "a treasure such as you found.
Then—then I had the Green Sick—and afterward I was
Ayyar, though I am also Naill Renfro." Could he make
her understand, he wondered.

"I am Ashla Himmer. But you called me by another
name."

"You are Illylle—or in part you are Illylle."

"Illylle." She repeated the name softly. "That is
pretty. But I sinned! I sinned or I would not now be
a monster!"

Naill took a chance. He stopped short and turned
to face her.

"Look at me, Illylle!" he commanded. "Look well—
think. Do you see a monster? Do you truly see a
monster?"

At first it appeared that she might answer that with
a ready affirmative. But as his gaze continued to hold
hers, steady and with all the demand he could put into
it, she hesitated. Frankly she inspected him from bare-
skulled head to mud-stained boots and back again.

"No—" she said slowly. "You are different—but you
are not a monster, only different."

"And you are different, Illylle, but you are not a
monster. You are not ugly. For an Iftin you are fair—
not ugly, just different."

"Not a monster—not ugly—for an Iftin, fair." She
repeated that wonderingly. "Please"—she held out her
bound hands—"loose me. I shall not run, you who are
Ayyar and also a sinner named Naill Renfro."

He slit the vines and threw them away. Her acceptance had come more quickly and more completely than he had dared hope a short time before.

"Tell me—do we go now to a city, a city of trees? I think I remember those tree towers. But how can I?" she asked, disturbed.

"Iftcan. Yes, there is such a city, but much of it is now dead," Naill told her. "What you remember is from long ago."

"But how—and why?" She asked his own questions of him.

"How—I can guess in part. Why"—Naill shrugged— "that I do not know. But what I have discovered is this." As they went he told her of what he had found in Iftsiga, of the treasure buried at her own holding, and of all he had learned or suspected.

"So—those who sin by taking the forbidden things"— she summed it up in her own way—"they are punished—by becoming as we. And so the Forest Devil does tempt us, even as the Speaker has always said."

"But is that so?" Naill countered. "Is this truly punishment, Illylle? Do you hate the forest and are you unhappy here as you would be if this was a punishment?" He was arguing awkwardly, perhaps, but he was sure he must alter her rationalization of the Believers' creed and her application of it to their own problem. If she believed that the forest was a punishment for the damned, then for her it might be just that.

"The Speaker said—" she began, and then paused, plainly facing some thought, perhaps not new to her but one of which she was still wary. She stopped short and put out her hand to the tree beside which she stood. It was an odd gesture she made, as if her warm flesh curved about a loved and beautiful possession. "This—this is not evil!" she cried aloud. "And the city of trees, of which I dreamed, that is not evil! But good—very good! To Ashla there was evil—to Illylle good! For Illylle there is no Speaker, no one to say this is bad when it is good! So"—she was smiling now, looking at Naill with a light in her eyes, on her face, the light of one making a discovery of a new and joyful freedom—"so now I am Illylle for whom the world is good and not filled with sin—always so many, many sins, so many sins where the Rule holds the listing."

Naill laughed involuntarily, and a moment later she echoed him. It was as if some of that feeling of joy had winged between them. At that moment Naill felt no weariness, no pain. He wanted to run—to cry aloud in this new feeling of freedom and delight.

But behind, the hounds bayed, and striking deeply into his mind came a warning from Hoorurr.

"They come faster, forest brother—go!"

Naill caught at Illylle's hand and started on at the best pace he could muster.

ELEVEN

TO THE MIRROR

The sun that had plagued them was veiled by dull clouds. Illylle was looking out over the open riverbed. By her shoulder Hoorurr perched on a tall rock, his head turning from Naill to the north and back again slowly, while he snapped his bill in small sharp clicks of dissent.

Across the water lay a rock-paved shore where a mist—or was it smoke from smothered fires?—curled in languid trails.

"What lies there?" she asked.

"I don't know. But—"

"It is evil!" That was no question, rather a statement of fact. The girl raised both hands to her head, bent forward a little, her eyes closed. Naill laid fingers on her upper arm.

"Are you ill again?"

121

She shook her head. The quarrin stirred, regarded the girl with a surprise as open as that which might be expressed on human features. From Hoorurr's throat came a series of small purring notes, which Naill had never heard before. The quarrin's feet lifted, first right and then left, as if he were engaged in some solemn dance in time to his own calls.

And now Naill saw Illylle's head move too, slightly but unmistakably in that same rhythm, back and forth, in time to Hoorurr's stamping feet and muted cries—or was the quarrin taking his lead from her? This was something Naill could not understand except that within him the conviction grew that at this moment the leadership of their small party was passing from him to her.

"No!" He tried to catch at her arm once more. But she was already gone, flitting ahead, to splash into the river shallows, wading out in the main current. Hoorurr voiced a great hooting cry and spiraled up, circling above the river and the girl. There was nothing for Naill to do but follow.

Illylle pushed on without hesitation, as if she knew just where she was going and why, swerving to avoid storm wrack, yet always coming back to a line that would bring her out on a rock ledge on the opposite shore. One of the mist trails drifted over the water, and Naill caught the reek of smoke: true enough, smoke from a fire fed by vegetation. Thin as that was, it made him cough and was raw in his nose and throat.

The girl scrambled up on the ledge, going on all fours to reach the crown of the slope. Hoorurr continued to wheel overhead, but the quarrin called no longer. At the top where that rock shelf leveled, Illylle halted and stood straight, her wet garment clinging to her body above her scratched and welted legs. She faced north, inland, her arms hanging to her sides, her eyes now wide open—yet, Naill believed, not fixed on

any visible point ahead. She was either seeing farther
than his own sight reached, or something that was
within her own mind.

> "Gather dark, gather dark,
>   Bring the blade, bring the torch—
>   Summon power the land to walk."

Her voice was very soft, close to a whisper, and she
accented the words oddly, chanted them into a song
without music.

"*Hooooorurrrr*—" the hooting cry of the quarrin was
her answer.

As Naill pulled himself up to join her, she turned
her head, and once more he saw the luminous spark
deep in her now wide-open eyes.

"The power is thin, perhaps no longer can it be
summoned." Her words meant nothing. Maybe she had
plunged so deeply into Illylle memory he could no
longer reach her.

"Come." He faced east—toward Iftcan.

"That way is closed." Now it was her hand that held
him back. "The barrier thickens." There was for a
moment a slow smile on her lips. "No warrior steel cuts
a path through the White Forest."

"What—?" Completely bewildered, but realizing that
her cryptic warning was indeed seriously meant, that
Ayyar memory stirred in him at the mention of the
White Forest, Naill hesitated. "How, then, do we go?"
he asked.

Illylle's head lifted; her nostrils quivered. Through
the dark mass of the cloud bank broke a flash of lightning. And the wind sang along the river with a wild,
rising voice.

"They gather—oh, they gather! And the power is
thin—so thin!"

Naill lost patience. To be caught in the open if the coming storm proved as severe as the last one was folly, perhaps close to suicidal. They would have to find cover. He raised his voice to top the wind: "We must have cover from the storm!"

She caught his hand and began to run west, along the rock ledge bordering the river. He found that he dragged back as his wrenched leg stiffened, slowing the pace she set. Then she studied him, came to some decision of her own.

" . . . not . . . run . . ." Her words were tattered by the rising wind. They were both lashed with whips of water from the river. Her pull was insistent as she angled abruptly from the stream edge straight into the murky portion of the wasteland. Naill strove to hold back, to argue.

His earlier distaste for that country was hardening into something a great deal stronger and more militant.

"To the Mirror—the Mirror of Thanth!"

Ayyar memory . . . for an instant he had a mind picture of silver, rimmed with pointed rocks. A place of power—not Forest Power, but power! Then that was gone, and the wisp of meaning it held for him vanished as the wind about them swept the mist murk out of their way, cleaving a clear path into the dreary overgrowth of the waste.

Naill was moving faster before he noted that what lay underfoot now was not the broken earth with its trap-tangle of vine and vegetation, but a pavement of gray stone, very old, with dusty hollows and grooves worn into its surface as if for many centuries feet had trod here. Old—and alien to even Iftin kind—but not forbidden.

Illylle ran a little ahead, having dropped his hand when he followed. There was an eagerness about her, not only in her eyes, in the curve of her lips, but in every line of her thin body. She could be one hastening to a long-awaited rendezvous . . . or home.

The pavement was not wide, and in places sand and earth had silted over it so that only the faintest traces were discernible. But the girl never looked down at where her feet trod; she watched ahead—seeking some other guide, or perhaps already moved by one.

Dark—the dark was drawing in. And with it . . . Naill's eyes moved from side to side. His night sight could not reach far enough in the storm's gloom. There were shades—things—which could be bushes swaying in the wind . . . or something else. Only none of those deceptive bushes touched upon the roadway, nor did they approach it too closely. It was framed by rock and bare earth.

And those rocks, mere rounded boulders at first, looked entirely natural in this grim country—until they crowded more thickly at the road edges, rising in rude walls, first waist high to the fugitives, then even with their shoulders, and on to tower above their heads, until those giant slabs on either side let in only a slit of sullen gray sky far above. Naill believed now they were a wall built with purpose—to protect the road, shelter those who used it?

Down in this trough between those rock ridges the wind was gone, but now and then a distant play of lightning could be seen. Rain began, funneled down upon them by the rock walls, running in streams to join a widening rivulet about their feet, ankles, calves.

"Illylle, if this water rises . . ." Naill broke out.

"It will not. Soon we come to the Guard Way."

"Where do we go?" He tried for enlightenment the second time.

"Up"—she sketched the direction with a rising hand—"to the Mirror. To the Earth's Center."

She was right; the road was rising, becoming steeper. But still it ran north and they must be well into the waste. No murk clung in this cut, nor did Naill smell any of the reek the drifting mist had carried. Here was only rock washed by the rain.

Now Illylle slackened pace. "The Guard Way—have you the word?"

"No." Naill stared ahead eagerly. The rocks in the wall arched, met to form a dark mouth of what might be a tunnel. There was shelter from the storm, but there might be other things to consider past temporary comfort of body. For some reason Naill's hand fell to his sword hilt; he drew the blade.

Slim silver in the gloom. A speck of green danced on its point, brightened, flared as if he bore a torch. Then Naill saw on the rock of the arch other green flecks come to life, flash but not die. On the sweep of the keystone a symbol waxed into life—glowed.

Illylle laughed. "Not dead—not dead—sleeping only—to awake—awake!" Her voice arose in a cry of triumph.

> "Starlight, swordlight, Ift-borne,
> Welcomes back the wanderers.
> Far travel, sleep long,
> But the Power returns. . . ."

She swung about, standing now under the vast curve of the arch with its glittering green symbol, held out her hands to Naill in a wide gesture of welcome.

"Sword-bearer, give me your name!"

"Naill Renfro," one part of him said with a desperate stubbornness. But he answered aloud, "I am Ayyar, tree born in Ky-Kyc—Captain of the First Ring of Iftcan."

"Sword-bearer, come, be free of the Guard Way."

They were faced by a stairway in place of the road, a stair that climbed up and up under the rock roof, leading where Naill could not guess. And the Ayyar memories did not supply an answer here. Together, shoulder to shoulder, they climbed those stairs. And as Naill faltered and limped, Illylle lent him her strength. There was a feeling of serenity and comfort that flowed from her arm under his, her nearness, into his tired body, keeping him climbing.

How long was that stairway? What space of time passed as they climbed it? They were outside normal time in a strange way Naill Renfro could not have produced words to explain, but which Ayyar found right and natural. Around him was the past, and any moment now some barrier would break, and the past would flow in upon both of them. Then they would know all the answers, and there would be no more questions to ask.

Only that did not happen; the end of the stairway came before they broke that intangible barrier. They came out into the open once more on a straight, smooth ledge in a cup, which might have been the cratered cone of a small volcano. Stark walls rose from a sheet of untroubled water, a silver mirror that did not reflect the light—for there was no light overhead now, not even a prick of star—but rather contained a glow within itself, as if it were a pool of fluid metal.

"The Mirror!" Illylle spoke softly, for they were in truth intruders, disturbing something vast—beyond human comprehension—something so old, so full of power, that Naill flung up his sword arm, hand still weighted by the drawn blade, to hide his face. Her fingers were warm on his wrist, drawing it down once more.

"Look!" she commanded, and in that order was such authority that he must obey.

Mirror still, mirror bright—vast as an ocean, small enough to be scooped up by his two hands—it spread, it shrank, it pulled, it repelled. And under all Naill's emotional stress—fear and awe—there grew an aching hunger. What he desired most did not come. Again there was a barrier between him and what waited just beyond, something so wonderful, so changing of spirit, that he could have cried aloud his loss and frustration, beaten down that wall with his sword. All knowledge was there—and he could not reach it!

Through his own depths of desire and sorrow Naill heard Ashla crying. And that sound drew him back to sight and awareness, not of what could have been, but of what was. The girl crouched on the ledge above the Mirror as she had beside the forest pool where the consciousness of her changing had first come to her. But there was no terror or horror here. No, like him, she was torn by the loss of what she could not have, for all her reaching.

Naill knelt beside her and drew her into his arms. Together they took comfort from the fact that this overwhelming failure was shared, was a part of each of them.

"What have we done?" she whimpered at last.

"It is what we are," he replied, and knew that he spoke the truth. "We are only a part of what we should be to stand here. We are Illylle and Ayyar, but we are also Naill and Ashla. So we are neither truly one or the other—to fear wholly . . . or to have all."

"I cannot—" She drew her hand across her tear-wet face and began again. "How can one go on—knowing that this is here and yet one cannot have it? We have been judged and found wanting."

"Are you sure that will always be so—the judgment is final?" Naill had begun that as reassurance; now he wondered for himself, too. "Suppose—suppose"—he put his groping into words and the words were like water to a sun-dried traveler, bringing their own comfort—"that Illylle and Ayyar will grow the greater, Naill and Ashla the less. It has been a very little time since we were changed."

"Do you believe that in truth, or is it only words said in kindness?" she challenged him.

"I meant them as words to be kind." He felt compelled to the strict truth in this place. "But now—now I believe them!"

"This is the Mirror of Thanth. And in it is the Power and the Seeing. Someday—perhaps the Seeing will be ours then. . . . And, oh, the richness of that Seeing!"

"Now"—Naill arose and drew her up with him—"it is better that we go."

Ashla nodded. "If I could only remember more— the way of the Asking and the Giving—"

"I do not remember as much as you do," Naill told her quickly.

"But you are a warrior, a Sword-bearer—for you it is the Giving, not the Asking," she burst out impatiently and then stood, hand to lips, as if startled by her own words. "Only bits do I remember . . . but once—once I knew it all! Illylle will come back fully, *then* I shall know again. But you are right. For us now this is a forbidden place. We have escaped the Wrath only because we came with clean hearts and in ignorance!"

They went down the stair, but when they reached the gate of the Guard Way, Naill slipped and lowered himself stiffly to the stone pavement under its arch.

"I do not think I can go any further, whether I provoke the Wrath or not," he told her simply.

"And I do not believe that shelter here will be denied us," she returned. "Give me your sword—for again I remember, a little."

She took the weapon by its leaf-shaped blade and laid it flat on the pavement directly beneath the archway. "The key will keep open the way."

Then Ashla opened Naill's pack, exclaiming over its contents. Together they ate of the bread, drank from the bottle he had refilled at the river. Naill's last waking sight was of Ashla shaking out the extra clothing, measuring it against her. He drifted to sleep, his head pillowed on an Iftin cloak. Outside, the murmur of running water on a road older than man-kept time was a soothing lullaby.

A glowing sword before him—a warning. . . . Naill moved, his shoulder grating painfully against a rock wall. He sat up. There was a sword on the floor, yes, and it was glowing—not green, as it had been beneath the gate, but coldly silver. He laughed. That was the reflection of daylight—pale, yet bright enough to be caught by the highly polished blade.

A stir on the opposite side of this nook and Ashla also sat up, to blink drowsily back at him. She was dressed now in the extra suit of hunter's wear, and she had belted on the long knife that had been at his side before he went to sleep.

"You are well?" he asked, hardly knowing what greeting to use.

"There were many dreams," she replied obliquely. "I have a feeling we will do better away from this place."

Now that she had put it into words, Naill was sure of the same thing. There was a chill in this stairway, the belief that intruders were not welcome—that they should be long gone. He strode back and forth to test his leg. Some of the stiffness held, but he could move, if limpingly. Naill broke a piece of bread in half and shared it with her.

"Back to the river now," he began. Yes, back to the

river, then west to the sea. They must find those others who had set the traps. Then they would know—as they must—the purpose behind all this.

"Back to Himmer's garth."

At first Naill was so intent on planning his westward journey that those words did not register in his mind. When they did, he stared at her. "In the Forest's name—why?"

"Samera," Ashla replied as if that made everything clear.

"Samera—the little girl?" Understanding was still beyond him.

"Samera—she is my sister. When they took me to the forest to die—as they thought, a sinner judged—she came with food and water. They would beat her for it if they discovered. Perhaps she is now sick, too. I must know, do you not see that? I cannot leave Samera! The new wife—she is the keeper of the House Rule now. Me she hated, and to Samera she was unkind always, for we are children of the first wife. While I was there I could stand between her and Samera. But now—now Samera is alone, and she is too young to be alone!"

"To Samera you are now a monster. It was she who put those hunters on our trail." Naill spoke the truth brutally, because it was the truth.

"That may be so. But still—I cannot leave Samera!" And he knew she was set in her stubbornness. "There is no need for you to go back with me," she continued. "I can hide in the forest, try to reach her by night."

"She would not come with you. She would be afraid."

"She would know me, and knowing me, she would not fear."

"And how would you get into the garth yard at night, find a child kept indoors? The hounds—watchers—they will be alert now for anyone coming from the forest."

"I know only that I cannot leave Samera—she will be lost without me."

"Listen—I am telling you the truth, Illylle. We are no longer of the same breed as your sister. You will not know her as you did; she will not know you." Naill spoke out of the wisdom he had gathered upon his return to Kosburg's. This girl would feel the same revulsion.

"In this I am still Ashla, not Illylle. I go for Samera!"

Naill set his teeth as he remade and shouldered a smaller pack. "Then, let us go."

"For you there is no need," she told him quickly.

"There is a need—we go together or not at all."

TWELVE

FIRE HUNT

"Tell me—why do you do this?" Slim in the forest dress, Ashla was almost one with the twilight shadows as she halted briefly between two drooping-branched trees. So much had she bent to Naill's will that they had gone west for a space instead of directly south, that they might approach the Himmer garth from that direction, thus taking what precautions they could against any sentries along the Fringe.

"Why do you seek Samera?" Naill countered.

"She is my sister. For her I am responsible."

"You are Ift, I am Ift—in that much we are now kin."

"Not blood kin," she protested. "You can go on to the sea, find those others who you spoke of. This is no work of yours."

"Can I?" Naill asked deliberately. "Am I sure there

133

are others of the Iftin after all? What proof have I? Some tracks, too loosely set to be sure of more than that something walked erect through sand and on earth; a signal on a cliff already burned to ash when I reached it; sight of a log floating out to sea. . . . No, I have seen no Iftin—I have only guessed and pieced together a story, and what I guessed may be very wrong."

He heard her breath catch, saw her head turn toward him.

"But there have been others with the Green Sick—others left such as we."

"How many?" he pressed.

Ashla shook her head. "I do not know. The illness was a punishment sent to sinners. No garth wished to publish the guilt of its people aloud. We would hear whispers of this one and that struck down. But of my own knowledge I do not know of more than five."

"Five—from this district alone?"

"From the south Fringe line—and that was in five years."

"A steady drain—but why?" He repeated the old question. "I wonder. . . . How many in all the years since a first off-world landing was made here? And are all those now . . . Iftin?"

"You are free to search and see," Ashla pointed out swiftly.

"I am not free. I stay with the Ift I have found. But in return I ask one promise."

Her chin lifted. "With Samera there, I promise nothing!"

"Then just listen. If you find that what you wish is impossible—that you cannot reach her, or that she will not come—then will you go without lingering?"

"You are so very sure she will not come with me. Why?"

"I cannot make you understand with words—you will see for yourself."

"She will come—if I can reach her!" Ashla's confidence was unshaken. "The dusk is now full. May we not go now?"

Hoorurr had vanished when they had taken the road to the Mirror two days earlier. Naill wished for the quarrin now. With the bird scouting before them, an invasion of the garth would not have seemed quite so foolhardy. But lacking Hoorurr, they must depend upon their own eyes, ears, noses.

He had earlier forced one concession from Ashla; that she would follow his orders in the woods until they reached the fields. And the girl kept that promise faithfully, obeying his commands and copying as well as she could his woodscraft. There was no moon showing tonight, and the softness of coming rain was again in the air.

"The cold may close in early this year," Ashla observed as they crouched together in a thicket. "When there are many severe rainstorms earlier, that is so."

"How early can it come?"

"Perhaps within twenty days now, a sleetstorm, after that others, each worse. . . ."

Naill shelved that future worry for the action at hand. "Listen!" His hand on her shoulder was a signal for quiet. The yap of a hound . . . they heard it clearly.

"From the garth," she whispered.

Naill's tension did not ease. One dog might be at the homestead; that did not mean that others were not patrolling the fields, accompanying a human guard. He said as much.

"No. To those the forest at night is a place of terrors. And Himmer is a cautious man; he will have all in the holding, the gates barred."

"But you plan to enter there." Naill thrust home the folly of her proposed move.

For the first time since she had made her decision at the foot of the Mirror stairway, Ashla's resolution showed a small crack. "But . . . I must." What began hesitantly ended in the firmness of a vow.

"Where in the house would Samera be?" Naill recalled his own expedition at Kosburg's when he had looked upon beings with whom he no longer had any common ground.

"All the little girls—they sleep together in the loft. It has two windows." Ashla sat back on her heels, plainly attempting to visualize what she described. "Ah—" She turned to him eagerly. "First there is the covered shed where there are two phas colts. And from the roof of that, it would be easy to reach the window. Then I can call Samera—"

"And if she sees you?"

After a moment of silence her answer came, a small ragged note disturbing her former confidence. "You mean—she will fear me—cry out as she did at the hut? But perhaps it was you she feared then. Me—I am Ashla who loves her! She would not fear me! And also, it is dark in the loft; they have no light there. She will hear my voice, and of that she will not be afraid."

Perhaps there was some logic in that argument. And—short of dragging Ashla away bodily, which he could not do—there was nothing left but to yield to her desire and do the best he could to take all precautions possible.

They circled farther to the south in order to move into the wind. There was only one wan light showing at the garth now—the night lantern in the yard. As far as they could judge, the inhabitants of the household were safe abed. The field crossings were made in rushes that took them from the shadow safety of one

wall to the next. Then they were close to the stake
barrier about the buildings.

Naill's nose wrinkled against the smell of the garth
and its people. Just as the human scent of Kosburg's
larger holding had awakened revolt in him, so did the
odor of this place. And this time the impact of his
olfactory senses was even sharper. He heard a small
gasp from his companion, saw her run her hand vigorously under her nose.

"That"—Naill tried to drive the truth home—"is the
smell of off-worlders!"

"But we—we are—" She was shaken, bewildered.

"We are of the Iftin, who do not kill trees or live
encased in dead things! Now do you begin to believe
that we are we—and they are they?"

"Samera can be like us also!" she said obstinately.
But Naill thought that she eyed the bulk of the buildings before her a new way—certainly not as one
returning to a familiar place.

The phas shed was set against the stake wall, or they
would never have made the entry. A running leap took
Naill within grasping distance of the top. Once up, he
lowered his sword belt to aid Ashla's climb. Below them
they could hear the stir of the animals, a snorting from
one of the beasts. Ashla lay flat on the roof and
crooned softly, a soothing rise and fall of small notes.
The snorting stopped.

"They will be quiet," she whispered. "I fed them
their mash, they know my voice. And—there is the loft
window!"

Still on her hands and knees, she scuttled across the
shed roof and crouched beneath the opening. Then she
arose slowly to look inside. Her survey took so long
that Naill wondered if the dark baffled her sight, better
than human though it was. Then, even as she had
quieted the phas colts, so she signaled again—a small

hissing of whisper, the separate words of which did not
even reach as far as his own post. Three times she
spoke. Naill caught a glimpse of movement within. The
windowpane swung out and a child stood there, her
arms reaching for Ashla.

Only, when Ashla's hands went out in return, the
child shrank back and Naill heard her frightened cry.

"No—no—not Ashla—a demon! A demon is here!"
Her screams were as wild as they had been in the
forest clearing. Naill moved, crossing the roof with a
wild thing's leap to catch at Ashla, force her back with
him to the wall drop.

"Over!" He threw rather than let her climb, following in an instant. There were other sounds in the garth.
Just as his expedition to Kosburg's had aroused that
other holding, so were Samera's screams doing here—
and now the hounds' bay drowned out her cries.

"Run!" Naill caught Ashla's hand, and they were well
on their way across the first field before he was conscious that she was not dragging back, that her flight
was as quick and sure as his. But she was sobbing as
she fled.

"Not—not—" She fought to get out words Naill
believed he already knew. "Not Ashla," she choked out.
"Never Ashla again!"

His own revolt against Terrankind had been complete, but he had had no ties with anyone at Kosburg's
beyond a kind of passive companionship. How much
harder this must be for someone who had to learn that
even close blood ties no longer held between settler-
born and Iftin. Would the shock be as great this time
as it had been when she had faced Illylle in the forest pool?

The main thing was to get away, back into the
shelter of the woods. The garthmen might bring the
hounds out in the fields, patrol for the rest of the night

in the open, but that they would venture far into the forest he doubted. And he intended to be as far to the westward as possible before the coming of dawn.

"You spoke the truth," Ashla said as Naill swung her down a gully, pushed her along that cut. "That was Samera and we—we were no longer sisters. She—she feared me, and when I looked upon her, it was as if she were someone I had known long ago but for whom I no longer felt in my heart. Why?"

"Ask that of those who set the treasure traps," Naill retorted. "I do not know why they must have their changelings—but changelings we are now. We have no longer any contact with off-worlders."

"It was so with you?"

"Yes. I tried to go back to Kosburg's when I recovered from the fever, after I was changed. When I saw them . . . I knew there was no going back."

"No going back," she repeated forlornly. "But where do we go?"

"West—to the sea."

"Perhaps that is as good a place as any," she agreed mechanically. And she did not speak again as they plunged deeper into the wood.

They kept on past the dawn, since the day was cloudy. Though no rain fell, yet there was a mist in the air and this turned chill, so they were glad of the hooded cloaks. Wearing these, they melted so into the general green-silver-brown of the forest, Naill thought any trailer without hounds would pass them directly without noticing.

The river had taken a bend to the north, and they had not yet reached its bank when Naill learned he had underestimated the enemy to an extent that might mean their deaths. A flyer's hum grew loud and with it the crackle of unleashed energy. Rising smoke and fumes marked the beat of a flamer whip wielded from on high! The pilot was cruising hardly above treetop level, using a portable flamer on the shorter forest growth of the river bottoms.

In spite of the dampness of the mist, the recent rains, no vegetation could resist that. And a fire so begun would burn until a storm of hurricane proportions would be required to quench it. No longer depending upon their own hunting methods, the garthmen must have appealed to the port officials for aid. If he and Ashla could be thus herded into the open by the river, they would be easy prey.

The ruthlessness of that flame lash was enough to panic a fugitive. Naill forced his fear under control.

"What is it?" The girl's attention was for the way they had come, the smoke, the sound of crashing trees as the ray ripped the wild.

"They have a flyer and are using a flamer from it." Naill reported the truth.

"Flyer . . . flamer . . ." She was bewildered. "But those are Worldly weapons—no garthman would use them."

"No—so they must have called the port officials."

"How could they? The Believers do not allow com units in any garth—those also are Worldly."

"Then the port police were already out—for some reason."

There had been that other flyer hunting over the river when he had first made his way to Iftcan. But that was days ago. Why would they still be patrolling the wild? Hoorurr had been wing-shot by a hunting party in the forest. Had that party failed to return? Such a mishap could explain some of this.

Nor did it matter how they had come; the fact that they were methodically lashing the forest with their destructive weapon was the danger. And about the Iftin fugitives other creatures were taking flight. A small pack of borfunds burst through brush, running beside Naill and Ashla for several feet before they plunged again into a thicket. Birds fluttered from tree to tree, and other things swung or winged from branches, moving north before the fire.

"What—" Ashla halted, stripped off the cloak to roll it over one shoulder so it would not impede her flight. "The river—we head for the water?"

Naill longed to agree that that was their salvation. But he could not be sure—not with the flyer above. Oddly, he never thought of attempting communication with the pilot of that craft. The mutual repudiation between changeling and settler had been so complete that he had no hope of any understanding from the off-world officials of the port. The river it would have to be.

They made for that, pushing their weary bodies to the limit of physical endurance. Luckily, the flyer pilot was engrossed in laying a crisscross pattern of fire. Ashla stumbled, nearly went down, her breath coming in huge, tearing gasps.

"Can—not—" she choked out.

"Can!" Naill cried with a confidence he did not feel. His ankle was paining again. But ahead was the river. As he pulled her to her feet, he held her so and demanded: "Can you swim?"

She shook her head. A shaggy animal hardly smaller than a phas lumbered past them, its heavy shoulder fur actually brushing against Naill's arm. The man began to run again, pulling the girl with him, in the wake of the animal, which blasted an open path straight through the underbrush.

Somehow they made a bank ten feet or so above the waterline. The shaggy animal had gone over, to half wade, half swim into the deeper part of the stream where other life splashed. All were heading downriver in a wild and vocal mixture of life forms Naill found largely strange. The forest for miles must have emptied its population into the dubious safety of that strip of water.

"We can't go in there!" Ashla clung to Naill, watching the struggle below with wide and terrified eyes.

Naill glanced across the river. The murk that hung over the waste was there stronger, thicker. In it he could see gleams of red he was sure marked flames. Even if they could win over there, passing among the battling animals, they would not be able to go ashore. In the water, a chance—over there, no.

"We have to!" he shouted in her ear, propelling her to the rim of the drop. "There—" he pointed to a piece of driftwood bobbing between two rocks, at any moment ready to be plucked out of its half mooring. "Get your arms over that. It will keep your head above water."

But they were to have no time for a careful descent of the bank, a chance to choose the method of their water entry. A garble from behind, the whiff of an only too familiar odor—Naill whirled half around, his outflung arms striking Ashla full in the back, to send her over the lip of the drop.

In the dark of the trap pit he had seen a kalcrok as it normally appeared to its victims. Here Naill faced a half-grown specimen of the same horrible species running in the open. The silky hair growth on its back shell was scorched away; it must have lingered in its den until the last possible moment, perhaps having had to break through a flame wall to escape. The pain of those burns must feed its natural ferocity into madness.

Naill used his cloak as a flail, beating at the head of the creature. The cloth was torn from his hold, and he stumbled back, over the cliff. He had one moment of knowing that he was falling.

Then he landed in a pocket of sandy gravel, his left arm under him, with enough force to drive the breath out of his lungs in an explosive puff, and he lay there dazed. From the ground above sounded a snarl spiraling up into yowl. Sand and soil sifted over the edge, but the kalcrok did not leap after him.

Shaken and weak, Naill got to one knee. Ashla . . . where was Ashla? A barrier of rocks rose between him and the small cove where that floating length of drift had lain. He thought his forearm must be broken. But he crawled sidewise along the stones to look for the girl.

There was a place of disturbed earth, marks leading to the lapping water. But those could have also been made by one of the animals. And the drift piece still bobbed by the water-washed rocks. No sign of her! Suppose she had hit her head, slid helplessly on into the stream?

Naill crept to the water's edge, but before he had a chance to look, a mass of reddish fur, torn and running with a brighter red from gaping wounds, rolled down from above. A fanged jowl dropped to emit one of those snarling yowls as the creature hit water, floundered, and then was washed on to sway limply against the very piece of drift which was to have supported Ashla.

There was just enough strength left in Naill to make him crawl on, away from that small cove. The dim hope that the girl might have gone so, instead of into the water, kept him going. Then came the sound of a motor hum. A remnant of self-preservation flattened him down on the earth. Naill lay there, whimpering a little as the waves of pain flowed from his arm, pulsed through his body—until he hardly cared that at any moment the flamer ray could hiss across him.

Inside him grew a full and sullen hatred for that off-worlder flyer—for all the species who killed trees, burned the land. These—these were of the Larsh breed! Should he live, by some miracle, should he come out of this fire hunt—then there would be a harrowing of these new Larsh, such a sword-feasting as the ancients had never seen! He was Ayyar and this was Iftin land—while still he lived, it was Iftin!

Pain. . . . The flamer? No, that would have finished him. And the flyer had passed over. For this small space—this very small space of time—an Ift had won, if the mere preserving of one's life was a victory.

THIRTEEN

THAT WHICH ABIDES—

"Ayyyyaaaarrrr—"

His cheek scraped gravel as his head moved. Why was he so aware of that small discomfort amidst the haze of pain that wrapped him in? The kalcrok—he had fought a kalcrok, won free of its pit. No, that was wrong; he had faced another kalcrok on a riverbank and had fallen . . .

"Ayyyyaarrrr!"

Against his will his eyes opened. There were smoke wreaths over him, the choking fumes making him cough. That coughing wrenched his body, bringing gasps of pain. Heat came with the smoke; scorching fingers of it reaching him. Water . . . there was water . . .

Naill began to crawl until the one hand he could use plunged into that water. Then, without knowing just how, he rolled into the stream, floundering, his head under so that he choked again.

"Ayyar!"

Something pulled at him. Naill tried to fight away from that clutch, which was torture as it tightened on his arm.

"No!" He thought he shrieked that protest.

Water. . . . Naill was in the water, but his head was above it, resting on a support that moved, spun, pulled him with it first in one direction and then another. But the haze had cleared some from his head; he was able to look about him with a measure of comprehension.

His injured arm lay along a water-worn log; his right one dangled across it into the water on the other side so that his head and shoulders were above the surface of the river. And when with infinite labor he was able to turn his head, he saw he was not alone. Green-skinned face, the eyes very large, and bright, pointed ears above a hairless head.

"Ayyar?" She made of his name a question. But as yet Naill could not answer; he could only lie quiet, letting her will and the river's current decide his future. That somehow he had found Ashla, that they were in the river—that Naill knew. The rest did not matter now.

There were other creatures in that waterway. A dripping head arose beside Ashla's for a space; a clawed paw strove to cling equal with her hands. Then both vanished again without Naill's really knowing what manner of animal had striven to share their very frail hold on the future.

"Ayyar—push!" Her voice roused him again.

Smoke—or dusk? The river was dim. Before them loomed a land tongue sprouting rocks and tangles of brush. On that were beached other fugitives above the water. Some still squatted above the waterline, others moved inland. The bottom rose abruptly under Naill, and his knees scraped on that undersurface, jarring his arm so that he cried out.

They crawled up among those other refugees from the fire. There were many rocks here arching high, and they squeezed into a pocket between two such. Naill collapsed; only the boulder backing his shoulders held him up.

"Your arm—" Ashla bent over him. "Let me see."

Red hot agony was a lance reaching up into his shoulder, down into his chest. He tried to evade that torture, but her body was braced against his, her two hands cupping his chin, holding his head steady as she spoke slowly, striving to gain and hold his attention, to reach his thinking mind.

"The bone is broken. I shall try to set it. Brace yourself so—and so. . . ."

Her hands were on him, shifting him a little, his right hand put against a rock, palm flat. Dimly Naill understood, tried to do as she wanted. Then—pain to which what he had earlier felt was nothing at all! He swirled away wrapped in that pain, losing the rocks, the stable earth under him—everything!

There was a weight across his body, a throbbing in his arm. Naill raised his head. Light—growing light. . . . His eyes squinted and then he forced the lids further up. The weight on his chest was his left arm splinted and bound. And the light was that of day.

"Illylle!" She had been with him in the river; that held through the haze and pain. And now she slid down a boulder at his call. In one hand she carried a leaf-twist container from which water splashed. As she held that to his mouth, Naill drank thirstily.

"Can you walk?" Her hands were under his shoulders, trying to raise him. She spoke brusquely, her question a demand.

"There is need?" Naill was alert enough now to measure what might trigger her concern.

"There is need."

He was on his feet, a little lightheaded, but ready to move. Matter-of-factly Ashla came to him, drew his right arm across her shoulders, and started him along between the rocks.

They appeared to have come ashore in a barren waste. No green showed, and the rocks glittered in the growing light. They would have to find a refuge from the sun or be blinded until evening. But where?

"Where do we go?" Naill asked her, hoping for some concrete answer.

"Up." Her reply was ambiguous. But climb they did, and that was a chancy business, though they went slowly and the terrain was rough and broken enough to provide a kind of natural stair in places.

They finished that climb on a height facing broken lands riven by crevices out of which curled, as might tongues of green smoke, twisted spires of vegetation, more gray than green, Naill's eyes told him. And there was no promise here of a welcoming forest. Suddenly Naill stiffened against the girl's steadying arm.

"Which side of the river?" He asked that with more emphasis than he had used before.

"The north."

"This is the waste." He did not need any confirmation from Ashla. The very feel of the place caught at him as might a breath of corruption out of a long-sealed kalcrok pit. All he could see were rocks and those ravines choked with ill-shaped growth. Yet—as he had before on the road to the Mirror—he sensed a lurking, a scouting—a spying. Not on his part, or Ashla's—but something . . . out there . . .

"This is a waste," she repeated almost stolidly. "But

the sun is rising. We cannot return to the river. And twice the port flyer has cruised overhead."

There were strong arguments for going to ground here, yet still they were weak ones in the face of what Naill felt as he looked out over this barren country and remembered Hoorurr's warning. They had gone undetected, unharmed, to the Mirror, and returned. But all through the latter part of that journey, Naill had known with a strange certainty that safety lay only on the ancient road between those two walls, walls that had been erected with a purpose of defense . . . against what? And that road had been so very old—could the menace it had been walled to resist still exist?

"There is no choice," Ashla continued, and Naill could feel a tremor in her arm about his shoulders. "We need not go far—and you have your sword."

Naill saw now that the belt of that weapon weighed down her shoulder. Where she had found it, or how she had kept it through their river journey, he did not know. But he believed that in this time and place that Iftin-forged weapon was small protection indeed.

However, they had no choice. Perhaps he could make the shade of the nearest of those knife-slashed crevices, go to ground under its growth to wait out the day. But that was the best he could do.

"Get me over there." He pointed to the nearest cut. "Then you go, keep close to the water and head as far west as you can before true sunrise. I do not know how far this extends—and you may be able to get out in an hour's travel."

She made no answer as she steered him ahead. What he suggested had only a small chance of success, but it was better, far better, than for her to remain here.

When Ashla did speak, it was to point out the easiest way down into the ravine, to warn against rough footing. And Naill was too engaged with battling through brush to argue with her. The stuff was brittle, oddly desiccated, as if, in spite of its appearance of life and growth, it was really dead and only preserved a semblance of what it had once been in truth.

There was an acrid smell to the snapped branches, crushed leaves, not the wholesome aroma of the forest country. As they neared the bottom of the cut, Naill saw pale, unwholesome plants close to ground level, puffy things with fleshy, tightly curled leaves.

"Here." Ashla steered him right and halted. Part of a tree trunk still possessing a look of the true forest protruded from the wall of the gully, its heart long since decayed and eaten away, but its outer shell making a kind of wooden cave, which, to Naill, offered more natural roofing than the still-living vegetation about it.

But when he put out his hand to that old bark surface, he touched not the substance of long-dead wood, but the hardness of rock. The tree was petrified.

"This will serve me," he told the girl quickly. "You must go, before the sun climbs."

She had eased him down under the curve of the stone bark. Now she settled herself beside him composedly.

"We go together—if at all."

Naill was alert to that hint of foreboding.

"If at all?"

All at once Ashla bent her head, covered her face with both hands. He was sure she was not weeping— not with running tears. But there was a kind of despair in the line of those hunched shoulders, that gesture with her hands, that held a hint of fear. Only for a moment did she sit so, and then her head came up, her hands dropped to lie on her knees. But her eyes remained closed.

"If—if it were only given me to remember—to know!" She cried out, not to him, Naill believed, but to the very circumstances of their being. "Illylle knew—so much she knew—but Ashla does not. And sometimes I cannot reach Illylle through Ashla! Naill, what do you know of Ayyar, truly know?" Her eyes opened, held his with a fierce intensity as if his answer was now the most important thing in the world, could lead to some salvation for both of them.

And it sparked in him a need to search his own mind for Ayyar and what Ayyar of the Iftin had known.

"I think"—he spoke slowly, wanting to be very sure of every limited fact, if fact could be the term for a recollection; he did know—"he was a warrior—and he was Lord of Ky-Kyc. But the meaning of that I do not remember. He was a Captain of the First Ring at Iftcan, and he battled there when the Larsh overran the Towers. He was a hunter and one who roved much in the forest. That is all I am sure of. Sometimes I pick a fruit, cross a trail, see or hear some animal or bird—and know what Ayyar knew of them. But of Ayyar I know very little."

"Enough knowledge to keep you alive in the forest, and a little, very little, more than that," she summed up.

Naill straightened. That—that made sense in a new way!

"Perhaps that was all Ayyar was meant to give me!" he burst out. "Enough forest lore to keep me alive! And all the rest—that about the fall of Iftcan was something that was meant to be forgotten but was not!"

"If one has a recorder and must leave a message in a hurry"—Ashla caught up the tossed ball of his idea—"and the message lies in the middle of another report, then one could mark it, but still part of the report would intrude upon it."

"A recorder?" Naill was surprised that she would choose such an example to illuminate her meaning. "But were recorders used by the Believers?"

"No. But when my mother had a blood affliction and the Speaker could not pray it away, her father—Bors Keinkind—came and took her to the port to see the off-world medico. I went with her, for she was unable to care for herself. But it was too late—had we gone earlier she might have been saved." Ashla was quiet for a moment and then went on. "It was there I saw recorders and many other things . . . things to make one think—and wonder. Many times have I remembered and thought on what I saw there. But suppose this forest lore was important for survival—so you were given part of an Ayyar memory . . . and other parts of that memory also clung."

"What about Illylle? Does she also furnish you with such aid?"

"Yes—knowledge of animals, foes to dread . . . of certain plants to eat, to use in healing"—Ashla frowned—"and some that may be weapons. But—Illylle was once a person of power. She knew of the Mirror, and she had a right to stand above it and evoke—evoke what lies within its waters. I think she was in some manner a Speaker of her people, one with weapons and tools not to be seen or felt. And it is in this place that I sense that the most, because I want to hold those weapons."

"Against what?" Naill demanded.

Her frown grew. "I do not know!" Her hands went again to her head. "It is locked in here, I know it is! And it is very important that I remember what Illylle knew. There is danger here—worse danger than the flamer, or the hounds and the garth hunters. It has rested a long time—or slept—or waited with patience . . . and now—" Dropping her hands, she faced

Naill with a dawning horror far back in her eyes, and her voice sank to the faintest thread as she finished that warning. "It would—feed."

Naill found himself listening, not with just his ears, but with all of him—as the hunted listen for the snuffling of a hound. Yet he knew that no animal, no man, threatened them. It was something older, far more powerful, far more complex than any life form he had known before. Was it already out there, teasing them? Or had it not yet awakened, become aware that what it so long had hungered for was now within reach?

"The White Forest!" Illylle spoke now, and Ayyar's fear flared at that name. "This is the Fringe of the White Forest!"

> "Iftin sword, Iftin hand,
> Iftin heart, Iftin kind.
> Forged in dark, cooled by moon,
> Borne by warrior who will stand
> When Ring breaks and tree tower falls—
> Iftin sword—Iftin brand!"

His voice trailed into silence from the rich swing of that chant, a chant that carried in its cadence the march of feet, the clash of swords, the purr of tree drums.

"Iftin sword!" she echoed, and with a swift movement drew the blade he had found at Iftsiga. " 'Forged in dark, cooled by moon!' If it were so—if it were only so!"

"That was part of Ayyar memory," Naill told her. "Do you know its meaning?"

"A little—only a little. It is a prophecy, a promise—made to an Iftin hero in the Blue Leaf day. And it was fulfilled. But that was in the Blue Leaf, and our leaf is Gray and withered." She turned the blade over and over in her hands, studying it closely. "This was a key at the Guard Way—we saw that, both of us. Perhaps it is more than a key. Perhaps it is the blade of Kymon, or akin to that blade. If so, it has a power in its own substance. Illylle, Illylle—let me know more!" That last was a cry that was close to a sob.

Naill took the sword from her. True—he had watched that green spark flare on the tip of the blade and the symbol glow in reply on the keystone of the arch. But in his hand he could see no more than a finely made weapon.

"What did Kymon do? Was he the hero of the prophecy?"

"Yes . . . it was so long ago—dim in memory. He dared the White Forest and won the Peace of the Iftcan, so that those of his blood could tower the Great Trees. And that which nourished the White Forest was bound by the Oath of Forgetting and Side-sitting. Then the Blue Leaf became the Green, and still the Oath held between Iftin and That Which Abode Apart. But when the Green Leaf was at its falling, the Iftin were fewer and That Which Abode stirred. The Oath was called aloud before Iftcan, so that the waste dared not advance. Only the Larsh—who had not sworn the Oath, because in the day of its uttering they could not mouth words—answered That Which Abode and came into *Its* light. And so they were established as a nation and grew the greater as the Iftin grew less.

"When the Gray Leaf budded, once more That Which Abode stirred and the Towers of Iftcan were shaken. The Oath was spoken and the Burning Light could not pass. But the Larsh, who had not given the Oath, became *Its* hands, *Its* weapons, and the Larsh were many, the Iftin so few, so very few . . ." Her hands were up before her, slightly cupped, fingers apart. Almost, Naill could see her try to hold water that trickled away to be swallowed up by thirsty earth. And in him Ayyar responded with a vast surge of anger and despair.

"Then came the end of Iftcan and the end of the Iftin. There was no more Oath-binding and That Which Abode was freed to do as *It* willed with *Its* servants—the Larsh."

"And this is the memory of Illylle?" Naill asked softly.

"This is the remembering of Illylle, though it comes to me dimly as one sees through hot bars of sunlight. Now—the Larsh. . . . Is this the Day of the Larsh, the Night of the Iftin having passed?"

"I think that perhaps the Day of the Larsh has also passed away. There is no tale of them since the first off-world ship put down on Janus a hundred planet years ago."

"The Larsh may be gone, but that which sent them has not! Old powers linger in this land!" Her voice grew stronger. "This may not be the blade that was forged by Kymon, carried by him into the great Sword-feasting of the White Forest. But within me is the knowledge that it has its power, and"—she paused, then nodded, as if she had been reassured by some voice or thought Naill could not share—"that you have a part in what is to come, a part of purpose. Now—it is well into day, and day is the time of That Which Abode. We must have rest. Give me the sword, Ayyar-Naill, and do you sleep, for in me there is a stir, and perhaps I can remember more—whereas if I sleep, I may lose—"

Her certainty was such that he could not protest. As Naill settled himself on the ground, the disconnected story she had told held in his mind—Kymon, a hero who had forced the Oath upon the Enemy, so that the trees of Iftcan could harbor his people, and the ages that that Oath had held back a burning, pitiless white light, until the Iftin grew too few—too few and too thin of blood-line, too burdened with ancient memory to maintain their fortress and their lives against the battering waves of Larsh, new-come from the beast and daring in their youthful ignorance, their fostered hate, to destroy that which they could never build, stamp out what they did not understand. Yes, Ayyar memory told him, she had the truth of that . . . Illylle-Ashla, Mirror Watcher that was.

FOURTEEN

CAPTURED

The bared blade lay across his knee, his good hand resting ready on its hilt. Naill sat quietly. Outside the vegetation-filled cut, the land was baking hot under a blazing sun. But here, within the trunk of the petrified tree, he could see. And always there was hearing to depend upon for warning. Ashla slept now, curled on her side, droplets of sweat gathering on her forehead. For if the eye-blinding glare of the sunlight did not reach here, the heat it generated did.

He had nothing to do but listen and stare out at the stretch of gully. Where the sun reached in splotches, the thick, fleshy growths opened, flattened out their leaves, ate. Naill watched insects, small creeping things, blunder onto those leaves, stick fast, be slowly absorbed into the unwholesome surfaces. This was a place alien to man in its very nature.

The country of the forest had been closed to the settlers, feared and hated by them, but home to the Iftin. This was a land closed to all life, save that which had been conquered—or had bargained and accepted the Enemy's terms. To Naill's eyes it was dead or dying. But that was not the truth. No, the life of the waste was merely frighteningly different.

Ayyar had given him hunter's ears, a forester's sixth sense. Now Naill was conscious of a stir, a kind of awareness. Then he caught a clicking, regular—faint at first, then louder, then fainter again. As if something had passed along the upper rim of the gully, something that had no reason to slink, or creep—something patrolling on sentry go.

Perhaps he was allowing his imagination too free rein. Yet Naill's senses were as certain of that as if he actually watched the thing pass there. The fugitives were to be kept in the pocket until—? That "until" might mean many things—an attack in force, a break on their part, the coming of higher authority.

Ayyar memory supplied Naill with no picture to match that clicking pace. It was louder again, coming now from the other lip of the ravine. Either the sentry was making a circuit of the gully—or there were two of them.

The wise thing might be to break cover while there was only one sentry—or pair of sentries. But neither of the fugitives dared try that. They would be blinded by the sun, unable to either fight or run. Some flying thing was gliding down to skim just above the growth in the gully.

Hoorurr? Naill, for an instant of time, held a very forlorn scrap of hope and so was tricked into a half betrayal. He tried thought-contact with that flyer. And in return met a force so outside his comprehension that it was a monstrous blow, hurling him back against the curve of the tree-trunk wall. Not a flying thing, he thought groggily, but an intelligence, and entity using a smaller and weaker thing to discover—him!

"No!" Perhaps Naill screamed that; he could not tell—perhaps he only resisted that invasion, with mind alone. But he was no longer in the tree. He was out in a space he could not have described in any words he knew—confronting a being, or an intelligence, that had no form, only force and alien purpose, a being to which he and his kind were an enigma to be discarded because they did not fit the pattern the being created.

And it was the very fact of that alienness that was Naill's shield of defense now. For he sensed that there was something in him that baffled the enemy, struck into the very heart of that overwhelming confidence.

"Ky-Kyc!" The old battle cry was on Naill's lips. "Naill!"

His head was against the petrified wood. Ashla's hands rested on his shoulders. Her eyes held to his as if by the power of that intent gaze alone she had pulled him back from the place where he had faced the Enemy.

"*It* stirs! *It* knows!" Her features were set, stern. For a long moment her gaze continued to hold his as if she thus searched into his mind, seeking some thought, some feeling that should not be within him. Then her head moved in a small nod.

"The old truth stands! *That* may kill, but it cannot break us—even when one is Naill-Ayyar instead of true Ayyar."

And he answered strangely, out of thought that was not yet clear. "Perhaps because of Naill-Ayyar, not in spite of Naill."

She caught his confused meaning. "If so—that is

well. Made to lose old knowledge, we should gain
some measure of return. But now . . . *that* knows of
us!"

Naill edged along the trunk's interior. He did not
know whether he could sight either of those sentries—
that which clicked, or that which flew. Ashla lifted a
hand in warning, pointing up.

The winged scout or spy was still above and now
it gave voice. Not with the carrying hoot or beak-
snapping of the quarrin, but in a long, shuddering wail,
more suitable for stormy skies and high winds than for
the sunlight of open day. And—across a piece of open
sky—Naill saw it fly. Saw—what? He was not sure. The
light was too strong for his eyes. And that thing could
almost be a drift of cloud. He only knew it was glittering white and its form hard to distinguish.

"Not a bird . . . I think." He qualified his first guess.

"It is a Watcher and a Seeker . . . " Ashla brushed
the back of her hand across her forehead. "Always only
bits of what should be known. In itself it is not to be
feared—only that it is an extension of That Other. . . . "

"Listen!" Naill shaped the word with his lips, afraid
that even a threat of whisper could reach the sentry.
The clicking—from the opposite side of the gully. . . .
He eyed the brush about the mouth of the tree trunk,
measured the distances and the height of the growths,
before he began to tug at the lashing that fastened his
injured arm across his chest.

Ashla would have protested, but he signed what he
would try and she loosened the tough ties of grass,
leaving his arm free. Naill began to squirm a few inches
at a time into the open, out of the protecting hollow
of the tree.

No clicking now—the sentry had passed, was at the
farther end of the gully. But Naill had discovered his
spy post, was belly-flat at a point from which he could

see a small portion of the rim. And now—that click was returning. Slowly Naill pulled down a straggling branch to form a screen between him and the patroller. With his green skin, his clothing meant to be camouflage in the forest, he believed he did not have to fear detection from above as long as he remained quiet.

It came into view and Naill stared unbelievingly. This was no monster from Janusan past, no alien nightmare. It was something he had seen before—many times! And yet, when his first bewilderment had vanished, he was conscious of small details that were wrong. Before he could count to ten the sentry had vanished past Naill's vision point.

A space-suited off-worlder—walking with the jerky gait of anyone enclosed in the cumbersome covering, the clicking sound coming from the magnetic plates set in the boot soles—an off-worlder in the common rig from any star ship. And yet there were differences about that suit. The whole thing was heavier, with more bulk. And the helmet had the Fors-Genild hump at the back of the neck. The Fors-Genild had been replaced years ago. Naill tried to remember back to the days when he had had free range of his father's ship. They had had Hammackers on every suit. Why, you only saw the Fors-Genilds now in museum collections of outmoded equipment. That suit could be a hundred years old!

He had to be sure—know that this was not some hallucination induced by the sun and his own faulty day-sight. Naill remained where he was, listening eagerly for the return click of those boots on the rock, thinking furiously. Why would the patroller be wearing a space suit on a planet where all conditions were favorable for his life form—because that was the suit of a Terran, or Terran-descended, explorer.

Click—click. . . . Naill raised his head as far as he

could without moving out from behind his brush
screen. Fors-Genild all right! And now that his attention was drawn to that anachronism, he spotted others. The suit *was* old! No modern planet hopper, no
matter how out of funds, would entrust his life to a
suit from that far in the past. Why, he would not be
able to service it, perhaps not even be able to operate some of its archaic equipment.

Which meant . . . ?

Chilled inside in spite of the heat that reached him,
Naill waited until those clicks grew fainter and then
wriggled back into the tree trunk.

"What is it?" Ashla asked.

Naill hesitated. Oddly enough, he could accept in
part that flying thing which was the tool of a reaching alien intelligence. He could accept his own physical
change, the presence of Ayyar memory to share his
mind, better than he could accept the fact that a
hundred-year-old space suit was methodically tramping about the edge of a gully in this wasteland. Was
it because the powers of the Iftin *were* alien and so
could be accepted as a believing child could accept the
wonders of an old tale—while science was represented
by that marching suit—an object which was concrete
and did not deal with memories or emotions but with
stark fact—and here that fact was . . . wrong?

The suit marched—but what marched inside it? Naill
had not been able from where he lay to distinguish any
features behind the faceplate of the helmet. All at once
he had an odd and completely disturbing vision of an
unoccupied suit, animated by what could not be seen
or felt, but which obeyed as the flying thing had
obeyed.

"What is it?" Ashla crept to his side, her hand on
his good shoulder. "What did you see?"

"A space suit—marching." Naill supplied the truth.

"A space suit. . . . Who?"

Naill shook his head. "What?" he corrected. "It is an old suit, very old."

"Old? They reported once that a hunting party from the port had been lost. . . ."

"Old. No hunter would wear a space suit, no crewman would have to wear one on Janus. This is an Arth planet, entirely suitable for Terran-descended life forms."

"I do not understand."

"I do—in part," Naill told her. "That which is here . . . has another servant—once off-world, but now his . . . or its."

"In two hours the sun will be gone." Ashla looked out of the tree trunk, measuring the planet shadows as they lay on the ground. "In the dusk we shall be the favored ones. That suit—it will be clumsy. What wears it cannot move fast across broken ground."

"True." Naill had already made that deduction. But he knew something else—that there was an arms belt about that stalking figure. If not a blaster, it wore tools that could be used as weapons. And he told her so.

"It is very old. Would the charges in the seamer, in the coilcut, still be active?"

Again Naill was surprised by her familiarity with off-world machines and tools.

"I was at the port for a double handful of days after my mother died. There was much to see—to keep one from thinking," she said, answering his unspoken question. "There was no one there to say such learning was evil."

"You had always this liking for worldly knowledge?"

"After the port—yes. Just as I wanted to know more of the forest—not to destroy, as was garth way, but to know it as it is, free and tall and beautiful. Before I was Illylle I had such longings. But that has nothing to do with this space suit and what it may do. I do not believe we can outwait it here."

"No." Naill had already determined that. "Our water is gone, and food. We move with darkness. And perhaps we can do it in this fashion. The gully is long and narrow, running roughly northeast by southwest—or so I remember it when we came in, though I was not too clearheaded." He made a question of that and she closed her eyes, as if better to visualize the territory.

"You are right. And the other end is very narrow—like a sword blade pointed so." She sketched with her fingers.

"If that narrow end can be climbed, it is our best try for a way out. The suit marches at a regular pace. We must creep under cover down the ravine as soon as the dusk is heavy enough, wait for it to be at this end, and then make our break to the west, using every shadow we can for cover."

"There are many chances in that."

"We take them, or sit here until we die or they dig us out like Jamob rats!" Naill snapped.

To his surprise Ashla laughed softly. "Ho, warrior, I do not question the rightness of your plan—for to my mind also it is the only one. But have we the fleetness of foot, the skill in hide-and-seek to bring us out of here?"

"That we shall see." For all his hopes, that statement did not sound as hearty as he wished. And as the long minutes crawled by while they waited for the coming of dusk, Naill experienced first a crowding impatience, and then a growing sense of the utter folly of what they must attempt. By counting his pulse beats he could gauge the pace of the space-suited sentry, judge how long it took the patroller to make the circuit of their ravine. Ashla lay down again, her head pillowed on her arm. Naill wondered, with a small amazement, if she were able to sleep now.

The sunshine could not last forever. Shadows grew, met, spun webs across the valley. And still the click-click of that patrol sounded regularly. At length Naill gave the girl a small shake so she looked up at him.

"We go. But keep down, well under the bushes. And do not touch any plants if you can help."

"You mean the eaters. Yes, I have seen what they do. But they are closing with the dark. Take care of your arm. Shall I re-sling it for you?"

"No, it is better at my side if we must crawl. Now—keep behind me and do not move the brush if you can help it."

It was one of those periods when every minute spun into an hour of listening, of movement kept agonizingly to a minimum. Naill longed to get to his feet, to run for the sword-point end of the valley in leaping bounds, yet he must make a lizard's sly passage. They cowered together, halfway down the length of their way, as the suit stamped by above. And again when only a quarter of their journey still lay ahead, as it passed on the other side.

Then they reached the point, facing a narrow crevice. Ten feet above—maybe a little more—the open rock of the waste plain would lie open. To get straight back to the river would mean passing the patroller in the open, and that Naill dared not try unless he was left no other choice.

"Now!" He started up the crevice, praying no slide would start from the clutch of his fingers, the dig of his booted toes. He pulled himself up, supported and steadied by the girl below. Then he lay across the rim and reached down with his good arm to assist her in turn.

They could see the sentry almost halfway down the right side of its return journey.

"To the left!" Thankfully Naill sighted an inky blot of shadow cast by a standing spar of rock.

It was the sword that betrayed them. Naill had set it back into the sheath before he climbed. But now, as he moved, weapon and scabbard scraped the stone and the noise was loud.

"Quick!" Ashla caught at him, pulled him on. "Oh, please—quick!"

Somehow they made it, to sprawl into that patch of dark. But the regular click-click of the space boots had become a rat-tat. Then—silence. Was the patroller readying one of the weapon tools from its suit belt? Would a lash of flame, meant to seal a break of ship skin, cut across their rock as a herdsman would use a stock whip to snap straying animals back to the herd?

"Ayyar—behind you!"

Naill twisted about.

No space suit marched from that side. These were pallid, leaping, moving things—resembling the hounds of the garths and yet unlike. For the hounds were animals, and their kind had long been subservient and known by mankind. While these were of another breed, outside all natural laws Naill understood.

"The Larsh wytes!"

Now Ayyar remembered—remembered such packs, hunting among the trees of Iftcan. That had been an ill hunting but one he had faced, sword ready, as he did now.

A narrow head with eyes that were sparks of sun, blasting yellow, snapped at him and he swung at it, to cleave skull, tumble the pack leader back among its fellows. There was no time to choose his next kill for bared teeth were reaching for his throat. Naill stabbed upwards, saw another of the wytes fall.

"Behind me!" he ordered Ashla.

"Not so! I, too, hunt wytes this night!" he heard her

cry in return. He saw her use the long hunting knife to cover them from a rush on the left.

Their surprise attack a costly failure, the pack withdrew a little. One at the rear raised its head to voice a long howl. From the dark sky came an answer . . . the cry of the flying thing which had earlier hung above the gully. And then, while the wytes held them fast to their rock spire, the suited sentry strode into view.

They were strange partners, the wytes and the metal-enclosed unknown. But the wytes accepted the suited figure as their leader, drawing aside to let it pass. It stalked into a space directly before the fugitives and stood there. Naill tried desperately to see the face behind the helmet plate. The once-clear surface of that section was fogged, webbed by a maze of fine cracks and lines, completely masking its wearer.

"Watch—oh, watch!"

But no warning could have saved them, Naill knew. The early suit might be clumsy according to modern standards. But it had been of the best engineering and design of its time, equipped for dangerous and demanding duty. Once that small object now spinning at them had been set and dispatched on its arc, nothing short of a blaster would deter it from completing its mission.

They were not going to be flamed out of existence. They were to be the helpless captives of what wore that suit, hid behind the cracked faceplate—or its master!

FIFTEEN

THE WHITE FOREST

A shallow bowl of valley stretched on down and away from where they had paused. And the reaching moonlight made a shimmering maze of glinting, prismatic light there. Naill shielded his eyes with his good hand. Ashla's fingers closed on his arm.

"The White Forest. . . ." Her voice was emotionless, drained, and not, he thought, by the fatigue of their journey over the broken plain of the waste.

Since that tractor beam generator had circled them back at the edge of this forbidden territory, they had marched straight on northward into the unknown, their space-suited captor in the lead, the pack of wytes padding at a distance but covering the rear—a weird assortment of travelers.

The beam had kept them docile enough, made them move in answer to the projected command of whatever lurked within the suit. And there had been no answer to all their attempts to communicate with that. Was their goal this forest?

For forest it was, if one judged that term applied to growths that arose vertically into the air from grounded roots, spread branches, grouped closely together. But this was a forest of branching, glittering crystals. No leaves rustled here, no color save the rainbow flickers that twinkled and sparkled in the moonlight. It was as if ice had chosen to reproduce trees and had succeeded in part.

The beam pulled them on, downslope, into that place of cold and deadly beauty. Because deadly it was. Ayyar memory in Naill brought fear, the terror known when a man faces something far greater than himself as an enemy—not personally, but to all his species. As early men of the Terran breed had feared the dark and what might walk in that blackness their eyes could not pierce, so did the Iftin-born hold an age-old aversion to stark light and what could dwell comfortably in its glare. But Naill and Ashla had no choice—there was no breaking that invisible pull between them and the space suit stalking forward, towing them as a man might tow a recalcitrant hound.

As they were drawn over the lip, down into that place of white light, the wytes no longer dogged them. Perhaps they, too, found this a place of terror.

Naill's boots crunched on a surface that gave in brittle fashion beneath his weight. He glanced down, saw that there was a trail of broken crystals powdered into sparkling dust. The ponderous footfalls of the suited guard were clearly marked, lying over other tracks—perhaps many of them.

Now there was another sound or sounds—a tinkling, coming from the growths or pillars making up the forest. As they drew closer, Naill could see that those horizontally branching shafts stood tall, not with the overwhelming height of the tree towers of Iftcan, but tall indeed compared to his own inches.

"The White Forest," Ashla repeated. "Tall it grows, straight it stands." Her voice held the queer singing note which Naill had come to associate with Illylle speaking through changeling lips. "But it is not real—it does not live. . . . Therefore—it is not!"

What she meant he did not understand, but oddly enough her denial of what they could both see was a lift to his spirits.

"Built—grown by a will," she continued. "It lives by a will, it will die by a will. But this will cannot make another Iftcan, no matter how it tries."

They had passed under the wide, stiffly held branches of the first "tree," and her words returned as faint, whispering echoes. The chiming tinkle grew stronger, a hiss of answering anger.

Ashla laughed. Her hand lifted to point a slim green finger at the next tree.

"Grow leaves—but you cannot! Nourish life—but you cannot! Shade the traveler—but you cannot! Feed with your fruits—but you cannot! Bend to the storm—but you cannot! Forest which is no true forest—beware the life, the storm, that which you have not . . ." Her voice sank again, and once more her hand reached for and clasped Naill's.

"Why did I say that?" she asked. "If I could only hold the old knowledge in my head as you hold the sword in your hand—then perhaps together we might follow the path of Kymon and—and . . . " She shook her head. "Even the manner of the triumph of Kymon is lost to me now. Only, I tell you, Naill-Ayyar, that had we the old knowledge we could fight. There is a secret that slips through my memory when I would have it forth. . . . Always it is just gone from me. This is a place of Power, but not the Power of Iftcan—and therefore one Power might be ranged against the other, had we only the proper key."

The hissing tinkle of the forest waxed stronger, making an odd rustling which lapped them about. But there was no change in the pace of the suit, drawing them after it in the grip of the ray-hold.

The faint path, which had wound down the slope, now led in a curling curve among the boles of the crystal trees, while the moonlight reflected and re-reflected on glittering nobs and surfaces confused and bewildered. If the lesser light of the moon proved so formidable, what would sunlight make of this mirror-trunked forest?

There was no evidence of any native life. As Ashla had accused, this was a dead place, dead without ever having held life as they knew it.

"Does Illylle remember this?" Naill appealed to the girl by his side.

"A little—far too little."

"Any idea where we may be going?" he persisted.

"No—save that it will be a place where there is peril, for this is the opposite of that which dwells in the Mirror—it balances this against that as a harvest is weighed on the Speaker's scales."

The ground still sloped down. Naill had not been able to judge during their short halt on the rim of the valley how large a territory the crystal structures covered. Perhaps whatever controlled the space-suited sentry, the wytes—the flying thing—lay in the very heart of this land.

Naill's mouth was dry; his ankle ached dully as did his arm. And he knew that Ashla must be as hungry, tired, and thirsty as he was. Food, water, a chance to rest—they needed those badly, might need them more before this journey came to an end.

Above their heads the crystal branches wove a criss-cross net shutting out the night sky. They were capped over by an icy cover. Could they some way mark a trail against a possible retreat?

Naill was shocked out of that speculation by Ashla's fingers biting deep into his flesh in a convulsive grip. Startled, he looked around, but her eyes were not for him. Her gaze was fixed on a tree ahead and to the left.

"Look!" The merest whisper directed him.

Naill obeyed. By some trick of the reflecting surfaces there was a mirror of sorts. And pictured on it . . .

At first he thought that greenish figure was himself—or Ashla. Then he knew that at such an angle their own reflection would be impossible. No—that was an Ift, but a stranger! Who? And where?

They were pulled ahead two steps and that shadow image was gone, vanished as if it had never been at all. But they were left with the knowledge that they were not alone in this glittering prison.

If what or whoever walked in the space suit had seen that momentary reflection, there was no hint of it, no pause in the steady pace it set. Almost Naill could persuade himself that he had seen nothing either, but Ashla held to its reality.

"An Ift—one of us," she told him softly. "Another prisoner."

"How can you be sure of that?"

"Because—an Ift in the White Forest could only be a prisoner. To us this place is death!"

Their captor crunched on, and the invisible tow cord on which he held both of them continued its unrelenting pull. The ground now leveled out. They must be at the foot of the valley wall, close to its heart and whatever secret it did hold. Here the crystal trees stood very tall, approaching the lower "towers" of Iftcan in size. And for much of their length their trunks were unbroken by branches. Those bare limbs existed close to their crowns, forming a roof overhead, but leaving much space underneath.

Abruptly the prisoners were at the head of a stairway, much like the stairs that had led up to the mountain-cupped Mirror, but which here reached downward into a second valley or crevice bitten sharply into the earth, as if some giant warrior had struck with a sword blade to divide a furrow in soft and yielding soil. Yet here was no soil . . . the ground itself had a glassy glaze that struck back at their eyes with punishing light.

Naill surveyed that stair with foreboding. The acute angle of descent would tax a strong man. He doubted if the two of them could make it now. For the first time since it had taken them captive and turned to march into this wilderness, the space-suited leader made a move other than just walking. Its metal-mittened hands rose to chest level. It lazily cast from it another beam disk.

Ashla screamed and Naill shouted. They were whipped after that spinning disk, their feet skidding and slipping on the slick surface of that glassy verge, pulled on out into the air above the crevice—with no hope of escape.

But a swift plunge to ghastly oblivion did not follow as Naill expected. Though their feet had left the surface of the ground and they lay extended forward on what he would swear was air alone, they were not falling—they were floating, as a man might in the free fall of a spaceship, descending into the gulf, that was true, but not at a speed to crush them when they met the surface below.

The walls rising about them were cream-white, smooth save for that ribbon of stairway. Naill spun his body around with memories of how it had once been

on board ship. However, when he tried to move closer
to Ashla, or "swim" toward the wall stairway, he was
still under inhibiting control.

Ashla was quiet after her first scream of fear, but
Naill could hear her breathing heavily, see that her eyes
were wide open, her features setting in a mask of naked
terror. She had had no defense against the strangeness
of this, no memory of free fall in space to sustain her.

"This—is—free—fall—as—on—a—ship," Naill got
out. His outflung hand closed about her wrist, so that
their bodies drew a little closer together. "This is
controlled—perhaps by the beam disk."

It was where they were going, not how, that mattered now. Below them, all he could see was a murky
billowing, darker than the walls, as if some fire steamed
or smoked there. Yet there was no warmth in the air.
As the first streamers of that murk engulfed them, Naill
felt no change in temperature. His initial nightmare
faded; they were not being wafted down into a furnace.

The murk grew thicker. He kept his hold on Ashla.
Close as they now were, it was difficult to distinguish
her features. They were as blind here as they would
have been in broad sunlight, if for a different reason.
How long had they fallen? Naill had tried to keep count
of the steps in that stair but knew that he had missed
out long since. And still they continued to float down.
Then, breaking through the fog, came more formations
of crystal. Unlike the trees of the upper forest, these
appeared in clusters of roughly geometric shape—they
could be towers, ramparts, the bulk of alien buildings—
while through them ran small pulsing lines of light, to
no pattern Naill could perceive, save that they formed
veins in the surfaces, as the veins carrying the blood
to serve his own body.

There was a bright flash of light at their feet while
they were still above the surface of the ground.

Whatever sustained them vanished in that wink, and they fell in a rush, landing in an angle between two of the now towering crystalline walls.

Naill sat up, pulling Ashla with him. The tinkling bell which had become a part of the world since they had entered the White Forest was silenced. They had ceased to note it consciously while they heard it, but the quiet that followed was so complete it awed them both.

"What is this place?" Ashla held tight to Naill, did not try to move.

"Illylle does not know?" He appealed for some scrap of memory to aid them now.

She shook her head. "Illylle sleeps—or is gone." There was a desolation of loneliness in her answer.

Naill strove to make his own contact. There was no touching any point of Ayyar memory. They were totally on their own, intruders, prisoners in an alien place. But that fact was no reason to sit and await trouble! One could choose a battlefield. And he had an idea that when the beam control had hit ground, it had broken, that they were now free of its bounds.

"Come!" He pulled her to her feet. His left arm in its splints was still fastened to his side as he had had her do before they set out. He would leave it so. At least he could use his right, and the sword he had sheathed after their capture by the ray had been left him by the space-suited enemy. What defense that blade could be against the intelligence responsible for their present plight Naill did not know. But the hilt felt good to his hand when his palm closed about it.

"Where would you go?" Ashla asked.

Her question was a just one. The fog swirled about the crystal walls, leaked through apertures in them. There was no visibility for more than a few yards in any direction. On the other hand every instinct in Naill warred against remaining where the disk had landed them. If the fog was a hindrance it might also be a help, giving them cover. He said as much.

"Which way, then?" Ashla did not protest, but turned as she stood, studying the hardly visible landscape.

"As we fell—that stairway was over there." Naill pointed. "Perhaps we can reach its foot."

"And is there also a chance of finding food"—her tongue ran over her dry, cracking lips—"and water?"

"I do not know."

"There is this, we were brought here carefully. Had our deaths been planned, what need to spare us that fall?" Ashla spoke slowly as if reasoning it out in her own mind. "So—"

"So—somewhere here is food and water? You may be right, but the price of wasting time in a blind search . . ."

"While one lives, there is always a chance. If we climb the stair, we only come out in the forest once again . . . to find that suited thing waiting—or the sun up! And the sun shining in there!"

She did not need to elaborate. To climb into sunlight blazing on those crystal trees would be climbing into sure death for Iftin bodies—even if they could drag their way up that long stairway.

"Which way, then?" Naill asked in turn.

"This is a time when perhaps we must depend upon chance." Ashla stooped to pick up an object she tossed from hand to hand. "This is what brought us here—let us see if, by the whims of chance, it can take us even farther!" She shut her eyes and turned rapidly around before she threw the disk from her.

There was a faint tinkle and they both saw the disk rebound from a wall to lie on the earth in an opening. It was an illogical and reckless way to decide their next move, but Naill accepted it. Together they went through the doorway.

It was a gate rather than a doorway, for the space beyond was as open to the air overhead as that where they had landed. This was a corridor of sorts running straight ahead. Walls of crystal stood higher than their heads, half curtained by the mist.

"Listen!" Perhaps some trick of those crystalline walls carried and magnified that sound. Ashla was already hurrying toward that unmistakable murmur of water.

They sped down that hallway, and the sound of the water grew stronger as they stumbled eagerly along. There was another doorway, and they came through it to a space Naill believed to be truly open, though he could see little of its area. Ashla sprang on.

"This way! Over here!"

What they came upon was no natural river as they had known before. Water flowed there right enough, but it swirled at a race through a trough of crystal.

"Wait—!" A remnant of Ayyar's hunter's caution made Naill call out.

She did not listen to him. Falling to her knees, Ashla plunged both hands into the flood. She might have been testing the validity of what her eyes reported. Then, the water running down her arms, she made a cup of her fingers and drank.

It might be the wildest kind of folly to trust the wholesomeness of what they found there. But Naill's resistance was swept away. He followed her example, and the moisture on his skin, the liquid he splashed one-handed into his dry mouth, smelled no different, tasted no different, from any that he had drunk from forest springs and pools. It was cold, clear—like new life flowing into his whole body.

"You see"—Ashla smiled—"in this much, chance favored us. We have found water."

Naill sat back on his heels, his first craving satisfied. "We may have found more than water." Now his wits were working again, weighing every small point that might operate in their favor.

"How?"

"The water comes—and it goes . . ."

"You mean—follow this stream to its source or its end? Yes, that is good—very good!"

"The water makes a good guide, a better one than any other we have seen here. And we have no means of carrying a drinking supply if we do leave it." He had been forced to abandon the remains of his pack, with its water bottle and food, back by the river.

"Guide and sustainer all in one. But which way do we go—upstream or down?"

Naill could see small difference in choice. Either way could serve their purpose. But before he could say that, Ashla gave a little cry and leaned out over the trough, her hand flashing down into the water, coming up with something in its grasp.

What she held was a fussan pod, empty of seed, but still fresh.

"Upstream! This came from upstream. Where there is one there may be more!"

Naill's hopes arose with hers. He got stiffly to his feet, favoring his aching arm. "Upstream it is—let us go!"

SIXTEEN
IFTIN PRISON

"I thought"—Ashla's tongue caressed her lips—"that I would long for nothing as much as I wished for water. But now I find hunger can also be a pain. And one cannot eat crystal. Is there no end to this stream or this place?"

"It looks as if we are coming to something now." Naill had been striving to pierce the foggy mist, and the vague outline he had seen through its swirls appeared to remain firm in spite of the coming and going of that tenuous curtain.

What lay before them was a wall of crystal, stretching, as far as they could tell, clear across the valley. And the water guide which had led them there poured in a rush through a conduit in that wall far too small to provide an entrance to whatever space lay beyond. Ashla dropped down limply.

"I cannot go back. I am sorry, but I cannot go back."

She said that simply, her sober tone underlining her surrender to this last blow.

"Not back!" Naill went directly to the wall. The crystal was not smooth but studded with irregularities, pocked with hollows. This could be climbed—not by a one-handed man, perhaps, but Ashla might do it. "Not back," he reiterated firmly, "but over! This is as rough as a ladder."

She was drawn by his confidence to approach the wall. Then she glanced at him.

"And you? Do you sprout wings to bear you over?"

"No—but there is this." Naill unslung the sword shoulder belt. "If you get to the top, hook this about one of those large projections. Then I will have a hand hold to bring me up in turn."

Ashla regarded first the wall and then Naill doubtfully. He strove to break through her hesitancy.

"We must do it now, while we still have a measure of strength in us. Or do you wish to remain here bewailing our fate until hunger is a finish?"

To his surprise Ashla smiled at that, a joyless grimace stretching her gaunt face.

"As you point out, warrior, struggle is always better than surrender. I shall climb."

Privately Naill was not sure that even with the aid of the belt he could make it. But this was their only chance. Judging by his own swimming head and weakened body, he was certain she was right; they could not now retrace their road down the valley.

Ashla climbed slowly and with caution, testing each hold before she entrusted her full weight to it. It seemed to Naill that the minutes of that climb lengthened into hours. Then her head and shoulders topped the edge of the wall and she was able to see over. Seconds later, her face alight and eager, she looked down at him.

"We were right! Here is true forest! We were right!"

Her report provided him with a last spurt of strength, enough to give him the necessary energy to reach the perch on which she now clung, her hands and the dangling belt at his service. Then they steadied one another as they gazed out over a section of welcoming gray-green, full of beckoning shadows. This was not Iftcan—it was not even the forest upon which the settlers preyed—but it was far closer to it than any land they had seen since they had entered the waste by the river.

Naill was not wholly conscious of anything save that green. Then the sudden rigidity of Ashla's body against his own broke his absorption.

The girl's head stretched forward on her shoulders. Her pointed ears flared wide from her skull, and her eyes were fixed in a probing stare on the forest before them.

"What is it?" Naill's first surge of relief was erased by a thrust of alarm. He heard nothing, saw not even a leaf tremble in that waiting woodland. "Tell me—what is it?"

But he was too late. Ashla had already moved, swinging over the barrier on the far side, descending by a series of reckless holds and half falls that frightened him. Then, without a single backward glance—as if he had ceased to exist for her—she ran on across the small strip of powdered crystal sand to the trees and disappeared among them as if a green mouth had gulped her in.

"Ashla! Illylle!" Naill's voice rang hollowly, a lonesome sound deadened and swallowed into a thin echo by some sonic property of this place. He dared not move as fast as she had. His descent was slow and clumsy, but at last he did reach the ground.

From this level the greenery ahead had a solid,

forbidding look. Naill studied what he could see of it. Here, too, the mists trailed, one moment hiding, the next revealing a section. But this was true forest growth, he thought. And—Ashla had already gone that way. He strode over the small traces left by her running feet on the sand.

Outwardly this was the same forest as that beyond the crystal growth to the east. His ears now picked up the small muted sounds of insects and other life within its hold. Muted—that was it! This place was shadowed, reduced, in a fashion Naill could not define, from the life of the other woods he had walked.

His hunter's eyes followed the signs of Ashla's head-long passage—snapped twigs, torn leaves, the print of her boots in the soil. She must have burst on as if striving to reach some goal with no care for any obstacles in between. Why? Just another of those endless questions that were a part of this world.

Naill used the sword to beat and cut himself passage in the same direction the girl had taken. Then the point of that blade struck into the open, and he followed it—into a clearing.

Two—three—four of them, counting the one who faced Ashla. Four green-skinned, large-eared—changelings? Or Iftin of the true blood? They were all men, clad in ragged remains of the same forest dress as Naill had found in Iftsiga. Two of them wore shoulder-belted swords like his own. One had a wooden spear headed with a crystal point. Naill took that in, in a quick evaluation of the company.

Then the man before Ashla drew his full regard and, studying him, Naill forgot the rest.

The stranger was perhaps by an inch or so the tallest of the group, but he was not otherwise physically outstanding. It was . . . Naill tried to be objective, tried to understand why, when looking at this ragged, quiet man, he was moved to respect, ready to surrender some of his independence and will. There was only a moment of such desire before Naill fought it down.

"Who are you?" The man spoke and Naill was about to reply when he realized the question was not addressed to him but to Ashla.

"Illylle—and you are Jarvas." She spoke with conviction, almost impatiently as one who found such a question stupid and unnecessary.

The man's hand came up in a gesture of warning, as if to ward off her words. "I am Pate Sissions."

"You are Jarvas—Mirrormaster!"

He moved then, swiftly. His hand clapped over her mouth, his right arm crushed her into captivity. Naill leaped out with ready sword.

Ashla fought wildly against her captor's hold, useless as that was. They staggered together and Naill hesitated, afraid to strike Ashla. That hesitation was his own undoing. His instinct warned a fraction of a second too late. The wooden butt of the spear struck against the side of his head, sending him down.

Cool . . . green. . . . He lay on moss in Iftcan, and above him boughs made the autumn wind sing. Tonight there would be the Festival of Leaf Farewell and he would go into the Court of the Maidens for the choosing.

Maidens—one maiden . . . a thin face, wan, always a little tired and sad, Ashla—no, Illylle! Illylle—Ashla, name balanced name. Ashla was Illylle, Illylle Ashla.

"So—it is thus, little sister. Here we are as we were—and so we must remain until we win forth."

Words out of the air. Naill made no sense of them. But he heard in answer, "I am Ashla—of the garths, then."

"You are Ashla always—here. Do not forget it. And I am Pate, and this is Monro, and Derek, and Torry.

And your impetuous young friend is Naill. We are off-worlders and settlers—no more, never any more than that."

"But we are not. Just a look at us would seal that truth."

"We are totally alien to this Power. *It* is the mind, the memory that mind holds, not the physical form that matters to it. Now *It* is doubtful, still uncertain concerning our identity. Once *It* learns the truth—"

"I understand."

Naill knew that he did not. But he forced open his eyes, turned his head. He lay on a mat of leaves under a rough lean-to, looking out at a small fire around which sat the four men and Ashla. The man beside her turned his head, his eyes found Naill. He arose lithely and came to kneel beside the other.

"How do you feel?"

"Who are you?" Naill countered.

"I am Pate Sissions—First-In Scout of Survey. And"—his hand gestured to the company by the fire—"that is Haf Monro, astropilot of the *Thorstone*."

Distant memory stirred in Naill. *Thorstone*—a long-lost cruiser by that name . . . what *was* the story?

"Derek Versters of Versters' Garth, and Ladim Torry, medico of the Karbon Combine."

Karbon Combine? But the Karbon people had been off Janus for almost a full generation! Yet the outwardly green-skinned Ift whom Sissions had so introduced appeared to be a man still in his first youth. First-In Scout, astropilot, garthman, Karbon medico—a wide range of occupations on Janus, covering perhaps the full length of time the planet had been known to Survey.

"You are all"—Naill broke out the word he had first heard back at Kosburg's—"changelings!"

Sissions' big-eared head swung slowly from left to

right in a gesture of negation made more impressive by the very length of that movement.

"We are off-worlders—from different times and worlds—who came to Janus for different reasons. That is what we are—and will be—*here*. And you are?"

"Naill Renfro—bought laborer."

"Good enough. Continue to remember that, Naill Renfro, and we shall deal easily together. Sorry we had to knock you out—there was not time to reason with you."

"Where is this place? And how did you get here?" Naill pulled himself up to rest on the elbow of his right arm. His head was thick and ached dully, but he was not so dimwitted now as not to realize that there was a method in Sissions' speech, that he had been warned against some very real danger.

"As to this place—well, it is a prison of sorts." Sissions sat down cross-legged. "We are not sure ourselves as to the reason for our detention here. Except that it means trouble. How did we get here? Well, we came in various ways at different times. Monro and I were hunting a friend who had come in this direction and vanished. We were picked up—"

"By an animated space suit?" Naill cut in.

"By a walking space suit," Sissions agreed. "We found Torry here already—he was first in residence. They caught him near the river where he tried to take a shortcut west. And Derek—Derek came later with a companion who chose to leave."

"You can leave?" Naill demanded in surprise.

"You can leave, provided you are intent upon committing suicide. An agile man with a great amount of determination and no sense can climb to the White Forest. Whether he can get through there . . ." Sissions shrugged.

"So you just sit around and wait for what is going to happen?" Naill's amazement grew. His whole reading of this man suggested that such a spineless course was so alien to his nature that Naill could not believe Sissions was in earnest.

"So we wait," Sissions assured him. "We wait, and we remember who and what we are."

Again that inflection of warning. Naill sat all the way up. They were watching him with a kind of detached inspection, as if waiting for him to make some move by which they would then be influenced into an important judgment and appraisal.

"How long do we wait?"

"We do not know. Perhaps until the opposition moves so we can learn who—or what—*It* really is. Or until we find our own solution. Now—" Sissions picked up a small bowl, handed it to Naill. Through the substance of the container he felt the warmth of the contents. Eagerly he savored and then gulped the stew.

"Light coming." Torry stood up, the crystal-pointed spear in his hand. "Best back to the burrow." He came to Naill and together with Sissions assisted him to his feet.

"Where are we going?"

"Out of the sun," the former medico told him shortly. "In the day period here we're as good as blind. To be caught in the open is bad."

"To be caught in the White Forest in the sun," Sissions added, "that's the end. And we've not been able to work out any way of crossing that in one night's time. That is the lock on our prison cell, Renfro."

Naill could see the right in that reasoning. The crystal forest in the moonlight had been hard enough to face. Its brilliance under direct sunshine would burn out their night-oriented sight.

"There was one of our kind up there when we came in—we saw his reflection on a tree," he reported.

"Halsfad!" Derek pushed closer. "Where? How near the edge of the forest was he? Pate—maybe he was able to make it after all!"

"We could not tell," Naill replied. "The reflections must be deceiving."

Sissions agreed. "Could have been from any direction. And even if he reached the edge of the forest before sunup—what then?"

What then indeed? The miles of baked and empty rockland ahead with no shelter—Naill though of that. Yes, it made an effective prison for all of them. And desperate flight was not the answer; he understood Sissions the better now.

"Home." Monro had been in advance. Now he stood before a dark hole, folding back a curtain woven of plaited leaves. Ashla crept after him, and they followed one by one until they were all within the shelter.

Its skeleton was a tree with huge exposed roots, roots that extended out of the bole well above their heads as might branches, but running down to the earth, rather than horizontally, so that the center trunk appeared to be supported by a fringe of props. In and out through that grid of exposed roots leaves had been woven, lengths of dried vine, and pieces of bark, to form a structure with the living tree as its center.

Ashla went directly to that trunk and set both of her palms flat against its bark.

"Iftin wall, Iftin roof,
    Wood lives, wood—"

Even as he had jumped her in the clearing, so was Sissions upon her again, his hand across her lips with the force of a slap.

She raised hers from the tree to twist and tear at his fingers until she had freed her mouth.

"You have forgotten too much!" That was Illylle speaking now with all the force of command she had shown at those times when the Iftin took precedence over the Terran in her. "This is Iftscar—from the true seed. It will not betray us. Though why it should grow in the White Land . . . ah!" She nodded, not at them, but at some thought or memory. "When Kymon journeyed forth, with him went a pouch blessed by the Counters of the Seed, and they gave him of their powers. So—here fell a nut of Iftscar, and through the long time of the True Leaves it has grown. Look into your memory, Jarvas, Mirrormaster that was—you have been too timid by half!"

She turned in his hold, her hands now rising to cup over his eyes. At first Sissions moved under her touch as if to push her away. Then he stiffened, straightened, and slowly—very slowly—his own hands went out to rest against the tree trunk as hers had done before him. Ashla stepped aside and left him so.

"Iftscar!" She flung up her arms in a gesture of welcome. "We shelter here. In the Leaf of the Gray we claim what you have to give us."

"Pate—Pate!" Monro would have dropped hand on Sissions' shoulder, but the girl fended him off.

"Let be! He takes the strength he should have drunk long ago. He forgot when he should have remembered! Let be—you have not the Seeing!"

Sissions' hands fell from the tree trunk. He turned, his eyes wide. Then he blinked and came back from some immeasurable distance.

It was to Ashla he spoke: "I am indeed a fool. There may yet be a key we have not tried, already set in our hands."

"If you had not the right memory then you were

wise not to hunt lost keys. Is it not with all of you as it is with Naill and with me—that you possess only parts of memories, but not the full recall of your Iftin selves?"

"Yes."

"And so you fear—and wisely—what you do not control nor know. I believe, Mirrormaster, that such caution is not folly but wisdom."

"Perhaps two memories knitted well together may supply us with the key to this prison!" Sissions held out both hands to her, and hers fell palm down on his.

Naill watched them with a strange lost feeling. Ayyar—who had been Ayyar after all? A fighting man who at the last testing had gone down to defeat. A warrior who dared not use the Mirror of Thanth, but had fled from its challenge. And Naill Renfro—a slave laborer from the Dipple. Neither part of him had been a man of victory or strength—perhaps the whole was less . . .

"Many memories"—Ashla's eyes went from man to man—"but maybe too different. To weave a power there must be unity. We can but try, you who were Jarvas."

"What's going on?" Monro demanded sharply.

"We may have been too cautious." Sissions was again the off-worlder in speech and idiom. "This tree house gives us immunity to certain forces here. Now"—his glance caught them, held them, demanded—"we shall try pooling our Iftin memories, and from such a harvest perhaps we can glean what we need—to tip the scales of fortune on our side."

"But you said—" Derek began and frowned at Ashla. "She appears able to change your mind quickly enough."

"We have never been able to decide whether we have these Iftin memories by plan—or by chance.

Perhaps we'll never know the truth of that. But today—for the first time—two of us who had certain powers in our Iftin identities have met. If we can join those powers, draw other knowledge from the rest of you"—Sissions' head was high, his eagerness was in his voice, mirrored on his face—"this can lead us to freedom! We can only try—but are you willing to join?"

There was a hesitancy, but one by one they gave their assent.

SEVENTEEN

LOST SHIP

Naill's back was against one of the roots of the trees which formed the refuge. He nursed his splinted arm across his knee. And thought.

They had carried out Ashla's suggestion, pooled their Iftin memories, only to discover that those memories were so diverse that they had little common meeting ground. Their Ift personalities appeared to have come not only from various places but also from eras well separated in time. So they had found no key to their prison.

One would need the protection of a space suit to travel the White Forest and its surrounding waste by day. And they could not hope to make that journey in a single night starting from this site.

Space suit . . . Naill battened down all Iftin memories and strove to recall those of Naill Renfro—a very

191

...g Naill Renfro. He had been what—six? seven? eight?—when the *Lydian Lady* had been caught in the orbital battle about Calors. Spaceborn and bred, he realized that planet time did not count much in his early days. And what did he know of space suits?

He had had one, made to his size, and he could remember how the instruction in its use had come by hyposleep. Twice he had worn it, going out with his father on one heat-baked, desert planet, and again when taken on a tour of the outer hull of the ship as part of his space training and discipline. Yes, he could recall that without difficulty—everything about the suit, its handling, servicing and equipment.

The point was that now there was a suit out there, mobile, in use—in use by something non-Terran, which might make all the difference. Even if they could not take that suit—and capture what used it—a suit meant a ship somewhere. And Naill was certain that no off-worlder had deliberately wandered far from a ship in that cumbersome rig, not all the way from the present spaceport—that was certain.

Item two was that this waste and what governed it was unknown at the port. And he had heard nothing concerning it from the settlers. None of those prisoners here had been taken until they crossed into the waste. Whatever ruled here did not venture forth to seek prey; it waited for it to come within short reach.

Therefore—the space suit meant a ship not too far away. And to Naill a ship meant a possible supply of weapons, a hope of defense and offense. Let Ashla and Sissions try to use Iftin methods against the enemy—that never-defined enemy! There might be another way altogether!

However, if there was, surely the men here had already searched for it. Sissions claimed to be a First-In Scout. Those explorers of Survey were noted for their flexible thinking, ability to improvise and experiment. And Monro was an astro-navigator whose attention would be centered on ships. They could not or would not have overlooked the connection between space suit and ship here.

Yet the thought of those two—suit and ship—continued to work in his mind. Naill brought up all the old arguments—that such a ship, did it exist nearby, could long ago have been stripped. The suit was an old model, very old.

"How's the arm?" Naill was shaken out of his thoughts as Torry knelt beside him. "Any pain?"

"An ache now and then." Naill realized that he had not felt much discomfort for some time now. The arm, stiffly bound and splinted, was a cumbersome nuisance, but otherwise it did not bother him too much.

"Let me take a look. You know—we all heal more quickly since we changed our skins. We're tougher in many ways. I wish I knew more about what happened to us. . . ."

"You're from the port, aren't you?" Naill asked. "How did you get the Green Sick?"

"The same way we were all suckered in—because I was curious. I went out on a field trip—trying to pick up some native plants to study. I found one of the treasure caches, came down sick before I could rejoin my party. As far as I knew, I might have something highly contagious—so I kept clear. Then it was too late—I was changed and I didn't want to go back."

"What's the purpose of the caches, the changes?" Naill watched the other skillfully unwrap and unsplint his arm.

"Any pain?" Fingers ran along his skin, exerting pressure.

"No."

"I'd say that had knitted true. Favor it a bit, but you

can leave off the rest of this. The purpose of the caches? Just what you've seen—to gain recruits."

"For whom and what?"

"None of us really know; we have only a general idea. Sissions was the first capture. And he's helped with the recruiting ever since. We have a compulsion at certain times of the year to set those traps; we can't help ourselves. As far as we can make out, there was a civilization native to Janus a long time ago. They worked with nature, did not seek to oppose or control her. No machines for them. There came a time when that race went into decline—finally they were overrun and wiped out."

"By the Larsh!" Naill cut in. "I remember!"

"Do you? Derek does too, but Pate and I and Monro don't—we're all from an earlier period. Anyway, after the fall of Iftcan there could only have been a handful of survivors. But that handful appears to have numbered among them some of their scientists. They must have developed the treasure chests then, planted a few to wait. They certainly had hope, or trust, or some inkling that another race would arise here, or come from space, to trigger those installations. Anyone who does handle cache things—with liking—assumes the personality and body changes connected with that particular cache. To this day *we* don't know how they work. But there has to be some bond of sympathy between the finder and one of the objects included in that collection."

"But if Pate Sissions was the First-In Scout of Survey, then he must have landed here—" Naill stared at Torry.

"About a hundred and twenty planet years ago?" Torry nodded. "Yes."

"But he's—he's a young man!" Naill countered.

"We have no idea of the life span of the original

Iftin, or what happened to our bodies during the Green Sick. As far as we can tell, after the change there is very little aging for us. I have been this way for nearly seventy-five planet years. But our numbers grow very slowly, since not all caches are found—and some take no captives."

Naill tried to digest the thought of agelessness. He was not unaware that some alien races had achieved life spans far beyond that of the Terran breed. But how could such a change be wrought in a Terran body?

"The caches can attract only certain types," Torry continued. "And the method of selection and control of such captives is another secret we have not broken. We number now only a few more than a hundred—just thirty of them women. Five children have been born—and they are Iftin from the beginning. Also—they have no memories. Still we are bound to set the traps. Sissions and I were here on such a mission when we were taken prisoner."

"You do not live in Iftcan?"

"We have a base there. That is where Pate found the first treasure which started us all along this road. But our new home is west, overseas. Until we learn more, we can only have patience and do what we can to re-establish our kind."

"Until?" Naill asked.

"Until we are again a nation. You know the First Law—a world having an intelligent native population and a civilization can be given a choice: to join the Federation or warn off all contact. In time we shall have Janus—we grow more Iftin with the years. And the off-worlders cannot hold this planet against our will."

"But the settlers—"

"Are not natives. They would change Janus, alter it to an off-world pattern, narrow, arid, and stultifying. They are slowly shrinking in numbers as more and

more of them come over to us. This world does not
welcome them, and those it can welcome speedily find
a cache and join our ranks—as you came, and Ashla.
What part of the treasure lured you so that you had
to handle it, wanted to possess it for yourself?"

"The tube," Naill replied instantly. "It was the
color—those patterns. . . . Something pulled me—I
cannot explain."

"For me it was the figurine." Torry smiled. "I held
it in my hand for hours the night I found it. Those
who cannot resist become one with us. And in each,
an Ift of old shares and moves. I am Torry but I am
also Kelemark of Iftlanser. I was a tender of young
growth and one learned in herbs and plant lore."

"Did none of you ever try to go back to the port—
to the settlement?"

"Did you?"

"Yes. But that was a garth; they have a superstitious
fear of the forest, of everything coming out of it. And
the Green Sick to them is punishment for sin. Naturally they hunted me."

"But you, yourself, when you went there—did you
want to stay? Were those humans *your* people?"

"No."

"We believe that this, too, was a part of the plan,
that in becoming Iftin we were also implanted with a
revulsion against our former kind. Thus, if the purpose
of the planners was to rebuild their race, independent
and truly Iftin once more, they deemed we must be
apart from the species we once were. None of us can
now force ourselves to return to the port—to any off-
world holding. And the longer we are in the forest, the
stronger that repulsion is. We are meant to recruit from
them but not mingle with them."

"And this"—Naill's hand indicated their present
situation—"what has this to do with it?"

"We don't know—more than we have learned from bits and pieces of memories. Your Ashla seems to know much more than the rest of us. She has taken on the Ift portion of some priestess or seeress of the last days. There is a force here—long hostile to the Iftin. *It* is stirring again because the Iftin also are reviving through us. As to what *It* is—or why *It* keeps us here"—Torry spread his hands—"we are not sure at all."

"The space suit?"

Torry was silent for a moment. "Your guess is as good as mine. I will say this much. I do not think any normal man wears that thing—though it is off-world and of a type I have worn myself."

"What are the boundaries of this place?" Naill wanted to know.

"We have a long narrow strip of forest, running for a good space north and south. There's that wall you came over, and beyond it all crystalline growth. We've explored in there at night. But we found nothing save the stairway and those walls and corridors none of which follows any pattern or sense we can determine."

"And that is all? Then where is this Thing in control?"

"We haven't been able to locate *It*. As far as we can discover, the crystal growth simply runs on and on. And we dared not follow it too far for fear of being caught out there in the day. Our night sight is limiting."

"So you've just accepted imprisonment, then?" Naill was once more amazed at what seemed a lack of enterprise on the part of the captives.

Torry smiled, a grim curve of lip. "We appear quite spineless, don't we, Renfro? But not quite. The way out is not always the most open. As you will see in due course."

"Ayyar—" Ashla came into the tree house carrying a holder improvised from a leaf. She showed him its contents. "Sa-san berries. Ripe sa-san berries here!" She shook three of the plump, red-black fruit, each as big as his thumb, into his hand. "There was a voice once in the Wind Forest." Her eyes were dreaming as she remembered. "Ah—how sweet its flowers smelled in New Leaf time!"

"Illylle," Torry said, "you remember a great deal, do you not?"

"Much, much, but still not enough!" Her dreaminess faded, she looked a little lost. "I thought—believed—that together we could break through, find what we lost. There was Jarvas, who had been Mirrormaster . . ." Her lost expression deepened. "But he was not enough Jarvas, he was too much Pate Sissions—and so we could not do it. And the rest of you—all different—different times, different powers. Perhaps it is the Turning of the Leaves which has made it so."

"The Turning of the Leaves, Illylle?" Sissions had followed her inside, and had taken one of her hands in his. "What is that?"

There was a small pucker set by impatience on her forehead. "There was the Blue Leaf when the world was young and the Iftin were strong in their might. Then did Kymon come to this place and strive with That Which Abides, and the Oath was taken between Power and Power. None of us here were of that Leaf time—those mighty ones must have gone long, long ago, too far to be recalled. There came after the Green Leaf and of that Leaf were you, Jarvas, though you seem to remember it not. And then there was a lessening and a trial of the Oath. But still the Word held; though it was stretched thinner with time, it was still a tie.

"Third was the Gray Leaf, and that was the time of ending in which Illylle dwelt and he who is here as Derek but was then Lokatath, a Sea Lord, and

Ayyar—who was Captain at the First Ring of Iftcan. And that was a dark, dark time, for the people were few and they were tired with many years—and the children of the race were fewer yet. Then the Larsh, who had not said the Oath, gathered and marched. At last the end came, and the Leaves fell. Thus we came together—not of one age or life—and united we cannot raise the Power as I had hoped."

These men were all older than he, Naill reflected, and, as Illylle's memories seemed to imply, they had once been of consequence in Iftcan. He was Naill Renfro, a worldless wanderer, lately a slave laborer. But a certain defiance rising in him made him speak now: "There is more than one heritage of power—" He was that far when he paused, a little shaken because they were all staring at him now. "We have a double heritage." He pushed on quickly. "And there is the space suit, made by our own kind. The suit could only come from a ship—no matter what wears it now—and the ship was also ours."

Pate Sissions smiled. "All very true. Torry, how is that arm of his? Is he ready for a journey?"

"If he takes reasonable care. Healing was quick, as usual."

"Then I think it is time we move." He glanced up at the tree bole around which this hut was fashioned. "Iftscar may be a natural insulation against arousing *that*." His hand pointed to the strip of forest outside. "Only tonight there is a stirring—I feel it. *That* may not know any more about us, but *It* senses something. *It* is uneasy—awake—"

"Yes!" Illylle interrupted. "That is the truth! *It* stirs— and *It* knows *Its* power and how to use it!"

Whatever she and Pate Sissions were able to pick out of the air was not discernible to the rest, but their sincerity in believing it existed could not be denied.

"We were very close to breakthrough last time," Monro observed. "And it is yet early evening—we have the whole night before us."

They were gathering up the few furnishings of the tree house, filling skin bottles with water, making small packs of dried berries and nuts. It would seem they did not intend to return. Naill accepted one of the packs, slung it across his shoulder, but asked no questions. He judged that they were about to carry out some long-projected plan, as the amount of their food supplies, the extra water containers, meant a journey of some duration.

Sissions led the line of march with Ashla behind him. She was seldom far from the man she had named Jarvas and claimed as "Mirrormaster." Then came Derek, Torry and Naill, while Monro brought up the rear. Their weapons were three swords and two spears. Something in Naill questioned the assurance with which Sissions pushed ahead.

Shade of trees gave way to a patch of open, and there the wall of the valley was not glassily coated but rose as a stark white rock broken by a fault from which the stream ran. Sissions splashed into the water which rose to his knees, stooped head and shoulders to pass into the cave from which it flowed. And in turn they copied his move.

The stream bed offered smooth footing but the current was fast, pushing against them. They were not long in the water, but climbed to a ledge to crawl on hands and knees along a wet surface. As they drew away from the entrance, even their night sight did not serve them well and Naill marveled that the others had ever found this path.

The ledge brought them at last well above the waterline, and finally Torry drew Naill to his feet, keeping one hand on his shoulder to steady and guide

him. Then they were out in a wide space where there
was a dim gray light. Two sides of that area were coated
with the slick crystal; the rest of the walling was rough
stone, wrenched and broken as by some explosion or
settling of the earth in a quake.

Light filtered through from well above their heads
where on one of the crystalline walls was a narrow slit,
coated with transparent material. To reach that slit a
ledge had been chipped along the nearest stretch of
rock wall. But still a space remained to be bridged
between that ledge and the slit.

Sissions climbed with the ease of one who had done
it many times before. At the highest point of the ledge
he slipped a fiber band about his waist, dropped loops
of cording over points of rock, and leaned back against
that frail support. His aim was to the left and out, at
a height above his own shoulder, an awkward angle at
which to work. His tool was one of the swords. With
swing curtailed by his position, he aimed the point of
the sword into the lower end of the slit, picking time
and time again at the same portion of sealing material.
Four swings . . . five . . . a full dozen and he rested.

"Any luck?" Monro called. "Want one of us to spell
you?"

"There was a give on that last punch. Let me try
just once more."

His muscles moved visibly under the rags of the
forest jerkin. The sword point thudded home with an
effort Naill himself could somehow feel. And—went
through!

The crackle of the breaking was loud. They could
see a net of cracks spread across the surface. Someone gave a cry of triumph. Sissions struck again and
there was no more resistance. A rain of splinters cas-
caded down, and wind—clear wind—whistled through
the opened window.

"Rope!" Sissions' demand was curt. Derek was already climbing with a heavy coil of vine fiber wreathed about his shoulder.

They were a long time making that fast, testing its securing over and over again. Then Sissions unlinked his support belt, to resnap it to the rope. He gave a small jump, and his hands closed on the lower rim of the slit. In a moment he was up in it, perched on the edge looking out.

"How is it?" Monro called.

"As far as I can see clear—and"—Sissions' head turned as he looked straight down at Naill—"your ship's waiting out there, Renfro."

He dropped forward, out of their sight while the rope was payed out between Derek and Monro. The former astronavigator followed, then Torry—Ashla—Naill—with Derek steadying the rope and seeing them all through the slit before him.

The rock wall through which the window broke was part of a ridge for another valley. But the land below was not crowded with crystal growths—it was bare sand and rock. In that sand a ship rested, straight and tall. Whoever had piloted her in for that landing had made it a perfect three-point one, and she had stood undisturbed ever since, by all outward signs.

Her hatch was open and the entrance ramp was run out. There was a tall drift of sand about the foot of that ramp, and the scorch of her set-down was no longer visible on the ground about her fins.

They advanced on the old ship cautiously. Naill gathered that they had spied upon her from the window slits over a period of several work nights. She was a Class-C Rover Five. Rover Five! That made her at least a hundred years old. She might have passed through many ownerships and, while she might have been considered too old to work on the inner lanes, she was still spaceworthy for the frontier. Perhaps she had been a Free Trader. There was no service insignia symbol on her hull, and she was too small for a transport or regular freighter.

"Dead." Monro stood at the foot of the ramp.

"Maybe so," Sissions agreed. "But was she stripped? If not—"

If not, more suits—supplies of a kind that would take them across the waste, weapons better than the swords and spears. Monro was on his way up the ladder, the others strung out behind him. Did it hit them all at once—or were some more immune than others?

Ashla cried out and stopped, clinging to the handrail with a grip that made her knuckles into pale knobs. She wavered, almost fell. A moment later Sissions echoed her wordless protest with a spoken "No!"

It beat against them all. The revulsion Naill had known at Kosburg's was here a hundredfold the stronger. To advance was to fight against his churning insides for every inch. Distaste—no; this was a horror of disgust!

They swayed, held to the rail. Ashla went down, edging past Derek, past Torry, on her hands and knees. Monro kept his feet but he was swaying as he turned to descend. Sissions stumbled behind. Naill gripped the support so tightly with his good hand that the metal bit into his flesh. He was first in line now and he held there, facing the open door of the space lock.

His body fighting his will, he began to pull himself along—not down but up!

EIGHTEEN

JUDGMENT DELIVERED

He was Naill Renfro. There was no Ayyar, no Iftin, in him! He was Naill Renfro, and this was only a spaceship—like his father's.

Suit racks—empty. Naill steadied himself against the corridor wall with one hand. Dust was soft under his skin boots. The smell of age—of emptiness. . . . He was Naill Renfro exploring an old ship. So—no suits. But there could be other things here adapted to their needs. He pulled himself on, keeping his thoughts rigidly fixed on those needs and his human off-world past.

Arms cabinet—also empty. A second disappointment. This spacer appeared to be stripped of everything that could serve survivors. Perhaps the landing had been an emergency one and the crew had departed with their equipment, never to return.

No weapons—no suits. Naill leaned his head against

the wall and tried to think clearly, to remember the
stores on the *Lydian Lady* and where they had been.
It was a struggle to do that with the awful horror of
this place tearing at his mind, churning in his stomach, rising in a sour taste at the back of his throat.

Where now? He shuffled on. There was one more—
just one more place to check. Naill was sure he did
not have the strength to venture any farther into the
spacecraft, to climb to another level. Here! He lunged
and his good hand pressed on the panel of the com-
partment he sought. Here were the tools, the supplies
of outer-skin repairs. The inner layout of the ships had
not changed so much over the years that they were
not arranged in the same general pattern. He forced
the panel open.

His cry of triumph echoed hollowly down the pas-
sageway. Then he had them in his hand, the protective goggles to be worn while using a welding beam.
Their key to freedom? Holding those tight to his chest,
Naill wavered down the passage, came into the open
and descended the ramp.

"What—?" Sissions met him.

"Listen . . ." Naill had the dim beginnings of a plan.
He waved the goggles at the former Survey man. "With
these on, the sun can't be too bad."

"One pair only—there are six of us." Torry joined
them.

"One man leading, wearing these," Naill explained.
"The rest of us blindfolded, linked together, by rope
if need be. We could take turns with the goggles."

Sissions had those now. "It might work! How about
it, Ladim?"

The former medico took them in turn, snapped the
protective lenses over his eyes and looked about him.

"Can't be sure, of course, until we try. Used at short
intervals, taking turns as Renfro suggests . . . well, we

may never have a better chance. Though how far we have to travel west before we find any decent cover—"

"Not west!" That was so emphatic that they all turned to face the girl. She had been sitting on the ground at the foot of the ramp, but now she stood erect.

"Westward *That* will be watching . . . waiting. . . . Once *It* knows we have escaped—"

"South to the river, then?" Derek asked uncertainly. The girl appeared so sure of what she was saying that it impressed all of them.

"No!" Her answer was as determined as before. "East!"

"Back to Iftcan?" began Monro.

Naill had been studying Ashla. She was gripped by that half-fey mood he had seen her display so many times during their flight together. Just as he had pulled on his human heritage to dare the ship, so was she now pulling herself into her Iftin personality.

"Not Iftcan." Her head moved slowly from side to side. "The day of Iftcan is done. That forest was withered and will leaf no more. We must go to the Mirror. This is laid upon us," she cried out fiercely, directly at Sissions. "We must go to Thanth!"

"I say get out of here and head west!" Derek protested.

"She's right about one thing," Torry cut in. "They—whoever or whatever controls this place—would expect us to do just that—west with no long way around. It might just be smarter to circle around by starting east, then south to the river."

"We go to Thanth!" Illylle repeated. And now Sissions added his will to hers. But not too completely: "East . . . for now."

They pointed eastward from the forgotten ship,

hastening to make the most of the remaining hours of darkness. The valley wherein the old spacecraft had set down ended in a cliff up which they climbed, coming out on a waste of crushed crystal sand, facing, some yards away, the White Forest where moonlight flickered and sparked.

"No trail through that," Monro pointed out. "How will we know we're going straight and keeping east?"

"Those branches"—Sissions indicated the nearest "tree"—"are all right-angled and they grow in an established pattern. See this one and that? We keep our eye on the third branch up on every second tree. Let's get through this before sunup if we can."

It was a strange way to trace a path through the crystalline wilderness, but the Survey Scout, trained to note just such oddities, was right. The third branch on every second tree pointed in the same direction—a long glittering finger to the east. And they took turns watching for it, the rest shielding their eyes against too much of the reflection and glitter.

Naill was in the lead on his turn as pathfinder when he saw mirrored on a trunk of a neighboring tree a dark patch which came into better perspective and stopped him short. In spite of the distortions of that reflected image, there could be no mistaking the space suit.

The fugitives clustered together, to stare at the broken vision on the surface of the pillar. How far away it might be they had no idea.

Illylle spoke first. "It is not moving."

"No. Could be that it is waiting for us to walk right up and get caught again," Monro commented.

"I think not." Sissions' head had turned from right to left and back again. He had glanced from the image on the tree to the other growths about them. "It is behind us and perhaps to the right. And it is not moving at all."

Torry gave a grunt. "Close to dawn now, I judge. That thing may believe there's no need for hurry, that it can round us up quickly enough when the sun rises. I'd say we'd best make tracks and fast."

Torry's suggestion was accepted. They did hurry their pace as best they could. And when they left the reflection of that space suit behind, it did not show again, though they kept watch for it. So the medico's guess could be right—the guardian of the White Forest saw no reason to hurry in pursuit.

When the fugitives paused again, it was to make their final preparations against the sun. Torry argued that because of his training and ability to judge properly the efficiency of the goggles, he must have first chance as guide. The rest tore strips from their clothing and adjusted blindfolds which were as light-reducing as they could make them, after linking themselves together with the fiber rope.

Their advance slowed to hardly more than a crawl with Torry supplying a running description of the ground ahead, warning of missteps and obstructions. In spite of that there were falls, bumps, painful meetings with crystal growths. It was a desperate try, and only the heartening assurances from Torry that they were making progress kept them to it.

"Sun's hit the trees," he reported laconically some time later.

They were all aware now of the heat of those rays on their bodies, of a measure of light working through their blindfolds.

"What results with the goggles?" Sissions asked hoarsely.

"No worse than moonlight—yet," Torry reported.

So they were working this far. But suppose that the wyte pack waited ahead? They could not fight those blindfolded. And that suit—was it tramping stolidly

along behind them, ready to gather them in as
easily as it had netted Ashla and Naill back on the borders of the waste?

"Ah . . ." Torry broke off his stream of directions with
a small cry. Naill tensed and then relaxed as the other
added, "End of the wood . . . open beyond. And—I'm
ready for relief."

They had drawn lots before they had started and
were linked on the rope in the order of those lots.
Naill's hands went out readily, felt the goggles fall
into them as Torry pulled his waiting blindfold down
over his own eyes. Adjusting the lenses and pushing up his blinder was an awkward process, but a
few moments later Naill blinked out into a bright
morning which the treated goggles turned into a
bearable blaze.

He hurried to help Torry and the others on the rope
and then faced into the open country. It was barren
rock and sand—the sand running in sweeps as if it were
the water of dry rivers. And one of those sandy streams,
while thick to plod through, ran east to give them
smoother footing. Naill plowed toward that, towing his
line of followers.

How far were they now from the valley of the ship?
Naill had no idea of how much ground they had covered. He glanced back at intervals, each time expecting to see the suited sentry emerge from the blinding
glitter of the White Forest, just as he listened for the
snarling cry of the wyte pack.

The river of sand, which had seemed a good road
away from the Forest, did not serve them long, for it
took a sharp turn to the north, and Naill was faced with
the fact that they must somehow make their way up
along a ridge. They rested, drinking sparingly of their
water, eating nuts and dried berries.

"No reason to think it was going to be easy," Monro

commented. "My turn to take over now. Maybe—if we went up one at a time—me helping—"

Naill's hands were fumbling with the goggles when he saw Ashla move.

"Wait!" Her word was an order. She was facing toward the Forest, which was now but a glittering spot behind them.

"*It*—stirs! *It* knows! Now *It* wonders . . . soon *It* will move!" Her hands were fists. Naill could see only her lips, tight and compressed below the edge of her blindfold.

Sissions was on his feet, too. "Illylle is right. Pursuit will come."

"We can't run and we can't fly. Looks as if we've had it," Monro commented.

"No!" The protest came from the girl. "Now!" She whirled about to Naill as if she could see him through her blindfold. "This is my time to lead!"

"Not your turn—"

"This is not a matter of turns—or of anything but the knowing. And I have the knowing, I tell you! This is the time."

Sissions spoke. "Give her the goggles." The tone of that order overruled Naill's rise of protest.

His own blindfold was in place again when she spoke. "I am ready. Now we link hands—we do not hold the rope."

Her own fingers tightened about his. He reached out his left arm with caution, groped for Monro's hand. Then . . .

Naill had no words to actually describe what was happening, and Ayyar recognized it only dimly as a flow of the Power. But it was as if he could see— not physically but mentally—that through him flowed an awareness of his surroundings which was coming not by the way of his own senses, but from the girl, to pass along that line of men hand-clasped together.

So linked, they began a scramble up and out of the sand river and across the ridge beyond. Naill could sense, too, the strain and drive that worked in Ashla. Yet she kept going and they followed, at a better pace than they had held since sunup.

"*It* has learned." Her voice was low and hoarse. "Now *It* will truly move! *Its* servants gather."

And Naill heard—as if from very far off—the soulless wail of a wyte.

"Will with me!" That came as a plea from her. "Iftin warriors, Mirrormaster, Sea Lord—once you all stood blade and power against That Which Abides. Now will with my will, fight with those wills as you did with your blades in a leaf time now gone!"

Naill could not guess what response she aroused from the others. But in him there was a glow of anger and above it a wild, fierce determination to stand against the Enemy. He shouted a long-forgotten battle cry and did not know he mouthed it, for now he was not hand-linked to a company of fugitives; he was marching with his men, going to the First Ring of Iftcan. And in him pride and belief were no longer dim but fiery bright and clear as the green spark that had tipped his blade to open the Guard Way of the Mirror.

Iftcan and his vision of the waste melted into one, fitting together so that green growth merged with rock, fertile forest soil with sand. And he was Ayyar as Ayyar had been in the greatest day of his life.

"The Mirror Ring—oh, my brothers—there is the Mirror Ring!" Illylle's voice cut through Naill's dream, and the vision she now saw fitted over the vision of Iftcan's Tree Towers—gray mountain with over it a patch of cloud growing and spreading to cut away the glare of the sun. They were all running, speeding across ground they did not see with their eyes.

Then—the Enemy struck! Heat—light—something akin to lightning cracked in their faces. That brooding fear Naill had felt waiting beyond the walls encasing the Mirror Road took on body—strength. The wailing of the wytes was no longer distant. And his long-ago battleground became here and now.

Why he did it he could not have answered sensibly, but he flung back his head, raised his face to a sky from which, through the fold of cloth, came a searing, baking heat. Then Naill called—not only with voice, but with mind, with every part of him. And the shrill "hooooorrruuuur" of that call carried, echoed and re-echoed.

"On—on!" That was Illylle's demand. Somehow she was keeping them moving, summoning up their will, their strength, projecting for them the road they must take.

There was a roll of sound—a muttering along the distant reaches of the sky. A puff of wind blew in their faces, swirling up sand and grit to score the skin. But it was not the furnace blast of the waste; it was cool, carrying with it the smell of the forest.

And with the wind rode other things—feathered things—hooting, protesting, yet coming. Wheeling, dipping above those who ran, the quarrin kind had answered Naill's summoning—not only Hoorurr, but perhaps all of his species still holding to the shadows and glades of Iftcan. The fugitives could not see them, but they felt the impact of the quarrin thoughts, heard through the wind the sound of their wings. Three times the birds circled the runners, and then they dropped behind to where the wytes howled on a fresh and open trail.

The heat about them was the heat of anger. It had

been so long since That Which Abode had roused to full participation in any struggle that *It* was sluggish, unable to summon quickly old strengths and powers. That was what saved them. For had *It* struck earlier with the pressure *It* could exert, they would have been stamped to nothingness in the dust of the waste.

"On—up!" Illylle's battle cry was a hacking sob. Naill's hand dropped hers; flung out his right arm and closed it about her waist. She was stumbling, hardly able to keep her feet. But before them was the barrier wall of the Mirror Road, and they had met it where the rocks were as high as his head.

"Here!" He drew all the runners together with a call as he held up the girl, felt her wriggle in his hold. Then she was out of his grasp, gone—and out of his mind in the same move. A curtain had fallen between them.

"Over this!" Naill pictured in his own mind for the others the barrier about the road as he had seen it days ago. He stood with his hand on the rock wall, drawing each in turn to it, starting them to climb.

The wytes cried very closely now, their hunting bays broken by snaps, snarls—as if they fought. Naill guessed that the quarrin harassed that portion of the enemy forces.

The invisible power was the worst. Naill was thrust back and back—pulled from the roadway which he knew meant safety. Another step and he would be lost in his blindness. The heat bit into his brain, spread a blasting numbness down nerve and muscle.

Out of somewhere came a rope; a noose settled about his shoulders, jerked tight about his arms, tight enough to wring a gasp of pain from him. Now the pull was in the opposite direction. Naill stumbled and spun, breathless, only half conscious of the struggle.

"Dark the seed, green the Leaf—
Iftin power, Iftin belief . . ."

Had he said that, thought it? Had it come from him
at all? A second in which to wonder, a moment of
release from pressure growing intolerable, then with
a bruising crash his body brought up against the rock
wall of the road. He climbed—to fall into a swift stream
of cool air and the welcoming hands of his companions.

The roll of thunder grew into a mighty beat of
sound. Naill dragged off his blindfold and followed the
others as they ran along the road. Above them was a
gray ribbon of cloud, the edge of a mighty sunshade
which stretched from the east as if it had its birth in
the sky above dying Iftcan.

There stood the gate of the Guard Way. No sword
had been drawn to open it this time, but the symbol
on the keystone glowed green. The stairs—they took
those stairs still at a breakneck pace, halting only when
they reached the shelf overhanging the Mirror.

A storm was coming, such a storm as had beaten
the forest when Naill sheltered in Iftsiga. No wind
reached into the basin which held the Mirror, yet the
water was troubled. It moved in ripples around and
around, rising with each stir of that circling.

Forces were gathering: forces such as Naill Renfro
had never known—forces Ayyar held in awe.

Illylle moved a little away from the rest. She had
swept off the goggles, stood watching the circling of
the water.

"There has been a seeding. There is now a
growing—soon will come the Leafing. But without the
seeds, there will be no Leaf! If a Leaf is willed—
protect the seeds and the growing. Give us now Your
judging. Shall the seeds endure until the Leafing?"

Was that an invocation of something—something utterly opposed to that which they fled—something that was the very life of Janus? Naill believed it to be so. And they stood to witness the answer to her appeal.

Up and up the water raced about the sides of the Mirror frame. It lapped against the edge of the ledge on which they stood, yet none of them retreated. Naill felt no fear. Once more he seemed on the edge of a great discovery. The time might not yet be fully ripe, but someday it would—and he was a part of it!

The first of those waves touched the peaks that cradled the Mirror—touched, lapped, spilled over. Faster and faster the water swirled. It was now ribboned and laced with green foam, spun by the speed of its boiling. Over through a dozen—two dozen— channels poured that flood, fountaining out into the waste beyond the boundaries of the Mirror frame. The wind howled, the clouds broke, pouring down a second kind of flood.

Under that deluge the fugitives gasped and reeled, but they did not seek shelter. It was a growing rain, a rain to encourage sprouting seeds—new life.

Lightning . . . lashes were laid in whip lines across the sky to the west. There was an answering blast there—a white glare flaring skyward as if to dry the clouds instantly of their water burden. A terrible consuming anger strove to strike them, even this far away, as a wave of expanding energy. Then the rain closed down. The Mirror continued to pour its substance out and down to water the desert plain.

How long did that continue—the Mirror spilling, the clouds emptying rain? A few hours—a day? Naill could not have told. He was only aware that in time there was an end to that fury. Clouds parted. Stars shone serene in the sky. Still they were together on the ledge above a now quiet Mirror. And they were awed and small before a power far greater than they could imagine.

"We have much to learn." Jarvas who had been Pate Sissions spoke first.

"We have much to do." That was Torry, again Kelemark.

"*It* has not conquered—this time." Naill-Ayyar's hand was on his sword as he faced west.

He who had once been Monro and was now wholly Rizak smiled. "Nothing is ever too easy, if it is worth the winning—and the holding."

But Illylle smiled and hummed gently.

Naill-Ayyar knew that song; the words to fit the tune dropped into his mind one by one. It was very old—older than Iftcan, that song—for Iftcan's Tree Towers had been evoked and nourished from saplings by its singing. That was the Song of the First Planting.

"There shall be again a city." She broke the song to prophesy what they all knew in their hearts would come to pass. "And it shall rise where there was desolation. And the Oath shall be spoken once again. For the Iftin are replanted and the Nation shall grow— though the seeds were not of this world. There has been a judging and a judgment. We shall see a Fourth Leaf come into full greatness. But all growth is slow, and the way of the gardener is never without battle against destruction from without." She began to sing again—the song which was only for the Mistresses of the Planting. They listened to her almost greedily.

She walked ahead, began to descend the stairway leading to the plain and the night. Behind they followed eagerly.

Victory on Janus

I

A winter sun was sullen red over Janus. Its bleak rays lit up the Forest that was being destroyed. Flame bit, grinding machines tore life from soil-deep roots. Quivering branches clicked together a warning that reached into Iftcan-of-the-trees, the city that once had been.

And in the heart of a mighty tree, Iftsiga, the last of the Great Crowns that still leafed and had sap blood, the in-dwellers it sheltered stirred from the depths of hibernation.

Larsh! Out of memory nearly as old as Iftsiga itself came that name. Death by the beast men. Out, brothers, defend Iftcan with sword and heart! Face the Larsh—

Ayyar struggled wildly with the covering over him, forced open unwilling eyes. It was dark here in the core of the giant tree. The summer festoons of lorgas, the light-larvae, were missing. Like all else they slept, snug in the crevices of the sheltering bark. But it was no longer quiet. About him like a wall was a trembling, a throbbing. And though Ayyar could not truly remember having heard it before, he recognized the alarm of the Forest Citadel.

"Awake! Danger comes!" Every throb of that great pulse beat through him. But it was so hard to move. The lethargy that had gripped him and his kin in the fall, that had brought them to shelter and sleep, had not lifted gradually as nature intended. Ayyar was not yet ready to face the new life of spring. Painfully he crawled from his nest of mats.

"Jarvas? Rizak?" His voice was hoarse and rusty as he called to those sharing this chamber. The force of the warning grew stronger, urging him to—flight!

Flight—not battle— That from Iftsiga, the stronghold that even the ancient Enemy could not reduce? Had the great tree not been seeded in the legendary time of the Blue Leaf, been grown to shelter the race of Iftin in the day of the Green, and of the Gray of the last disaster, outlasting the wrath of the Larsh, preserved to help awaken the Iftin anew? This was Iftsiga, the Eternal—yet the warning was—

"Flee! Flee!"

Ayyar crept to the nearest wall of the tree, put his shaking hands on that living surface. Now it was warm beneath his cold flesh, as if its life arose to fever pitch.

"Jarvas?" He clawed his way up, swaying. There was movement in the other two bed places.

"The Larsh?" That question from the gloom on his right.

"Not so. Remember, the day of the Larsh is past."

Once again his memory had to be welded—for he bore the memories of two different men, as did all those now within Iftsiga. In an earlier time, he had been Naill Renfro, an off-world labor slave. Ayyar's lips drew into a snarl in reaction to that memory. As Naill he had found a treasure within the woodland. And because he had dug it up, the dreaded Green Sick had struck him down.

From that terrible illness he had emerged as an Ift, green-skinned, hairless, forest-attuned, provided with the tattered memory of Ayyar, Captain of the Outer Guard in the last days of Iftcan. And as Ayyar-Naill he had found others like himself—Ashla of Himmer's garth or settlement, who became Illylle, one-time priestess of the Mirror, Jarvas-Pate, Lokatath-Derek, Rizak-Monro, Kelemark-Torry.

Over the South Sea were still others who had earlier undergone the same change. But they were such a very few, for not all off-worlders were to be drawn into the net of the buried treasures set by the first Iftin-kind at their dying; only those who had the right temperament. And none of the changelings were truly whole. In them was an uneasy balance; one past set against the other. So was he now sometimes Ayyar, sometimes Naill, though for longer periods now Naill slept and he could draw upon the knowledge of Ayyar.

"There is death abroad." Ayyar spoke now. "The warning—"

"True. And the time of sleep not yet done." Jarvas answered him. "But we must have the awakening draught—"

In the gloom Jarvas crawled on hands and knees to the opposite wall, his hands fumbling with what was set into the living fabric of the tree.

"Ah—Iftsiga denies us not!" His cry was one of wonder and hope.

Ayyar lurched across the chamber. Jarvas drank from the spout set in the wall, not waiting for a cup, but catching the sweep sap in his hands, sucking it avidly from his palms. Ayyar followed his example.

The chill in him vanished, warmth sped along his

veins, spread through his body. He could move easily, and his mind cleared.

"What is it?" Rizak crept up to drink in turn.

"Death—death to Iftsiga!" Jarvas stood tall. "Listen!"

The murmur, the crackle of branch against branch, was a struggle of the ancient tree to communicate with the Iftins—or the half-Iftins—now within it.

Jarvas swung around. "From the east it comes!"

To the east lay the clearings of the garths, the settlements that were black death blots in the Forest. There, too, were the buildings of the port where off-world spacers set down.

"Why—what?" Rizak turned, refreshed from his sap drink. "They do not clear land in winter, and this is not yet spring."

"We shall find the answer only by seeking it," Jarvas replied. "Iftsiga would not wake us, except in extremity. This is grave danger—"

"The others—" Ayyar went to the ladder which led both down and up in the center of the chamber, linking all levels of the tree tower.

"Jarvas? Ayyar?" A soft call from below, even as he set foot on the ladder rungs. He looked down into a face turned up to his.

"Haste, oh, make haste!" Illylle's voice arose. "We must haste!" She moved before him, descending to yet another level where many small chests stood stacked against the walls.

There were the others, Kelemark and Lokatath, pulling at those boxes, moving in frantic haste to drag them to the ladder which led on down, deep into the earth and root chambers of Iftsiga.

"The seeds!" Illylle lifted one of the chests. "We must save the seeds!"

With her words a sharp urgency struck Ayyar also.

Every one of those chests contained seed for the regrowth of the Iftin. In them were the treasure traps to draw new changelings into their company. Should anything destroy these chests their dream of a new nation would die. Yes, above all, the seeds must be saved.

"Where?"

His night-oriented sight had grown keen since the sap-drink, and he could read the sorrow on Illylle's face.

"Into the root chambers—"

Dreadful indeed must be the peril! To use the root chambers meant that Iftsiga had no hope of survival. How could Illylle be sure—yet she was.

"The seeds—" She turned to summon Jarvas and Rizak now on the ladder.

Jarvas nodded decisively. "The root chambers." He did not ask, he ordered.

So they toiled, using their new-born strength, stripping Iftsiga of the meaning it had held as the Citadel during ages more than Ift or man could reckon, carrying those precious chests, each with a sleeping memory and Ift personality, to the farthest limit of the long roots and, in doing so, killing the tree that had been the refuge and shelter of their race. And ever, as they worked so feverishly, the warnings heightened; the need for speed enveloped them, so that they ran, pushed, carried as they cleared one chamber, two, three, a fourth—

Then they were done, and Jarvas and Illylle, working together, sealed the cramped ways through which they had crawled and pushed their burdens, using the substance of the tree, with earth and certain words to bind with power.

Then they came up into the entrance chamber from which they could emerge upon a limb and let down a ladder to the ground. There they gathered supplies to make packs. Jarvas took command.

"Iftsiga dies; by what means we shall learn. But in its dying, may it also fight against those who destroy it. Thus—"

He and Illylle went, one to each wall, laying their hands against the tree's now shuddering surface, to speak almost as one:

> "Let your spirit not depart gladly,
>   Great One,
> But harshly to those who come
> Of all the days, may this be the worst
> For those who ill use you.
> Die in battle; make of your branches
>   swords,
> Of your twigs needles to tear,
> Of your sap poison to burn,
> Of your trunk a crushing weight.
> Die as you have lived, Ift-friend,
>   Ift-protector,
> That your seedlings may spring anew.
> This be our promise, Iftsiga—
> Your seed shall sprout with ours.
> Ift-blood, sap-blood, shall be as one.
> Ift to tree, tree to Ift!"

Around them the tree swayed; a sound came from trunk and branch that was not a groan but rather the growl of beast aroused.

Then Jarvas gave his orders. "We must know the enemy, whence he comes, what he strives to do here. Scouts to east and north! And you, Sower of the Seed"—to Illylle he gave the old title—"to that which is our help, to the Mirror, that mayhap you can call upon what lies there to our aid—"

She shook her head slowly. "Once I did so, yes, but twice perhaps not. Illylle is not wholly Illylle. I have too many memories not rooted in Ift. But what I can do, I shall. And"—she faced them—"brothers, let not death choose you. Ill-faced may be our stars, but still are we the new seeds, do not forget that!"

It was night, the time of the Iftin, as they came into the open. Around them was a flow of movement. Peecfrens slid swiftly along branches, leaping in bounds from one limb to another, their fur silver in the moonlight. Borfunds grunted and snorted below. Flying things sought the air. All the Forest dwellers were on the move. Most of them had roused from hibernation, but they were alert. None of them need Iftin fear. But other things, deadly enemies, might also be on the move.

"Hooo-ruurrru—"

It was a welcome cry that was also a querulous complaint. A large bird settled beside the Iftin, turning its tufted head to survey them sleepily, sullenly. The quarrin was an old hunting companion. Ayyar opened his mind to its thoughts.

"Break—tear—kill!" Red savagery answered him.

"Who?"

"Things that crawl! Hunt the false ones! Kill, kill, always kill!"

"Why—?"

The quarrin hissed, was gone on wide-spread wings.

"Things that crawl," Rizak repeated. "Earth-grubbers?" Out of his off-world past he made tentative identification.

Machines could alter the face of any planet, given the time and the determination of human will. But such machines were few on Janus. This world of trees had been settled by the Sky Lovers, a dour religious sect who worked with their hands and with the aid of animals, refusing to allow machines anywhere but at the port site. Earth-grubbers were not for Janus.

Unless, since the Iftin had sought their winter sleep, some powerful change had been wrought in the world they wished to reclaim as their own.

"The port lies northeast," Kelemark said. "But why would they be using machines? The forces there keep within their own boundaries. And—in the winter—the Settlers would not be hunting 'monsters.'"

No, the Settlers on the garths would not stir after those they called "monsters" and who enticed hunters into the Forest.

"The garthmen would not use machines." Lokatath spoke positively. He had been one of them before the Green Sick change.

"Guessing will not provide us with the truth," Ayyar-Naill returned. He had been a soldier; his answer was action.

"Do not play your life too boldly," Illylle called after him.

He smiled at her. "I have been knocking on the door of death since I first walked this world. But I do not throw aside a sword when I go to face the kalcrok," he said, naming the most fearsome of the Forest enemies.

"Split up," Jarvas said as they moved through the frosted vegetation. "Then return to the Way to the Mirror. I think that is our safeguard."

They became a part of the Forest, each to find his own path north and east. Fewer animals passed now; some moving sluggishly as if their awaking from hibernation had been so recent they had not had a chance to drink sap.

Ayyar's nostrils expanded, cataloguing scents, wary for the stink of kalcrok. There was the stench of man to beware of also—for man to an Iftin was an offense, carrying with him the smell of the death he dealt to Forest life—and perhaps they must now quest also for the odor of machines.

Kalcrok he did not scent. But man—yes—there was the taint of man on the air, to be easily trailed. He passed two of the Great Crowns, but these were bone-white, long since dead—probably from the time the Larsh stormed Iftcan. Ayyar had been one of the defenders, but no small spark of memory remained past his first standing to arms. Had that first Ayyar "died" during that attack? They had no knowledge of how the personalities they now wore had been set within the treasure traps and then transferred by the Green Sick to off-world men and women. But Ayyar had been a captain of the city guard in the old days and now it would seem that Ayyar-Naill must play the same role.

The smell of man now mingled with an even worse stench as a pre-dawn wind puffed about him. It was the smell of burning, such as the garthmen did to clear their lands.

Dawn was near. Ayyar reached into an inner pocket of his green-brown-silver tunic. Kelemark, who had once been the medico known as Torry Ladion, had devised a daytime aid for light-dazzled Iftin eyes, goggles made of several layers of dried leaves. So equipped they could travel in all but the brightest sunlight.

That thick stench of burning could mask the odor of men. He must now depend upon sight. Around him the saplings, the brush, were leafless. Patches of blue-tinted snow lay in shadows. The air warmed as tendrils of smoke wove ribbons of mist from smoldering mats of blackened fibers. He looked through a shriveled screen into widespread desolation and again his lips were a-snarl.

When they had gone to sleep, the river had divided the remnants of Iftcan from the land of the garths. But now burnt paths stretched well back into the Forest. Each ran spear straight from a heat beam. This was no garth work, but that of machines. Why? The officials at the port had no reason to clear land, in fact they were forbidden to.

Ayyar flitted along the edge of the ash-powdered strip, now and then covering nose and mouth with his hand as he passed some noisome pocket. The beaming had not been at random, but laid down with definite purpose. It was plainly meant as an assault against the whole of the Forest.

He now fronted open charred ground on which stood a machine, a dark box squatting sullenly on treads to take it across rough and broken ground. Farther off was an earth-grubber, its snout at present raised and motionless, but behind it lay soil, gouged and ravaged.

Dawn was very bright to Iftin eyes. Even with the goggles on Ayyar squinted. Beyond the machines was a hemisphere, as if the tortured soil had breathed forth a stained, dun-colored bubble. A camp!

Again this was no garthman's shelter, but the kind the port men brought with them. Ayyar called upon Naill memory as he searched for any official symbol that might identify the camp.

After the discovery of Janus the planet had been given to the Karbon Combine for exploitation, almost a hundred years ago. But they had done little with it. Then a galactic struggle, which had torn apart old alliances, devastated worlds, and made of Naill Renfro one of the homeless wanderers, had given the Sky Lovers a chance to buy out the Karbon interest, since the Combine had gone bankrupt. The war had given a death blow to many thrusts of space expansion and cut back for a time mankind's outward flow. Janus, with its wide, thickly forested continents, its narrow seas, its lack of any outstanding natural riches, had been easily relinquished to those who wanted it as a homeland.

Once it was assigned to the garthdwellers, off-world powers would have no reason to meddle with the planet. Their jurisdiction extended no farther than the port. Yet now they were carrying on a systematic battle against the Forest.

There was no symbol on the bubble-tent, or on the other two smaller ones nearer the river. Ayyar settled himself to wait and watch. He knew the danger of over-confidence; yet he was sure that no man in that camp, or any garth of the tree-hating Settlers, could match an Ift in woodcraft. The dogs of the garths were to be feared, but here he did not smell dog.

The light grew stronger. He glanced back now and then at the Forest. The dead Great Crowns were bones. Around their huge trunks, roots spread out in high buttresses, taller by far than his head, dark caverns between their walls. In the old days one beat upon those, and the call would be repeated, so that in moments signals ran from one end of Iftcan to the other. But if one sounded such an alarm today, who was to answer? Unless troubled ghosts would gather, unable to defend their graves. Scraps of Ayyar memory stirred.

"Take into your hand a dead warrior's sword and beware, lest his spirit come to claim it—and you!"

Naill had such a sword. It lay smooth and straight against him now, its hilt ready to his hand, its baldric across his shoulder. Naill had taken the sword, so he was Ayyar, to be claimed by Ayyar's battles.

There was movement at the nearer of the bubble shelters. A man came out. It was no garthman—he wore no brush of beard, nor their sad-dull, coarse clothing. He had on the uniform of port security. Then this *was* an official expedition. What *had* happened during Iftin slumber?

Ayyar measured by eye the distance to the machines,

to the camp. The ground was far too clear to risk any advance on his part. And that physical and mental change that had so forcibly altered Naill into Ayyar had also planted deep in him a revulsion toward his former species. Even to plan close contact with them made him giddy with waves of sickness.

Yet the only means of learning the truth was to get within listening distance of those men. And once they manned the machines he would not dare to linger— there was too good a chance of being caught by the sweep of a heat beam.

More men came out of the sleeping quarters. Two wore guards' uniforms, the others the clothing of port workmen. But, Ayyar noted, they all went armed. Not with the stunners that were the usual planet side weapons—but with blasters, only issued on inhabited worlds under the most imperiled conditions! That was another reason to keep well out of range. Iftin swords were not equal to blasters.

The men went into another bubble—mess, probably. Then Ayyar heard the hum of a flitter. He froze under his change-color cloak. It was coming from the port and would set down not too far from his place of concealment.

Two men dropped from its cabin door. They walked, not to the camp, but to the beamer, one of them sighting along the dead paths it had cleared.

"—take us months to char this off. There is a whole continent to clear!"

He who did the sighting glanced over his shoulder. "We cannot wait for off-world help. You saw the Smatchz garth. And that was the third. As long as they have these forests for cover, we cannot track them."

"But *what* are they?"

The other shrugged. "Ask me after we catch one. As far as their *word* is concerned they are green devils.

I"—he hesitated, running one hand along the ray tube almost caressingly—"was on Fenris and Lanthor during the war—and the Smatchz garth was worse than anything there. We face the hardest kind of war, hit and run attacks where the enemy has all the advantage. The only way to drive those green demons out is to blast away their cover!"

"Well, the sooner we get to it then . . ."

They turned back to the camp. Ayyar watched them stop a little way from the shelters. There was a shimmer in the air; they stepped forward, once more the shimmer—but it was behind them. A force field! The camp was ringed by a force field! Which meant that those inside that barrier were guarded against some greatly feared danger.

Green demons from the forest? Ayyar glanced down at his own slender hand, at its green flesh. Could they have meant Iftin? No, that could not be. The only Iftin, except for those wintering across the South Sea, were those who had sheltered in Iftsiga. The "green demons" could not be Iftin—but then who or what?

II

For the Iftin there was an older, greater-to-be-feared Enemy than any from garth or port, That Which Abides. Of old the Larsh had been *Its* army, issuing forth from the noisome Waste. Yet in that same grim desert stood an Ift refuge, the sanctuary of the Mirror of Thanth. Now under the sun, *That's* weapon, Ayyar entered the time-worn road leading to the crater-cradle Mirror.

Could they summon again the Power of Thanth? Illylle and Jarvas had called up that force months ago, to battle by storm and flood the servants of *That*, pinning the Enemy back into *Its* own place. And the flood that had spilled over the rock lips of the Mirror has washed across part of the waste, cleansing much of it from evil.

So much the Mirror had done for them. What more it might accomplish they did not know. Could it be used against off-world men and machines, bound by no natural law of Janus? To each planet its own mysteries, powers that were tools or weapons for its natives, but that had no meaning for invaders from other stars. To the Iftin, the Mirror and that which acted through it were things of majesty and force. To others this might only be a lake of water in a basin of rock.

"Ayyar—"

He raised his head, for his eyes had been on the age-worn pavement under foot.

"Kelemark," he acknowledged. So he was not the first here.

As Ayyar, Kelemark wore cloak and pack and carried sword. But over his arm lay a length of cloth, stained and torn. From it came a smell that wrinkled Ayyar's nose.

It was a smell, not of man, nor the taint of machine—this was something else—insidious. So, having once filled his nostrils, the smell remained to poison each following breath. Yet otherwise that rag appeared a portion of Iftin cloak, for it was green-brown-silver, each color flowing into the other.

"What—?" Ayyar pointed to it.

"I found it caught on a thorn bush." Kelemark stretched out his arm. Suddenly the rag writhed, twisted as if it had life. With a startled exclamation Kelemark threw it from him. Now the odor was stronger, and they both moved back, standing instinctively on guard.

Ayyar's sword was out, though he did not remember drawing it. He held the blade, not with its point to an invisible foe, but gripping it just below the hilt, slanted skyward.

> "Iftin sword, Iftin brand—
>   Light fails, Iftin stand.
>   Cool of dark, fire of noon—
>   Green of tree, evil's doom!"

From his mixed memory came those words, as did the movements of his sword, back and forth, up and down. He was no Mirrormaster, nor Sower, nor Tender, nor Guardian—but a warrior. However, there were ancient safeguards against *That* as all men knew.

Now the sword he held blazed and dripped green fire, and those droplets ran along the ground to encircle the rag. Yet the fire did not destroy; it only enwalled. He heard a cry from the stairway that led to the Mirror, the thud of running feet.

Illylle came in haste, and with her, Jarvas. But when they saw what lay upon the pavement, fire imprisoned, they halted.

"Who found this and where?" Jarvas asked.

"It was caught in a thorn bush near the burning," Kelemark answered. "I thought—I feared it was of ours. Then, when I picked it forth, I knew it was not, but that it was important."

Illylle dropped to her knees, staring at the rag. From her belt pouch she brought a white sliver of wood as long as her first finger. Though water had ofttimes washed this way, yet still were there pockets of sand, and one of these was nearby. She pointed the end of her sliver to that which lay within the ring of fire; then she touched that same end to the sand.

Her hold was loose, merely designed to keep the sliver erect. Now it moved, marking the sand. And the symbol that appeared there was a tree with three large leaves—Ift! But the sliver was not yet done, for it jerked between Illylle's supporting fingers, scoring out the leaves it had just drawn, altering them into angular bare branches.

Ayyar studied the marks. Those sharp branches, he had seen their like before.

"Ift—not—Ift—but of the Enemy!" Jarvas half whispered. "What is the meaning of this?"

He looked to Illylle who studied the drawing on the sand. She shook her head.

"This"—she pointed to the rag—"has the semblance of Ift. Yet it is of the White Forest! I do not understand." She dropped the sliver and put her hand to her head. "So little can I remember! If we were of the true blood, more would be clear. But of this I am sure, what lies there is wholly evil and a weaving of deception."

Jarvas turned to the men. "What did you learn?"

Kelemark reported first. "They are on this side of the river, first burning and then grubbing. They are determined to erase the Forest—to kill it and its life."

"There is a camp of port men," Ayyar added. "And—" he repeated the conversation he had overheard.

"Green demons raiding garths!" Jarvas broke in. "But—*we* are the monsters their ignorance has feared for years. And we of Iftsiga are the only ones this side of the South Sea."

"There is one way to learn more—" Illylle arose. "I shall water-question the Mirror. But"—she looked to Kelemark—"do you remain here, for until you are purified you may not approach Thanth."

She put no prohibition on Ayyar, so he followed as she and Jarvas climbed the stairway that led to the ledge above the silent, brooding lake in the crater cup, the repository or focus of a power they did not understand.

Once more Illylle went to her knees on the edge of that ledge, stretching out her arms over the water.

"Blessing upon the water which is of life," she said and then fell silent. She stooped to wet a finger tip, and this she raised to her lips that her words might give them the needed answer, her mind now open to the Mirror. When she spoke, she did not look at her companions but across the lake, and upon her was the aura of one who is a vessel of power.

"Ift is not Ift. Evil wears the semblance of right. One defeat in battle does not end a war. The seed is endangered before the sowing—"

To Ayyar it made little sense. But he saw that Jarvas, perhaps by the power of interlocking thought the Mirrormasters once had, gained knowledge, his expression now being grimly dark. He put forth his hand to lay on Illylle's head. She blinked as an awareness of self flowed in.

"Come!" Jarvas brought them back to the walled road. Now Rizak and Lokatath were also there.

"Jarvas, there are Iftin—" Lokatath began.

"Not Iftin, true Iftin!" Illylle cried. "They may wear Iftin shapes, but they do the will of the White Forest, not the Green!"

Jarvas nodded. "It is so. That has not been defeated, only awakened. It has set the off-worlders against us in this manner."

"They have overrun garths," Lokatath reported. "I hid in the river rocks and heard those at the camp speak of it. They have slain and destroyed, these false Iftin, in a manner to arouse garthmen and port against them, so that old differences are forgotten and all off-worlders unite to wipe out the Forest and any Iftin found there—without mercy."

"The Forest is very large," began Illylle. Then she looked to Jarvas. "Can they really do this thing?"

"There are few of them here now," he replied soberly. "But they must already have summoned off-planet help. Yes, they can do this, if such aid comes."

Ayyar's hand fell to his sword hilt. "If *That* uses them, as *It* used the Larsh—"

"Yes," Jarvas agreed. "It was after my time that the Larsh became the weapons of *That*. My memory is of the Green Leaf, not the Gray. Now, it seems *It* would use these off-worlders in the same fashion, perhaps to the same victorious end."

"I wonder"—Ayyar put into words his thoughts— "does *That* always have to use others as tools? There was the space suit that herded Illylle and me into captivity— we never discovered what wore it. Was it not the same when *That* took you prisoner before us? Those wytes, *Its* hounds, hunted us, and we felt the drawing of *Its* power when we escaped to the Mirror. In Ayyar's day the Larsh were sent to pull down Iftcan. Now the off-worlders are provoked into serving *Its* purpose. But never does *That* venture forth Itself. Why? What do you remember from the Oath of Kymon?"

"As to the nature of *That*?" Kelemark asked. "That is a thought, Jarvas. If *It* is so strong, why—?"

"Kymon went into the White Forest and strove with *That* and forced upon *It* the Oath, which held during the Blue Leaf and the Green, to be broken in the Gray." Illylle repeated well-known history.

"And the nature of *That* which he found in the White Forest?" Ayyar persisted.

She shook her head. "Jarvas?" she appealed in turn.

"Nothing," he replied. "It uses mental control; we all know that. Beyond—" He shrugged. "Now, apparently, *It* also has Iftin, or beings resembling Iftin, fighting for *It*. Those Iftin we must seek."

"Our noses should lead us." Rizak nodded to the rag.

"Meanwhile, the Forest dies," Illylle pointed out. "What has been our hope? To raise up a new nation, then seek our freedom from an off-world colony under the law. If they continue to destroy our home, there will be no chance for us ever to treat with them."

"She is right," Rizak agreed. "We have to make them understand what is really going on before they reach a point of no return for any of us!"

"And just how will you do this?" challenged Lokatath.

"By capturing one of the false Iftin," Ayyar said, "and proving the difference."

They stared at him, and then Jarvas laughed shortly. "Simple, yet perhaps the best solution. So now we go ahunting for the Enemy, and I think that means prowling along the river."

"Can you foresee their trail there?" Kelemark asked Illylle.

"Not in this. While they move, they are encased in their master's protection, and I have not the skill to break that. We must do this by eye, nose, and ear."

It was decided to follow the shore south from the entrance to the Mirror, along the river. Night would favor them most, since Iftin senses were nocturnal and already the day was far sped. Thus, wrapped in cloaks, they lay against the road wall and slept.

Swiftly at dusk they sped along their chosen route. Winter-dried reeds, far higher than their heads, made a small woodland. But these beds they skirted. The change in temperature from day to night, as always, altered odors. Some were sharper; others faded. There were sounds; the scratching which was an earth-lizard dragging a river worm back and forth across gravel, the calls of hunters winged and four-footed. Once they crouched in silence, waiting while one of the great carnivores swung its muzzle under the water at the river's edge, champing jaws meanwhile, to wash out its mouth after feeding. And the fresh blood smell of that meal reached them.

But no unusual scent tainted the air. The land the Mirror had cleansed was now behind them, and the darkness of the true Waste lay to their right. In the north the sky was bright.

"Now they beam at night." Lokatath stated the obvious.

"They grow impatient or more afraid," Kelemark replied.

Was Iftsiga already burning? Ayyar wondered. And what of the seed chests? Would their hiding place among the roots of the Citadel be deep enough to protect them from the earth-tearing snout of the grubber?

Water vapor clung to the river at this point. And here they picked up the trail they sought. Lokatath spat, and Ayyar tasted bitter moisture gathering in his own mouth. The stench from the rag had been bad, but this was infinitely worse. Drawn into one's nostrils, it seemed to fill one's lungs with a lingering, loathsome residue.

"Fresh?" Rizak commented.

"Yes, and leading over river to the garths."

Ice-rimmed logs and rocks, their surfaces just above the winter-shrunken stream, made a bridge of sorts. The Iftin used it.

"Ah—" The soft exclamation from Illylle drew Ayyar's attention. She was frowning, her head turning from right to left and then back again, as one who tried to discover some half-forgotten landmarks.

"What is it?"

"This way, does it not lead to Himmer's?"

West and south— Yes, not far from here he, newly Ift himself, had seen the transformation of Ashla Himmer into Illylle, had aided her through the worst of that discovery that she was now alien to her kind. Though she had not believed—not at first—that she was alien. She had insisted upon returning to her garth, to seek out the younger sister she cherished. Only when the repulsion each felt now for the other had been made plain had she been convinced that kin of Ashla were not of Illylle's. Yet perhaps now a faint stir of that old affection worked in her.

Over the river the trail did not run straight. It was almost as if that which they hunted had quested, like a hound seeking a quarry of its own. Then, far away, sounded the barking of garth dogs. From Himmer's? Ayyar could not be sure. But he hoped it lay more to the west.

Now the trail straightened, and they fell into a half run natural to Iftin. A woodland engulfed them though this was not the Forest. Yet it was good, like unto a drink of cool water in the day's heat, to have trees close about them—bare of leaf, winter-ravaged as those were.

This was a forest already emptied of many of its inhabitants, for garth clearings had gnawed at it steadily to north and east. And the creatures that were wary and shy had long since departed. Not all, however. Some still holed up in tree or ground burrows. Now these slept through the dead season.

Strong was the scent and louder the clamor of the dogs. At least those sentinels must long ago have aroused their masters. Remembering the fate of other garths, they would be doubly alert. Armed with blasters, they should be able to turn back an attack.

The Iftin party must take care. It would do no good to be caught in some fight and mistaken for the Enemy. Ayyar caught Jarvas' sharp hand orders, dividing them into two parties, right and left. It was right Ayyar turned, Illylle beside him, Rizak a little behind.

They detoured about the clutching, dangerous branches of a large thorn tree. Now the scent was not so strong. Ayyar sniffed another odor, the death that surrounded each garth where tree, bush, all green life died in ragged cuttings gouged out of the true beauty of Janus. And he knew again hatred for those who thus slew.

Was this Himmer's garth? He asked Illylle. She looked about her. But now she shook her head.

"This is too far east. Perhaps it is Tolferg's." But was she sure or only wished it so?

It seemed to Ayyar that the barking had lessened.

Fewer hounds giving tongue? Now, flickering light among the trees—torches?

They slackened pace and kept to cover until they looked through a screen of withered brush, out over raw land where huge stumps stood, charred from the dogged burning of fires kept going for weeks, even months.

The light came from torches blazing on a stockade wall. Behind that was the garth building. Several of the torches had been pitched down to set fire to dried material heaped in the open, so that the stretch of cleared land was as light as the besieged could make it, though every half-burned stump provided a pool of shadow. With their hind-quarters pressed against the now barred gate of the garth enclosure stood four hounds, showing their fangs to the night. They had not come to that stand easily. Wounds bled on their flanks and shoulders, and another dog lay struggling to win to its feet but unable to do so.

Between the edge of the wood and the gate lay at least six more of those vicious four-footed guards. It looked as if they had been loosed to buy time for their masters.

"To the right, beside the forked stump," Illylle whispered.

The black clot of stump had been fire-hollowed into an unusual shape, its center portion burnt away, but the two outer rims rising in projections, giving the remaining stub the appearance of an animal head, ears up, alert to any sound.

Between those ears was movement, a rounded shadow arising for an instant. From the rear the skulker looked Ift, cloak spread out in the concealing sweep Ayyar used upon need. The head turned—Ift! Illylle's fingers tightened on Ayyar's arm. The counterfeit could not be detected, at least not here and now. Rizak whispered.

"Could *That* have captured some of the old true race, made them *Its* servants?"

"Who knows? But this is of the Enemy." Of that Ayyar was sure. "How many?"

He searched the ground with hunter's eyes and used his nose to locate five more before him. Since they were certainly not all bunched here, perhaps double or triple that number might be abroad.

Illylle drew a sharp breath. "They wait—for what?"

A scream answered her, such a cry as only extreme fear and pain might tear from a human throat. Out of the brush to their right stumbled a weaving figure, rags of clothing still about it, but not enough to conceal that it was a woman. Shrieking, she staggered on between the hidden attackers who made no move to pull her down.

"She is their key to the gate," Rizak said.

Would it have worked? Perhaps, had not the hounds moved. Two of them sprang, almost as one—not at the creeping shadows, but for the woman. Their fangs ended her screams as she was borne to the ground. Then the hounds howled as ray beams from the stockade crisped them. Their masters must have believed them mad.

One of the false Iftin sprang into the open, caught an outflung arm of the woman, hurled the body back into the shadow of a stump where two of his fellows pounced upon it and dragged it away with them.

"Aloft—over there!" Rizak's head was up.

One of the port flitters was in the night sky, and from it lashes of fire beat the ground.

"Back!" Ayyar pulled at Illylle. They ran from the death that would spare nothing in the ignited woodland.

"Down river—south—" panted Rizak moments later. He was right. The rock and sand there would not burn; they might find shelter if they could reach it. As yet the beams struck only about the garth clearing—but they would work out from there.

In this much they were favored, the trees took long

to ignite. It was only when the flame lash touched the lower growth that danger spread.

They heard sounds in the brush, the flight of other things. Then two figures burst into a glade on the left—false Iftin, one wearing the rags of a smoldering cloak about his shoulders, as if he felt no heat or pain from that burning garment. They were heading for the river, too.

Were those the only survivors among the attackers? Some must have been caught in the first lashing of the flitter, Ayyar was sure.

"We—can—not—make—it—" Rizak coughed through the smoke.

"To the right!" A momentary glimpse had suggested salvation to Ayyar.

One of the trees, almost the size of a Great Crown, had fallen here ages past. Its roots pointed to the sky on one side of a deep pit. From that hole came a smell Ayyar knew of old, kalcrok. He had been web-captive in just such a burrow. But this scent was old. The burrow could not have been used lately. Perhaps the absence of large game, driven away from the garth, had led to its abandonment.

"In!" He followed his own order, pulled Illylle with him, to land on a mat of evil-smelling debris, Rizak sliding down behind.

What Ayyar sought lay directly before him, the entrance to the inner burrow. The webs about the walls were only tatters. This was safely deserted and could save them. He scrambled forward into the heart of the kalcrok nest hole.

III

It was a tight fit as they wedged into that runway in the deep earth. Somewhere along was a side chamber wherein the once owner had had its nest. This should house them from the fury of the flames. When they lay together in that evil-smelling hole, Ayyar's heart still pounded heavily.

"Jarvas, Kelemark, Lokatath—" he heard Illylle whisper.

Yes, what of the others? Had they found the small measure of safety offered by the river lands? But Rizak was thinking ahead.

"Burnt-over, this land will be bare for any searching. If they loose hounds . . ."

"These burrows have more than one door." Ayyar could speak from his fearsome earlier experience. "And they run straight. The other door will open nearer the river."

"Rizak, when will the brethren now over the South Sea return?" Illylle asked.

"We roused early. They should come with the true spring."

"To find the country arrayed against them."

"They do not come openly ever," he defended their fellow changelings, the ones who were moved by implanted instinct to invade the Forest, set the treasure traps and wait thereafter to find and aid the new Iftin who emerged from the Green Sick as their kindred.

"But neither have they yet faced such danger as this," Ayyar pointed out. "They may return to find no Forest and all off-worlders hunting them down. *That* plans well, striking in winter when we do not move."

"I cannot believe," Illylle's head lay on her arm, her mouth in these close quarters so near to his cheek that Ayyar felt the warmth of her breath with every word she spoke, "that the Mirror failed us! We saw the flooding and the storm and what struck the Waste. That could not have escaped—"

"But we do not know the nature of *That*," Ayyar interrupted. "It may be that danger arouses *It* to greater strength and efforts, to the summoning of more servants and warriors. With the Larsh *It* brought down Iftcan. Now with these off-worlders *It* will hammer the remains of that city into black ash. There is only one way to face *It*—"

"Yes—deal with those at the port, see that they know the truth!"

Ayyar could feel the shiver run through Illylle. His own body reacted thus as well. To go among the unchanged, to speak to them face to face, to be so close— that was an ordeal that perhaps none of them could stand up to, physically or emotionally. If there were some other way, one that did not include a meeting—a communication, until that could be used at long distance.

It would seem that Rizak's thoughts marched with his for now the other asked Illylle:

"These garthmen, they mount coms to keep in touch with the port, do they not?"

"No, that is worldly." The former garth girl made swift answer. "Only at the port will you find such things."

"Or perhaps in that camp," Ayyar amended.

Again Rizak picked up his thought. "Any camp would be well-guarded. They would expect attack in retaliation for the Forest spoilage."

Ayyar's memory of the port was such a small one. He had landed there but had still been groggy from the deep frozen sleep of a labor transport. All he could recall was standing in the line of human wares while that bearded giant Kosberg looked them over critically to make his choice. Then he had helped to transfer bundles of bark from the carts of his new master to a loading platform. He had never seen Janus port again.

"You know the port?" he asked Rizak.

"The port? No, I did not planet there. I crawled out of a lifeboat that downed in the Forest, sent from the space ship *Thorstone* as she passed through this solar system. The plague had hit us, but we kept going, hunting help. When we reached here I was barely living. They threw us in lifeboats to get rid of us. I landed with a party of dead, but I lived. Then I found one of the treasures—and became Ift. So I do not know Janus port at all."

"Lokatath was a garthman." Ayyar ran down the list. "But Kelemark, he was a medico there."

"But back in the days of the Karbon Combine," Rizak reminded him. "A lot can change in more than fifty years. And Jarvas was a First-in Scout before the port was established at all."

"But I was there for four hands of days," Illylle said.

"And that was only a small tale of seasons ago. I know the port. Is it in your mind, Ayyar, to go there?"

"To go there for a com. If we can get even a travel-talker we are that much closer to communication."

"The port," Rizak repeated, "I do not know. But your thought of a com to talk to them is good. Only we must first get out of this burrow. Let us put our minds to that."

And he was right, for there was a time during which Ayyar feared they had chosen their grave rather than a refuge. They found breathing hard as the flames outside fed on oxygen, and they lapsed into a comatose condition near to what they had known during hibernation. But when they stirred again there was more air, though it carried the reek of smoke.

Illylle was coughing, and Ayyar felt the choking fumes biting his nose and throat. They had better move, unless it meant going into the fire. He rasped out as much and pushed into the passage.

"Listen!"

But he did not need Rizak's cry. It was raining beyond. He had not expected such a heavy downpour. Perhaps the season was later than they had thought. The floor of the burrow was wet with a seepage of water. It must be pooling in the old trap pit. Ayyar crawled on, the others following.

A smoking mass of half-consumed vegetation had fallen across the outlet. He thrust at it with his sword and made them an exit. Although it was now day, the clouds were so massed that they emerged into twilight and around them the storm beat icily. The beam mounted on the flitter had accounted for the under-brush and the crowns of the trees, but the great trunks, charred and blistered, yet stood. Among these they made their way to the river bank.

It was between two rocks at the improvised log

and rock bridge that they came upon a body. A white arm outflung, the flaccid hand turned up as if to cup some of the flooding rain, was what Ayyar saw first. He turned quickly.

"No!" With one hand he tried to fend off Illylle, but she had already seen it and pushed past him to look down at what lay beyond.

Horror faded, she leaned closer as Ayyar and Rizak joined her. There was a human face, with no expression now, but rather a queer blankness that Ayyar did not associate with the peace of death. There could have been no peace, however, for the throat and upper breast had been shredded away by the hounds, and that attack had uncovered metal, wires, and broken bits of cogs.

"Robot!" Naill memory supplied the proper word.

Rizak hunkered down, ran exploring fingers along the arm. "More—feel this!"

With distaste Ayyar followed his example. The "flesh" was cold, rain wet. But its texture, to his inexpert touch, felt the same as if it had been part of a real body. Yet the rips in it were not bloody, and there was no denying that metal lay beneath.

"A made thing!" Illylle gave verdict. "But unless one knew—"

"Their key." Rizak nodded. "Send her in screaming and garth gates would open. Only this time, something went wrong. Those hounds knew, poor brutes, and died proving it. The false Iftin must have dragged her this far because she was important to their plans. Then, for some reason they had to abandon her. Which may be the worst mistake they have ever made!"

"How?" Illylle wanted to know.

"We needed some proof. Well, we may not have a false Ift, but we do have something here to make any off-worlder think. This is unlike any robot I ever saw,

but it is a robot. Now, suppose we put her out in plain
sight. In time they will send a snoop scouter over here,
perhaps more than one. Let them find her and begin
to wonder!"

He was right, Ayyar knew. Give the port authorities
a mystery such as this, and they would be more ame-
nable to belief in a difference between Ift and false Ift.

"Those false Iftin—are they as this?" Illylle wondered.

"Perhaps. But—who made this and where?"

Illylle leaned still farther over the battered robot,
drawing deep breaths. "There is no need to ask, brother.
The stench of evil has not been washed away by the rain.
This, too, is of the White Forest."

"I do not see how it can be," Ayyar protested. What
did he know of the Enemy? He had been once taken
prisoner by a walking space suit of antique design
which had herded him and Illylle through the Crystal Forest to imprisonment at the depths of a chasm.
But—this robot, it could only be the work of a high
technology of a type of civilization he could not equate
with Janus at all.

"Do you not see," Illylle demanded of him now, "we
know so little of *That*. Remember the space ship that
sat on the desert sands— Perhaps there are other ships
lost in the Waste, things from which *That* may use at
will!"

Possible of course. But there was no use wasting
time in speculation now. Ayyar helped Rizak free the
robot woman from between the rocks, stretch out the
body face up in the open to be clearly seen. If Rizak
was right concerning the coming of a scout snooper,
this ought to be in port hands soon. Meanwhile, they
must get back across the river and find the rest of their
own party.

"Let us trust that they made it across." Rizak glanced
back in the direction they had taken when they had

reached the other bank of the river. "With this weather that dam-bridge will not last long."

"Where do we look for them? At the Mirror?"

"No." It was only a feeling, but the belief that it was right made Ayyar put force into his answer. "To the south."

The narrow sea lay south, and somehow its dune-hilled shore promised safety. To the port men the Forest would be the proper place to hunt their demon fugitives. Perhaps the others agreed with him, for they did not dispute.

Here where there were no trees, the brush and rocky outcrops must provide them with cover, and they kept to what was offered, listening always for any sound of a flitter. They had worked their way well downstream from the crossing when they heard a hum and lay flat among the stones. "Hovering," Rizak murmured. "I think they have sighted our lady."

"Ahh—"

To their night-oriented eyes that flash of flame was almost blinding. Those in the flitter were laying about with a beam, making sure that the body was not bait in a trap, or, if so, that the would-be trappers were taken care of before they landed.

"Move!"

With the flitter so occupied, they must put more space between themselves and it. Ayyar trotted around a shelf of rock to halt and look down. This gravel held no tracks, but just as the stink of the false Iftin was to be easily scented, so did his nostrils now inform him that those of the true blood had passed this way, and a very short time ago. Some of their party, if not all, had also won to this side of the river and were heading seaward.

When they were well away from the vicinity of the flitter, Ayyar whistled. To ears not trained in Iftin calls, the notes were a song of a river bird. And he continued to whistle so at intervals until he was answered. The replying trill took them into a maze of shrub, winter-thinned but still walled into thickets. And here, in a wide nest of marsh grasses and cut reeds, which had once been the lair of a finkang, they found Jarvas and Kelemark.

"There—someone is hurt!"

The third form in Ift clothing lay to one side, and Ayyar started forward. That could only be Lokatath. But why should he be tossed so—and there was something strange about his body— It took Ayyar a minute of sharp study to see that that strangeness was due to the fact that the supine form lacked half a skull!

Rizak strode forward to gaze down. "So we have another machine!" His mouth puckered wryly as if he wished to spit upon the body.

"Another one? Then you have also found one of these things?" Jarvas demanded.

"A woman—fashioned to resemble a garth dweller. She must have been used to open the gates, but the hounds finished her. Or did you not see?"

"We saw. What did you do with her?"

Rizak smiled. "We left her where she has already been found. To give the off-worlders something to think about." He went down on one knee to inspect the Iftin robot the closer. "Clever! Meeting this one face to face, I would say he was Ift. Until I saw this—" He jerked a thumb at the broken head and the mass of melted wires and other material it contained.

"No, you would not!" Illylle corrected him sharply. "This is evil! Your nose would tell you that."

"But off-worlders do not have such noses," Jarvas reminded her. "And the false Ift could seem true to those not of our kind. Clever indeed, with a devil's cleverness. In this fashion *That* has set a barrier between us and any garthman or off-worlder."

Rizak agreed. "But Ayyar suggests we try contact by com—"

"Com!" Kelemark swung around to look at the younger Ift. "And where will we find one of those?"

"At the port," Ayyar returned. "All we need is a hand-talker—get one of those and—" He spoke to Jarvas. "You were a First-in Scout, you know the official codes. Suppose you broadcast, would they not hear you out? Really listen?"

"They might. If we had a com. But to pick one up at the port—" Jarvas stopped. His expression changed from one of irritation at stupidity to thoughtfulness.

"Where is Lokatath?" Illylle asked. "Did he—was he lost?"

Kelemark shook his head. "No. He has gone to the signal rocks on the coast. There must be a beacon set there to warn the brothren."

She smiled. "Wise, very wise. But we cannot look forward now to an early planting—and perhaps they will not come soon."

"That is it. We do not know how early we have been awakened. So we dare take no chance."

Jarvas seated himself cross-legged in the deserted nest and brushed aside the fabric of its stuff at one edge, clearing a small space of ground. On it he laid out small pebbles.

"This is the port—am I right, Kelemark?"

The former medico looked over his shoulder. "I have not seen it for many years—"

"But Illylle has," interrupted Ayyar. "She went there not many seasons ago for medical aid when her mother was dying. Illylle?"

"Yes." She sat down in turn to face Jarvas across the cleared space. "Here is where the ships land and of those there are never many. Once each tenth of a year a government cruiser comes in. Between times, at the harvest season—the traders."

"Do not forget," Rizak warned, "that by now they may have beamed a call for off-planet help."

"Concerning that we shall have to take our chances," returned Jarvas. "So—the ships land to the west. What else?"

"Here"—she put down a larger stone—"is the building that houses the customs and the other government offices. Next is the hospital, then the barracks of the police, beyond—the quarters of those others who work there. Here are the sheds for the storing of the lattamus bark waiting to be shipped—that is all. Oh, yes, another building here to house and store the working machines."

"That is farther north, and now it must be empty," commented Ayyar.

"North," Jarvas studied the plan. "They are blasting into Iftcan from this direction." A sweep of his hand indicated east. "And they patrol along the river. To the northwest is the untouched Waste and *That's* stronghold. Also we are haunted by time."

"The garths must all be alerted." Illylle rested her chin upon an upheld fist, her elbow based on her knee. "Perhaps they have offered the safety of the port to any of the garthmen who care to come there."

"And would any?" asked Ayyar.

"I do not know. All their beliefs are against it, but perhaps in great extremity some would. Himmer's lies here—" she gestured to the north and east of their present camp.

They waited for her to continue, aware some purpose moved in her mind.

"Himmer's I know. Also, I know the animals there. Himmer has two phas broken to ride. They will come to the call—so mounted . . ."

"Too wild a chance." Jarvas denied her plan. "Every

garth will be standing alert for attack—they would have hounds out."

"How did the garth that was attacked call the flitter?" Ayyar asked suddenly. "The flyer came in ready to blast—they must have been ready for trouble."

"Maybe the garths have coms now, because of this," mused Rizak.

"And if they have—" began Ayyar.

"No—trying to get to one of those, undetected, would be like walking bare-handed into a kalcrok web, expecting to talk that double mouth out of fanging one!" Kelemark protested.

"There is the scout flitter—and that—" Rizak nodded to the robot Ift. "Plant that out in the open as we did the other. Let them see it."

"They will take good care to flame lash all around before they ground, and everyone in the crew will be wearing a blaster," Kelemark pointed out.

But Illylle looked thoughtful. "Suppose we have a way to defeat such caution?"

"How?" Ayyar wanted to know.

"Sal bark—"

Old lore was what she called upon now, the Forest learning. Bark stripped from a small, red-brown tree with leaves so tiny that even in the full life of summer it never looked to be more than autumn-bare, pounded and fed into a fire, made a smoke which stupefied and bewildered. It had been used to finish off kalcroks, when those monsters could be kept from retreating into the deep corridors of their dens.

"They will expect one trap, give them a different one—" she began when Ayyar picked up her idea and elaborated upon it.

"Pick a place that is open but that has brush around it at a little distance. They will fire that before they land. The sal bark will be in that brush. If we have any luck, we can then use the com of the flitter or the personal travel-talk of one of its crew."

"And the sal fumes, the fire, how do we ourselves walk through those?" Rizak asked dryly.

"We find a place close to the river," Kelemark chimed in. "One of us takes to the water and waits. The sal smoke will not last long—we shall not be able to find too much of the bark—if we are lucky enough to discover any."

Jarvas laughed shortly. "As bizarre a scheme as I have ever heard—but—"

"You are forgetting something. Are you now more men than Iftin?" Illylle frowned at them. "Men must depend upon what their two hands hold, their eyes see, their ears hear. There are other powers that can root in those senses and by belief grow beyond the visible and the touchable. I have lost much, but once I was a Chooser of Seed and a Sower, and from such planting there was growth beyond the normal. It was our gift and we used it well then, as we must do now!"

A little of the awe that had touched Ayyar at the Mirror of Thanth when this slim girl had called upon powers truly beyond mortal sight and sound again shadowed his mind. Illylle seemed so sure of what she said that her confidence carried over to the others.

The search for sal bark sent them out among the rocks, though not into the fringes of the Waste. For a thing of such virtue could not be found in that garden of all ill. Kelemark was right; any harvest would be a scanty one. Ayyar had perhaps two handfuls, taken from one small seedling, when he returned. Illylle herself had done best, for she had made a bag of part of her cloak, and it was a quarter filled with the aromatic twigs.

Jarvas vanished up river in search of a proper place to set out the bait and the rest worked with care, using one of their cloaks to keep off the rain which was now a drizzle, as they shredded each tiny piece of precious bark into one pile. When they had done, Illylle ran her hands back and forth through it, crooning in a whisper. Ayyar did not strive to distinguish her words, for this he knew was a growing chant. Not *the* chant, of course; that was too sacred for any such use, but still one to send virtue into their small pile of sal.

Rizak shared out supplies, mainly the flat nut-meat bread from the Iftsiga stores. The refreshing sap which had awakened them had sustained them for long, but now they must turn to real food.

"With the night our chance passes for now." Kelemark leaned back against a rock.

"There is always another sunset." Illylle shook bits of bark from her fingers.

Yes, thought Ayyar, there was always another sunset. Yet time did not linger for the good of any man— or for Ift—or for *That* which moved back there in the Waste, the thing they had gone into winter sleep believing muzzled, defeated— Defeated? It would seem that they had witnessed only a small opening skirmish in that spectacular meeting of powers when the Mirror had overflowed its basin, not a final battle. And *That* had resources beyond any they had dreamed.

The knowledge that had gone into the making of the false Ift—that was not born of the half mystical, otherworldly influence Ayyar thought pertained to the realm of That Which Abides. It was far closer akin to offworld technology.

What had Illylle said—other ships planeting mayhap, out in the Waste, their cargoes open for *That*'s use? The woman robot, yes, that could have come from such a ship. Not the Iftin, however. Those were of Janus. Someone or something had fashioned those to be used for this purpose—to set all Iftin apart as outlaws and the hunted. Was this off-world—not part of *That* at all? No—they knew the stench of old, and it clung to the false ones.

They must learn what their half memories continued to deny them—the nature of That Which Abides. If *It* was not a power beyond description, like unto that which arose from the Mirror, then *It* must be force of another kind. But they must *know!*

Ayyar turned his head, looking westward to the Waste. They had seen, other than the false Iftin attack, no sign of any movement out of there. The flying thing which had once spied upon him and Illylle, the walking space suit—none of those had appeared. This strip along the river was normal healthy ground. But—there was the White Forest, and the chasm, and somewhere the true lurking place of *That*.

Jarvas slid between two rocks, joining them after a whistle announced his coming.

"There is a good place not too far away. Also, the flitter continues to patrol. But we must wait until midmorn—"

"Morning!" Rizak grunted. "Very well, we wait."

It was difficult to reverse the natural order of things, to sleep through the cool of early morn until dawn and wait for the deadening sun and the light of full day. But they had to adapt to man's time again if they would accomplish their purpose.

Ayyar took the last turn at guard, watching westward. Nothing stirred there. In the Forest there would have been life which he could understand, with which he felt kinship, which would bolster the spirit. There, there was nothing—save the feeling that storm gathered. Not a gale of wind and rain and massed cloud, but another kind. And they must be prepared to face it as best they could. From it there would be no shelter, no hiding place.

IV

Gullies of sand, hardened by winter frost, ran between rocks as might rivers of water. And the water—Ayyar looked at it with little favor. There was ice in it. At least the rain had stopped and the clearing sky gave promise of a bright day—far too bright for Iftin tastes. In the dawn, still comforting to their eyes, they were setting their trap.

The robot body was placed to sprawl convincingly half across a rock. Its protective camouflage cloak was ripped away, the form could be plainly seen. Around it were winter-dried brush and reeds, and into this they wove their sal, putting the larger amount to the north from which the wind blew.

Jarvas made a last adjustment to the bait and stepped back. They had drawn lots for the one who must lie in the water to spring the trap, and Ayyar did not know whether to be glad or sorry that the banded stone had been his portion.

Now, stripped of cloak, pack, everything save his clothing and his sword, he lay at the water's edge, ready to take to the stream when and if they heard the coming of a scout flitter. So loosely woven a trap, yet it was the best they could devise.

Ayyar put out a hand the let the chill of the river flow across it as he cupped his palm and brought it up, spilling drops. Illylle was not the only one to remember old invocations. Once Ayyar of Ky-Kyc had held a curiously marked cup and poured its contents thus upon the earth and spoken such words as Naill-Ayyar whispered now:

"As thus I pour this water by my strength and will, so may my enemy be poured, to lie helpless and spent upon the earth!"

That prayer had not influenced the Larsh, nor would it probably be any more effective against off-worlder, garthman, or *That*. But man—or Ift—needs must cling to some belief or hope in something greater than himself at such an hour.

He clipped the leaf goggles down over his eyes. They had been right in their fears; the day would be bright. And there was some taste of spring in the air, as if the heavy beat of rain had unlatched the prison door for another season.

Spring in Iftcan! Ayyar caught at scraps of memory dim and faded, yet his blood ran quicker, like the sap rising joyfully through the Great Crowns and all that grew in the Forest, as he remembered this small picture and that. Spring was for seeding, not for death. Yet death had been forced upon Ayyar once before and now faced him again. He had his hand and a sword in it—that was the way for Ift to ever front the Enemy!

There was a buzz—davez, his mind identified—very early for that insect to seek the river. He lay very still.

If one did not move, the stinging blood-sucker would not attack.

Then came a sound greater than any insect buzz—the flitter! He did not need Jarvas' warning whistle to send him into the water between a storm-battered tree and rocks. The hum grew louder. Now—surely they would sight the robot! And if the woman thing found earlier had aroused interest—

Yes! Ayyar sank beneath the water as the hiss of a flame beam lashed across the water-logged tree, swept the rocks, onto the brush screen now between him and the robot. The wind and the height of the riverbank should keep the sal fumes away from him, but it was a chancy thing.

With a whisper of displaced air, they were landing. Now he must angle around a rock and crouch again. Ayyar jerked and almost cried out—he had forgotten the davez, and the pain of the sting was sharp. He struck at his shoulder, flattening the insect feeding greedily, and then was ashamed at his lack of control. What if that movement had betrayed him to those in the flitter?

"Over there—cover me!"

The words in Basic sounded odd, as if in a foreign tongue once well known but just slightly remembered. Ayyar pulled himself between two rocks. Above, the smoke swirled. Would enough of it reach the men—one climbing out, the other still in the small cabin? Ayyar watched the off-worlder stride confidently to the robot and put out a hand to settle on its hunched shoulder. Then he coughed, shook his head vigorously, and fanned smoke away from his face. He tugged one-handedly at the false Ift before, with a mutter of exasperation, he holstered his blaster and used a double grip to work loose the leg Jarvas and Kelemark had spent so much time wedging tight.

"Another robot," he called back over his shoulder. "It seems to be caught fast—" He staggered against the rock. Then he turned and took a step or two toward the flyer before he slumped to the ground.

"Rashon!" The hail from the flitter brought his head up, but he could only crawl, and before he reached the cabin door, he lay face down and still.

"Rashon!"

A hand holding a blaster swung into Ayyar's line of vision. Sal smoke had knocked out one of them, but his fellow had been in the cabin. Had enough of the fumes entered there? The off-worlder emerged crouching, his eyes darting from side to side, surveying the smoking brush wall. Hooking one hand in the fabric of his fellow's tunic, he tried to drag Rashon back to the cabin. But the fact that his comrade was a larger and heavier man made that difficult. However, he made a valiant try, refusing to put up his weapon.

Wind drove smoke about him. Ayyar heard a desperate burst of coughing. Then the would-be rescuer half fell, half flung himself at the cabin door, to fall across the entrance.

Ayyar whistled. They had no idea how long the narcotic effects of the smoke would last. Thus he must search at once for what was needed, and the others were prepared to pull him out if he too succumbed. With a wet-sleeved arm held across nostrils and mouth, Ayyar approached the flitter. It would seem that that last burst of smoke was the end product of the burning sal, for Ayyar could smell nothing now but the brush afire.

He forced himself to the flitter, revulsion for the off-world machine weakening him. There was a com unit in there, right enough, but it was built in. Perhaps Jarvas could command his antipathy long enough to use the broadcaster for a single message. But on the other hand, either man might wear a travel-talk.

The shrinking in him was worse pain than any davez sting, but Ayyar dared not surrender to it. Putting out his quivering hands, he turned over the man lying in the cabin doorway. What he wanted was fastened to one outflung wrist. Shuddering, Ayyar fumbled with the seal-catch, jerked free the strap, and brought away the call disk. It was as though he held unmentionable foulness against his Ift flesh. So greatly had the change conditioned him against those who had once been his own kind that he could hardly continue to grasp that small round of metal, the strap still warm from the arm against which it had been locked.

But grimly holding on, he plunged down the riverbank to the place beyond the smoldering fire, where the others waited. He dropped the com on a rock, unable any longer to stand its touch, and then tramped away some paces to retch and retch again.

When, sweating and shivering, he returned, only Jarvas and the girl were there. Jarvas, beads of moisture gathering on his hairless head, was examining the com.

"Where are—?" Ayyar began hoarsely.

Illylle nodded to the now almost dead fire. "They send the off-worlders back to port. Rizak sets the automatic return. They will carry with them the false Ift."

"But why—?"

"He says"—she nodded to Jarvas who was still rapt in concentration over the com—"their safe return there shall prove our good will. They will now believe more in his message if they receive it."

They saw the flitter rise, swing about, head in the direction of the port. Then the other two Iftin came unsteadily to join them. Rizak sank down, his head

thrown back, his eyes closed, his mouth hanging open
a little, his chest heaving. To have entered the cabin
and set the controls must have taken a strength of will
such as Ayyar was sure he did not possess. Why had
the change set in all of them such a terrible aversion
to those who had once been blood, flesh, and bone kin
to them? Jarvas had said it must be a safety measure
provided by those master Iftin biologists—to keep the
new race apart until they were in such numbers they
could not be reabsorbed by their own kind. But the
master biologists had not foreseen this present difficulty. How *could* Iftin deal with those who made them
physically ill to approach, mentally disturbed? Perhaps
all their communication could come only through such
a device as Jarvas struggled now to make operative.

"Can it be used?" Illylle dared to ask.

Jarvas' face was drawn, wasted. He kept his place
near the rock by manifest effort.

"We can only try," he mumbled. The cover of the
com had been raised. Instead of speaking into its tiny
mike, Jarvas held two twigs together just above its
surface. Now he clicked those together in a pattern of
sound that meant nothing to Ayyar.

Twice he looked up, his twigs silent, a lost, wondering expression momentarily crossing his face, as if some
supposedly well-rooted memory had failed him. Then
he went on, less confidently, but with dogged purpose.
It was in mid-click that he was interrupted by the com
itself. The voice was thin, metallic:

"Vorcors! Vorcors! What are you doing?" There was
a peremptory sharpness, a demand for the truth and
that speedily.

Once more, and more slowly, Jarvas clicked.

"Vorcors! What in the name of the Seventh Serpent?" Then there was complete quiet, save for Jarvas'
clicking out of a code once almost better known to him

than the name of Pate Sissions, how long ago, how far
away? And Pate Sissions was no Ift.

"They ought to be taping it," Kelemark remarked.
"Once let them decode it—"

"If they can." Rizak's answer was a half whisper. He
pointed to Jarvas. The clicking grew ever slower, the
moments of puzzlement longer, closer together. It was
as if the longer he strove to use his off-world memory,
the more difficult it became.

At last he turned to them with a wry grimace. "That
is my best, I am afraid. One more run through. And
let us trust I did not do as poorly as I fear!"

He readied his twigs, but that metallic voice came
from the com:

"You—whoever you are—we have a fix on you!"

Rizak glanced up and over his shoulder as if he
feared to see a scout already hovering to descend.

"Why should they warn us?" Ayyar wondered.

"Perhaps," Illylle answered him, "because Jarvas is
not as inept as he fears. Perhaps already they have read
or found someone who knows his code. Shall we wait
to meet them?"

Jarvas shook his head. "Not now, not until we know
more. However—" The twigs he had used for message
sending he now put to another use. Wet and dipped
in the ash of the burned bushes, they provided him
with clumsy writing materials. And around the com on
the rock he put some symbols, not in any off-world
writing Ayyar knew but in one that must have potent
meaning, or at least Jarvas believed so enough to take
pains over the inscription.

They headed south, their cloaks and packs weighing on them. Ayyar had lost all the strength he had
gained from drinking Iftsiga's sap. His head whirled
giddily at intervals, and he wondered how long he
could keep the pace Kelemark set. Somewhere

before them was the sea, but still the Waste brooded on their right hand. And in it things stirred; he was as sure of that as if he could see them.

A small copse provided them with a breathing space. Even so limited a stretch of woodland was refreshing. Ayyar rested on the dried leaves of other seasons, but he dared not close his eyes. Sleep was too close, weighting his eyelids, slowing his body.

"What will they do? Will they come?" Illylle questioned.

"I do not know." Jarvas twisted a scrap of moss he had picked up absently. "I do not doubt they had the fix. And they must believe in the code, or they would have attacked without warning. In a short time the flitter will come home with the crew safe, plus the robot. That should prove our good will. When they come, they will read what I wrote about the com. Even in a century, the scout recognition symbols cannot have altered too much. They may then send a message off-world, to trace one Pate Sissions."

"But all that will take much time!" protested Illylle.

"Yes. And time we may not have. But just now I see no better way. Do any of you?"

Even Illylle was forced to concede he was right. But Ayyar noted that she turned her head now and then, to stare out over the Waste. He wondered if she also had that sensation of a watcher there, biding time for a purpose that in the end would do them no good.

Though they listened, there was no sound on the com of any flitter homing. Ayyar could not deny his disappointment, though he knew that it was foolish to hope for such a quick reply. As Jarvas had pointed out—the port authorities must be checking and rechecking.

The Iftin did not go any farther than the edge of the dune land. And it was there that Lokatath came to them. A raw and bleeding scratch crossed one cheek, as if some branch had laid whip to him, and he breathed with the heavy gasps of one who had gone a distance at a speed he had to drive himself to hold.

"They muster!" He pulled himself to a sliding stop by holding to a bush.

"The off-worlders?"

Lokatath shook his head in answer to Jarvas' question. "Those—from there—" He pointed with his chin to the west.

"The wytes are out coursing the Waste. And they hunt with the false Iftin—who move toward the river!"

"How many?"

Lokatath shrugged. "Who can tell? They weave in and out, and it would seem that the ground itself sometimes moves to hide them or to confuse—"

"As it can," agreed Illylle. "*That* has many strange powers. But why do they move in the day—?"

"Because time is our enemy; can you think of a better reason?" Rizak wanted to know. "*That* is aware that we are here somewhere, that we were unable to follow the brothren overseas last fall. So *It* has launched this attack. Thus when our kin do return, they must land in the thick of it, perhaps to be burned down before they know the why or even that they have any enemies!"

"And what of our com messages?" It was Ayyar following the old pattern of marshaling his thoughts aloud. "If those from the port find the false Iftin waiting there when they come, they will deem it a trap."

"Yes," Jarvas acknowledged. "Therefore—we must discover wherefore this horde moves and if they plan to leave the Waste." He balled his right hand into a fist and ground it into the palm of the left. "If only our memories were sharper! I had thought *Its* servants did not venture beyond the Waste—yet the false Iftin crossed the river."

"Never forget the Larsh. They moved at *That*'s will beyond the barriers of the Oath. What seems to bind the master does not prevent the servant from carrying out orders," Illylle replied.

"One of my last clear Ayyar memories is that of slitting a wyte at the very foot of a Great Crown. Yet in an earlier day such would not even bay at the distant shadow of Iftcan," added Ayyar. "I say again, what of any who are drawn to the com? Trap of our setting it will not be, unless unwittingly, but trap it may well prove!"

"Therefore"—Jarvas got to his feet—"trap it must not be! If we lose this chance to tell them the truth, we might as well flee before the wind like leaves, with no hope of a seeding. So—now we must spread ourselves. Illylle, you most of all have need to fear attention from *That*. What would *It* not give to have even a memory-crippled Sower within *Its* hold. Therefore—back to the seashore for you."

"And for the same reason"—she rose to front the standing Jarvas—"must you be careful, Jarvas. Oh, yes, you remember less of the Words and the Gift even than do I, but once you had them. And who knows whether *That* might not have *Its* own ways to awaken more memory than you wish. Therefore, run not into a net."

He smiled, but grimly. "Perhaps I alone have other memories to convince those from the port of who and what we are. Therefore, I have no choice but to return to our ordained meeting and there do the best I can. Now—" He faced the rest of them. "Rizak will come with me. And Kelemark, do you go seaward with Illylle. For you twain"—he looked now to Ayyar and Lokatath—"scouting—one north, one along the river. Decide which between you."

"And west?" Lokatath asked.

"West we shall leave, for now. To track the enemy on his own ground is a risk we are not yet driven to taking. It is more necessary to see what garthmen and port force are about."

They stripped off their packs but kept their cloaks for cover. Illylle and Kelemark, loaded with the supplies, started south, the rest, north.

"Smell it, brothers?" Lokatath's nostrils were wide, his head up, as he tested the air from the west.

"Yes, false Ift—and others—" Ayyar made identification.

"I will take cross river if you agree," Lokatath said. "That land is known to me." Out of the garths as he was, the choice was sensible.

So once more Ayyar trotted north. At first he would share the trail with Jarvas and Rizak. Then he would be on his own with perhaps the remains of Iftcan as his final goal.

The sun was high and bright. Even wearing the leaf goggles, they suffered. But they saw nothing move, save now and then a bird in the air, an animal or stream dweller going about its business. Burnt lengths of wood drifted down the current, bringing the rank death stench with them. Ayyar did not doubt that those destroying the Forest were still about that murderous business. And could the Iftin hope to prevail in any argument against the hatred and hysteria of the garthmen? Or the determination of those from the port?

"Flitter! Northeast—"

As one they took to such cover as the ground afforded at Rizak's warning. The hum they could hear, but it was a second or two before they saw the machine against the too-bright sky.

"Too late! We cannot get there before they ground—" Jarvas muttered.

"In more ways than one, too late!" Ayyar added. From the Waste came a shrill yapping that roughed his skin, brought hand to sword hilt, and blade half out of its sheath before he was conscious of that move. "The wytes are coursing."

Garthmen had their hounds, so did *That*. But the wytes were not any hound such as honest flesh would own. Once before in this time he had faced them as they bayed at Illylle and him in the Enemy's seared land. They could be killed or sent to what they knew as death, but only one by one, whereas they hunted and slew as a pack.

"They close in—" he cried.

"Seeking— Ah, look you!" Rizak's cry was even louder. The flitter was larger than the scout they had grounded to gain a com. It was coming fast. But from somewhere deep in the heart of the Waste, there flashed a searing beam to meet it, envelop it with incandescence.

All three of the Iftin fell upon their knees, their hands to their eyes, blinded for a moment. Ayyar knew a stab of fear. Were they to be blinded in truth? Painful tears trickled from beneath the lids he kept tightly closed. All he could see was red, blood red, filling the world.

"Is it—is it gone?" Out of the red world he heard Rizak ask that. Against his will he opened his eyes. Red, more red. But through it dimly he could distinguish rock and brush. He was not blind!

The hum of the flitter he no longer heard. The machine must have flamed into nothingness in that beam. But now he was dragged to one side as a hand fell heavily on his shoulder and gripped him tightly.

"It—it is still flying—landing—!"

Blurred as his sight now was, Ayyar could see that Jarvas was right. There was the flitter, no longer concealed by a dazzle of light, descending as if normally piloted. Yet the hum of motor was gone. And now the shrilling of the wytes arose to a scream that hurt his ears, to add to the pain of his outraged eyes. That pain acted as a spur. He got to his feet and started to run, though he staggered from side to side, toward the place where the flitter would ground. Behind him he heard the others coming, at intervals during that awful baying.

Why he was so bound and what he would do there, Ayyar had no idea. But that he must do this, he knew. And he swayed out into the open as the flitter touched down, without thinking for the moment that he might well be running into the fire of blasters. Only, as some measure of sense came back to him, he stopped. There was no opening of the cabin door.

"Dead?" Rizak asked from his right.

"Perhaps." Jarvas advanced to the flyer, walking in an odd, stiff-legged fashion, his body rebelling against the orders of his mind.

But before he could set hand to the flitter, the cabin door slid back and a man crawled into the open on hands and knees, falling the few feet to the ground. Scrabbling for leverage, he then advanced, still on hands and knees and crept back to the side of the flyer where he pulled himself up. He wore the tunic of the port security police, and officer's star on the shoulder, and he stared straight before him as if he were as blind as Ayyar had been moments earlier.

A second man emerged in the same helpless fashion. This one was older, and he had a civilian's tunic. He sprawled forward, lying face down, moaning a little, providing a stumbling block for the third man, this young one in a pilot's uniform.

"In shock, I think." Rizak supplied one explanation. "Listen!"

A wyte bay, very loud and clear. To the hunters from the Waste these off-worlders would prove easy prey. Jarvas clutched the arm of the pilot.

"Get them—we must take them away before—" he ordered in gasps.

To touch—to hold and support one of those men— he could not! Every atom in Ayyar screamed that. But he must! He had to! They could not be left for the wytes.

He stooped and caught at the outflung hand of the elder man, pulling at him. To his surprise the off-worlder arose, as if he needed only Ayyar's tug to bring him to obedience. He got to his feet and allowed the Ift to lead him back among the rocks where they had a small, a very small chance at defense. And as easily, the other two came with Jarvas and Rizak. But they continued to stare straight ahead, no change in their blank faces, as if they were now the robots.

Once among the rocks the Iftin set the off-worlders at the back of that small space and faced outward, their swords drawn and ready.

V

They had chosen, to the best of their ability, that temporary fortress, and, it would seem, with luck they had chosen well. The off-worlders were backed by rocks, and nothing could come at them from that side, while—before the sword-armed Iftin—the passage was narrow. Not more than two of the wytes could storm them at a time. There could be no pack maneuver there to drag them down. Only—perhaps servants of another species followed. Would it be this day that the true Iftin faced the false?

Ayyar listened until it seemed to him that his whole body was one giant ear. For a long moment now the wyte had not given tongue. He could hear the murmur of the river, other sounds all normal. Why were the Enemy running mute?

Then he drew a sharp breath. From here they could see the flitter. Something slim, white, narrow of head,

long and bony of leg, pattered into the open and
rounded the flyer to sniff at the open cabin door,
thrusting its head and shoulders into the interior in
search. The wyte withdrew to nose the ground over
which the off-worlders had stumbled. Now it swung
around to stare at the rocks and sighted the waiting
Iftin. Its jaws opened; a thin, pale tongue showed. The
creature flung back its head, voiced one of the shrill
howls that hurt Iftin ears and rang inside Iftin minds.

So having summoned, it trotted forward to hunker
down well beyond the range of any prudent sword. A
movement beside Ayyar caught his eye. Rizak fumbled
at the belt of the off-worlder he had guided. His hand
moved jerkily, force of will tensing his body until his
fingers closed about the butt of the blaster holstered
there. With strained, clumsy movements, he brought
that hand around, as though the light weapon in his
grip was an almost intolerable weight. The barrel rested
on a rock top, pointing at the wyte. Rizak fired.

Fire sped to dazzle and hurt their eyes, their goggles
notwithstanding. There was no cry from the wyte—the
beam had been too swift. It left death behind in a
twisted thing resembling the gnarled roots of a long
dead tree. Ayyar rubbed his smarting eyes, goggles
pushed up. As he snapped them back into place he
waited, tense, for some answer to the summons the
wyte had voiced. Rizak had finished off the pack scout,
but it was only one of many. And could blasters deal
as well with robot Iftin?

"Riverside—to the south—" Jarvas ordered suddenly.

Ayyar was dismayed. To leave this shelter, small as
it was, for the open was rank folly. But—perhaps to
wait for untold odds could be stupid too.

"Come!" Jarvas spoke in Basic to the off-worlder of
the police. He raised the other's limp arm, placed its
hand upon his own shoulder. But now Ayyar saw the

eyes in that slack face move, fasten on Jarvas. And surely there was dawning intelligence—awareness in them!

With each of them guiding one of the off-worlders, the Iftin went down slope to the ice-packed gravel of the water's edge.

"Look!" Ayyar whirled, knocking his charge back and down. But Rizak needed no warning. He sprayed the beam of the blaster, and the things that had moved in upon them from the south twisted in its flame. Wytes— three of them—running mute.

"What—what— Who—are—you?"

The voice speaking halting Basic startled Ayyar. He had come, even in that short time, to think of the off-worlders as semi-inanimate, without any claim to a share in this, mere burdens for the Iftin. Now he looked at the man he had knocked to the ground. He was older than the flyer and his face was no longer blank. He raised a hand, reaching for a weapon; Jarvas spoke first.

"Get on your feet, if you can. Here they come again!"

No warning bay from the wyte, nothing but a flicker of movement from among the rocks. Rizak cried out. In his forearm hung the quivering shaft of an arrow. He dropped the blaster, and in the same second Ayyar stooped to scoop it up. He rayed a green-clad figure standing among the rocks, but it did not fall, though the beam crisped away its clothing.

"The head!" Jarvas shouted. "Aim for the head!"

Aim? It was hard to hold this alien weapon at all. It shook and wavered. He rested the barrel on his forearm to steady it, shivering at its touch. But the second sweep of that beam went in across the head of the archer. The false Ift did not stagger, but it began to run back and forth with small jerky steps—until its

erratic course brought it to the top of a small cliff and
it crashed over and down, to be hidden from their
sight. Another arrow clattered against the stone at
Ayyar's shoulder. There was no going south into that.

"Back—upstream—"

The off-worlder who had spoken got to his feet and
obeyed Jarvas' order as if he were one of them.
He had his blaster out and accounted for the second
silent rush of wytes as they flowed down upon the
party. Ayyar's hand shook so he could not aim properly, only sent a beam spraying across the rocks.

Then, as suddenly as the attack had lipped toward
them, it was finished. Nothing stirred among the rocks,
and even that heaviness of spirit that had been a cloak
about those who served *That* lifted from them, though
whether this could be depended upon as a signal of
the Enemy's retreat Ayyar could not be sure.

"Who are you?" Again came that demand from the
off-worlder. His blaster was now covering the three of
them.

"We are Iftin—of the Forest," Jarvas replied.

"More robots—" The pilot's hand struck the blaster
from Ayyar's hold.

"Not so. Your robots are out there." Jarvas pointed
to the west. "You have just seen them and their hounds
in action. We left you one of them to let you know
the truth—"

"As if we believe you—"

"Hanfors!" The third of the flitter crew—he of the
police—cut in sharply. "Who signaled thus—" He
repeated a stream of numerals.

"Two, seven, nine," Jarvas added. "Pate Sissions,
First-in Scout."

"Where is he?" the pilot demanded.

"He is with us; he sent that message," Jarvas said.
"We are not the robots, nor do we have any alliance

with *That* which controls them. They are being used to create ill feeling between us and you off-worlders."

The man who had halted Hanfors' outburst lowered his blaster an inch or so. He looked to the oldest of their number inquiringly and the other spoke:

"You brought us down—to tell us this?"

"No. *That* brought you down, to be an easy kill for *Its* servants."

"And just what is *That*?"

"I can give you no answer. Only *It* is a power which has existed for ages, which has always stood as an enemy to my people, and which moves against us now through you."

"Through us?"

"You fire the Forest, grub out its roots—why?"

Hanfors snorted. "Why? To uncover the burrows of the vermin who raid the garths—you—you Iftin, if that is what you call yourselves."

"We Iftin have not raided you."

"We have these now, at any rate!" Hanfors spoke to the others. "We can take them in and get the real truth—with a snooper. I will set the flitter on ready; you bring them up—"

He holstered his blaster and ran up slope to the machine.

"Those swords," the older man said. "Suppose you drop them now."

Rizak supported his wounded arm with his other hand. There was a dark patch growing around the arrow shaft. Jarvas unbuckled his shoulder belt, dropped the sheathed blade on the ground as he asked:

"Will you let me see to his wound?"

"All right. But disarm him first!"

Rizak's sword followed Jarvas'. Then Jarvas laid hand on the protruding shaft.

"You!" The off-worlder pilot looked to Ayyar. "Put yours down, also."

But as Ayyar raised unwilling hands to put off his weapon, there was a call from the flitter. Hanfors came out of the cabin and down slope with greater speed than he had gone up.

"The controls are dead. We cannot raise her."

"Send in a call—" suggested the older man.

Hanfors was already shaking his head. "Everything is dead, no motor, no com—nothing—"

"Can you repair it?"

"Repair what? Hanfors demanded. "There is nothing wrong that one can see."

"Nothing wrong except that it will not work," commented the third man. "If that is so, we are also off the port beam, and they will come looking for us."

"Just when, Steffney? And"—the older man glanced to where Jarvas was dealing with Rizak's wound, snapping the shaft to draw through the point—"we cannot believe that this is a particularly healthy spot in which to be grounded. I would suggest we start north. The clearing squad working on this side of the river must have put a com-find on us as we went over. They will be looking for us first. Also"—he tapped one finger against his blaster—"we have these. It would seem that the weapons mustered against us"—he looked pointedly at the swords, the broken arrow—"are less efficacious. And we now possess three hostages."

"Three prisoners. You, drop that sword!" Steffney ordered Ayyar. "We will not have too far to march, and it is all along the river, sir."

The older man looked upstream and then glanced at the remains of the wytes. As if he could really read his mind, Ayyar knew what the other was thinking. As they glided overhead, swinging well above the Forest, where men of his species were triumphantly wreaking their will, over the Waste that had no meaning for an off-worlder, this country held no fear. To be set afoot here, after a brush with strange enemies, that was another matter altogether. The Waste spread wide; the Forest was no longer just a nuisance to be swept from a man's path; man himself was reduced in size and power. To tramp north through a wilderness, guarding three prisoners, not sure of what might lurk behind or of anything else in the wild countryside, that was an undertaking this port official for one did not relish.

"This is not empty land. *That* and what and who serve *It* are on the move." Jarvas must have read the same thoughts and was prepared to build upon them as an aid to some mutual understanding.

"We have you. They will not attack us—" Hanfors grinned.

"Will they not? And from whence came that arrow?" Ayyar asked. "Did our own comrades shoot at us? If so, to what purpose?"

The older man smiled slightly. "Do you know, those are questions to be answered. Of course, you may have been sent here to bring us down, stage a fake rescue, and so win our confidence."

"There is one answer. Look at the one he did shoot," Steffney interrupted. "If it is a robot—then why would he worry about blasting it? They could sacrifice a robot to make the story good. And that nick in the arm, that is nothing to howl about. You may be right, Inspector Brash!"

Jarvas shrugged. "There is no opening minds willfully closed. Only this I tell you, we are no hostage for anything out there. To them we are the enemy, and you cannot use us for shields."

"Maybe not. But we shall find other uses for you," Steffney declared. "Now let us be on our way—march!"

Ayyar reluctantly shed his sword, watched Hanfors gather up all three sheathed blades and sling their baldrics across one shoulder. At an impatient motion of the blaster in Steffney's hand they began to walk north along the river. Now and then a faint breath of burning wood came to them, marking the death of the Forest.

They had not gone out of sight of the flitter before Ayyar knew that the attention of *That* in the Waste was again turned upon them. But they heard no more baying of wytes nor saw any movement there. The off-worlders might not be scouts or woodsmen, but they went warily enough and did not relax caution.

Jarvas was nearest to the river, Rizak next to him, while Ayyar was the closest to their guards. Ayyar's mind began to play with the possibilities in that line up. Suppose he were to stumble, tangle with Steffney. Could Jarvas use that momentary confusion to get to the water? And would the river protect him from blaster fire? No, there was Hanfors moving up to the right, only a step or so behind Jarvas. Rizak must have been more badly hurt than they first guessed, for now and then he staggered, lurched over against Jarvas, though he made no complaint. If they only had a chance to plan—!

How far were they from the devastation about the Forest? It must be more than a day's journey away on foot. And with the coming of night the Iftin would have the advantage of clearer sight. But would *That* let them travel without another attack? It was watching, and not far from here was the road to the Mirror—

No! As sharp as any order shouted aloud, that denial shot through his mind. One does not lead the enemy into the fastness of one's strength. The Mirror had served them against *That*, but it would not open its protection to them if they came with off-worlders. It

was as if the revulsion they themselves felt against their
one-time kin was multiplied a thousand times in protest.

It was sunset now, and the slow pace Jarvas, now
supporting Rizak, held grew even slower, in spite of
the urging of the off-worlders to hurry. Brash took the
lead, but suddenly he paused and looked west.

"Hear that?"

Was it sound or something more subtle? Ayyar had
that second or two of warning, perhaps because he had
once faced its like. A shadow in the air, winged. One
of *That*'s messengers. As it flapped lower, Brash shook
his head violently, his hands to his ears. And behind,
Ayyar heard Hanfors cry out.

He threw himself back, crashing against the pilot,
bringing them both to earth. He tried to hold onto the
other in spite of the revulsion that sapped his strength.
Perhaps his head came in contact with one of the rocks,
perhaps the other landed a blow. But a night no Iftin
eyes could pierce swallowed him up.

Waking came piecemeal. He was being dragged
along, and he was sick, very sick! Did he cry out in
protest or only think he so cried? In either case, his
plaint did no good. He continued to be pulled forward.
He fought against his sickness, trying to stabilize his
private world so that he might learn what had happened.

At last he made a vast effort and opened his eyes.
He hung between Hanfors and Steffney; before him
moved Brash. About them was a weird interplay of light
and shadow, which he could not understand but which
made him giddy and light of head.

Jarvas? Rizak? He could not see them. Had they
indeed escaped into the river? Or had blasters cut
them down? He still marched along the river, but as
his head cleared a little, Ayyar saw the difference in

the off-worlders. Although they moved easily, they had an odd look. No longer did Brash glance to right or left, displaying the caution he had shown. Rather did he walk with disregard for the ground underfoot, with a straightforward stare, as if all that mattered was some waiting goal.

That last moment before the melee—Ayyar could remember it all now: the coming of the flying thing which was an extension of *That*'s eyes, as he had learned when Illylle and he had encountered it. And as it had then, so did it now strike a mental bolt, probing at the party of Iftin and off-worlders. With Ift it could not prevail, but with the men from the port? They moved as if under command—*That*'s!

There was no pause for rest. They might have been tireless robots as they kept to the steady pace. Ayyar did not struggle in their grasp. It was all he could do to control his aversion to that hold and keep his mind steady.

There was no howling of wytes but a sound alien to this side of the river, the rumbling clank of heavy machinery. And as if that had some particular meaning for those he traveled with, they halted, but to no spoken order, standing to face north whence that sound came. It grew sharper, stronger.

Some of it came from upstream, yes. But there were other sounds across the river, among which were faint cries, surely from human throats. Through the thin woodland there came the crackling of small trees and brush going down before the not-to-be-withstood force of a machine's advance. What pushed its nose through into the open was no flamer or grubber, as Ayyar had expected, but something that had no place in this wilderness, as if one of the space ships had fallen over to creep reptile-like across the land.

This was a loader, combining in its body, force

enough to pull a heavy-laden truck, with the crane
mast and other fittings to transfer those burdens into
waiting cargo ships. The mast was now tilted askew,
half ripped from its moorings, ragged banners of
broken branches and winter dried vine caught up
and wreathed around it. The same woodland debris
was caught in every crevice of the machine as it
ground forward, breaking through the edge ice along
the river, advancing as if the force of the current,
under which it shuddered and shook, meant nothing beside the necessity for crawling through that
flood to reach the other shore.

It was pushed downstream by the current, yet it
continued to fight doggedly to reach their bank, though
now it traveled at an angle which, if the machine did
finally manage to breast the full force of the river,
would bring it out not far from them. Ayyar watched,
hardly believing that truth of what his eyes reported.
The blind determination of the loader was amazing.
There was no driver in the small upper cabin which
had been bashed and twisted, perhaps by the fall of
some tree with which the machine had argued passage.
It was as if the loader itself was imbued with brain-
less life!

The clamor from upstream on their own bank grew
louder as the loader continued its fight for river passage. There, too, vegetation was being crushed. Finally
they caught sight of the flamer, its nozzle covered with
the same debris the loader bore, not belching flames
but pointing with a slightly crooked finger obliquely
toward the Waste.

Cleaned by the stream of most of its ragged covering, the loader's treads caught on some underwater sand
bar and it splashed up the bank. All the time, the off-
worlders with Ayyar stood, staring straight ahead.
Whether they watched at all he could not be sure. But

they showed no surprise or alarm at the coming of the machines.

The flamer blanked into the open, turned to point to the Waste, began a ponderous march westward. After it, ground-eating prongs erect, a third machine, the grubber, came into view from the forest clearing and turned in the same direction. The loader made heavy business of bringing up the rear.

From over the river the shouting that followed in the wake of the loader was loud. Blazing, waving torches showed there. Then Brash came to life, as did the two men supporting Ayyar, moving away from the stream, up slope in the wake of the three machines still grinding into the Waste. They did not turn their heads to look as the torches reached the water's edge, but Ayyar strove to do so.

He did not believe that the garthmen with their night limited sight could see the four men from that distance. The Settlers did no more than move up and down on the bank. There was a large party of them, and Ayyar saw the light shine on metal. Gleaming scythes, axes, and the long knives used in clearing brush could also be weapons in the hands of desperate and determined men.

Perhaps their party was sighted as they reached the top of the rise, passing in the rutted track left by the loader, for the shouting grew louder. But Ayyar, unable to turn in the merciless grip that held him prisoner, could no longer see what happened behind them.

However, now they were no longer alone, for, amidst the wreckage strewing the path that the machines had broken, came other men, walking with the same unseeing tread of his captors, staring before them. All wore port clothing and plainly were now controlled by some influence that did not claim him.

Ayyar stiffened, drove his booted feet as deeply as

he could into the rutted track, strove to twist free from the grip that dragged him on. He might have been struggling alone to delay the loader. There was no loosing of that hold. They continued to compel him forward.

Was *That* summoning an army obedient to *Its* will?

Cries from the river! Ayyar could not see if the garthmen had conquered their hesitation or were also caught in *That*'s net. He could only fight for his own freedom as best he could, digging in his feet, struggling, useless though his resistance seemed to be.

Two of the company that had followed the clearing machines caught up with Ayyar's party. Neither group looked at their new companions nor gave any sign they knew the others existed. Both the newcomers wore uniforms of the police. They were armed with blasters, but those were holstered, as if here and now there was nothing to fear. And their calm march had a quelling effect on Ayyar, as if he were being borne along in a company of men who were both invincible and deathless.

They came to the edge of a gully into which the loader had plunged and was now making violent efforts to get up. Hanfors and Steffney turned sharply to the left, bearing Ayyar with them. The other men headed for the stalled machine, put their shoulders to it, lending their strength to free it, though their efforts made no difference to the wallowing of the loader. Now came others, first port men, all blank of face, all going directly to the machine's aid. After them, four, five, of the bearded, dully clad garthmen, all wet with river water, dripping as if they had swum the flood.

Without a word exchanged between them and the men from the port, they joined in the task of striving to free the loader. Groaning, scraping with its treaders, the machine struggled. Then those treads caught—it heaved, gained a space, another, pulled over the top, leaving behind it men who had fallen and lay panting and spent but who struggled to their feet to walk blankly onward in its wake.

VI

Behind those who freed the machine came Ayyar, between his two guards, still at that mechanical, unvarying pace. They were now at the tail of the motley mob heading into the heart of the Waste. Ayyar saw to the north the shadowed rise of the mount that was the frame of the Mirror. But it might as well hang like a moon out in space for all it would serve him now.

The way was rough, the soil soft so that the machines crawled through it slowly, leaving deep ruts. This was where the Mirror flood had cleansed and swept free the land. But it was desert still, though the evil growth that had once formed leprous patches had withered into dried skeletons.

On and on. Now and again the flying thing that was the projection of *That* swooped over the straggling line of men and machines. If the wytes or false Iftin also roved this land they did not show themselves.

Ayyar no longer struggled. Better to conserve his energy for any chance fortune might bring. But his mind was clearer, more alert, and he studied both the land and the men about him carefully.

It must be near midnight. The moon looked oddly pale and far away. To off-world eyes the terrain must be very shadowed. But it would seem that the purpose that united his captors made them also impervious to day or night. Now and then a man did sprawl forward in the ruts, only to regain his feet and go on, with no sign that he was aware of his tumble.

Suppose one—or both—of his captors should so lose their balance? Could he guide them into any pitfall? Ayyar began to search the ground ahead for any promising hole or unevenness. Experiments taught him that he could not vary their progress route by much in spite of any struggle on his part. But perhaps only a handsbreadth right or left might serve his purpose.

Then came another halt; men tramped around the machine just ahead, as if alerted by some signal. Ayyar caught sight of the grubber in much the same difficulty in soft ground as the loader had been earlier. The strange army gathered about it, lending their strength to aid the trapped machine. Ayyar caught his breath in a gasp of horror.

One of those pushing it had fallen under the treads of the grubber. Not one of his companions, even those nearest, made an effort to pull him out of danger. Instead, the machine lurched on and over him with crushing force. Then only did the men stand aside, their hands hanging idly by their sides, their faces blank, their eyes fixed on some point ahead invisible to Ayyar, while the grubber ground on. When the loader, too, had passed, they took up the march once again.

There had been no cry from the man who had so gone to his death. If the false Iftin were robots, then these were now even more alien for they had once been men and now were—what?

Ayyar's revulsion for the off-worlders increased a hundred-fold. Had the Larsh been so? He strove to make memory obey his will as he had so many times in the past. In this company it would seem that Naill was growing more clear, Ayyar less. He looked upon these men and machines as Naill would consider them.

Psycho-locked! That came out of Naill memory— and just what did it mean? There were drugs, it was rumored, that could turn a living body into a mindless robot-like thing. They deadened brain and personality so completely that the thing left had even to be ordered to eat, to carry out the other processes necessary to keep the body alive and serviceable to the master. But these men could not have been drugged, at least not those with him.

Left, right, left, right— Suddenly Ayyar realized that his feet were moving in time with all the others. This . . . was . . . right . . . this was meant—let go—be one—with them—with *It*—

With Larsh declared another memory struggling in his mind. Not one of the Iftin-kind; they did not share minds with Larsh!

Naill—Ayyar—he was torn between the two who were one in him. Naill who would be united with this plodding company, Ayyar who felt toward such companions only disgust and fear. To be Naill now was defeat. He must cling to Ayyar as a man in a spring-flooded river would cling to a floating log. He was Ayyar, Ayyar of Ky-Kyc, once Captain of the First Ring, who had dwelt in Iftcan. That city—Iftsiga—

Close to drowning, he clung to the thought of Iftsiga, its centuries-withstanding strength, its healing, its sheltering. Iftsiga's sap had fed him only a few days ago. He was one with the Great Crowns, the Forest,

not with these who would and did despoil that
beauty.

As one who stumbles through smoke murk into clear
air, so did Ayyar emerge, by strength of will, from Naill
who would betray him into the hands of *That*. He
dared delay no longer, for every moment of time he
marched with this company locked him more
securely to the purpose that animated them.

Deliberately he moved his feet to break step. He
did not try again to weaken their hold upon his body,
but once more he set to studying the ground ahead.
He decided upon one of the dried skeleton bushes—
for lack of anything better. Half of it had been driven
into the soil by the track of the loader. But to the left
of that rut projected a stub of the center stem that
looked as if it might hook a man at shin level. Exerting pressure slowly, Ayyar began to move his captors
inch by wearying inch into the position where the stub
could trip Hanfors.

So small a thing on which to build any hope! But
he had not fought their grip for a while. They might
have relaxed a little when they no longer had to brace
themselves to defeat his pull.

So—just a little more— Ah, it looked as if he had
planned better than he knew. Hanfors was walking in
the depression of the left loader track, Steffney, on the
other side, in the matching rut. This left Ayyar a little
above them on the uncut ground in the middle, making
their hold on him harder to maintain. He waited to
see if they would adjust that to defeat his purpose, but
they did not. Now if Hanfors would only trip on the
broken bush— Ayyar made ready to take any advantage.

Three steps—two— Now!

The broken stub caught Hanfors on his shin. Fortune favored Ayyar, for the stub was stoutly enough

bedded not to yield. The man staggered, tumbled forward, and at the same moment Ayyar jerked back with all his might.

He broke the hold the young pilot had on him. Steffney still kept his lock grip on the right, but Ayyar swung around, struck the other's undefended face as hard as he could. Steffney went down in turn, and Ayyar staggered back a step or two. Then he turned and ran, expecting any moment to hear them pounding after him. But perhaps the fall and the blow had slowed their reflexes, for after a few tense moments, he knew that they were not following.

Which way? Toward the river where the garthmen had gathered on the opposite shore? North to the Mirror? Or south to the sea? At least in the south were those of his own kind, and perhaps Jarvas and Rizak had escaped there also.

Ayyar had covered perhaps a third of the way back, angling southward, when movement before him sent him into cover. He tried to see or scent what waited there. Did the false Iftin and the wytes now patrol the shore? There was no baying.

"No!" He cried that aloud. Another company of marchers from the world beyond the Waste. Garthmen these were, carrying axes, any sharp-edged tool that could serve as a weapon. But they moved with the same thudding lock-step as had the earlier group. And with them—Iftin! False Iftin herding captives?

Then Ayyar caught sight of the face of the nearest guard—Jarvas! Was he caught by that compulsion? Had he reverted to Pate Sissions, and so was susceptible to whatever influence stirred all the rest of them? Beyond him was Lokatath who should have been scouting beyond the river. Jarvas was the nearer.

Ayyar skulked close to that line of marchers, crouched behind a tangle of dead and dried brush.

Then he leaped, his hands closing on the taller Ift, bringing the other down under his weight on the ground. If Jarvas had been under the influence of *That*, it was now broken. He heaved under Ayyar, caught him in an immobilizing infighting hold that was of Pate's knowledge, not Jarvas'. Then their faces were near together, and Jarvas' slitted eyes widened.

He loosed his captive and sat up, Ayyar beside him. Coming at a swift stride was Lokatath. They were truly Iftin then, not controlled. Ayyar said as much in his joy, and Jarvas nodded.

"What compels them does not affect us—"

"Unless," corrected Lokatath, "we allow ourselves to remember that we were once as they. But what happens anyway? These—they were on the track of a raiding party—suddenly they became as you see them—marching as if to order, swimming the river with only the purpose of reaching this shore in their minds— What would *That* do?"

"Marshal an army, I think." Swiftly Ayyar told what he himself had witnessed.

"Machines, men—?" wondered Lokatath.

"*It* has given up more subtle tactics such as the false Iftin and now *It* moves to open warfare—" Jarvas got to his feet, stood looking after the marching garthmen. "*It* is gathering all the servants and tools *It* can garner—to prepare—"

"For what? To root out the Forest tree by tree?" Ayyar asked. "Already those from the port and the garths were doing that for *It*. To fight us? We are but six on this side of the ocean. *It* need not forge an axe to destroy a blade of grass. Why then?"

"Yes, why?" Jarvas gazed now not after the marchers, but north to that shadow of the Mirror's setting. "There is another power, another opponent *It* would consider far more worthy of *Its* full attention than us.

Months ago that power struck, and perhaps that blow—
or blows—was what aroused in turn this desperate need
for retaliation. No, I do not think that these march
against us, nor against the Forest any longer. Just as
That once sent the Larsh to defeat Iftcan, so now *It*
will send what tools *It* may gather to defeat the cen-
tral point of all that opposes *It* here—the Mirror of
Thanth!"

Ayyar memory quailed from even considering such
sacrilege. Always there had been the power invested
in the Mirror or focused by it. And by that power
had seed grown, Iftin-kind lived, Iftcan tossed great
branches to greet seasons' winds throughout centuries of life. And, likewise by the will of *That*, had
death and decay and desert crept, always threatening that life, ever held at bay. Now when they were
so few, and *That* so strong because of the many *It*
could summon to *Its* banner, there was a chance
that the final overturn of all was before them. And
even to think of that sent a man's brain close to the
edge of madness.

Words out of the long past were on his tongue now.
He had no sword any longer, but his hand went up
as if it held such a blade—point out.

"This is Iftin answer then—any tribute will be
bought at sword point."

He heard a high excited laugh from Lokatath. "Well
said, brother! It is better to die fighting than to give
over-lord's salute to *That*!"

"Better still," Jarvas cut in sternly, "to live and ask
what our swords can do for Thanth. We go crippled
into any battle, for we have not the powers nor the
knowledge of those we replace, while *That* has all
memories open to *It*. But whatever we can do, we shall.
And in this hour we must not be divided. Rizak is
hiding by the river; his wound is not such that he

cannot join with us. But Illylle, above all, we must have with us!"

"My journey that," claimed Lokatath. "Though"—he glanced at the sky—"day comes and it is *That's* time. I will not risk too great speed."

"You must not!" Jarvas agreed. "It is in my mind that *That* will take no chances, even though the weight of advantage is now *Its*. Forget not that the false Iftin still prowl, and the wytes. Also perhaps *That* pulls more Settlers. Run a broken course through this land of danger."

"Perhaps two of us—" began Ayyar.

"Not so! We must not separate too widely. For you and me and Rizak, the Mirror and the burden of waiting there."

They did not seek the river end of that road which led to the Mirror, but struck directly cross country, passing from the shriveled part of the Waste at a steady lope into that part where clean greenery had begun to find root, though this was now winter dried. The wall of the way, which grew taller the nearer one drew to the Mirror stair, was about shoulder high at the place they elected to cross it. Once that had been an effective barrier between the brooding menace of the Waste and the sanctuary of the road. For Ayyar, now, there was a difference on this side of that barrier. In the slot of the road he had had no sense of peace, nor of refuge, rather of withdrawal as if some hunter was hiding to watch and wait.

Jarvas made no move to approach the stairs that led to the Mirror, nor did they urge him to it. They were three, having brought in Rizak on their way. Over the arch which led to the steps glowed the symbols Ayyar had seen there months ago when a spark from his Iftin sword had turned some unseen key to bid them enter.

Then that symbol had been green; now it was darker in shade, and it pulsated as if behind it some energy flowed and ebbed or built by degrees. They watched it; but none spoke.

If their question had been, "What was *That*?" now it could also be, "What moves the Mirror or uses it to communicate at Iftin call?" Ayyar decided. And he knew the wariness of one who crouches in open ground between two hostile forces, so far beyond his own puny strength that he could not even guess at any bonds laid upon them.

Jarvas sat crosslegged in the road, his eyes fixed. Ayyar guessed that he was now fighting for memory, to be all Jarvas, to know what that Jarvas who had been Mirrormaster had known. Mirrormaster? Not truly, no Ift could master that which reached through Thanth.

Rizak leaned against one of the wall stones, nursing his hurt arm across his chest, his eyes closed. But Ayyar—his restlessness was such that he prowled along the wall, first east and then west, looking out into the Waste. Dawn was coming fast and the heat of day was *Its* own time. What was that in the graying sky?

No winged follower of *That*—rather a flitter from the base port flying straight out westward. Was *That* summoning all machines? Or did some foolish off-worlder come scouting here? The course would bring the flyer directly over the Mirror. Ayyar's hand half raised in an instinctive warn-off gesture. But even as he moved, the flitter veered sharply, swooped as if control was momentarily lost, then rose again to make a sharp-angled flight to avoid the mount and its crater.

Once past the Mirror, the flyer followed the route of the vanished army. There were no other signs of life outside their refuge. But the rising sun sought out glittering spots here and there to the west—too far for

Ayyar to make out their nature but brilliant enough
to hurt his eyes. So as he made his voluntary sentry-
go, he watched only the space beyond the walls of the
road.

How long it was before Jarvas stirred, glanced at his
two companions as if he saw them, instead of looking into an inner well holding only thought, Ayyar did
not know. The sun was well up and they were hungry. But their supplies as well as their weapons were
gone. Ayyar was thinking of that loss when Jarvas asked
a question:

"Anything out there?"

"No."

"Consolidation of forces." Rizak, whom Ayyar had
believed asleep, spoke without opening his eyes. "And
what do we do—march in to face what waits there?"

"If necessary, yes." And they could not dispute
Jarvas' answer, for they knew it was true. There was
no turning back now; perhaps there never had been
a chance to since each of them in his own time had
reached out his hand to take up that portion of the
"treasure" that had made him a changeling. This was
an old, old struggle for the Iftin-kind, and they were
Iftin now.

"Sleep if you can," Jarvas said to Ayyar. "The watch
is mine."

Though the sun glared, the road still held shadows
along its walls, and they were shelter. Thankfully Ayyar
lay in one such dusky pool, closed his eyes. Slumber
came, though he had not thought it would.

Of what had he dreamed? Of something that might
answer all their questions, that he was sure of when a
hand shook him into reluctant wakefulness. But that
answer was gone with the opening of his eyes to the
refreshing dusk of evening. On the arch the symbol still
burned, but steadily now, as if the gathered energy was

complete. And there was such an atmosphere of expectancy that he looked about him, seeking to see what or who had been added to their company.

It was Rizak who had roused him. Of Jarvas there was no sign, but the other answered Ayyar's unvoiced question.

"He has gone—up there."

Ayyar stood to follow, but Rizak shook his head. "For us not yet."

Looking upon the symbol, Ayyar knew he spoke the truth. For them the summons had not yet sounded.

> "Blue the leaf, strong the tree,
>   Deep the root, high the branch,
>   Sweet the earth, lying free.
>   Gather dark—"

With the words Ayyar's hands moved as one who wished to finger a curtain, draw it aside—

> "Gather dark, hold the night,
>   Stars hang, the moon is bright.
>   Blue the leaf, life returns.
>   In the end, sword never fails—"

But that song was not true. Swords had failed once; they could again. And swords against blaster were no match at all. Naill thoughts troubled Ayyar's mind. From behind him came other words:

> "Blue the leaf, rise and grow,
>   Deep strike old roots to reach.
>   Star shine, moon glow—
>   Ift seed—"

Rizak stopped. "It is gone," he added a moment

later. "With so much else, all the wise words, the power songs. In bits and patches they come to mind and then they are naught. If we could sing together the tale of the sword of Kymon, well might we guess the nature of *That* and how Kymon forced upon *It* the restraining Oath. But we cannot."

Why did they speculate now on wisdom that might or might not be hidden in an ancient hero tale, Ayyar wondered. Of course it could well be that Kymon had once walked this very path of Thanth. Or was he a legend who had never lived? No, old songs would not help them now, nor tatters of memory. Yet still in his mind rang the words that did have meaning for all Ift born or changeling made:

"Blue the leaf, life returns—"

For blue had been the leaf in the golden age when the city of Iftcan had been root-set and the Ift, masters of Janus.

The night was long as they watched and waited, knew hunger and thirst and must set aside as best they could such demands of their bodies. They watched the Waste where nothing stirred, and listened, always listened for anything that passed outside the road.

Even with dawn Jarvas did not return from the Mirror. But Ayyar found a depression in the rock where drops of dew gathered, and those they licked to dull their thirst. He remembered more and more the rich, life-restoring sweetness of the sap in Iftsiga's walls and wondered how much longer they could deny the needs of their bodies.

It was deep in the second night that they heard sounds from the east. Ayyar armed himself with a stone, the best weapon chance now granted him, only to drop it again at a familiar soft whistle. Three came along the road. By some great good fortune Lokatath had bettered the time allowed for his mission. Illylle and Kelemark, each carrying a small pack, ran beside him, straight for those who waited in the glow of that purplish symbol and what lay behind it for good or ill.

VII

For the fourth time in his life as a reborn Ift, Ayyar stood on that ledge overhanging the Mirror of Thanth. Each time the lake had been different—the first time when he and Illylle had come that way it had awed him, making him wish to creep quietly away, lest he disturb the meditation of something far greater than his imagination, human or Ift, could encompass. Then, the second time, when they had all fled to Thanth as they would to the last refuge left on a hostile world, it had been a cup of rising power, again awing them, yet with that which had sustained them through the fury that followed.

This time he might be looking down, not at a flood of water, silent, untroubled, fathomless, but rather into a mist that writhed and billowed and was, he was sure, a substance not of Janus nor any world his kind knew. And there was no welcome, no security, only restless tossing and—not fear, no—but an uneasiness, a tensing, as if before battle.

Even Illylle who had climbed here light of foot, as one who expected communication, halted self-consciously and stood at a loss with the rest. Jarvas had not turned his head to greet them as they advanced on the ledge. He stood there, statue still, his arms at his sides, his whole stance that of one who waited, and waited, and waited—

It was Illylle who moved first, joining Jarvas. Perhaps she did remember more, perhaps she was daring to improvise now because of their need. Both thoughts came to Ayyar as she raised her arms, held out her hands, palms up, as one who asks alms.

Words she chanted. Some he knew, others were of the Hidden Speech, sounds to evoke answers from powers beyond their ken.

Up from the Mirror came a mist, not a surging as it had been when the water overflowed. It formed a tongue to lick down the presumptuous, to wipe out those who would demand an answer. All fear Ayyar held in memory from both his lives was as nothing to what he knew now. For the fear one holds for an enemy is naught to the fear which comes when that which one believes to be a strong protector turns against one, and there is no refuge left.

Yet none of them broke and fled that ledge as the tongue of fear swept closer to them. And now Jarvas chanted also, as if Illylle's words had unlocked his own past priesthood.

The tongue did not lick them from the stone as Ayyar thought it might. It curled higher in the air, menaced—but it did not strike. And then Illylle moved her hands as one who sows seed, and the tongue began to swing in the same way, following her gestures. While from Ayyar fear passed, leaving only awe. They were accepted. In the midst of a great and abiding anger such as his kind could not measure, the force that found focus in Thanth recognized and accepted them.

The tongue of mist withdrew, and they were alone. But a chill which was not of winter was about them. Shivering, Illylle spoke though she did not look to them, staring instead into the Mirror.

"I have said—we are ready. Now we must wait to see what task shall be laid upon us."

What is time? In the life of men a numbering of sunrises and sunsets, of days, years, seasons, plantings and reapings. Man makes times, dividing it into narrower and narrower portions as he needs it for living which becomes more and more complex in its demands. Naill Renfro was space born; thus time had not laid so tight a bond upon him as upon most other men. And when he had become Ayyar he had walked into a time that was reckoned by seasons, by growth and winter sleep. Now he was caught up in another time in which his body was nothing, in which he was only to wait. And how long was this time he could not afterwards have told, nor did he remember it clearly.

There came a moment when the mist below lay quiet, collapsed into water. But now the water was not a smooth, set mirror. Through it ran ripples of blue and green which thinned and paled into silver, and these formed lines and patterns which were not normal for any water, if the Mirror of Thanth was, or had ever been, mere water.

Illylle and Jarvas chanted together—the girl's lighter voice rising, the man's making a lower, stronger note, yet both fitting, one to the other. And again the words were not to be translated but were meant to be sounds in which the meaning lay only in the melody.

The silver lines moved back and forth, tracing the fantastic pictures one could almost understand, but never entirely. Now the whole of the flood lapped higher about the walls of the crater, as it had on the day when it had spilled over to cleanse the wilderness about and to challenge *That* with storm and flood.

From it arose another tongue, this not of mist but of substance, lifting higher and higher into the air as it circled the wall, thinner and thinner, until it could have been a vine of the Forest. And into that writhing, curling vine of water poured all the silver, so that it was alight throughout its length, although the gleaming brilliance of it did not strike harshly on Iftin eyes.

It approached in its round the ledge on which the Iftin stood, and its tip was star bright, curling down over their heads. It quivered, swinging back and forth, lingered for a moment above each in turn, sometimes for only a second, sometimes longer. Twice did it so quest, and then it struck at Illylle. Down over her head and body ran the coruscating silver, beading shoulders, limbs—

Then it raised again, and once more swung out over the rest of their small company, seeking—seeking—

Ayyar started. He was the target this time. He did not feel the touch of the water as it chose him, rather a tingling through flesh and bone and blood, as if the silver flood had entered into him. Then that was gone, as was the tongue itself, fallen back into the Mirror.

And the turbulence of the Mirror died away so that they looked down into a calm surface. Ayyar knew that what had dwelt there for a space had now withdrawn into the place which was its own, and that a door between was closed.

But the reason for what had just passed was what he must know. He looked down at his arms, his shoulders, his body where that river of silver had run. He was warm, and the hunger, the thirst he had known, was gone. Instead he was alive as he had been after his draught of sap, filled with energy, with the need for action. But what action? In the answer to that lay the importance of all that had happened here.

Illylle turned away from the edge of the ledge and came to him.

"Thus has it been ordained. As it was with Kymon, the Oath Giver, so is it now with us. We go to where *That* abides, that we may be the vessels through which what lies in Thanth may loose wrath upon the Enemy."

And the choice had not been his at all, was Ayyar's first thought. No, that was not the truth either. By coming here he had indeed offered himself for battle. Now he could not protest when he had been accepted. But why? He was no Mirrormaster; he was only a warrior who had once fought in a lost cause against this same Enemy. But—Kymon also had been a warrior—if Kymon ever truly *was*, inside the wrapping of legend and hero worship. And there was no denying that the choice had been made.

He turned to Illylle. "We go now—?"

"Now."

"Take this." Kelemark drew off his baldric, pushed it and the sheathed sword it supported into Ayyar's hands. It would seem the others accepted the fact of their out-faring.

Jarvas drew his cloak closer about his shoulders. "What can be done here is done. We must not linger."

"Then where?" asked Illylle.

"To the bay at the shore, if fortune allows us to win there. If the brothren come overseas we shall meet them." He paused and looked for a time-stretching moment into her eyes and then into Ayyar's.

"I know not what you face, save that it is peril indeed. And one which none can share with you, no matter how much they wish it. What good fortune may come from willing and from our desires shall march to your right and left, but whether that can arm or defend you"—he shrugged. "Can any man tell? This has been laid upon you to do—the best with it—and you!"

They crossed into the Waste where the road walls were waist high. Day sky was above but there were clouds; by so much did the weather favor them. But— where were they to go? Venture without plan into *That's* stronghold?

"Where we go, that I can guess," Ayyar said. "But what we do there, that is another thing."

"We shall know that also when the hour is come," she replied.

Her confidence grated against his doubt. "To run blindly into *That's* hold is to perhaps throw away every defense we have."

Illylle looked at him over her shoulder. "Defense? Is it 'once a warrior, always a warrior,' Captain of the First Ring of Iftcan that was? There may be other ways of fighting than with blade—"

"Yes," he told her grimly, "with blaster and flamer! Have you forgotten what army has drawn ahead of us into this land? You say we are weapons in ourselves, carrying in us some potent force to meet that which the Enemy can muster. But it is in my mind that we must do as the songs says Kymon did, win directly to *That*, face to face. And in so doing we must pass any defenses *It* has set. Do you not remember how it was when that space suit took us so easily prisoner? And that may be the least of the dangers now ranged against us."

"So, what then is your answer? We have no time to creep and lurk, seeking out some unknown safe path—"

"Can we not? I say we have to or be finished before we are fairly begun. This is no Forest hunt, this is in a land the Enemy has made. There is one way—" He had been thinking, fast, clearly, more clearly, it seemed, than he had for some time.

"And what way is that?" she demanded. Already she had pulled well ahead of him on into the Waste, her impatience a goad.

"Does not the Enemy have the false Iftin? Are they not to the eye even as we?"

He had caught her attention. She looked back at him, a frown on her face.

"The false Iftin—but how—?"

"They are sent out to raid from whatever camp *That* keeps. They come and go—if we can track a returning pack, join it as stragglers—"

"They do not live as we, cannot *That* detect the difference?"

"We must take our chances. But they are no more, and they may be less than the perils we may encounter going blindly. There is no reason not to try this."

"And where will you find them?"

"They have been raiding across the river. Lokatath was with those who pursued them, garthmen caught in turn by the compelling of *That*. Therefore, if we strike southwest we may cross their trail."

Her frown deepened. "It is not good to waste time for something so uncertain."

"For us all the future is uncertain. But, in this, accept warrior wisdom, Sower of the Seed. One does not run blindly into a kalcrok's den because of a need for haste. And to my mind it is better to enter into *That*'s city by *our* will, rather than *Its*, if that may be."

She yielded to his arguments, but reluctantly, and they went south, still also to the west. The day remained overcast, clouds serving them by so much. Ayyar remembered those glittering points he had sighted from the road, but they came upon nothing that could have given off those flashes. Finally they crossed the deep-rutted tracks which were the trail of *That's* captives.

Ayyar watched the sky, fearing to sight one of the flying servants. But so far they appeared to move through a deserted land. At last he asked:

"Do you know what we must do when, or if, we reach *That*?"

"This only do I know, that we are in the service of the Mirror. It is my hope that when we reach that last moment we shall be moved in a pattern that will serve for good."

Tradition granted Kymon more knowledge of his battle. If he had been merely a tool to carry one force to face another, legend did not say it. But legends were the shadows, not the mirrors of truth. And it might well have been that the hero of the White Forest had walked even as they, uncertain and unenlightened.

Ayyar's nostrils took in a new scent. Ah, in so much he had guessed rightly. False Iftin had passed. With wytes or alone? The answer to that might make a wide difference to any would-be trailer.

"They—" Illylle's voice was a half-whisper. Ayyar nodded, signaled her to silence.

A little more to the west—yes, the scent grew stronger, almost a thick reek! But which way had they gone—eastward-traveling raiders would not serve their purpose. He slid cautiously around a rocky outcrop, saw narrow boot prints in the soil—west! Again he signed to Illylle and looked ahead with a scout's eye.

Here the Waste was cut by gullies, with curiously shaped stone outcrops on guard along their rims or at their mouths. It would seem that time and weather erosion alone could not have sculptured those grotesque boulders, that some purposeful hand had pointed up the suggestion of a demonic face or beast. This was a land that had nothing in common with the Forest. It might have been on another planet altogether.

The soil underfoot was not quite sand, but it was barren of plants save for where, here and there, some bunch of long dead roots protruded from the side of a small rise in a way that made them seem to be clutching, misshapen tentacles. And here and there, uncovered by the wind, were patches of ground very hard and dark, so encrusted that a stone falling upon them gave forth a metallic ring. Ayyar was reminded of the scars left by thruster blast on space fields. But these patches were too small, too scattered, to be the marks of some ancient port, whatever strange activity they stood monument to.

A red thing with a scaled body surveyed them with bubble eyes set high on its narrow head and then skittered away between two stones. Ayyar watched it go suspiciously. He feared that all life here could in some way report to the ruler of the Waste, make known the passing of any who were not servants of *That*. But on the other hand birds, beasts and scaled things had shared the Forest yet been apart from Iftcan and those who dwelt there.

"It is a wild thing only." Illylle must have guessed his thought.

"How can you be so sure?"

"Do not those who serve *That* give off the shadow of their master? Though it is well to suspect all within this land. I wonder—"

"Concerning what?"

"What do you propose to do when we see this quarry we now trail? False Iftin certainly will not accept us. And they will—"

Ayyar swept her back, holding her half imprisoned against the gully side with his body as he listened, sniffed the air. The reek of false Iftin was suddenly so

nose-filling as to make him gag. They must be very
close to those they sought, and he had better have a
quick and efficacious answer to the question Illylle
proposed. She squirmed around to face in the same
direction, her body rigid against his. Then she spoke
in the thinnest of whispers:

"Just beyond that projection—"

The wall of the gully thrust out here in a sharp
promontory. Behind that was an excellent site for an
ambush. Ayyar searched the face of the wall against
which they stood. One of the bunches of dried roots
stuck out there within grasping distance; with such aid
he might be able to climb above. He pointed to the
crest and Illylle's eyes narrowed as she measured the
distance in turn. It all depended upon his ability to
make that climb undetected. To spread himself against
the wall as a clear target was not good to think about.

Illylle drew her sword. She gestured for Ayyar to
stay where he was, but she need not have made that
warning signal for surprise kept him still. Along the
blade of the Iftin weapon, seemingly coming from the
hand curled about its hilt, ran a series of sparkling
ripples, silver as the questing finger of Thanth. Now
the girl swung the weapon back and forth, its tip
up-pointed. She did not turn her eyes from the sword,
but her lips shaped a word:

"Go!"

Ayyar jumped and his hand closed about the roots.
They held against the pull of his weight. Then his other
hand dug deep into the soil, and he climbed. Belly
down he crawled along the rim. Illylle leaned forward.
Now and then her sword dropped its shimmering point,
and to his eyes it appeared that she had to make a great
effort to force it up again. What she did he could not
guess, but at least he had won to this advantage without
being a target for attack.

Now he could see the other side of the buttress. Green, hairless head, tall pointed ears, Iftin cloak outspread—and in its hands no sword—but a barreled object not unlike a blaster. And with, Ayyar did not in the least doubt, perhaps the same force as that off-world weapon.

The creature's head was held high, though it was not searching with its eyes the rim of the cut. Instead that head was shaking slowly from side to side, even as Illylle wove her blade. And its eyes stared blankly at the stone against which it crouched.

Ayyar freed his own sword, though what effect that might have against the metal under the robot's concealing "flesh" he did not know. Only, the moment the hilt was in his hand, the silver ripple he had seen on Illylle's blade dripped from his own fingers. Not memory, but some command deep within launched him into action. He raised the sword so that its point was aimed at the false Ift's head. Ripples spread down and down until it would seem that what made them must drip onto that green covered skull below. And with the ripples there was a drawing within him, a feeling that some inner strength of his own went surging along that conducting blade.

The false Ift jerked, raised high upon its toes, and then fell forward, its limbs loose. On the ground it continued to jerk at intervals but it made no move to rise. Ayyar slammed his sword back into the sheath, a little afraid of the weakening ebb.

In a last spasm the Ift raised a little from the ground, fell heavily back. Ayyar slid down not too far from it. When it no longer moved, he approached it cautiously. The barreled weapon had been released from its grip during that last convulsion and he stooped, would have picked it up, when Illylle's order came.

"No!"

She came slowly, one hand against the gully wall to support her. Now she added:

"You bear within you one power. Dare you deny that after this? You cannot take to yourself the weapon of another!"

There was something in what she said. He picked up a stone and brought it down on the weapon, smashing it to bits. It broke brittly which he had not foreseen. He then looked to the false Ift, bringing a larger rock to batter the head of that inert creature. The substance of which the skull was formed split. Inside were fused wires, slagged metal. Ayyar squatted on his heels to study the wreckage. Energy, some type of energy, had dripped from the sword in his hand to accomplish this! Yet with that stored within him he had felt no ill, suffered nothing.

"Do you not yet understand?" Illylle demanded. "You are the vessel to carry a force. But it must not be wasted. Now where do we go from here?"

"The same road—with care."

"It would seem we are going to be favored— unless they can sniff us out in turn. Look you above."

Those clouds that had kept the sun from troubling them were massing ever darker. Whether the turbulence coming was born from some machinations of the Mirror or not, they did not know, but that it promised them a concealing cloak was plain.

For a space they traveled the upper ridges of the gullies, crawling serpentwise when they would have been plain against the sky. If other false Iftin or their master had any knowledge of the finish of the one they had accounted for, they did not show it. But Ayyar was willing to proceed upon the assumption that that might be true.

Above the third valley they so avoided, they came upon the first sign that other protection against Iftin

had been set up in the Waste. Only the dimming of
the storm clouds saved them. Once they had been led
captive through the White Forest—where trees of
crystal mimicked the rich growth of true life—a dazzling reflection of the true world. Here was raised a
pillar of that same crystal, mounted on a headland—
to blind Iftin eyes with sun-reflected brilliance. Ayyar
warily circled around it, being thus forced to lower
levels. The chill of the storm was changing scents. He
was not sure they could depend any longer upon their
noses for warning.

Then the fury of the breaking storm drove them to
any cover they could quickly find. Darkness Ift could
face, but not such tearing winds, such buffeting of hail,
such numbing sleet.

Together they crouched in a crevice, their cloaks
drawn up so they might pull the corners over their
heads, hiding their eyes as lightning leaped across a
wild and riven sky. And to the wrath of the storm there
seemed no end. Whether it was loosed by one power
or the other, it had about it that which Ayyar deemed
unnatural.

Illylle stirred. Her lips were very close to his ear,
but he could hardly hear her words as she said:

"This will hide all trails—"

She was right. Perhaps when they could go on they
must simply head west and—

She started; her arm dug into his side. But Ayyar
had seen it also, illumined by a flash of lightning.

It had not been there when they had taken refuge,
that he could swear to. Yet now it stood on the western wall as if as fixed as the crystal pillar.

Man—no. Nor Ift. But it had four limbs and it stood
erect upon two of them. Memory stirred within him.
Once he had known or seen its like. Where—and when?

VIII

It continued to stand there, facing east, if such a thing had a face to turn east, west, any direction. Danger might lie in awaking Naill memory consciously, but Ayyar was forced to that in order to learn the nature of the Enemy. He told Illylle his plan and what might come of it.

"But that—I have Ashla's memory, and nothing such as that walks through it!"

"Garth memories do not know off-world well," he pointed out. "For years I was in the Dipple on Korwar. Prison though that was, still we had contact with half the galaxy. Korwar is a pleasure planet, save for those condemned to be planetless and so to live within the waste heap of the Dipple. Now and then I had a day's labor at the port and we saw there many strange things. And this—this moves deep in my memory. What we can learn now, anything we may learn, must be to our advantage. But if awaking Naill brings me into a trap set for off-worlders, then do you be ready for it—"

She smiled. "I do not truly believe that one who has been washed in the substance of Thanth can be so taken. But, I shall be ready—for what, Ayyar? To thrust a sword through you?"

He gazed at her with full soberness. "If I were to become such as those who marched through here— then, yes, I would welcome such death at the hands of a friend."

Illylle's smile vanished. "You do not jest. Do you wish to have me swear?"

"There is no need. Only, if I strive to move from here, then do what you must to stop me, at any cost."

He fixed his gaze upon that thing. There appeared no division between head and body, if head and body were terms which could be applied to a rectangular box supported on two stilt legs, two arms or like appendages dangling by its side. It was difficult for even his night-oriented eyes to see it clearly for the storm distorted it. A box on legs. Now that he studied it, he could also make out a series of small sparks of light set in a row across the section comparable to the breast. Also, he was very sure, it was metal, or metal encased. And he had seen its like. Where, when?

Naill Renfro—deliberately he set about recalling Naill Renfro— What were Naill's first memories, so deeply buried that they must be mined with effort bit by bit?

His father's ship—he made himself visualize it, cabin and corridor, his own small cubicle which was the only true home he had ever known. Captain Duan Renfro, Free Trader, and Malani, the wife he had brought from a warm, smiling planet of shallow seas, many islands, endless, gentle summer. The worlds they had visited— then the end with their spacer caught in a battle that was none of their war—Malani and Naill in the escape boat—picked up and brought to Korwar—and the endless gray life-in-death of the Dipple, the dumping place for those displaced by the war with no worlds to return to.

The ship—resolutely Naill-Ayyar turned memory back to the ship, combing it by recall. Nothing like that thing above had been in the ship. Then, on some world where they had gone trading. But that was hopeless. His faded mental pictures of those were past disentangling now. So—the Dipple was all that was left.

Not in the collection of barracks itself—then in the city—or the port. He settled for the port. There had been wide landing aprons on which set down fleets of very differing spacers—traders bringing luxuries from a thousand worlds, passenger liners, private yachts of rulers and the wealthy. They reeled through his mind until— He caught upon one of these fragmentary memories, strove to pin it down. Yes!

A long bank of computers—he had seen that in the heart of a liner. The ship had been put in quarantine because of a new illness detected aboard. But laborers from the Dipple, hungry for the work, had been sent through a blocked-off passage to bring out some highly important sealed cargo. He had looked into the computer room as he passed, and just such a robot had stood there. It was a service type, meant to deal with computer repair—more than that he did not know.

What was it doing here? The best thing to do would be to follow it—for it must return soon. He was needed—it was most necessary to join the others. What was he doing here in the storm and rain when he was needed, greatly needed? He must be going—

"Ayyar!" A hold on him kept him from rising, from going as he should go. Angrily he strove to break that grip. He was Naill Renfro and he had that which he must do—now!

Look, the robot was turning—leaving— Unless he followed he would be lost! He would never find the others, be one with them as he should be!

"Ayyar!"

Desperately he pulled against the hold. Then something flashed before his eyes, its brightness blinding, searing. Now he was in the dark where there was no Naill—nothing—

"Ayyar!" Very faint and far away that calling. Why should he answer it? To make any effort was too much to demand of him.

"Ayyar!"

The calling would not let him be, pursued him, herded him up, out once more into the world. Very reluctantly he opened his eyes to look into a green-skinned face, into slanting eyes that held concern. Malani? No, Illylle! Slowly, painfully his mind matched a name to that face.

That was Illylle and he was Ayyar—Ayyar of the Iftin. And they were in a shelter between the rocks of the Enemy's Waste while about them the storm raged and from above—

He struggled to sit up though the girl's hands on his shoulders pinned him back with all the strength she could muster.

"It is all right. I am Ayyar—"

She must have read the truth in his eyes for she released him so that he could move, look to where the robot had rested. It was gone and he was not surprised. Had it been spying upon them? What *was* its function in the Enemy's service, for that it belonged in the ranks of *That* he did not doubt.

"It went—that way." Illylle pointed west. "Do you know now—what it is?"

"Very little. I saw its like once—long ago and on another planet—in the computer cabin of a liner. It is some form of service robot, though its real function I do not know."

"But what does it here?"

"Be sure, nothing to our advantage."

As Naill he had thought to use the thing as a guide. As Ayyar he must also do that, and the prospect of such a journey was not easy to think about.

"Come!" At least the storm was slackening, and he felt they dared not lose track of the robot.

They scrambled out of the crevice, winding their cloaks about their heads and shoulders. Rivers ran down the gullies, but the robot kept to the heights, moving as if it were programmed for some independent activity.

Perhaps more than one spacecraft had in the past landed in the Waste to be used by *That*. They had found one on their first escape, an older type of trader like those Naill had known. But what if there had been more complex vessels, even a liner?

There was a crackle in the air, a blinding burst of light. Illylle cried out, stumbled against her companion. Ayyar rubbed his eyes, striving to wipe away blindness, unable to go on in a black world. Through his body ran again a hot tingling such as he had felt when the tongue from the Mirror had touched him.

Half blind, Ayyar supported the girl, peering about him. There was continued brightness from behind; he dared not turn to face it. Some instinct for preservation sent him staggering to a rock outcrop, dragging Illylle with him.

"What was it? I am blind! Blind!" Her assurance was gone; she clung to him with both hands, her shivering body pressed close to his for comfort.

"That may be temporary," he told her. "Close your

eyes, wait. I do not know what it was, but there is now a bright light behind us. If we go forward we must keep to cover."

"Blind I cannot go," Illylle said. "If you can see you must leave me—you must!"

"I, too, cannot see—very much," which was not altogether a lie. This weakness of their Iftin bodies might defeat them yet. "We must wait, hope it will pass."

During that waiting, Illylle's hold on his arm was tight and painful. She said nothing after her outburst, and he did not dare to ask if she had any glimmer of returning sight. His own was clearing, but very slowly. And over such broken ground they dared not venture, not when they must go with two kinds of caution, against a misstep, and in fear of being sighted by some guard of the Enemy.

The storm cleared. Whether it was still night or day Ayyar could not have told. But around the rock against which they crouched still streamed the light from the east, making a fan that was shadowed by break of gully, rise of rock. Seeing that Ayyar knew that his sight had cleared. He spoke softly to Illylle:

"What can you see now?"

Her eyes had been closed. Now she opened them, blinked, and her fingers dug into his flesh. "Some— a little—but all is blurred. Ayyar, what if—?"

"If you can see some, then it is clearing," he hastened to assure her, hoping he spoke the truth. "Do you see enough for us to go on?"

If Illylle's sight cleared no more, then he must find a better hiding place for them both and soon. Who knew what might roam this land? A cave, a place in some gully where one man with a sword could bar the entrance— that was what they needed. Yet he dared not go to seek it. They must stay together.

"Guide me." She spoke with determination, her will plainly in control. "Guide me and let us go."

So began the worst of their journey, taken with many pauses as from the shadow of each bit of cover Ayyar studied the way ahead for the quickest and easiest route to another. Long since, he had surrendered his hope of tracing the robot. Their only direction was west, and they took it in a weaving pattern, zigzag.

"Any better?" he asked at what might be their tenth halt.

"Only a little, a very little."

He hoped she spoke the truth, was not saying that for his encouragement. So far, he had found them no place for a refuge. They rounded a wall of rock and Ayyar saw glitter ahead. It was not as brilliant as the beam at their back, but it warned them of danger. He put on his leaf goggles, helped Illylle to don hers. That reduced the glitter, but Illylle stumbled even more.

"What can it be?" she asked.

"There is one thing—the White Forest."

The crystal trees, certainly those would pick up light from the east, produce just such points of glitter. And the White Forest, if it did not guard the heart of *That*'s domain, must lie very close to it. Could they penetrate the Forest without a guide? They had come out of it once because the alignment of the branches, always straight-angled from the prism trunks, had given them a check upon their direction. But into it they had gone as prisoners guided by the walking space suit.

"There is the wood—" Illylle said longingly.

Yes, the wood, that spot of green life that lay in the Enemy's own country, that had kept alive the Iftin captives. But that lay at the bottom of a chasm and down the stairway which led to it— Ayyar knew that they could never descend that steep way now.

"Come—"

He led her on. The glitter became more intense, but still there was something odd about it. The trees Ayyar remembered had stood tall and straight. This light lay close to ground level. And when their painful crawl brought them still closer, he saw what did face them— a truly insurmountable barrier. For those tall trees were now broken shards, splintered and riven, covering the ground in heaps to cut to rags anything venturing in among their ruins. So must the fury of the Mirror have wrought when it had unleashed that storm months ago. And *That* had either not been able to, or had not wished to—repair the wreckage.

"All broken—" Illylle looked at what lay before them. "We—there is no way through that!"

"None." So much they had lost when the robot outdistanced them. There was nothing left for them to do but cast along the edge of the shattered Forest seeking some refuge. Let the sun rise, strike those pieces—they could not face such reflected light, even if their lives depended upon it. Which well they might.

North or south? North lay the Mirror and the way they had once fled this place. South was unknown land. And was *That* watching? South Ayyar turned now, guiding Illylle, searching for any hint of refuge. They could not hope for clouds and storm a second day.

"Ayyar!" The girl's head was up; she was sniffing.

But what scented the air was not the stench of false Iftin, nor of any of the creatures of *That*. It was cool and clean, and it spoke of real growth and life. But here—in this desert—?

"That way!" She swung her head to the left. "Oh, hurry! Hurry!"

But before them lay the murderous shards of crystal, and Ayyar held her back. He was not sure he could pick a free path through without knowing how far they must travel, nor what lay beyond.

"This way is dangerous—" he began.

"That it is not!" she returned emphatically. "We must find—"

To take that way demanded such an agony of concentration from Ayyar that he held to his strength of purpose only by great effort. Illylle came behind him, heeding his words as to where to set her feet. Time and time again he had to set aside, with infinite care against slitting his hands, a jagged splinter too large to avoid. Yet to encourage them always was that scent of free earth and growing things.

"Growing things?" wondered one part of Ayyar's mind. This was winter; there should be no green here—anywhere. Another trap of *That* with bait no Ift could resist once he had journeyed through the Waste? No, that was one thing which *That* could not produce by *Its* will—a counterfeit of true life real enough to deceive the Forest dwellers.

There was a lighting of the sky, or was it intensified radiance from the east? In either case it turned the crystal into a fire about them. Illylle's hold upon him tightened again, and Ayyar knew without any voiced complaint that her eyes suffered from the glare. How much longer—?

The shards vanished, pulverized in two beaten tracks, ground down to pave a roadway. Ayyar was tempted to turn into that road, to follow it. But the scent lay ahead. He looked up and down that road. On it nothing moved—yet—

"On!" Illylle pulled at him. "Let us go—"

They crossed that open space and then passed, while Ayyar closed the way behind them with chunks of crystal. Wytes hunted by scent, but other patrolling sentries here might only scout by eye. Luckily, on this side of the beaten road the wreckage of the Forest was thinner.

Then there was a dip in the ground, and they looked down into greenery. Illylle loosened her grip on Ayyar—held out her hands.

"Tell me true," she whispered, "oh, tell me true—are those trees?"

They were not Forest giants. In fact they were far removed from the growth of Iftcan. But that they were trees and bore leaves in winter, he could not deny, though why they grew in the midst of territory which belonged to *That*, he could not guess.

Illylle turned her head. Her leaf goggles effectively masked her eyes and the greater portion of her face, but her mouth smiled as he had not seen it do in days.

"Do you not understand? *That* could not grow *Its* own works without the force of true growth somewhere to draw upon. There must always be a seed, even if what is drawn out of it is unnatural. This is the seed from which the Enemy's White Forest grew, the energy on which it fed when it was small. But because that was false, it died when the Wrath of Thanth touched it. But the true seed was nourished, not slain in that hour. Nor, having once used it so, could *That* destroy it."

Where she got that knowledge Ayyar did not know, nor even if it was true, though he knew that she believed it so. However, there was no denying this refuge of green in the midst of a desert of death, and they needed it as a man dying of hunger and thirst needs food and drink. So, with only the remnants of caution acting as a brake upon their need and their eagerness, they went down to be swallowed up in the shade of leaf and bough. Illylle dropped, to lie upon her back, her arms outspread, her fingers digging deep into the rich earth as if they were now rootlets to sustain and feed her.

Food—drink— Ayyar leaned his back against a tree

trunk, and nothing he could now remember had ever felt as good as the toughness of that rough bark. He had known the need for neither since he had left the Mirror, nor did he now. The scent, the sounds, the feel of the wood were enough to renew his strength, his confidence—

"That road"—he began thinking aloud—"that must be the way the off-worlders and the machines passed. But any Ift on it—unless a false one—"

"Ahhhh—" She sighed. "Here it is difficult to think. One must give oneself up to feeling, just to being—"

Ayyar was tempted even as she, but that inheritance from the Ayyar who had been Captain of the First Ring, a warrior in a desperate lost war, was his conscience now. They could believe welcome of this wood, surrender themselves to its healing, and be lost to the mission that had brought them here. No, somehow the road must provide them— Ayyar's thoughts hesitated, changed direction. This was a safe place in which he could leave Illylle! He did not know how far her eyes had recovered, but he suspected that now he must act without any responsibility for another. If he scouted along the road, he must do it alone, fortified by the belief that she was safe.

How to tell her? She was moving, bracing herself up on her arms. Some of the contentment was gone from her face, a shadow veiled the brightness.

"How well can you see?"

She sat upright; her hands came slowly, plainly unwillingly, to the leaf goggles. She took them off, turned her head from left to right, her lower lip caught childishly between her teeth.

"It is dim, still dim."

"Then you shall stay here for the present—"

"But we were both chosen to carry—"

"I do not say," he compromised, "that in the end

we shall not both go. But first I must scout the road ahead—"

"In the day? Even my poor eyes can mark that." She pointed to a sun finger creeping into their green nest. "With the broken Forest to make the glare a hundred-fold worse?"

"Be sure I will not move in folly. I would but see the road and if aught travels it by day. If I find the sun too great a torment, I shall return."

He put on his goggles and reclimbed the hill from the clean green into the hard glare of the Waste. The sun was up above the horizon, but as yet it did not pierce too keenly into the places where he crept, careful of every move, lest he cut hand, foot, or body on the jagged bits of the ruined trees.

He heard crunching sounds and pushed forward, lying in a small space between two piles of rubble. And he had been not a moment too soon in his coming, for there was travel on the road. Ayyar was past surprise at anything he saw here. Also this newcomer he knew of old. A space suit, its face plate fogged so that none knew what was within, or if anything was, stumped stolidly along headed east.

Ayyar lay very still. Once before, that thing or its twin had found and taken them captive, using the off-world weapons clamped to its belt. Was it coming to round them up a second time? He waited fatalistically to see it turn aside from the road, come clumping to his hiding place. So sure was he that this would happen that he blinked after it in disbelief as it continued along the track.

Then to his amazement, a second such apparition appeared. Space suit? He thought so. But the proportions of this had never been designed to fit a form of humanoid build. It was short, squat, abnormally broad across the shoulders, and it possessed four walking appendages, but no arms at all, unless the coiled tubing about its middle section represented those. The whole helmet must once have been a clear bubble, but, like the face plate of the other suit, it was now misted to hide what might be inside.

With the same unvarying stride it followed behind its companion eastward.

Although Ayyar lay there until the reflection from the crystals warned him of the danger of remaining in the open, he saw no sign of any human from the port or the garths, nor any of the false Iftin. But he counted four more of the ambulating space suits. Two were old style from ships of human occupancy. There had been another of the four-legged type and one of still another sort. This moved on small tracks, as might a machine. An ovoid body poised above that means of progress. Small openings like miniature portholes ringed it around, but all those were closed. From the top projected two antennae which might once have been limber and moving, but which now hung limp, bobbing against the outer shell of the ovoid.

All of this weird company headed east, two at a time, with an interval between each pair. Ayyar suspected that they were on patrol, but whether this was a regular form of sentry-go, he did not know. With this the full sum of his information, he returned to the restful green of the refuge and reported what he had seen to Illylle. She listened eagerly.

"These strange suits, you have not seen their like before?"

Ayyar laughed. "Even when I was Naill Renfro I did not know all there was to be known about the space lanes. The human suits are old, of a type long since discarded. It may be that the alien ones are the same."

"And those in them?"

Ayyar hesitated. "Somehow I cannot think that they hold life—as we know it."

"That is my thought also. Listen." She put her hand over his on the ground. "In the space of time I have been here alone—there has come a message for me. Not in words, no, nor even in clear thoughts. But this is a place of power, and we carry the fruits of power within us. I believe now that if we open our minds we may learn more of what has been striving to reach me—"

"*That?*" He was alert, remembering only too well what happened when Naill memory opened the doors to suggestion.

She shook her head vehemently. "Never *That!* Not here. But we were sent as tools and perhaps that which has entered into us will now work to open Illylle memory, Ayyar memory, when we have so great a need for more and more of those."

He was still wary, yet her earnestness influenced him, and at last he agreed to try.

IX

They lay on ground, which was not the seared covering of the Waste, but dark and rich, welcoming to seed. And as Illylle had done earlier, they dug their fingers deep into that soil as if striving to root themselves, to be a part of what grew here. Ayyar still feared to open his mind. To do so was to loose a door through which *That* might attack. Still, in this green place, it was hard to think that could be so.

Iftsiga—none of the saplings growing here were of the stock of the Great Crowns. No, if what Illylle thought was true, and this was the germ from which *That* derived power to grow the White Forest, then none of that seed would root here. But in that other Forest place, deep in the stronghold of *That* where they had been prisoner, they had found one of the old stock.

Iftsiga, Iftcan—the home Forest—his mind kept returning to the green there. Spring, and the rise of renewing sap—the awakening of Iftin bodies. Summer, with the long beautiful nights for hunting, for living. Fall, with the last securing of the Crowns, the coming of the need for sleep. Winter, when one's body was cradled safe within one of the Great Crowns, one's mind traveling—traveling through dreams.

Where had dreams led during the bodies' slumber? Memories—so faint they were only wisps, which, when he strove to catch them, melted. Winter—winter slumber, one learned then—much—much—

Such as—

One of those wisps of memory became solid. He could read it as if he watched a story tape. Yes, one could learn so. As thirstily as he had drunk Iftsiga's sap, so did Ayyar now hold to that memory. This and this— but could they do it? He was no Mirrormaster. What power had he to call upon?

Through the maze of dream memory, his body answered that doubting thought with a warm surge of life, a demanding of something within him for freedom of action. Ayyar opened his eyes upon the here and now, the green roof of boughs over his head. The need for action still spurred him. Beside him Illylle stirred, gazed into his face.

"Now we know," she said softly. "Now we know—"

"One of the space suits—" His mind was already weighing possibilities.

She frowned. "They are alien. Can they hold what we must send?"

"Where will we find a better key now? I do not think there is another. We can only try that first—"

"You shall be the one to go."

He accepted that readily. Ayyar the warrior, not Illylle the priestess. His life force could accommodate the energy that would burn her out if she strove to use the tool they must put hand to—her degradation would be so much the greater. Yet also with him, through him, would go that part of Illylle that the wave from Thanth had bestowed, so their double share of energy would march to confront *That*.

As yet he was not sure just how that could be done. Only his own part was clear in his mind from that strange communication with the dreams of the far past. Now—for one of the space suits—a humanoid one.

Would they return from their patrol soon? And how could he capture one? The false Ift had been destroyed by the energy transmitted in sword touch. Could one of the marching suits be so deactivated? And dared he waste power so?

"The power—" He turned to Illylle. "If I must use some of it to capture a suit, will I then be the weaker?"

"For a space, yes. Were we not both so when we took the Ift? But it renews its flow again. I do not think that we would have been sent on such a mission without that assurance."

"And you?"

"When the time comes that I must give all I hold of Thanth's touch unto you, then I shall be as one asleep. So we must search out a bed wherein I may rest until you return for my awakening." She spoke with such serene confidence that he wondered. For to him it did not seem that even victory would bring about his return. Yet he did not voice that doubt.

"We do not have much time," she continued. "If the suits do not return, then we must hunt another key—"

To spy upon the road meant going once more into the sun and glare, but he had no choice. Ayyar hoped the goggles would shield his eyes enough so he could see, when the time for action came. How did one bring down a walking space suit? With a lump of the crystal? No, in the sun he could not be sure of his aim

or even if such a blow would topple it. And what if
the suit was occupied? By—*what?*

He could only let inspiration guide him at the proper
moment, Ayyar decided. Illylle said no more, but she
watched him climb from the pool of green into the
desert of the Waste. He wriggled back to the spot where
he had lain before and covered his eyes. Listen—his ears
must do duty until the very last moment, and the suits
had made noise enough before.

The heat of the sun was a burden on him, pressing his body to earth. From moment to moment he
feared he could not stand it, that he *must* return to
that slit filled with green or die. Still he listened and
fought his misery of body and the nagging thought that
this was useless, that only failure waited him.

His ears did not betray him. There came a steady
crunch-crunch. Shading his eyes Ayyar looked to the
east. One of the roll-footed suits was returning, and
after it, several feet to the rear, a once human
covering.

Wait—if they came back in the same order as they
had gone, he wanted the last in line—the one that had
led before. To take that might not alert the rest of the
squad.

Number three was coming, one of the four-legged
trampers. Again a human, then a four-legged— Ayyar
waited, sword drawn and ready. One after another they
rolled or stamped by. Now! This was the last if the
count remained the same.

He crouched for a leap. The space suit was
passing—now!

Ayyar gained the rutted road in one bound. His
sword swung up and out so that its tip touched the
helmet on the space suit. There were sparks and the
suit halted while its unheeding companions marched
or rolled on.

The Ift waited for any sign that they knew of the loss of their rear guard, or for a hostile move from the suit. But the rest continued on and the suit was statue still. When the others were out of sight in a road dip, Ayyar sheathed his sword and caught the suit by the shoulder. At his touch it fell, startling him into a sidewise leap in wary defense. As it lay still in the road he returned to drag it back to their green hideaway.

To touch the metal made him sick, and he doubted whether he could ever force himself to do what must be done. But he could see no other way. The inert suit fell from his hands at the rim of the valley and rolled down, breaking branches as it bounced and flopped from side to side. Heavy as it was, he thought it did not cloak any body.

Ayyar came to where it lay and straightened it out on the ground. Although it was archaic in style, much older and more clumsy than those of the Renfro ship, the general shape was the same, and he was able to master the old sealing locks.

The fogged helmet came off. From the hollow within issued a small puff of vapor. Ayyar dropped the helmet as he choked and coughed. It was a sharp, metallic smell, combined with acrid, nose-tickling ozone.

Plainly the suit did not cover any living, or once living, thing. Seeing that, a little of the lurking nightmare, which had always been in his mind since he had seen the first of these a year ago, vanished.

Ayyar set the helmet to one side and opened the rest of the protective covering. In that portion where the chest of the original wearer would have been there was a small box suspended by wire—almost, Ayyar thought a bit wildly, as if the suit had been equipped with a mechanical heart.

This was scorched and blackened and from it came

small trails of smoke. Not wanting to touch it, Ayyar used broken branches to lever and break the wires, wrench it free. Still holding the box between branches, he hurled it out of the valley.

For the rest the suit was empty. Illylle pulled handfuls of leaves from bushes and saplings, selecting certain ones. With pads of these in her hands she came to the emptied suit and held them out to Ayyar.

"Rub these on the inside," she suggested. "They will cleanse it, perhaps make it easier to wear."

The leaves she had chosen were aromatic, good to smell. And he obeyed her with a will, making sure the whole interior was so treated. The mass left green stains on the lining, but he could no longer smell the taint of off-world when he had finished.

He guessed that the suit would fit him well enough, though he was more slender than its one-time owner. To walk planetside in its bulky weight was another matter, it would make him slow and clumsy. He only hoped that that awkwardness would not betray him to those or *That* which had set the unmanned suit on patrol.

Now—what about sight? The face plate of the helmet was fogged and he could not go blindly. Picking up the helmet Ayyar used leaves to rub the eye space. And, to his satisfaction was able to clean away some of the mist. He would have limited sight, but no worse, he believed, than through the goggles at midday.

No longer dared he delay. He turned to Illylle.

"It is ready now."

"Then, before you put it on—come—"

She led him back through the wood to the opposite wall of the narrow valley. "There—" She pointed.

"There" was a hollow recess in the wall. And at hand was a pile of stones, newly gathered, to judge by the broken moss and earth stains on them.

"When we are done with what we must do, then wall me up so that I may sleep undisturbed until you come to wake me."

"And if I do not—?" It was time to say that.

"We did not ever believe that this was a light task, laid upon us for pleasure or our profit. We do what must be done, that the Seed be not destroyed, and that that which raised us from the dust of centuries to walk again be served. Is that not so?"

He bowed his head, for this was truth. "That is so."

"Then"—she drew a deep breath—"give me your hands—and wait."

His hands in hers, Illylle stood with her back to the wall of the valley, singing—not loudly, rather as a murmur. And the words were not for him, but for a loosing, a surrender, a resignation of her will and strength.

Along her head, her shoulders, her body, into her arms, came a silvery flowing, as what the touch of Thanth had placed in her she now passed to him. From her hands into his came that tingling, spreading on into his body. So did they stand until the last of the ripples was gone from her. Now her eyes were closed, her face pale and haggard, and she swayed, falling forward against him.

Ayyar took up her light body; it felt very fragile in his arms. Gently he laid her in the hollow, wrapping both their cloaks about her. Swiftly then he built up the wall of stones, wiping away all the signs of disturbance that he could, lest they guide some hostile eyes to the sleeper.

Having done thus, Ayyar went back to the suit and began to clothe himself in it. Illylle had been right— the scent of the leaves with which he had scrubbed the interior made him able to stand wearing it, though it still took all his courage to fasten down the helmet, encasing him so snugly in the Enemy's covering.

To move so hindered was hard for his Ift body, used to the loose and supple clothing of the forest hunter. He took up his sword and managed to fasten the scabbard to the waist belt. He trusted that this might be thought a trophy of some victory and not a reason for suspicion. This done, he climbed awkwardly out of the valley and tramped to the road. He would lag far behind the rest of the patrol, but there was nothing he could do to remedy that.

It was good to reach the better footing of the broken track, for walking in the suit was a tiring process. Luckily he was able to see enough to avoid the pitfalls of the ruts.

The road descended in a series of dips as if it ran down a giant staircase of wide ledges. And on either side, the shards of the shattered White Forest covered the ground. Ayyar began to watch for the great chasm that had been the end of their journey on that former occasion.

But the trail he followed, when it did come to the edge of that break, turned south and ran along the rim. Mists curling below hid from his eyes the strange place of crystal walls through which he and Illylle had once sought a path, or anything else that might lie in those depths.

Now the path descended again, at a gentle incline to the left of the wall of the chasm, which rose higher and higher as a barrier. And along it were patches of that same crystal that had formed the trees of the White Forest—these protruding as if they were like unto the shelf fungi one saw in the Forest.

On one of these lay something dark, and Ayyar moved closer. A man from the garths by his bush of beard, his clothing—though that was rent into tattered rags—rested there. He was curled upon himself, his head turned away, and Ayyar thought that he was dead.

He halted by the quiet stranger to look over the way that still lay ahead. There was a valley—wide. And from its floor were raised mounds which differed sharply in color from the red-yellow of the sandy soil on which they were based. They were black, a dull, lusterless black. And they had been shaped by design, not nature, in sharply geometric forms. From this place he could see them in part. From the sky above they must be very plain indeed. The labor that had gone into their making must have been enormous.

Among those mounds things moved, perhaps the men from the port and the garths, or other space suits animated by the will of *That*, but they seemed to do so aimlessly and without purpose. Machines did likewise. He saw the grubber rumble along a mound foot, dwarfed by that rise of earth.

What this place was or its use, he did not know, unless it was merely a keepsafe for the servants of *That* until they were wanted. Perhaps as one among many he would not be detected. But he must find a way to *That*, wherever *It* might dwell, and to that he had no clue at all. If it meant searching through all the Waste and every wonder in it, then that he must do. He went on down into the place of mounds.

If this could be so clearly sighted from aloft, he wondered as he trudged along, why had none of the early explorers of Janus mentioned it? Why had it not shown up on any of the survey visa-tapes made before the planet was open to settlement? Such signs of a native intelligence would have kept the planet off the first auction held by Survey when the Combine had acquired rights here almost a hundred year ago. The trees of Iftcan could easily have remained a secret to explorers, as they had, but surely not this!

The closer Ayyar came to the plain of the mounds, the more he wondered at them. As far as he could detect, they were not buildings—but solid piles of earth. The burial places of some long vanished race? Iftin memory peopled Janus with naught besides their own kind, *That*, and the Larsh. And the Larsh were beast-men, only just emerging from the animal in the final days of Iftcan. Though perhaps the Larsh had a thousand years or more after their final victory to rise in civilization under the domination of *That*. Maybe these monuments were raised in honor of their ancestors or the power that had led them against the Forest.

Loose sand rose about the boots of the suit as he came out into the valley floor. His pace was now a shuffling crawl for it was labor to plow through this. Ayyar stopped short as a man approached. The other wore the tunic of one of the port security police, and in his tanned face his eyes were set, staring dully ahead as he walked, shifting and skidding in the sand unceasingly, as if he were a mechanical toy set to go and then forgotten, to walk so until he ran down into death.

All the others Ayyar could sight near enough to see clearly were like this man. They twisted and turned, went this way and that, with no reason, merely keeping on their feet and moving. He looked about for the animated space suits, but there were none about. Nor in this sand were there any tracks he could follow. Perhaps to circle the walls of the valley— In that way he could keep out of the path of the restless walkers.

Those walls were perpendicular, and on their surfaces the protruding crystals formed irregular splotches. Twice as Ayyar went on his slow survey of the wall, he sighted other men lying still, usually fallen face forward, arms outstretched as if they had collapsed, never to stir again. And both times these were garthmen, not from the port. Ever back and forth, into the shadows of the mounds and out again, walked those others without rest. And the machines crawled and rolled in the same aimless fashion.

Ayyar plodded on, the suit heavy on him, every movement demanding more and more effort. But he feared to stop among that ever-moving company, lest that halt alert any watcher. Only fatigue drove him at last to that danger and he rested, back against the wall, studying what he could see of the valley.

The sun marked afternoon. Ayyar longed for the coming of night. Nowhere in that crowd did he note any false Iftin. Perhaps both they and the space suits had their own place. Doggedly he began to march again.

There was something odd upon the top of a mound he now neared. He strove to raise his head within the lock of the helmet, straining to see better. That was a flitter resting there. At least it did not buzz about as did the rest.

Change came suddenly. Had he not paused from sheer fatigue, Ayyar would have had no warning at all. So close that he might have reached out a hand to lay on his shoulder, a garthman stalked stiff-legged. Now he halted, one foot still readied for the next step. For a moment he stood thus, then toppled to the ground. And he was not the only one. They were all going down, falling where they stood, some skidding forward as momentum carried them along. Ayyar was now the only one on his feet on the plain where activity had ceased in an instant.

He sensed what— A searching thought? Questing for him? Or just for anything foreign to the valley? Apprehension made him do the only thing he could, dampen his thoughts, blank out Ayyar as best he could. Perhaps normally he could not have accomplished that;

perhaps it was due to the virtue that had flowed out
of the Mirror that he was saved. He was conscious of
a hovering, seeking thing, as if he could actually see
some great hand, with crooked fingers ready to grab,
high over his head.

Moments passed; the shadows of the mounds spread
larger and darker, swallowing up many of those who
lay upon the sand. Still that thought sought, hunted—
And never dared Ayyar believe that truly he could
escape that hunt.

Then, as swiftly as it had come, it was gone. Yet
none of the captives rose again or moved, and the plain
was deathly still. Dared he go on? Or would the very
fact that he moved reveal him? He could not look in
another direction without turning his whole body. Must
he play statue here for perhaps hours? But with the
night, surely with the night, he might draw the dark
about him as a cloak and dare to walk again!

Ayyar did not have to wait for the night. From
between two mounds came a couple of space suits, one
human, one of the four-legged type. They halted now
and then by some of the supine figures, though as far
as Ayyar could see they did nothing else but stand so.
Finally the humanoid figure stooped and picked up one
of the limp men, held him on his feet, until the rope-
like appendages of the other suit flicked forth and
steadied him. Together they marched toward the end
of the valley, holding the helpless body between
them. And, daringly, Ayyar plowed through the sand
to follow.

The man they carried wore a uniform tunic with
officer's insignia on the collar. Perhaps *That* had drawn
all the port personnel to *It*, had the off-world force
in its entirety here. The two space suits turned to the
left, putting one of the smaller mounds between them
and Ayyar. He kept on along the wall of the valley,

striving to hurry a little to catch up with them when they came to the end of that mound. Only when he reached that spot, no space suits with prisoners were to be seen!

Ayyar waited, but they did not appear. Now he ventured away from the wall, shuffled through the sand to the side of the mound and edged along that, thinking that when the others came into sight he would fall in behind them. Still they did not come.

The mound ended, and he turned its point and looked back along the other side to where the others must be, fearing that they might have taken off in another direction while the pile of earth had been between them.

There was nothing there—nothing at all! The suits and their prisoner might have been wholly illusion. With the mound wall now on his left, Ayyar started down the side that had been the path of those others. Several of the garthmen and two from the port lay prone in the sand with no signs of life. But Ayyar thought he could make out, some distance away, a dragging path, grooving the sand, perhaps cut by the feet and legs of a man half carried, half pulled.

He came to the end of that indentation, for end it was, midpoint of the mound wall. Either they had flown from here or simply disappeared. For loss of anything better to search, Ayyar lifted his arm in the stiff sleeve of the space suit and thumped a mittened hand against the earth of the mound. A clod was dislodged and fell, showing plainly against the lighter sand. Now he saw other such clods about the end of the trail.

Had they climbed? Swinging around to face the side of the mound, he inched along, squinting through the dim face plate at the earth. Only such a close inspection showed him the hollow, nearly at eye level. He raised his hand and set it into that.

Under his feet the sand stirred. He was moving down! Already he was knee deep, his hand pulled from that hole, sand pouring in about him as he sank. Waist deep, and now the sand was stopped. There was a ridge rising above to hold back that dry flood. Under the sand on which he stood was solid footing, and that platform, or whatever it was, was descending smoothly as if through a shaft.

There was no way of escape. In the clumsy suit he could not hope to climb out quickly enough. He was as much of a prisoner now as the man he had seen dragged to this place.

X

He was not really in a shaft, Ayyar decided, for he could see no walls. And the sense of insecurity that that discovery gave him kept him very still on what he hoped was the center of the platform. It was dark here, even for Iftin eyes. And he could not lift his head, imprisoned in the helmet, to see the outer world above.

At last the carrier touched bottom, but for a long moment Ayyar made no move, almost hoping it would ascend. When it did not, he slid his right foot forward carefully, not raising his boot from the flooring. Sand from the surface grated under his weight, then his foot met another level, the floor of this burrow.

Ayyar took a chance, freed the helmet catch so he could push that back to hang between his shoulders. His head was free, his sight no longer dimmed by the plate. Now he could strain back, see that oblong of light above. It looked very far away, and now, though he flung the weight of his body to stop it, the platform, showering sand from its surface, began to rise.

His weight made no difference. Ayyar rolled off the un-railed surface. He stumbled back to avoid the flood of sand and bleakly watched the platform go. However, he could see a little more now that he was not prisoned in the helmet. He looked about swiftly before the source of light above was sealed by the platform.

Walls faced him fore and aft within touching distance were he to extend his arms. Right and left was darkness. Which way should he go to trail those who had preceded him? Two choices—with no clue to influence him one way or the other. He became aware of a kind of humming in the walls. This place had life, and awareness that was surely not the emission of any human or Ift mind.

Above, the opening closed, leaving him in the dark, but that blackness did not last. To human eyes, Ayyar decided, it might still be totally lacking in light, but he picked up a throbbing along the walls. If darkness had shades, then he saw one passing over another, blacker. Energy—could one see energy? He breathed in. The air carried faint, strange odors. But—yes, his guide—the scent of man! Could he depend upon his nose to track the off-worlder and his captors?

Ayyar started down the left-hand path, sniffing. That odor held, though it grew no stronger. Under his boots sand crunched and shifted. Within a few feet he traveled on smooth surface with now and then a ringing sound, in spite of his efforts to move quietly. The shadow pattern on the wall did not change. If he had set off any alarms by venturing into this place he had no warning of that.

There were no breaks in the walls. Looking back a short time later, Ayyar could not be sure where he had entered. If this was a trap, then he was surely and firmly taken. He was conscious that not only his nose, his ears, and his eyes were on guard, but also that inside him some other unnamable sense now did sentry-go, waiting for what he could not put into words. It too quested, waiting for—what?

On and on—only his nose continued to tell him that he was not on a false trail. Walking was easier with no sand to impede. And a compulsion grew to hurry as fast as those weights on his feet would let him. Ayyar fought that, determined to use a hunter's, a scout's caution.

He had begun to think the passage had no end when he saw the faint gleam beyond. Finally he came to a round plug door, intended to seal off the passage, but now swinging ajar. It was familiar enough to give him pause. This was the kind of barrier one found guarding an air lock on a spacecraft. Ayyar carefully put out his hand. It gave easily to his slight pull. He flattened himself as well as he could against the wall of the passage while he sent the door flying open against the opposite wall.

Light—thin, grayish, but still light. He waited alertly. This was far too much like a trap. Man or machine or whatever prowled these ways could be in ambush there. But they could not disguise what betrayed them to his nose, and he sniffed.

Acrid fumes—faint—linked unto that which had arisen from this suit when he first opened it. And other things, among them still the smell of man. But none strong enough to warn.

Ayyar stepped over the raised threshold, looked about him warily. To Iftin eyes this light was good. He stood in a space that was perhaps as large as Iftsiga's spreading girth. The bole of that Giant Crown had not been perfectly round, but this area was. Into it fed three other passages, or so he guessed by the doors he saw. There was, in addition, a curling stairway, hardly more than a ladder, made to rise about a wide center pillar. This too was familiar, of space ship design. Ayyar moved to the foot of that ladder, raised his head high, sniffing. Then he bent forward awkwardly to smell the steps.

The scent was there. But he eyed that rise dubiously. Unhampered by his suit, he would have had no fears about the climb. Within this casing, such movement was another matter. But to shuck the suit might be far more dangerous. It might even be deadly dangerous to continue to go helmetless here. Only the need for sight made him dare it.

As he had foreseen, the climb was difficult, and he had to pull himself up and along by grasping both rails. The ladder was metal, a smooth surface on which his boots, unless planted very carefully, were inclined to slip. Space suits were equipped with magnetic plates in the soles to counter just such perils, but on his suit they were no longer in service.

He traveled through another tube now, this rising straight up instead of running horizontally as had the first. Again there were no breaks in the walls, no landings giving on any level. Ayyar continued to climb, pausing every few steps to listen, sniff, await a warning from his inner alert.

The light grew brighter as he advanced, near that of a moonlit night in the upper world. Ayyar marveled at the walls; there were no signs of plate seams. The whole great tube might have been cast in a single piece. There was a chill here, an alien feel that triggered his old revulsion. Yet he was sure that the technology Naill Renfro had once known had nothing in common with these burrows.

There was an end to the ladder stair at long last.

He came into a second round area from which again ran hallways. But none of these were doored by locks. Here he made the daunting discovery that he could no longer depend upon his nose for guide. Too many odors, all foul by Iftin standards, fought one another. He could take any one of those passages and not be sure that it led him aright. Which way—?

"Try—"

Ayyar half crouched, his hand on the sword hilt which was to him the natural weapon. Then he knew that word had not been spoken in his ear as it had seemed for one wild instant, but rather had formed in his mind.

That?

"Try—sword—" Again, and very faint, a shadow picture only, of a thin face, an Iftin face—the eyes closed in slumber—or something deeper than slumber—the cheeks a little sunken—Illylle! Not quite as he had seen her last, but still—Illylle.

He did not cry her name aloud, but he strove to make it carry along his reaching thought of her to bring him assurance that it was she who had sought him thus.

"Try—the—sword—" The lips of that shadow face in his mind did move.

Ayyar drew the sword, swung to face the nearest hall. He did not know what he expected, but there was nothing—just the sword pointing. Slowly he turned to the next, again nothing. But at the third—ahhh—

Not the green light that had once dripped from it, no, this was a spark only, flashing and gone again in an instant. Warning—or guide? He must believe the latter.

He passed at his suit-dictated shuffle into that passage, the sword, pointing now to the floor, giving him no further sign. This was not a round tube. The ceiling was higher. And now and then he saw scratches

on the walls as if large, moving objects had forced their
way along with some difficulty.

"Illylle?" Once more he mind-called.

"Watch—sword—" No longer her face, just those
words, and with them a sense of danger, as if this
communication could awaken some peril. So he broke
contact. Yet he was heartened; he no longer walked so
alone in this place.

The hum in the walls was stronger. He could feel also
a kind of pulsation in the air. The stink of
machines, a strong stench that gave him the impression of age, of long entrenchment in this place was heavy.
There was the outline of a door in the wall to his left
and above it a shuttered slit. He paused to look within.

Vast dusky things he could not identify—machines,
he guessed. And from there the hum was a muted
roar—not truly of sound, but of vibration. It was hard
to equate this place with the White Forest, with *That*
as he had thought of *It*—a power beyond such toys of
men, as was the Mirror of Thanth, and what reached
through it, far beyond the knowledge of the Iftin who
had followed another path of life altogether.

What was *That*? He was beginning to revise his
ideas. Or was all this merely used by the servants here?
Who had built all this—and why?

After Ayyar left the place of machines, there were no
more doors. But shortly he passed between two crystal plates set facing each other. And his sword sparked.

Suspicion was triggered. He swung to the right,
touched sword point to that sparkling panel. A touch
only, not hard enough to mar it, or so he had thought.
But from the point of that Iftin-forged blade, cracks
spread in a web. The block became dull in an instant.
At once Ayyar turned and served the other panel in
the same fashion. If that had been some warning or
control, as he suspected, then it would not operate

again. But had the warning of his coming already flashed ahead? Perhaps he had thus offered a challenge to what dwelt here.

He watched for more of the panels, intent upon breaking them before they could relay his advance. There were two more such.

Perhaps he gained too much self-confidence by his small successes. He was not prepared for what followed when he paused to rest by that last panel. Suddenly he found himself walking, or rather the suit was walking, carrying him with it. In spite of his struggles, his attempts to throw himself out of stride, even to the floor, it continued to carry him ahead.

By concentrating all his will on a single bit of action, Ayyar was able to force the hand holding his sword to return that weapon to its sheath. He was afraid that whatever now controlled the suit might drop or throw away that blade—upon which he centered all his hopes of ever coming out of this place alive. He had thought that the "heart" he had removed from the suit had been its control. But it would seem that the covering in which he was now a prisoner was still sensitive to outside command. It even moved more quickly, with greater ease than he had been able to use. Ayyar was being transported, as much a helpless captive as that off-worlder he had seen brought into this maze.

The suit bore him steadily past other doors, with only a short chance to look inside. More machines—but these smaller—and always totally unfamiliar. Now, here was another of the curving stairs and the suit confidently climbed.

Illylle, he longed to reach to her. Not that she could give him any answer to this last disaster, but because he needed, oh, how greatly, some contact with reality. What was here was not life as he knew it, rather something opposed to his species for all the ages.

Yet he dared not give his spirit that bolstering. How he knew that, he was not certain, only that it was as true as any oath laid upon him. His hands lay helpless within the gloves, reaching for fresh holds to draw him up each step his unwilling feet took. Up and up—where?

When he came out of that second stairway, he was not alone any longer. One of the ovoid space suits rolled along. Ayyar waited for recognition, for the thing to make some move toward him. Not until it had passed, was several paces away, did Ayyar realize that it had not been sent to deal with him. But his suit thrust him along in its wake.

His inner sense was a warrior waiting battle, the kind of battle which is the last stand against the assault of the enemy. Ayyar snarled. About him was a choking stench. His fear was cloaked and armed with anger. Already he knew that it was all of *That*.

Ahead another space suit came out of a door, moved diagonally down the corridor. Ayyar gasped as he caught sight of what that metal monster carried. For slung across its shoulder, arms and head swaying lifelessly back and forth, was the unclothed green body of an Ift!

Illylle! How had they—?

He could not hasten the pace of the suit to catch up with that other and its burden before it had entered another door. But as he passed that opening in turn, Ayyar turned his head far enough in the unyielding collar of the suit to look within. The green body lay on a table there, face up—not Illylle!

Nor any one from their own small band. Then he saw that slit at throat level, the metal arms rising up and out of the table slab to work—false Ift!

Ayyar witnessed no more for his suit went past, on down that hall which gave on many rooms, the contents of which he saw but did not understand until at last he came to one which the suit entered. Ayyar shut his eyes against dazzling light. He felt the suit move at its controlled march, then turn around, take two steps back, come to a halt. Cautiously Ayyar tried to move. He could wriggle a little within that shell, but that was all. To raise his arm was impossible. He was a locked-in prisoner as ably kept as if he lay chained in a cell.

Through slit-open eyelids he tried to see what lay about him. The light came from a series of reflecting surfaces, but luckily the spot on which the suit had elected to take root was not facing any of those. By turning his head Ayyar saw he was one in a line of robots and suits. Next to him was one of the ovoids on rollers, beyond that a repair robot such as he had seen at ports, but of a slightly different pattern, and fourthly another humanoid space suit. There were still others, but he could not see them clearly.

The line of mirrors or reflecting surfaces was on the opposite wall to the right. And facing the midpoint of that line was a tilt-top table, now moved from the horizontal to the vertical. Strapped on that table was the off-worlder from the sandy valley. His eyes were open, staring into the surface of the mirror in which he was reflected in every detail. But he was not struggling against the bonds that held him, and Ayyar was not even sure he was alive. He could see no reassuring rise and fall of his chest.

There was only one table fixed so, only one man. But in the mirror to that captive's right, there was another reflection! It was as bright and clear as if the one who was so pictured still faced it. Garthman— bushy beard, untrimmed hair, dun colored clothing—

Only no man himself!

Ayyar's suit began to move, pacing out from the wall. From that line a second humanoid suit followed. Was he to stand before the mirror? He had to close his eyes; the glare was punishing. Yet there

did not seem to be any great amount of light elsewhere in the room.

His arms were raised by the suit, the gloved fingers flexing and curling. They grasped small projections,
turned them, and his own fingers felt the pressure of
the grip. Ayyar stole a look beneath near-closed eyelids. The suit that held him prisoner and the other
humanoid one were freeing from the wall the mirror
that bore the reflection of the garthman.

The panel was a head taller than the suits and none
too easy to unclasp. They worked slowly until they
could pull it from the frame, swing it horizontal
between them. On the surface, the representation of
the garthman did not move. It could have been a tri-
dee picture of Naill Renfro's knowledge. The suits per-
severed until they could carry it between them. Then
they turned and walked from the room, paying no
attention to the off-worlder on the table.

The other suit was in the lead and strode back down
the corridor up which Ayyar had come only minutes
earlier. Not too far away it turned into another
chamber where were a series of tables. Two were
occupied. On one lay an Ift body, but only in part. The
hands were still blobs of jelly-like substance, the head
shaped but still featureless, the tall, pointed ears only
flaps.

It rested on a mirror surface such as the one the
two suits carried between them. And on that smooth,
sleek table, showing only in part, Ayyar caught a
glimpse of a picture, as if the reflection were a pattern to induce the growing of the thing resting on it.

On the second table was a mass of quivering jelly
spread out to hide whatever pattern lay below it, and
over that lights played in swift, sharp flashes or a steady
glow, each touching but one portion at a time.

All that was Ayyar, the Ift, shrank and rebelled

against what lay in this chamber. His sickness of mind, body, and soul was so great that he could have spewed forth even his identity if that were possible. The stench of *That* here was more than he could bear, and afterwards he thought that he had lost consciousness for a space.

The gloves were moving, and so perforce his hands, snapping up catches about the rim of an empty table. Thus the mirror they had brought was immobilized. When their task was completed, the suits walked away, returning to the place of the mirror to take their stand again in the line of waiting servitors. Ayyar's head cleared a little, away from that foul place of unnatural growth. He swallowed the sourness in his mouth by will. For the moment at least, he mastered his unsteady stomach. He must free himself from the suit—but how?

He had come to believe during this excursion that whoever, or whatever, moved the suit either did not know he inhabited it or thought him so securely a captive that it did not care about his presence. If the first guess was the truth, then he might have a way to force escape, though afterwards he would have to continue in these burrows without the small protection the suit might afford.

But—to get out—?

The energy in his body, channeled into the sword, had incapacitated the suit the first time. But the sword was in the sheath at his belt, and he could not raise his hand to free it. His hand— Ayyar strove to turn his wrist within the glove. Since their return the glove had hung limp. The fingers did not answer to the pressure of his as they once had, but by using all the strength he could muster, Ayyar was able to move the hand a little until the fingers brushed the hilt of the sword.

So far—but no farther. The sword had to rest against

his bare flesh before the energy would drain into it. His bare flesh—

Ayyar stopped struggling with those stiff fingers. The sword had conducted the energy—but did he need that? He had that energy within him. For moments he fiercely willed to release that power through any part of him that touched the suit. But with no result.

The suit came to life as it had before. This time as it stepped from line, a four-footed space suit accompanied it. They headed for the table where the off-worlder faced his replica on the mirror. And once more Ayyar closed his eyes against the glare. They loosed the clamps which held the silent captive. Ayyar made a great effort. And because the movement he planned was in tune and not in opposition with the suit's ordered duty, he achieved his purpose. The Ift sword hilt caught in one of those clamps and was drawn from its scabbard as the suit moved away.

Now—his one lone chance! The suit leaned forward to loose the clamps about the off-worlder's ankles. Ayyar threw himself forward, over-balancing the shell that held him so it crashed to the floor. He turned his head, and his lips felt the coolness of the sword hilt. His teeth closed about it with a frantic grip. Already the suit was moving ponderously to regain its feet. And, as it came up, the sword swung back, with all the skill Ayyar could summon, to touch against its breast.

This—this was it! As he had striven to aim that energy along his hand and into the blade, now he attempted to send it forth from his mouth. And there were silver ripples answering, flowing down to the suit. Would it work?

The other suit was going about the business of freeing the prisoner from the table. But his had stopped. Tentatively Ayyar raised his hand and was able to take the sword hilt from his mouth. He was free

from the will that had used the suit for a servant. But
how long would that precious freedom last? Once
before he had thought the suit his, only to be trapped
in it. He began to loosen the seals.

Finally he stepped forth, and the suit, now an empty
case, lay on the floor. While he had so labored, the
four-footed suit had put off the final bonds of the
captive, and had taken up the limp body to bear it
toward the door, leaving behind the mirror vividly
imprinted with the reflection.

Ayyar caught up his sword, freed the baldric from
the suit and hurried after, down the corridor but now
in the opposite direction. Should he short-circuit that
suit, strive to free the man? But the off-worlder had
not moved; his eyes still stared as his head rested on
the suit's back. To all appearances he was dead.

The suit entered another chamber, and Ayyar paused
on the threshold, staring at what stood within. Row
after row of tall cylinders—to his right clear and empty.
But others were filled to the brim with a murky, pink
fluid, then capped with heavy domes of dull red metal.
In that liquid were half-seen solid cores. The suit he
had followed approached one of the empty cylinders.
One of its waist tentacles snapped out, pressed a stud
in the base of the upright column. The huge container
swung out and down. Into the waiting receptacle the
suit slid its burden. Once filled, the container returned
to its original position. A cap was lowered from overhead and, from a pipe in its crest, liquid trickled down
to rise about the body.

Ayyar shrank to one side. The space suit had turned,
was coming back to the door.

XI

Could or did it see him? He had no chance against an attack with only a sword for defense. Then his mind steadied. If the suit was inhabited he might have to fear it, but if it were empty the sword energy ought to render it helpless. His confidence flooded back. But prudently he stepped to the left, out of its direct path.

It did not pause or show any interest in him, but stamped on into the corridor, leaving Ayyar free to explore the room. All the cylinders with liquid in them were so murky that he could only see shadowy forms floating within. But the number was astounding for the chamber was very large and the filled containers stood like a forest of evil trees. There were surely more here than the numbers of false Iftin they had seen, unless those formed a real army. But these—if the patterns for the false Iftin were bottled here—who were they? Changelings caught in the net of *That*? Or—Ayyar's heart beat faster—were they from the old days, captives taken by the Larsh? And if so—could they be restored to life again?

As he returned, he glanced at the container that had so recently been given an occupant. The red liquid flowed now about the chin of the motionless offworlder, lapping against his lips. In him was no sign of life.

Where was *That* which controlled all this? Ayyar had seen nothing moving except the suits. Should he seek a higher level or a lower? And where did these burrows lie—under the mounds or the rock walls of the valley cliffs?

He turned left as he came out, heading into the unknown, watching for any wall plates. There was a pair farther on, and this time he did not shatter them. Rather, he went to floor level, wriggling past on his belly, rising only when he was well beyond their frames.

Some time past, Ayyar had stopped depending upon his nose, for the mingling of what were, for him, stenches blocked his ability to select any to follow. But now he did smell something, and it was like the clean blade of a knife cutting a foul kalcrok web.

For an Ift, you could not disguise the smell of growing things. He needed that as he had needed it in the valley where he had left Illylle. So he followed that scent eagerly, yet not so headlong that he failed to take note of his going and of any pitfall that might lie ahead.

No stairs—but a sloping downward of the passage, and ever the scent of true life. But—this was winter—and what he drew into wide nostrils was the odor of spring! Caution dampened his first excitement. It would seem that in *That*'s domain even the seasons could be controlled.

He crawled past two more of the wall crystals and

then was out in the open. From a point below rose the heady fragrance of what might have been the Forest of Iftcan itself!

The light was silver moon radiance. Ayyar sighed with relief and pleasure as it refreshed his tired eyes, just as the scents restored his body. Slowly he relaxed, was content.

Content? Deep in his mind the alert sounded. This was not Iftcan—this lay in the hollow of *That's* hold! Be not fooled by an outer husk—any more than by the false Iftin. Had he not seen how one thing might be fashioned to resemble another?

Still, what lay below beckoned him past any self-control. This was of his knowledge, his natural home. He began to descend a narrow path, so steep that he needed full attention for his footing. There were trees below, a dense growth of them, their crowns making a green floor for the eyes. And Ayyar's questioning nostrils picked up no evil scent.

He dropped from the path and moss rose about his ankles, made a cushion for his feet. Among that thick growth he saw here and there the night-closed bud of the tottlee, its blue so pale it was a small ghost of its daytime self. And here and there, by the foot of the wall, stood tall bargor lilies, light green with the darker spots fading into the leaves. Odd—these seemed to have no detectable scent while the night-blooming bargor of Iftcan could perfume the air for a wide area. So small a thing—

Ayyar stood staring at the lilies. Then he reached down, touched a finger to one of those velvet petals. It was alive—real. Yet where was the scent? A small thing, but one that broke through his unity with what grew about him. Now he studied what else was rooted there. The moss, yes, that was real.

And there was a sal bush. The moisture in its thin

leaves exuded at night to form luminous drops, tiny water jewels. One by one, Ayyar catalogued the plants, saplings, flowers, strove to find them wanting in some particular. Only the lilies—

No! The fragrance of bargors, cloyingly sweet, rising about him in an instant, as if someone had released it from a hidden fountain within the lily clumps. Released? Ayyar licked his lips. He thought of the scentless lilies, found them unnatural and so was led to examine more closely the place wherein he walked, and here was the scent coming as if by order—only too late to allay suspicion.

He pulled one of the drop-hung leaves, crumpled it in his hand. It gave forth the proper aromatic odor, felt completely normal. But now he did not believe in it or in this whole woodland. This was a trap of sorts.

Ayyar returned to the path down which he had come, fearing this place that had seemed to promise what he needed most. The wall along which that narrow footway had descended was bare. What had seemed solid rock under his feet had vanished as if it had never been. So *That* must know he was here. But at least he was warned and alerted—by so small a thing as a scentless flower.

He looked to the ground and the trees. Those were not tall though he might walk under their lowest branches with good head room to spare. But to one knowing the Great Forest, this was a wood shrunken into a miniature. To off-world eyes the gloom under the massed leaves would have been close to total darkness, but to an Ift this was not unusual. He picked out the gleaming grains lying in clusters along trunk and branch—fjot eggs filled with the inner light that would also grace those delicate insect bodies that would issue from the tissue shells.

Where he now stood was the only open space. There

was no way to skirt the wood by going along the valley wall on either side, and any retreat to the burrows was closed. His way must be forward unless he proposed to remain in the moss-carpeted pocket forever. He had his Iftin senses and his sword—and a very clever trap to penetrate. With a shrug for all folly, including his own, Ayyar walked under the first tree.

For all his careful examination, he could see no discrepancies between this wood and those natural to Janus. Almost, he began to suspect his own discovery concerning the lilies. He threaded his way between trees and came to another opening, a glade where there was a small pool, molten silver in the moonlight— moonlight!

Ayyar stared up to the patch of open sky. Yes, there was the moon. But—he shivered. Just as the lilies had been a warning, so did that moon appear not quite right. Though what was missing or had been added, he could not have sworn to. The water of the pool invited, lured him with the promise of a deep draught of clear, cold water. But that which had sustained him since he had been touched by Thanth dulled that lure, made it easy for him to put aside thirst.

On a rock by the pool rim a skeleton leg equipped with a hooked claw shot out, dipped into the water, arose grasping a struggling, finned creature, and disappeared again. A fisher-tonk—normal again in this place and hour. Ayyar listened to all the sounds. He identified hunters, both furred and feathered, all save one—no quarrin sounded its mournful night cry here.

Quarrin and Ift, long partners in the Great Forest— not as servant and master, but as equals of different, but intelligent species. And he had heard no quarrin call. Was he watched, traced through this wood? Would they now produce a quarrin as they had the lily fragrance when he had noted its absence? But though he stood and listened, that mournful "hoo-ruurrru" did not sound.

He skirted the pool, reentered the wood, trying to fathom its purpose. So far he had not been menaced by any danger, and there were some native to the Forest that could reasonably have been used here to imperil him had "they" wished to do so. Who or what lay behind all this—and also why? In the burrows, machines did *That's* bidding. Here the Forest grew in miniature, Ayyar firmly believed, to *That's* will. Illylle must have been wrong to believe it could not do so. He stiffened, leaped instinctively to set his back against a tree trunk. Fragrance had come from lilies when he had noted its lack, but this was not any perfume; it was that rankness that matched with false Iftin.

Could it be that those robots must be nourished by a wood of illusion as if they had that much kinship with the ones they imitated? He waited. There was no sound of footfall, but the smell was stronger and he was sure that the creature came his way. A bush trembled as a rounded arm swept aside a branch, and she stepped into the open beyond one of the buttressed roots of the tree where he stood.

Out of memory she was, not like Illylle who had worn hunter's dress and been a comrade under the dark cloud of danger. This was an Ift maiden such as once had been at the Choosing in the courts of the springtime. And she wore the flower robe of that day, living blossoms spilling their perfume as she moved. Her face was oval, her slanted eyes dark, and there was all the beauty of her race in her. She gazed at Ayyar, she smiled and beckoned with the old, old gestures of the Choosing. Memory worked in him, and an old excitement his present changeling self had never known awoke, drew him away from the tree, his hand out to meet hers without his willing.

"False—"

A whisper in his mind, a face to match the whisper, though much faded now.

"False—" So thin and far away a warning, while before him swayed the maiden, her feet moving in the first steps of the Choosing dance, her hands reaching, reaching, but now her smile a little uncertain, almost hurt—

"Vallylle, I am Vallylle—I am yours, strong warrior—" The flower robe rustled; its perfume was so thick that Ayyar found it hard to breathe. Yes, once there had been a Vallylle, and he had searched for her at the Choosing. This was not false—it was true, true! Ayyar memory said it was true.

"False!" The whisper deep in his mind was despairing, urgent.

"Come!" She was imperious now in her call to him. "Vallylle does not wait for any warrior—many wait for her!"

Neither was that false, nor any boast, memory told him. There were many who would give much, very much indeed, to dance the Choosing with Vallylle. To hesitate now—

She reached again for his hand. He was not conscious that he had taken another step to meet her.

"False!" His hand jerked. It was for an instant as it had been when the suit controlled him, not he the suit.

The suit—the maze of the burrows, the place of mirrors! And—Ayyar blinked awake—the stench of false Ift! His hand went to his sword, drew that weapon. Before him the girl ceased to smile; fear made a stark mask of her face; beauty fled from the whip of terror. She shrank away, her hands raised as if to beg for life. If she was some creature of *That*, she played her role well. Ayyar hesitated. False Ift, yes, of that he was certain. Still he could not raise his arm, strike the blow to cut her down. They had chosen well which opponent to send against him.

"You are mad!" she cried out. "Mad!"

For the first time Ayyar spoke. "I am not mad, but you are made—made for That Which Abides, or by *It*." Still he held the sword, knowing that prudence dictated "Kill," but unable to swing the blade. He watched her slip around the tree trunk, run from him, knowing bleakly that so perhaps he had not bought life, but his own failure and death.

All was quiet; yet the hum of the usual night noises underlaid that quiet. Like the scentless lilies, that was a small, revealing mistake, for in the real Forest the sound of their voices, Vallylle's flight, would have brought true silence for a short space. Almost, he was tempted to try the energy power of the sword on the tree at his back, upon all that grew about him, save that to waste the force was rank folly.

If there were any watchers in that wood, Ayyar sighted none of them as he moved on with hunter's skill.

No more Vallylles came to woo him, but he was increasingly conscious of the fact that he was under observation. Turn, twist, look about him as he would, he could sight none of those invisible watchers, or watcher, which he was sure followed. So keen did that feeling of being observed come to be that at last he went no farther, but once more put his back to a tree and stood waiting.

He longed to shout down the aisles of trees: "Come out!" But he curbed his fears enough to remain silent.

A vine caught his eye, and he studied the loops along a limb over his head. It curled also about the trunk, anchored by tendrils to the branches. In so much it resembled any parasite one could sight in some parts of the Forest. If it did not die, then, in time, its weight would bring down the limbs and trunk that so easily supported it now.

Only a vine—yet there was something about its leaves—

Small beads of moisture gathered there and along its stem; or maybe, as with the sal, it exuded sap at night. Ayyar raised his head to sniff. There was a faint odor, yes, and strange.

Those shining drops grew larger. They gleamed phosphorescently. He could see them even where the moonlight did not touch. Several drops ran together, formed a larger one that fell from the vine to the ground. Then Ayyar drew a deep breath. Where that drop had fallen, a tiny curl of vapor arose. Had he not been so intent he would have missed it.

More and more drops—larger. The hiss of their fall was like the sprinkle of rain. Ayyar muffled a sharp cry. Fire licked at the back of his hand. He saw the oily globule there. Even a flick of the wrist did not dislodge it, and the fire ate into his flesh with a pain so intense he could not believe it came from just that one small bead of moisture.

He was about to wipe his hand on his thigh and then hesitated. What if that drop of liquid agony soaked into his clothing? Instead he went to one knee, smeared the back of his hand against the earth, only to straighten with a cry as another spatter struck his shoulder. Rain—a rain of fire! There was not only one vine. The tree under which he stood supported another. There were more, festooned about him, all sprinkling their poisonous moisture. Ayyar ran. For moments he feared there was no end to that tangle of vine. Then, breathless, he gained the middle of another glade, stood under the open sky, free from that terror for a moment.

Once more he knelt, grabbing up handfuls of leaves and earth with his left hand, holding his sword with the right, smearing that mess wherever he could reach. Red sores remained when he wiped away the moisture.

Move two for *That*, he thought grimly. He might not understand the motives behind the moves, but that they were part of the other's game he was sure. Mankind had played many games across the roads of space, taken boards and counters, and the knowledge of moves and mates in their minds, gambling fortunes at times on skill and luck. Now he was playing a game, with life as the stakes, perhaps more than his life alone. And the game itself, its rules, if rules it had, were not known to him.

If he had any pieces to play, he knew not how to move them or against whom. What *would* be the next move? And from what direction? Ayyar crouched in the soft forest mold, hand on sword, looking round him as might a hunted animal.

Always the hum of a wood that was normal—its hidden inhabitants going about their business. About their business—

Ayyar turned so quickly in the soft earth he had stirred up to use as plasters for his hurts that he skidded and lost his balance. And it was that which saved him. For the sticky line that flicked out at the place where his head had been an instant earlier fell to the ground without touching him. This—this Ayyar knew. He squirmed away, his sword ready. Kalcrok! Not denned up and waiting for what might plunge into its noisome hole, but, far more dangerous, wandering loose during one of its periods between such in-den life.

He heard the snorting gibber of the creature, but there was no warning smell. Another of those sticky ropes dropped, this time across the point of his sword.

The blade flashed and the line shriveled into ash. He
had forgotten the power the sword could unleash. He
pivoted, searching in the shadows for some movement
that would betray the nightmare, only to see nothing
at all. But it was against the nature of any kalcrok to
give up so easily.

Only, he could not judge what inhabited this wood
by what he knew of the normal life of Janus. He could
try to withdraw under the trees where the branches
would be protection against the web ropes. Yet on just
such branches could the beast crouch in waiting—

Ayyar balanced one danger against the other. There
was a third way perhaps. He set the sword blade firmly
between his teeth and ran for a tree in which he saw
no loop of poison vine. His hands caught on a low
branch, and he used old skills to draw his body up
among the leaves.

Now, along this limb, and the next, then jump for
the next tree, always making sure that no poison vine
coiled there. Listen for any rustling behind, a sound
of a horror scuttling along his trail—

The next tree, and the next—Ayyar was not even
sure in what direction he headed. Always he must make
sure that no danger lurked along his aerial path. Oddly
enough, his passage flushed no birds, none of the small
tree-dwelling creatures, the sounds of which he could
still hear about him. Sounds—but not those who made
them. How much of this wood was illusion? His burns
pained him, the one on his shoulder making him
awkward in his swings from tree to tree. He continued to feel no thirst, nor hunger, nor had he yet tired.
But how long that would continue, Ayyar did not know.

He saw now that the ground under the trees was
sloping gently downward as if the wood sank to some
center core. And this made it more difficult to take
the tree road. Dared he try ground level again? He

squatted on a limb, sniffing and listening. There were
growths of fern-like leaves, rank and tall, below in
scattered patches. Like the vines, he found them new,
thus suspect. Their fronds were tightly curled, the
heads like balls, and their color quite dark, a dull green
veined with black.

Ayyar broke free a branch, lay belly down on the
limb, and poked at the ball head of the tallest fern.
There was a soft pop, and it vanished in a small cloud
of black dust. Ayyar grimaced. By so much was he
warned to keep to the trees while he could, until the
ground under them held life that at least looked
familiar.

Perhaps if he climbed higher he could see more of
what lay ahead. If the land was sinking he ought so
to be able to scout ahead.

The fourth tree had what he wanted, a fairly easy
way to climb and an old broken limb, lacking branches,
from which he could see. Below, the ground sank even
more sharply though it was still tree-covered. He gazed
out on a moonlit floor of tree tops, much like the view
from the passage mouth before he entered this wood.

Moonlit? How long had he been wandering here?
Time had no measurement. But the moon, or what
served for a moon in this nightmare, held the same
position overhead. Perhaps no day ever broke here, no
sun rose. This might be a weird sector intended for
Iftin life alone, yet not the Iftin he knew.

Something caught the rays of the moon, held them,
drew them, until they made a glory in outline—

Iftsiga! No, of course that could not be Iftsiga standing there, towering far above the rest of the wood. But
there was no mistaking one of the Great Crowns! Here
in the heart of *That*'s holdings was what any Ift would
seek for salvation and life.

The shimmer of moon on those green and silver

leaves—Ayyar could almost believe he heard their welcoming flutter from where he sat perched in this lesser, this inferior, tree. A Great Crown here!

It looked so close, yet the distance between him and it was not a short one. And what traps might lie between, he could not imagine. Yet that he must cross that expanse Ayyar did not doubt or question.

Could he keep to his path if he descended to the ground where the tops of lesser trees would veil it from his sight? He continued to study that distant tree, striving to pick out some landmark below to serve at ground level.

Finally he started on, keeping above the floor of the wood, continuing to move in the branches. But, in the end, to find limbs sturdy enough to support his weight he was driven lower and lower, until at last the trees about him were hardly better than tall and thickly leaved brush, and he was on the ground once again.

Ayyar rubbed his burned hand back and forth against the breast of his tunic. The brush was thick. To force a path through it would be hard. He was afraid to use the sword to slash for fear that some of the virtue would depart from it. He had to burrow and twist and use his own strength from now on.

For some time he fought so. Then he came through that barrier into smaller, weaker growth. It was as if the roots of the Great Crown ahead had taken the full nourishment of this ground, leaving only support for small, weak things. Still this vegetation was tall so that only once in awhile did he see his goal, the tree. And the shimmer of moonlight around it appeared now and then to distort that straight trunk, warp or veil it. Ayyar believed that he did not front an illusion but reality, his inner warning was stilled at last.

Still the ground sloped toward the tree. Ayyar could see it fully now—tall, silver, alive as Iftsiga, as the trees of Iftcan had once been in the height of that city's glory. It was a promise, a hope to fill his mind and all the world, so that he knew only it.

Ayyar pushed on, unaware of the sharp whip of branches about his body, of the times he was shaken by falls. Kalcrok and poison vine might lie in his path now; he would no longer see them. Nor did he see the chasm that opened before his feet. With his head still up so that his eyes could feast on the tree, he plunged forward into darkness.

XII

Ayyar was seated in a confusing place of fog. There was a game board before him plainly marked with circles, in some of which stood playing pieces, like chessmen, wrought into shapes he knew. There was a miniature Larsh, its hairy face up-turned, as if the tiny, glinting eyes set therein could actually see him. And there were a garthman, an off-worlder in port uniform, and small machines. All faced him from the opposite side of the board in an array that, he knew without being told, meant attack. On his side of the playing space were pieces that did not differ so widely one from the other. Iftin were there, flanked by trees like the Great Crowns.

In him was the knowledge that there was no retiring from this game. Yet he did not understand its complexities, and win he must. Only if he learned its meaning before a final defeat was there a chance for him.

A Larsh figure strode forward on its own tiny feet. Quickly, into the place it had just vacated, trundled one of the ovoid space suits in miniature. Somewhere off the board, out of Ayyar's sight, there was confident satisfaction.

That stung Ayyar into reply. He put out his hand and placed a green warrior to face the Larsh. Unlike the beast man, his piece had no semblance of life. It was a small doll in his fingers. As he put it down in a circle, there was a flash on the board and between the figures arose a barrier, mirror bright. On that mirror appeared the reflection of his Ift, holding so for a long moment. Then the green manikin was gone. The mirror slipped down into the surface of the board. But in the ranks of the army facing him was now a green Ift.

Again that sense of satisfaction flowed toward Ayyar. Yet he could see no opposing player across the board.

What did that move mean? Had it marked the original victory of the Larsh over Ift? The using of the mirror, the transfer of his piece to the ranks of the Enemy—were those echoes of what had once happened?

Memory stirred. How had he come here? Where was *here*? There had been a wood surrounding a tree, and he had been seeking that leaf-crowned beacon. Then—nothing! His eyes were on the board, the figures there. But his thoughts were elsewhere, striving to make some sense out of what had happened. Movement on the board—he must be alert, warned his inner sentinel. This was no time to seek answers but to attend to what lay here.

But who was he to play such a game? He was Ayyar, one of many who carried swords in defense of Iftcan, no dreamer of prophetic dreams, no Mirrormaster. Who was he to—to speak for—

"Thanth," whispered a faint voice within his mind, "the power of Thanth borne hither in your body and in mine—"

"Illylle!" His seeking thought called upon her. "What must I do, Illylle?"

"That which you see to do. But seeing is twofold, Ayyar—inner sight, outer sight. Be not deceived."

Outer sight—the board, the players on it? Inner sight—be not deceived—deceived? He was confused, and confusion was a weapon in the hand of the Enemy.

Board—there was really no board, no thin line of green pieces lined up to face a force thrice their number. He would deny all illusion. Ayyar put out his forefinger, set it on the semblance of a playing board, and willed—

Light spread out from his touch, sweeping across the rows of pieces. Then the board and the figures were naught, and he faced empty space.

The space was filled—with white things that rose out of the ground. He lay on his side looking at a rock wall that was studded with crystals, glistening in frosty light, until he raised his hand to cover his dazzled eyes. His body ached, was stiff, so that any small movement was painful. But he sat up, peered about. There was sand under him, the red, powdery stuff that had paved the valley of the mounds. He put out his other hand, and it fell upon chill metal, his fingers fumbling with the hilt of a sword. He snatched it up as a man in a river would seize upon a log to keep himself afloat.

Inner sight—outer sight? This was outer sight. Ayyar put his head back and gazed up. There was a rim to this ravine and over it dangled a torn branch. He had fallen here in his race to reach the tree. Thought of that jolted him into full consciousness. Only let him

reach the tree and he would be renewed, able to face
aught *That* sent against him! But the game board in
the misty place—what had been the meaning of it? An
arrogant promise that whatever went up against *It* was
absorbed into *Its* forces as the mirror had switched the
Ift piece? The mirror—that was the heart of *That's*
mystery, but one he could not solve.

Now—the tree waited.

Ayyar hobbled to the wall, strove to climb it. He
could manage with the aid of the jutting crystals to gain
part of the way; then an overhang closed the last few
feet to him. Find a better place— He limped along
the bottom of the cut. As he went the walls grew
higher, steeper. Discouraged, he returned, went in the
other direction, only to have the walls narrow over his
head until they touched to make a dark cave.

Back again—if he could not climb the far side, then
perhaps the one down which he had come would offer
footing. Ayyar made the attempt only to have the loose
earth slip, half burying him in a slide of dust. There
was no way up over the wall, only a path in the cut.
And at last he gave in and turned down that open way.

It was not only guarded by steadily heightening
walls, but it also began to slope downward and more
to the right. By that much was Ayyar heartened for
the tree stood in that direction. Then, looking up,
he saw those mighty branches, far, far above,
between him and the sky. He had entered the
shadow of the tree.

More and more to the right that way turned, denser
and denser the shadow of the tree. The old lore of
Iftcan—that a tree's shadow had power to harm— Yet
here, in the heart of *That's* domain, this tree stood—

Ayyar paused now and then, just to gaze up into that
canopy, to savor the good feeling of being once more,
even by so little, in the presence of a Great Crown.

Then the knowledge came slowly to him that this was not like Iftsiga, not what his heart longed for.

Not one of those leaves above stirred. They kept ever the same. He waited for the feel of life, of the out-flowing with which one of the Great Crowns would welcome Ift. Instead there was silence—nothingness.

He knew the dead towers of Iftcan, standing bone white and terrible, heart-rending with the sense of loss they awoke in all passing. That was death as the Great Crowns knew it. And now he would have welcomed that.

For this emptiness was not the death of what had once been life—it was a nothingness of that which had never lived at all! At the same moment that his Iftin sense told him that, Ayyar realized that those banks towering far above his head on either hand were no longer earth but the buttress roots of the tree. He was coming to its very foot.

To his eyes those buttress roots were no different from any he had seen in Iftcan. This might be Iftsiga he now approached, save that that lived and this did not. Like Vallylle, it was false, a mirror-image of the truth, but as hard and lifeless as the surface that reflected it.

Was it both bait and trap to draw any Ift who sighted it as it had drawn him? In Ayyar's hold the sword hilt warmed, from its tip the silver spark flashed. This was the road he was intended to march; there was no turning back.

The root walls were so high they cut off most of the light as he neared the trunk of the tree. And he was not quite sure when he did pass within it. There was such a feeling of loneliness, of being cut off from all his kind—perhaps for evermore—that closed about him as he went into the dark, that he sent forth a silent call born of fear and foreboding:

"Illylle!"

He had not really expected an answer, yet when none came he was chilled, feeling like one who enters a prison and hears behind him bolts lock, knowing that for him there will be no going forth again. But he could not turn back; he was under command as when the suit had carried him into the burrows. Only this was not *That's* ordering. It came from the energy stored within him.

Ayyar passed through the outer wall of the trunk into a space where a thin red light issued from the ground under his feet. It was as if he walked over live coals on a dying fire. Thus he came face to face with Ift again. This time it was not one like Vallylle, meant to allure, to entice. Rather it had a worn face, scarred with a great slash that had healed badly, that of a man and a warrior who had fought—to little purpose by the bitter lines about his mouth. And in his hands he held not a sword, but the shaft of a banner that hung limp, torn and stained from a pole ending in splinters.

Memory awoke in Ayyar.

"Hanfors—"

His whisper of that name was a thin sound. He whom Ayyar had once known and followed into battle did not move but stood statue still. And beyond him was another and another, all warriors who had led Iftin forces in glory and defeat. Some Ayyar knew, for they were from the last days when he, too, had had Larsh blood on his blade. But others were earlier, and yet earlier—

Then a small doubt crept into his mind. Hanfors had led them in defeat, yes. And there was Vanok, also of the last days, and Selmak. But others—they were of the Green Leaf when *That* was still Oath-bound, and they had known the glory, not the end of their race.

Therefore, if this was meant to be a triumph of *That*, it was not one that spoke the truth. And that small discovery was important, though as yet Ayyar did not know why.

Whether he fronted statues or the remains of living Ift set up to so glorify their conquerors, he could not tell, nor did he care to learn by closer examination. Then he saw on the other side a second line of figures, and these were armed—first with sword and spear to match the Iftin, then with other weapons. But those nearest to where he stood were Larsh. Slowly Ayyar walked on, peering at them in wonderment, for they changed. The beast men became different; they stood straighter and taller, their shaggy body hair thinned and disappeared, until he stood at last between those two who were the last in both lines. The Ift wore a type of clothing Ayyar had never seen, yet still he was wholly Ift—while that one to the right was no longer Larsh at all. And the clothing on its slender body was—it must be—a space suit! In its hands was clasped a weapon vaguely akin to an off-world blaster!

But the order in which those figures stood— The Iftin line plainly ran forward in time since Hanfors was first by the entrance. But the Larsh sequence was reversed, showing the slow evolution from the very primitive to a civilization high enough to aim for the stars.

How long then—how long since the Iftin had vanished from Janus? How many centuries had passed for the Larsh to climb and then in turn disappear? To think about that vast roll of time frightened Ayyar. For changeling that he was, the last frantic answer by the Iftin to the stamping out of their species, he carried the form and part of the memories of a man who had marched with Hanfors when the Larsh were part beast. And to cut such a great span of time into years,

seasons— His head spun, and he pushed such speculation aside in haste.

So the Larsh under *That*'s guidance had at last
tried for the stars? But then what had happened to
them, brought an end to their civilization, wiped all
traces of it from Janus, so effectively that no signs
of it remained? While the trees of Iftcan, or some
of them, had lived to guard the Iftin seed? It would
seem, for all the self-confidence of *That*, this very
chamber proved the superiority of Ift knowledge. The
Larsh had come and gone, but Iftin once more
walked the Forest.

For how long? So small a company of changelings—
a handful here, and few more overseas. No nation, less
even than one Company used to muster at the First
Ring. And with *That* now ready to play *Its* game against
them—what chance had they, in spite of all the craft
and skill which had brought them to life?

Ayyar did not want to look again at the lines of Ift
and Larsh. Only that tantalizing thought remained, that
the latter marked one failure of *That*—the Larsh were
gone. Could it be that now *That* wove its own magic
to bring them to life again in its present captives?

There was another doorway, another chamber. Again
the red light glowed, and in it were machines, strange
things, meant, he thought, to fly, others to pass over
the ground. They stood there, thick dust on their
surfaces and piled about them—the dust of time so
great that no mind might truly contemplate it. These
had been born of Larsh brains, made by Larsh hands,
and now they were as dead as those who had conceived
them.

But he was pulled from his survey of the machines.
In his hand the sword turned, pointed to the floor, and
from that position he could not move. Instead it grew
heavier, dragging his hand, his arm, his body downward

as the tip dug into the flooring. There was a crack-ling; light sped out in a star-burst from the meeting of point and ground.

Where that crackling had centered the ground began to sink. It was another platform such as he had found in the valley of the mounds. It moved slowly, creakingly, not with the swift sureness of that other.

Down, he balanced carefully on the unsteady plate. Above, not too far away was the open floor and the red glow. Around him though, it was dusky. There was a jar as the platform grounded. A trickle of earth shifted from above. Ayyar stepped off, and his boots were now on smooth surfacing. He must be back in the burrows or diggings like them.

As he moved to the left, his sword glowed and from the hilt, up his body warmth spread. The platform did not rise to seal the opening as had that other. This time a possible retreat was not closed to him. The sparkle of the blade was not green or silver as he had seen it before, but yellow, and the energy did not drain from it, but, Ayyar was sure, now ran the other way, from it into him.

He went along the passage, guided, he was certain, by the will which had sent him into *That*'s domain in the first place. And he went with rising confidence.

The passage ran straight with no doors along its walls. And the force continued to feed back into his body, making him ever more alert and alive. Yet Ayyar was certain this was no power native to that which reached through Thanth but rather something here that it could draw upon to recharge him.

He came to one of the lock doors, and this was firmly set, past any effort of his to move it until he touched the sword to it. The answer was a blinding light; so he shielded his eyes. And he smelled an acrid, stifling puff of air blown into his face. When he dared look again the door was ringed with a glowing line of molten metal, and at a nudge from his shoulder it fell forward.

Bright as the sword torch was, here its gleam was swallowed up in the vast space into which he came. Close to him he could see upright, slender rods of metal and, resting between them, row on row, packed closely together, yet with smaller rods keeping them from touching one another, were mirrors. They were covered with a cloud of dust. And, as he brushed it aside with an exploring finger on the nearest, underneath was a second opaque film. But it was dry and brittle, flaking off in great ragged pieces.

Ayyar held the sword torch closer. The mirror lay upon its side in the lock hold. But still he saw clearly the reflection of a face thereon—staring wide-eyed, as the off-worlder had looked at the gleaming sheet that had sucked his image into itself. Not Ift nor Larsh, but, he thought, what the Larsh had evolved into. It was a woman with ivory skin and massed yellow hair. He drew upon Naill memory. In the port of Korwar races of a thousand worlds came and went—some of them human, some of other species. Yet this face was unlike any he had seen before. And so mirrored with those staring eyes—it was as if he gazed upon a living thing who might at any moment speak to him.

The Green Sick, which had made of him a changeling, had also bred revulsion against humankind into him, now newly Ift. But what he felt at this moment, looking into those unblinking eyes, was hatred. Why? What harm could this mirrored reflection do him or his kind?

Unless—cold spread through him—from this mirror could be reborn the semblance of the creature so portrayed. Was this what had happened to the Larsh—

they had been reduced to mirrors and kept in storage? But if so—why did *That* now seek new mirrors on which to build servants, as he had witnessed? Here— he swung the sword light—were racks upon racks of mirrors beyond his counting, an army waiting, perhaps a whole nation.

Ayyar passed on down one aisle, but there were other aisles to his right, his left. How many he could not see, but all of them were filled with racks. Twice more he stopped to cleanse a mirror from dust and film. Once a man of the other race stared at him, but the second time he was startled to face a furred head, a sharp snout, unmistakably another species altogether, and one he would have named animal.

Then Ayyar noted that that rack had a red tube end while others were clear without coloring. Now he watched the tubes as he passed until he saw a rack marked with blue. Once more he cleaned a part of the nearest surface, and for the second time a weird face, if one might name it face, was revealed. This mirror was smaller, less than half the size of those that had pictured the people, and the creature on it was white and hairless with a pointed muzzle, small round ears. Its jaws were a little apart, showing fangs—

Wyte! No, not exactly like the hounds he knew, but enough wytes to once have been of common stock. Perhaps the wytes, too, had changed through the centuries, those sleeping here being of a later development. But That still used wytes to course the Waste, and those were like unto the ancient breed Ayyar had known in the days of Iftcan. Then what was this which was wyte and yet not wholly wyte—? He did not understand.

He was a long time walking the aisles in the dust and silence of what could truly be termed a place of the dead. Yet there was other than clean death here;

something which to his spirit stank as the stench of false Iftin fretted his nostrils.

Ayyar quickened pace until he was running through the drifts of fine dust, past rack on rack of the mirrors. Still there appeared to be no end to this storehouse. The glow of the energy which the sword still seemed to attract to it filled him. Almost he expected to see small sparks appear at his finger tips when he moved his hand. But the reason for his coming hither made no more sense than all his other adventures since he had left the Mirror of Thanth, that living Mirror so unlike those which walled him now. Still there was a kind of teasing in his mind, the feeling that there was an answer to all his questions, and it lay before him if he only had the wit to see it clearly. That teasing was, in truth, a gnawing irritation.

There was an end at last to the cavern or the chamber of the mirrors. The sword torch showed him a wall arching overhead, and here was another sealed door that Ayyar did not hesitate to burn free. He had no liking for where he was and would be elsewhere as soon as possible.

The corridor beyond was wider than any other he had found in these burrows, and there was undisturbed dust on its floor. Still the sword pointed him ahead. Then he came to another door and this was open, giving on one of the round terminals with a ladder climbing above. But the sword twisted down, tugging as it had under the tree, but with even more force, bringing him to his knees. Only, what had once been the continuation of the ladder stair there was sealed. Not by any door, but by a jammed mass of twisted, half melted metal. Had it been done deliberately to close off that way? Ayyar thought so.

He tried the power of the sword, but the energy pouring through it could not free even the top layer

of that fused mass. And at last, almost as if the power
which energized that blade relinquished all hope of
effecting an entry, it went loose in his hand. But he
knew that below lay what he sought, the guiding brain
and heart of all this place. By himself he could not
force an entrance to face it, while it would seem that
That's power could easily operate beyond this place of
its source, in the Waste, and farther, through servants
and tools.

Had he come so far into the heart of the Enemy's
territory just to know defeat as Hanfors and those
others of the last days had met it? Ayyar sat back on
his heels, the sword across his knees, studying that
fused stopper. He had a feeling that through him the
power that had activated the Mirror of Thanth to bring
him here was also considering the barrier and other
matters. No one Ift could do this alone. There were
tools, however, within *That*'s own territory that might
be brought to bear—tools known to the off-worlders.

But could Iftin use them? The conditioning that
separated them so sharply from those they had once
been surely would not allow it—any more than they
could approach the port itself through the confusion
That had forced upon Janus. Yet they must reach what
lay below.

There were machines, men with the knowledge to
use them in the valley of the mounds. But those men
were under *That*'s control.

Time—Ayyar got to his feet—this fretting over what
he could not do in the here and now was only a waste
of time. Somewhere, somehow the Iftin must find the
allies or the skill to dislodge this barrier, seek what lay
below. None of them—Iftin, garthmen, off-worlders
from the port—had any future here, save as mindless
servants to *That*. And to meet death trying was better
than just to accept defeat.

He sheathed his sword and turned to the ladder stair. He would have to find a way out, back across the Waste to Illylle and then to the others. Together they would decide. Perhaps all the changelings were from such varied backgrounds that they could put together their memories and so come to a plan. That which had looked through Ayyar's eyes moments earlier was gone, though he had not felt its passing until he was left empty.

Up he climbed, passing two more levels. Then there was more broken metal, some of it hanging in strips, the sharp edges of which threatened him as he squeezed between, to hack with sheathed sword at earth above. Dodging a shower of soil which poured around the ladder, he continued to push through until sun dazzled his eyes and the freshness of open air was in his face.

His efforts had brought him out on a height, and he wedged his body through with caution. A mound crest! Flattened to earth he crept along, shading his eyes to gaze down. The burrows under the earth must have confused his sense of direction, but he certainly now lay on the top of just such a mound as he had seen in that other valley. Or was he back in the same area? He tried to study the mounds about, seeking a landmark. Yes—there was the grubber from the port rumbling into view, no one in the operator's seat. He was again in the red valley. Now it only remained to cross that to the road beyond. But this was day, and he wore no disguising space suit.

XIII

Where were the men who had roamed here before? Ayyar peered between his fingers. Though the grubber trundled along, no one walked or lay prone on the sand. He could not be sure, but he believed that the road out of the valley lay on the other side of the mound. He brought out his leaf goggles, put them on. The glare became bearable. Ayyar looked down the shaded side of the mound.

It sloped steeply, with no fiber of any covering growth. To slide straight down might afford him the easiest and quickest descent—he could use the sheathed sword as a brake. The grubber had crawled on, veered away to his right. Now—!

He pushed over, the soil rising in ridges about him as he gathered speed, a small hillock growing ahead of his feet. The substance gave off a peculiar odor of old rottenness, which made him swallow convulsively. He

loathed the greasy feel of it on his flesh. Twice he braked
with the sword driven into that dank stuff—he no longer
thought of it as earth. At last, with a cloud of it stirred
up around him, Ayyar reached the sand and crouched
there on one knee in the pile he had brought down with
him, listening, smelling, looking for any guard.

This one mound he must set so deeply in mind he
would have no hesitation over its position when he
returned—if he returned. For this was the doorway to
the Enemy, even if he did not now carry the key.

It stood close to the cliff wall at one end of the
valley, the last in line, and it was circular in shape. He
must count the number as he crossed the valley floor,
set its place in relation to the other wall. Ayyar brushed
the unwholesome dark soil from him as he arose, every
hunter's sense alert.

He kept in the shadow of the mound as he shuffled
through the thick sand which puffed up ankle-high
about his feet as he went.

Ayyar had passed two more mounds without seeing
either men or the machine which had crawled away,
when without warning, attack came. A numbing shock
struck him thigh-high, hurling him off balance against
the earth wall. He looked down to see a feathered shaft
protruding from his flesh. Ift! Where?

With shoulders braced to the dank substance of the
mound he managed to keep his feet. But for how long?
Ayyar could not see the bowman. Doubtless the other
could pin him without effort. He tried to catch the false
Iftin scent. There was no breeze here to bring it
helpfully to his nostrils. And the blood was running too
freely from his wound.

False Ift—sword— What had Illylle done back there
when one of the robot monsters had stood in ambush
waiting for them? Ayyar tried to calculate from where
that shaft had been loosed. In his hand the sword

swung slowly as he poured his will into it, for that was the only word he found to describe what he now did. Back—forth—

There had come no second shot. Was the Enemy so confident of his disablement to wish to take him alive?

Out—by what lies within me—come from Thanth—out and show yourself!

He had not quite believed it would work, but he was answered. The shadow of a bow stretching across the sand, then that of him who held it. And the shadow's head moved back and forth in time to the swing of Ayyar's weapon.

Out! He strove to make that thought an order, a cord to pull his attacker to him. Out—here!

Ift, yes, to the outward appearance. But no Ift to Ayyar's nose, his mind. The other came with jerky steps, feet lifted oddly high as if the sand were some flood it must breast to reach Ayyar. Always the green head weaved from side to side, echoing the swing of the blade that shimmered silver in his hand. While through his body he felt the ebb of that strength which was the alien power.

The blank face, its Iftin features expressionless—from what mirror had it been born?

"Come," he called softly, hardly daring to believe that he could draw it within striking distance. Every jerky step spelled its unwillingness to obey.

"Come—"

It had stopped, was teetering back and forth as if caught between two strong compulsions. The hands raised the bow, slowly, so slowly. Was his power over it failing?

He dared not wait. There was a trick once known to Ayyar for infighting. With his left hand he dug fingers deep into the foul dust of the mound, swung his weight for a moment onto his wounded leg, and then hurled himself at the false Ift. The black dust went before him to blind the other. And though he crashed short of the leap he had intended, his out-thrust blade touched the green body, scored along it, if only lightly, as Ayyar went down.

The false Ift shuddered, its bow dropping from its hands as it went into a weird, stamping dance. Grimacing with pain, hardly sure he could make it, Ayyar got to his feet. His fall had broken the arrow shaft, driven the head deeper into his flesh. But he had no time for his wound now. He lurched on, swung once more at the twitching head of the false Ift. There was a shrill sound which hurt his ears, though he was sure it had not issued from between the thing's twisting lips.

It leaped forward, past him, running full face into the mound where it dug its hands deep into the earth. Then it was still, began to slide down, taking with it a fall of soil to partly cover its body when it hit the sand.

Ayyar watched, but it did not move again. Then he turned to examine his own hurt. He could force out the arrow head in spite of the keen pain. And he hoped it would not disable him past walking though he must go slow. He used a strip of his tunic to bind it and picked up the Ift's bow as a support.

How many more of the monsters lurked in the mound valley? He searched the shadows, to be startled by a clanking behind. The loader he had seen cross the river—how many days ago—rounded the mound, came straight toward him, almost as if intelligently guided to run him down. Ayyar limped as best he could around the end of the embankment.

The loader ground ahead, came to where the broken robot Ift lay. Almost Ayyar expected it to hesitate. It was difficult to believe that the machine was not under control from the driver's seat. But it trundled on, driving the crushed robot deep into the sand. Ayyar lifted his sword, though what good that would be against tons of mindless, moving metal—

If it turned left at the end of the mound, there was no escape; he could not scramble away. He had to wait, and that waiting was an endless horror out of sane time.

As the nose of the loader appeared, Ayyar could shrink no farther away. He waited. But the turn he feared did not come; the loader proceeded on a straight course. And Ayyar, using the bow as a cane, limped as quickly as he could farther left, putting the next mound in line between them.

He went as a hunted man, watching. His shoulders were a little hunched, as if he feared the bite of another arrow. The pain of his wound was as nothing to that apprehension.

But save for the loader clanking along at a course parallel to his, he saw no other moving thing. In spite of the need for speed his hurt kept him to a hobble, with pauses for rest. But finally he saw the road down the cliff wall. Did the patrolling suits still come this way?

Movement at the crest of the road. Ayyar again sought cover—but there was only open space between the last mound and the road. The need for reaching the only exit sent him limping to the valley wall. And there he crouched, knowing his choice had been impulsive and bad. There was a company coming down the slanting path. Not the suits of the patrol as he had feared but—women!

He stared unbelievingly. Some of them still wore the face masks forced on all of the garthwomen when they went abroad—the strips of cloth with eye holes and thin slits for mouths making them seem even more robot-like. Others had lost or tossed away the coverings, demanded by the standards of modesty among the garths, and went bare of face. The blankness, the lack of expression on their faces were as much of a mask as the cloths they had lost.

Women from the garths, who never walked abroad by any chance. And with them children! Ayyar drew a deep breath. It would seem that *That* was making a clean sweep, bringing to *It* all the Settlers on Janus.

They walked with the same staring eyes in the same unheeding march that the men had earlier shown. Some carried the smaller children; others led little ones by the hand. Yet they never looked nor spoke to their charges, and the children too, were caught in the spell. It was awesome, terrible, far worse to watch than the first parade of men. Ayyar kept firm his self-control to prevent his staggering out to meet them, seize the nearest woman by the arm, strive to awaken her.

He counted twenty in the party, and they did not pause upon reaching the floor of the valley but continued steadily out over the sand, taking the same path between the mounds as he had followed. He watched them go despairingly. They were no longer his species, and his aversion to them operated as they passed. Still Naill-memory pricked at him, urged him to some action that might restrain them from whatever fate they now faced. Only there was nothing he could do, save try to find his way to *That*, for the control of all this was *That's* alone.

And to do such a thing he must have help, not of those who could be so ensnared but of his own kind. He began to climb the road resolutely, refusing to look back at that small company shuffling through the sand below.

This had not seemed so hard a road when he had descended it, but now he must favor his wound and the progress was a struggle. Ayyar did not know how much of the energy he had exhausted in his knock-out of the false Ift, but he was aware that his strength was steadily ebbing.

Up and up—then he could not stifle a cry as the glare from the shattered bits of the White Forest blinded him. Even wearing the goggles he was afraid to try to look far ahead for any length of time. The sun was hot on his body as he crept along, dragging his wounded leg, unable to lean too heavily on the bow staff lest it break under his weight.

The crushed and rutted way was a guide. And he listened, tested the wind for any hint that there were others ahead. One of the outcrops of crystal was close. He put out his hand to steady himself and snatched back his fingers from its heat. But it was the only shelter nearby. He drew into that pocket, willing himself to bear the heat reflected from it, listening to a crunching that came closer.

He did not dare to look too long, but his sword was out and ready to thrust. Whatever came was heavy footed—one of the suits—or was a machine about to pass?

The black snout that now pushed into view was vaguely familiar. Ayyar tensed. Moving on its own treads was no machine intended for the subduing of land or forest, but one for the destruction of men. This was a vibrator from the defenses of the port, designed to beam at human or humanoid bodies, to break the normal control of muscles, to render the victim for a matter of hours, even days, a helpless jelly! He had not known that Janus mounted one, but apparently the port defenses had been so equipped. And now, like the blank-eyed garthwomen before it, the vibrator ground steadily ahead, answering some summons from the valley which made it more mobile than its human masters had ever intended it to be.

This insweep of people and machines alike meant only one thing to Ayyar, the building of an army. Against what? The pitiful handful the Iftin changelings could muster? Even if they brought the rest of their company overseas, they could not hope to match *That* in open field.

Ayyar waited until the vibrator crawled well down the road before he renewed his painful, half blind struggle in the opposite direction. Suddenly a speculation that made sense came into his mind. Did *That* feel *It* was in danger? In some way, could his own penetration of *Its* burrows have triggered a deep alarm? But no, this ingathering had started earlier—

How much earlier? He frowned, fitting one memory to another. They had awakened to the warning of Iftsiga. The port men had already attacked the Forest. But those men had not been under open and complete control then. The men he had seen at the camp had been normal enough. And the raid of the false Iftin which they had witnessed—then there had been no attempt to capture the garthmen as allies. No, they had not seen this type of control in action until they had called the flitter from the port, tried to establish contact with a mutual understanding against *That*.

This began to spell out the truth, Ayyar thought. *That* had learned of their attempt, and such an alliance was a danger to *It*.

They had gone on to Thanth and wrought there after the immemorial Iftin fashion. And *That*'s answer must be this sweep of off-worlders, this ingathering of each and every person or thing with which the Iftin might make common cause. But again and again his logic struck head-on against the one question he could not answer—what did the Iftin possess which was so feared by *That*?

Once a hero of the Iftin blood had gone to *That* and forced a restraining Oath upon *It*, an Oath that was repeated again at a later date and that held *It* impotent in *Its* own place. Then *It* broke the Oath, and the Iftin of the latter day could not stand against *Its* might. So Iftcan fell before the Larsh. But could *It* still fear that Oath; was *It* now preparing an army of "Larsh" to make an end to all opposition?

The Oath! If there had ever been a history of what it was and how Kymon had administered it to the Enemy that secret had been so enfolded in legend that Iftin of a later day could not learn it. Ayyar had entered the burrows, he had found the plugged stairway, he suspected that below that lay the lair of *That*. This much he could offer those he sought now but no more.

Illylle—he must find Illylle. Then they would cross the Waste, reach the sea and the others. It would be hard to speak of failure, but that was all he could carry them, save a true account of all he had seen. And the others, one of them might have knowledge from the days before he became a changeling that would enable them to make a plan—

Ayyar was very tired. It seemed that with every limping step more of his energy drained from him. Perhaps that power or strength had been given him for only one purpose. And since he had not achieved that, it seeped from him as did the blood stiffening his improvised bandage.

He had to depend mostly on his hearing or sense of smell for a warning, keeping his eyes closed to the glare, though he believed it was now well into afternoon. Night—how he longed for the coolness, the dim comfort of night. How long it had been since he slept through the heat of day he could not remember.

Watch now—he must watch lest he miss the turn to the valley where the true trees grew.

"Illylle?" He tried to call with his mind, as he shaped
her name with dry, cracked lips. Hunger and thirst
grew in proportion to his waning power. There was no
answer, no stir deep within his brain.

He searched for the place where he had set a forked
spike of crystal as a mark. Almost he was afraid he had
missed it, gone too far, when he sighted it. He staggered out of the road, zigzagged painfully among the
shards. The scent of the wood drew him, promising
shelter, comfort.

Then he lost his footing on the slope, fell and rolled,
and the pain of his wrenched wound sent a sharp red
thrust of agony through him, whirling him into the dark.

"Illylle?" Was it his own voice, hoarse and husky?

Dazedly, Ayyar opened his eyes, grateful for a sweet
shadow across his face. It was good to lie there with that
green screen between him and the punishing light.
Tired—he was so very tired. And there was pain— He
tried to lift his hand to his body to seek that source of
pain.

Dark—the good dark—he would plunge into the
dark as one plunged into the sea—

Sea!

He must get to the sea—with Illylle. The shell about
him broke—Illylle—the sea—the others—

It was hard to struggle up. His injured leg was stiff
and too weak the first time he tried to rest any weight
upon it. Ayyar clutched at a tree trunk and drew himself up along it as a man might cling to life itself.

> "Great the tree, green the leaf,
> Iftin need beyond belief!
> Strong the tree, stout the branch—"

The old invocation spilled from his lips. Not that
it held much meaning now. He did not have the bark

of one of the Great Crowns rough under his hands. Yet the words and the prayer behind them came to him, and he clung to his sapling as he would have to Iftsiga.

Perhaps his will, his need, aroused in him the dregs of that energy with which Thanth had filled his body. He was able to push away, to stagger to another tree and another, making his way in such haphazard fashion to that portion of rock and wall where he had left Illylle lying in something deeper than any sleep he had known.

He fell to one knee, straightening out his wounded leg, began to work loose the stones he had left to shelter her. His hands shook, and he had to think of each move, impress his will upon his fingers, wrists, arms. But it was twilight, and that growth of shadow was comforting, just as the scents of his oasis of green refreshed his lungs, starved for Forest air. Four more stones and he could look upon her.

She lay just as he had seen her last, her face wan, sharper of feature, an odd kind of sorrow upon it.

"Illylle—" he called softly, coaxingly.

But those heavy lids did not rise. He could not even see she breathed.

"Illylle!" He spoke sharply, with a demand born of fear.

His hand on her shoulder shook her, and in his grip she turned a little, her right arm falling limply out, so that her hand rested palm up on his stiff leg.

"Illylle!"

Awkwardly he drew her into the open. She was a soft, limp weight, her flesh cold to his touch. He sat there, her head resting against his shoulder, her legs trailing back into the crevice.

Remembering how they had parted he caught both her hands in his, pressing them tight, willing that that

force she had passed to him would now flow back to
arouse her. But there was no answer. Had he drawn
so heavily on that store that he could never wake her
again?

This was a new kind of fear, different from that
which had been his constant companion since they had
left the Mirror. He had feared for their safety and then,
after leaving her, for his own, and now—for hers, but
to an extent that blotted out all else.

Jarvas—the Mirror of Thanth—a man, a place,
either might hold the answer to her revival, and
neither were close at hand. To reach the Mirror's aid
Ayyar would have to take her there, and he could not
bear her across the Waste with his injury. The answer
was bitter. He must leave her here again and get to
Jarvas, not with just the news of *That*'s domain, but
for Illylle!

Moving painfully and slowly, but with as much care
of her as he could, Ayyar placed her slight young body
back in the crevice, began wearily to replace the stones.
He fitted them with the best care he could summon,
using all his skill to hide any trace that would suggest
they concealed something. He did not know whether
the servants of *That* might penetrate here, but it was
possible.

When he was done, Ayyar sat where he was for a
long moment, unsure now if he *could* move away.
Food—drink—where was that to be found? And without either he dared not leave. The green about him
made him wonder dully if some food and water could
not be found. Ayyar forced himself back to his feet,
staggering along, pushing through bushes, under trees
in an almost aimless search. He clutched at a bush for
support before he was aware of the pods ripening
there. Winter it might be in the outer world, but here
was a more kindly season. Fussan seed! He pawed at

the cluster of pods, managed to break one free, opened it and chewed at the seeds within. They were still tart, not sweet, but even their tartness revived him.

He ate and then set about picking the rest of the pods, tying them into a corner of the cloak he had brought from Illylle's crypt.

Water? Head up, he tested the air—the scent of water—? Yes! Faint—in that direction.

He limped heavily on to a place where a spring bubbled through the earth to feed a trickle of brook. There Ayyar buried his face in its coolness, drank, felt it wash from his skin the stain of the burrows and the mound valley. He had no way to carry water. What he drank now must last him through the Waste. Clutching the bag of fussan seed to him with his left hand, his right ever close to his sword hilt, he struggled for the valley wall. East and south now, the stars to guide him.

Ayyar did not pause as he passed where Illylle lay. If he did, he thought, he might not have the courage to go on. So small a hope, yet it was all he had. It was necessary to go on all fours to win to the top of the slope, emerge into the Crystal Forest. But the night was a second cloak, comforting and encouraging him.

South—east—under the stars at a crippled crawl that not only slowed him but also would act against him if he were charged by wyte, false Ift, or any other servant of *That* which might roam the night. He limped on, tightening his lips against the pain of movement. Now and again he chewed upon a fussan seed, making it last as long as he could.

Time passed; he was out of the crystal shards and into the desert beyond. And he was crossing this, watching for every bit of cover to aid him, when a light flashed up into the sky from some point in the east— a beam that might be a beacon—for what?

XIV

Steadying himself against a pillar of rock, Ayyar watched that light. It came from somewhere on the boundary between the Waste and the clean lands beyond. Now it pointed a finger straight into the sky, but at intervals a ripple surged along it. And when that happened, deep inside him, Ayyar felt an answering, an impulse to go to it, though that urge was well within his power to control.

However, as he watched, that pointing finger suddenly swung down, aimed no longer into the sky, but rather across the river at the land where the garths had been carved out of the wilderness. It appeared to hover for a moment before it settled, stark and still, while along the beam pulsations built up faster and faster. The light became so bright that Ayyar dared no longer look. But he guessed it was aimed at some garth, perhaps to summon the inhabitants into the hold of *That*.

Yet the Enemy could not control the Iftin so, and thus they had this small advantage, though who knew what else was abroad in this blasted land, serving *That*, able to influence or capture his own kind? Lurching away from the stone, Ayyar continued his journey at as fast a pace as his wound would allow.

The ground was rough and well provided with lurking places for trouble, so he went warily, sniffing, listening, alert to any sign that sentries or scouts were abroad. Once he heard the cry of a wyte afar off and stood to harken for any near reply. But that was the only sound save for the soughing of a wind.

Clouds scudded across the sky, veiling the moon. It was chill. He had come out of the valley wherein summer abode, and here that season was yet well ahead. Ayyar stumbled on a stone, leaned too heavily on his bow shaft cane and it broke.

Dawn was close, and he knew that he must hole up for a rest. He could drive himself no farther. There was a patch of leafless brush, and with the Ift's instinctive turn toward growing things, he managed to force a way into the center of this, breaking out a small nest, bending branches to close the opening he had made. The need for sleep was heavy on him, as it had not been since he left the Mirror. He chewed upon some seeds, settled his injured leg as best he could, and yielded to that need.

Once more he was in that misty place facing the game board. It seemed to him that the Iftin and the tree pieces had drawn together in a closer setting on his side, as if massing for a last stand, while on the side of his unseen opponent there marched an army in depth. Off-worlders, Larsh, false Iftin, garthmen—some of them pushed forward in moves meant, Ayyar believed, to tempt him into some rash sally. But he did not move; instead he studied the

oddly constituted army of the Enemy, fixing each in
his mind.

Of them all two held his attention the longest—the
false Ift and the Larsh. Iftin and the mirrors— Who
had made the mirror patterns from which these robots
had been constructed? Were the patterns reflected
from true Iftin, captives from that older time? If so,
were those captives still preserved within the burrows,
to be perhaps aroused and freed?

And the Larsh, who had risen from shambling beast-
men to the space-suited one he had seen in that line
under the counterfeit tree. It appeared to Ayyar now,
as he stared at one of those, that the piece changed
in outline as if one image for an instant or so fitted
over another, that the core of the beast was the man—
That puzzled him, was disturbing, for it reversed the
logical process. Once more thought teased him. By the
thinness of a dried leaf was he separated from an
explanation, yet it eluded him.

He waited for that invisible player to move, to
threaten his small defensive army. And then he knew
that, though he sat by that board, waiting, the other
was not here. Yet he felt no elation; it was rather that
the other had set aside the board and his pieces, to
pass on to a bigger and bolder game that Ayyar dared
not essay.

Larsh—Iftin—

Ayyar awoke—if it was awakening, not a return from
a place outside life as he knew it. Iftin—false! The stink
of them was on the wind. He did not move, using his
ears, his eyes to serve him.

His sight was limited by the brush walls of his
hideout, but he could hear. The Enemy did not
attempt to hide their coming: a ring of boot heel
against stone, the brush of a cape edge or leg against
bush, were clear to the ear. Stealthily, moving by inches,

Ayyar brought up his sword; he had gone to sleep with its hilt in hand. He feared that all the energy that had charged it had gone out of him. And without that additional safeguard how could he stand against these robots?

Now—he saw a figure in the gray dawn light. It turned its head, and Ayyar's eyes went wide. Almost he shouted a name aloud:

"Amper—"

Time whirled about him in a dizzy dance. This friend who had once been as close as blood kin, who had stood with him at the last battle for Iftcan— Amper! First Vallylle and now Amper, who had been far more a part of his life. Even seeing his face unlocked more of the Ayyar memory, flooded his mind with an array of pictures, all warm, glowing, drawing him—

The false Amper stood there, but he did not face the bushes where Ayyar crouched. And that fact saved Ayyar, giving him needed time to remember who and what this semblance of Amper was. The false Ift bent his head a little to the right, his attitude that of one intently listening.

Ayyar bit hard upon his lower lip. Let that one turn ever so little and, if his Ift sight was like unto the body he now wore, surely he could pierce the leafless covering behind which his prey crouched, to cut Ayyar down without hesitation.

Far off—a whistling, thin, shrill, like unto a true Iftin scout cry, yet also was different. Now this thing that wore the guise of Amper raised its head and echoed that cry, sending it on, to be picked up in the Waste behind by yet another. A net of the Iftin—hunting him? Or were they merely on patrol, ready to pick up any wanderers the beam drew into their master's service?

Steeling himself against any move, hardly daring to breathe, Ayyar watched as the other lingered. It seemed to him as if Amper might be playing a ghastly game, that the false Ift was well aware Ayyar lay there, was waiting for him to reveal himself when the tension built too high to control any longer. Still that other did not turn its head and look to him.

Ayyar could not believe he had escaped, for the moment at least, when Amper, drawing his cloak more closely about him, darted away, at a loping run. He waited, listening, testing the breeze for any warning of another one of the monster band being close at hand. It was hard when his nerves urged him away, to put more distance between him and that replica of his one-time comrade.

By so much had he learned another scrap of *That*'s secrets—the false Iftin must be mirror-made, copies of those who had once walked Iftcan. Shells, undead, evil shadows now of those who had once been loved, honored, had lived and breathed as did he. It would seem that the Iftin had not vanished from Janus. In one way they came as changelings, in another as the soulless slaves of *That*.

Ayyar crawled from his brush hole and stopped to uproot a stout piece of it, which, stripped of its small branches, made for him another cane. Day, with the sun coming. But he dared not wait for the night now. The false Iftin and those who traveled the Waste were not dependent upon the dark, and he could not allow their advantage to limit him when it came to the matter of time.

Still, as Ayyar hobbled on, he tried to make the land work for him. There was cover enough, the many eroded gullies, the outcrops of rock and brush and other ragged growth, though some of the latter looked so odd and evil he avoided any contact with them.

He huddled in the shadow of a stone at high noon, chewing the last of his seeds, trying to find in their tiny portion of moisture relief for his dry mouth. It was hard not to think of water. Memories of cool Forest pools, of the tumbling, rushing river, haunted him. The wind was growing stronger, and in it was another scent, the salt of sea. He could not be too far from his goal, though where along the shore he would find those he sought, he had no idea.

The glare of the sun was too much for him now. He had to remain under cover during its height. However, there was no cover from his thoughts.

Amper—how many more of those Ayyar had known, liked, loved, were now weapons and tools of *That*? The hall filled with mirrors, all picturing those strangers whose like he had never seen on Janus—had there once been here another race? Older than the Iftin, the Larsh, these late come off-worlders? How old *was That*? Had *It* any age as mankind conceived of age? Had *It* swallowed up, to hold in such bondage, whole nations of others?

The wind filled with the sea's breath curled about him, promised freedom from the stench of *That's* Waste and the things that prowled there. It was not Forest-sweetened air, but the Iftin had once also known the sea and found it good. What did lie beyond the shallow finger of the ocean toward which he traveled now? The changeling Iftin withdrew there each cold season. With the return of spring a handful of them ventured to this shore to set out those "treasures" that would in time add to their company. So slow a way to reseed the Forest race, yet the only one they knew.

Would they ever be able to do that again—with the garths emptied of the Settlers, the port men all drawn into *That's* net? But suppose it would be possible to revive and bring forth the captives of the mirror patterns? So might the seeding grow amain! Could one ever seize *That's* meat from within *Its* jaws?

Ayyar waited out the afternoon impatiently. Then, as the shadows grew longer and thicker, he ventured on once more, his face to that wind with its promise of soon reaching his goal. The land was changing, showing more and more patches of sand. Then, before him, were the dunes. He recalled that bay from which he had seen the log ship of the Iftin depart months earlier, having reached that spot just too late to join the brethren he knew existed but whom he had not then seen. But whether that lay east or west from here he could not tell.

The closer the sea, the colder the wind. He pulled his cloak tightly about him and kept to cover where he could. But that cover was very sparse now.

He threaded between the dunes to the flat outer beach. In spite of the brilliance of the sunset, the sky over the rolling waves was darkly sullen, and for the first time since his change Ayyar found himself preferring light to dark. There was loneliness and foreboding in that sky and the dusky, leaden-hued ocean.

Wave marks laced the edge of the sand, scudding around tangles of drift flung up in past storms. And above, flying things cried desolately as they soared and swooped. A long scaled creature crawled slowly from the pull of the surf, lay as if exhausted on the damp sand, then scuttled with an amazing burst of speed to hide in a pile of drift. Here Ayyar memory could not supply much in the way of identification, for Ayyar of Ky-Kyc had been Forest hunter, not seafarer.

He did not venture out too far on the beach. It was barrenly open there, which made him feel naked and vulnerable. Rather did he skulk among the dunes, searching ahead for those cliffs that had walled in the bay he remembered. A shadow to the left looked promising. With no better guide than that, he turned east, limping slowly, his cane slipping in the loose sand.

Cliffs began to rise ahead of him, stretching into the sand like extended arms, the hands of which were buried in the wash of ocean waves. And from one of those rugged heights Ayyar caught a whistle that was no cry of bird.

That sound drained the last remainder of his strength, as if, having managed at last to come into communication with his fellows, the will and determination that had kept him going seeped away and he could not take another step. He swayed, leaning heavily on the cane, his weight driving it so deeply into the loose sand that he lost balance, tumbled forward, and lay unable to regain his feet.

The whistle sounded again, this time from a different direction. Ayyar waited, almost past caring, for their coming.

Lokatath was the first beside him, to be followed by Jarvas, and then another, strange to him. So, he thought dully as Lokatath raised his head and the Mirrormaster knelt to look at his bound leg, those overseas had come, ahead of time, and into danger.

Ayyar wanted to spill out all he knew, to set action going—Illylle—the blocked door to *That*—the scraps of knowledge he had learned so painfully in the burrows. But now that the time had come for speech, his dry mouth and his cracked lips could not shape the words.

They brought him around the cliff, half carrying, half supporting the body that refused to obey his will. There in the bay rode the huge log that might have been one of the Great Crowns tossed so to be the sport of wind and wave but that he knew was a ship of Iftin. Safe in the small skiff at the water's edge they settled him and paddled out to the opening in that log. He could not climb in; they had to use a sling to bring him in.

He tried to whisper, but they would not pause to

listen. Instead they carried him down a wood-walled passage and into a cabin, which was like unto one of Iftsiga's chambers. Its comfort closed about him as a cloak might shelter one against the bitterness of a storm wind. So he sighed with relief as they laid him on a bunk.

Then Kelemark bent over him, and there was a time of darkness, which was good, which he welcomed, pushing aside thought—

Illylle? Into that warm dark came first the saying of a name, and Ayyar stirred unhappily, reluctant to acknowledge the need to answer. He tasted sweet warmth, healing his dry mouth, his aching throat as he swallowed. Through his body spread new energy and well-being. It was as if he again quaffed Iftsiga's blood.

"What of Illylle?"

Ayyar opened his eyes. Jarvas stood by his side, his eyes intent and searching, as if he could see into Ayyar's skull, bring out the answer to his question.

"She lies in hiding—I could not wake her," he replied. "It was thus—"

Once launched into his story, the words came easily. Ayyar discovered that he could build pictures for the others' seeing, beginning with the journey from the Mirror into the Waste. He told of their finding the true wood within the Enemy's territory and how they sheltered there. Of Illylle's giving to him that which had been set in her by the power of the Mirror, of his journey in the suit, and of what else he had learned in the burrows.

He was aware as he spoke that others gathered behind Jarvas, listening to his words. But it was to the Mirrormaster that he told this tale, for to him in that company Jarvas was the leader.

When he described the mirror patterns and their use, the evil wood of illusion, the false tree and the company under its roots, Ayyar heard their quickened breathing. Then he was interrupted for the first time. One who was behind Jarvas spoke, and his tone carried authority.

"This company of Larsh—tell us again of them—"

Ayyar was impatient, eager to finish his report. But he reacted to the note of command and once again described the silent line of the Enemy's servants, beginning with the bestial Larsh, ending with the space-suited figure of one who was wholly man.

"And these, you say, stood in reverse order to the company of the Iftin, beginning with the Larsh, ending with true man, while an Ift of the final days faced the Larsh?"

Ayyar nodded. Jarvas turned his head to ask of the questioner:

"You believe that this has some special meaning, Olyron?"

"It might. And what was beyond that, Ayyar?"

He continued with the room of the machines, of how his sword had unlocked the lower passage, of the place of stored mirrors. Again he heard the quickened breathing of those who listened.

On he continued to the stairwell, which was closed past his power to open. And now Jarvas asked:

"Are you sure that what you were sent to seek lay below?"

Ayyar did not doubt that in the least or that skill beyond his must be applied to draw that cork of slagged metal. He told them the rest—his fight with the false Ift, the coming of the garthwomen and children, his return to Illylle, and finally his sight of Amper in the Waste. When he spoke of that, he heard them stir uneasily.

Once his story was told, weariness again descended upon him. Kelemark must have sensed that, for he offered a wooden cup, and what it contained was tree sap, spring sweet, to clear his mind and wash away his fatigue.

"So—" Some of the company had gone, but Kelemark, Jarvas, and the man called Olyron remained. It was the latter who spoke. "So, it would seem that the task yet remains to be done." His tone was bleak, and Ayyar read into it criticism of the tool that had been chosen by the Mirror and then failed in action. And he regarded Olyron with answering coolness. But Jarvas smiled, if fleetingly, with a warmth for Ayyar.

"We know much more. And we cannot hope to win a war with a single small skirmish. Tell me, Olyron, who of those with us now holds in his other memory a knowledge of tools or procedure such as would clear that plug for us?"

Ayyar sat up and cautiously swung his wounded leg around. He found it stiff, but only a small ache remained, and there was already a scab formed, no need for bandage.

"To use off-world memory there," he pointed out, "is to come under *That*'s control."

"Then a memory of a memory, perhaps," Jarvas returned. "A memory recalled, given to another who will use it second-hand and not be caught in the web of his own pre-Ift self. Possible, Olyron?"

The other nodded. "It might be. This—this has such tangled roots that it is hard to trace any one stem from their supporting. I feel deeply that the line of Larsh has meaning for us—if we could only read it! And these mirrors that can pattern a man, then build a robot from his image—store it as you saw in the cavern— An Ift you once knew— So do they remain or only the mirrors? We follow a force that reaches us through a Mirror—yet that is a Mirror of water that lives and even wars upon occasions, while these reflectors slay or imprison."

Jarvas looked beyond them—to the wood wall of the cabin. "Tolhron," he said softly.

> "Place of sorrow and of fasting,
> Of evil everlasting.
> Chained are they who lie on Tolhron
> By the blood and by the bone
> Of those who set the spell
> Delving deep into the well
> Wherein all nothingness doth dwell—"

Ayyar saw that Kelemark and Olyron were as much at a loss as he to interpret Jarvas' chant.

Then Jarvas laughed shortly. "Memory again. That is an old tale, one for children, concerning a master of wayward arts who set up a place wherein he kept captives. And they could not be freed because the floor of his prison was mixed with blood and bone over which he had evil control, so that only when similar blood and bone were brought there might the prisoners be freed. I do not know why this rises to mind now."

"There was in this story some connection between this Tolhron and *That*?" asked Kelemark.

"Not that I can remember."

"In many legends there lies a grain of true history," Olyron commented. "And the fact that it comes to your mind now— If only we knew more of the Oath of Kymon! But your idea of shared memory has merit. You are sure you can find the right mound again?" he demanded of Ayyar.

"I made as sure of that as I could. And Illylle?" He turned to Jarvas.

"She can be brought here. Then, I believe, we can

restore her. Two parties, one to rescue her, one to go to the mound—"

"Why not one, picking her up on their return?" Olyron wanted to know.

"Because that one might not return!" Ayyar slipped from the bunk, stood up, one hand braced on the wall. They did not try to hinder him.

Olyron went to the door. "I will ask for any memory that can aid us."

"And what if he cannot find such?" Ayyar perversely saw all the stumbling blocks in their path.

"Then we shall have to do the best we can without—" Jarvas began when Kelemark interrupted him.

"There are tools, all we might need—at the port—"

"A second choice, though whether we could use them is another matter," Jarvas pointed out. Would their revulsion hinder that?

"Illylle had me rub the interior of the suit with leaves. I could bear to wear it then," Ayyar said.

"A good thing to keep in mind. We have substances here that might serve as well," Kelemark replied briskly. "Suppose I collect a few. We have not tried that before." He, too, left them.

Jarvas was staring at the wall again, past Ayyar as if he were now invisible. Tolhron or some kindred half memory again? If they did not have to depend upon such broken patches of Iftin history, they would be better armed.

"It is there—or here—" Jarvas held out his hand palm up and curled the fingers slowly inward as if he would clasp something tight and hold it so. "There is an answer before us in what you have seen, but I cannot discover it! If and if and if—! Are we always to be haunted by ifs?"

XV

There was a pooling of memories, both Iftin and human, among those gathered in the ship. As Ift after Ift was eliminated from that council, Olyron spoke to those left.

"Does it not strike you as strange, brothers, that while we seem in memory to be divided more or less equally between the age of the Green Leaf and the Gray, there are none among us from the Blue, which must have been the golden age of our nation? And that all we have in memory of the Oath between Kymon and *That* is legend only? If those who made changelings of us could draw from two ages, the vigorous Green, the fading Gray, why not from the third and, by their belief, the best—the Blue? Was that time so far back that they could not evoke the personalities of any living then to 'haunt' one of their treasure traps? Or is there an important reason why that age was barred to them?"

"Of what importance is that here and now?" one of the brothers asked.

"I do not know. Save that a memory of Kymon's time could guide us so well. To go blindly into this struggle is to be chain-bound from the start."

"If we lack knowledge of Kymon," Jarvas reminded them, "at least we have that of Jattu Nkoyo." He nodded to the Ift on his left. Out of all the men questioned only Jeyken, he who had once been Jattu Nkoyo, robot-service tech, had training that might aid them. His was the best off-world memory they could find, and now it must work secondhand into the bargain, lest Jeyken, turning to Nkoyo's recall, be swept up by *That*.

"You must not depend too much on what I can give you." Jeyken spread out his hands as if refusing some task beyond his strength. "What you really need is an engineering tech and his tools."

"Since we can summon neither out of thin air," Olyron commented dryly, "we shall do our best with you. Give us what you have, let Drangar learn it from you, going over in detail Ayyar's observation of what may be needed."

"I have been thinking of that pillar in the Waste and its beckoning beam," Jarvas cut in. "It may be near time for supply ships at the port. Do you suppose that signal could bring a ship? These animated space suits came from ships. We found one such landed back in the Waste last season, an old one. There could well have been others."

"So you propose making plans for an assault on the beacon? Just on the chance that it may be of some disservice to us?" inquired Olyron.

"If it is now being used, as Ayyar believes, to pull the rest of the Settlers into the Waste, then it is already a menace," Jarvas replied. "Yes, I believe that we must make that also an objective—for a third party."

Olyron looked skeptical, as if he wondered just how Iftin without machines or tools was going to accomplish such a program. And Ayyar could agree with him. Jattu Nkoyo might be a master robot-tech, but more engineering knowledge than he ever possessed could well be needed to unseal that stairway—let alone down the beacon pillar.

But he detailed for them again his best observations of the plug. At last the one-time robot-tech leaned back and looked to the Ift who would carry what technical assistance he could supply.

"It may be impossible. If you had a cutter set on high beam, you could go for the edge around the plug. Or if the passage below paralleled those above, you could cut through some feet back and drop down. But without a cutter—" He shook his head doubtfully. "You say these space suits still wear their equipment belts, with tools in them?" he asked Ayyar. At the other's nod, he continued. "Any plug put in that way would be too well set to burn out with hand tools—the way the sword energy handled the doors. Doors—" he repeated thoughtfully.

"What about them?" Jarvas wanted to know when Jeyken did not continue.

"This place, these burrows, as you call them, they must have been set up by space men. You had that impression, did you not—I mean, they seemed familiar?"

"Yes, they did!"

"And you came up a ladder, past how many levels?"

"Two."

"Did the corridors on each radiate in the same pattern? And how far apart were the levels, how many steps between?"

Ayyar closed his eyes and tried to visualize the mound stairs. Could he be sure that the pattern had been the same on each level? Never had he flogged his memory harder.

"I think that the next level up had a like number of passages running in the same directions. Of the other I am not sure. There were—no, I cannot tell the number of steps—" Another failure to report, and this one he could have avoided. Why had he not taken greater care to be sure of such details?

"Then—I would advocate a break downward from one of the passages."

"Through this metal lining and rock—using what—our fingernails?" Drangar snorted. "I have dug fields in my time, but that was earth and I had a plow—"

Jeyken did not answer him directly. He spread out his hands on the table top, framing the rude sketch Ayyar had made there of the passages and the stoppered stairway as he had seen them.

"Here is your weak point." The former tech pointed to the door of the passage. "If it is to spacer design, then these doors on all levels will be hung on a column straight down, each above the other. And around here in the wall somewhere will be an opening to repair any jammed control. On a ship a servo-robot is generalized, which means it is bulky and well armored, to work inside or out in space. So it needs plenty of room. Thus a repair space must allow for that and so would be large enough for a man to enter.

"You burn out the lock there, just as Ayyar burnt the doors, giving you access to any control cable. This will be strung in a well, and that will be your passage down to the sealed-off level."

"If and if and if again," commented Jarvas. "Always supposing that this is all made to a spacer design."

"Short of bringing in a large-size cutter, brothers," Jeyken answered, "I do not see any other way."

"But I no longer have the sword energy," Ayyar pointed out.

"Then you will have to capture a suit and get a blaster from it," was Jeyken's reply. "At a high voltage that will cut you in. Now, Drangar, this is what you are to look for—" He went into detail concerning the service doors and the machinery to be found within.

Ayyar slumped on the bench and stared at his hands resting limply on the table before him. He did not believe that they would have much profit from plans that left so much to chance, and guess work. Better accept defeat in this, rescue Illylle, retreat overseas, and leave the destroyed Forest, the Waste, and the off-worlders to *That*.

"We cannot—"

Ayyar raised his eyes to meet those of Jarvas.

"We cannot, or we would! Think you, are you able to set aside the thought that the seeding will fail, that our nation, now only a weak handful, will not have another springtime?"

Within Ayyar was a stirring. The sap drink had awakened and strengthened his body, not his weary mind. Now he knew Jarvas was right, that there had been planted in the changelings the need to perpetuate their kind, to set the treasure traps, to thus produce more and more Iftin. They could no more turn their backs upon that urge than the off-worlders he had seen could escape the call of *That*.

Perhaps if this was to be the end of the seeding, it was better that it came in battle with *That* than in slow decay. He got to his feet. That sense of purpose that had wrapped him, given him confidence when he had left the Mirror with Illylle, had ebbed. He had left in him now only a kind of weary determination to see this to the end.

"Illylle?"

"Kelemark and Lokatath will bring her back after we find her."

They waited upon the night. Two parties left the bay where the ship was already making ready to return overseas, after disembarking a third small force to remain at shore line concealment. One of the parties would go upriver, to deal with the beacon as well as they might. If any of them really believed that could be done, thought Ayyar, watching them disappear among the dunes.

The larger group, with him as guide, headed straight into the same trap from which he had come. His wound made him walk a little stiffly, but without the pain that had made his flight a torturous ordeal. Each of them carried at his belt a flask of oily spicy-smelling mixture that Kelemark and some of the other Iftin believed would overcome their repugnance to any off-world tool they used.

Undoubtedly they made better time than Ayyar had on his way out, covering the ground with their usual agile speed. Always they listened, sniffed, scouted for the enemy. It would seem that *That*'s servants did not patrol so far south. At least they crossed the trail of no prowlers.

"*It* does not seem to care." Ayyar spoke his thoughts aloud as they finally halted, to drink from their sap bottles and eat sparingly of nut meal wafers.

"So it appears," Jarvas agreed, and then he added, "or else *It* is so occupied elsewhere and believes us so weak as opponents that *It* can grind us into nothingness under *Its* boot sole when more important tasks are behind *It*—"

"But *It* began the attack against the Forest." Ayyar

blinked. Had there been a shift of purpose as Jarvas suggested, *That* turning from the eradication of the remains of Iftcan to more pressing matters?

"Suppose that the struggle against a dying Forest is no longer important," Jarvas continued. "Suppose *That* discovered the off-worlders and Settlers, set in motion against us, made such excellent servants for *Its* purposes that *It* could easily forget Iftin and use these to build what lies in *Its* mind. Suppose the Larsh were a tool which failed, that *It* has slumbered through the ages, waiting the coming of stronger metal—"

"But *It* is the ancient Enemy against Iftcan, against Ift—" protested Drangar, almost as if he resented the thought that they were as grains of dust, to be brushed contemptuously away to free a site for the building of another plan.

"To Ift, *That* is the great Enemy, yes. We know that we held *It* static or powerless for generations, until *It* fought us on our own plane with the Larsh. But perhaps *That* has another purpose, and our long struggle merely postponed it. Now *It* has found material with which to carry out such plans."

"But the garthmen, the port crew, have been here for years. Why wait until now to use them?"

Jarvas shrugged. "Perhaps *It* was not aware of them, not until the Iftin arose once more to disturb *Its* quiescence. Then, triggered by old memories, *It* moved against us. It may not even know how few we are. Needing servants to take the place of the Larsh, *It* found them. *It* may be experimenting. I believe that the false Iftin are an experiment, perhaps not a fully successful one. Remember the robot woman used to open the garth defenses? So *That* needs raw material for further experiments, summons it, molds it—"

"And, becoming so entranced with such a quest for knowledge, may not concentrate upon us?" Kelemark asked. "A welcome thought, but not one we dare to build too much upon."

"Look!" Rizak pointed to the northeast. The beacon was on, but this time it did not beckon from the garthland but turned in the direction of the port.

"Still gathering in," Jarvas said softly. "First the garths, now the port, or maybe from a ship there—"

Watching that beam, Ayyar wondered at their own rashness in believing that they could dispose of that, put down even so small a portion of the Enemy's works. And he could not see any success for the party pledged to try it.

They trotted on, glancing now and then at the distant beacon, which showed no change. There was no other sign that *That* was awake and aware. The Waste appeared deserted. At daybreak they sighted the glitter of the White Forest's ruin, and Ayyar picked up one landmark after another. The green valley could not be too far ahead.

"Scout first." He drew level with Jarvas. "I have been thinking if *That* does look for true Ift within its country, *It* could use the valley for a trap."

"True. Take the point then, Ayyar. I will come in from the north. The rest of you, move with caution."

There were five others. Kelemark, his small bundle of healing supplies humping one hip under his cloak; Lokatath; Rizak—of their original company; Drangar and Myrik, another Ift volunteer, from the overseas party. Now they all faded into obscurity, using shadows and the rough ground to cover their passing.

Ayyar moved out, intent on reaching the valley, not from the direction of the road but from the south. The shattered spires and stumps of crystal rose about him, and he had to pick a careful way, not as concealed a one as he could wish. He relied upon his nose, and so far none of the stench of the false Ift or *That*'s other servants had come to his nostrils. But an early morning breeze blew, now and then raising a weird sound in its path across the crystal needles, and those forces might be downwind.

On this side of the green valley the rim was higher. He saw none of the welcome, leafed branches showing above it. Then he reached the edge of the drop, staying as close to the earth as he could huddle, searching all that lay below with a probing eye. To his most suspicious examination there was nothing to signal danger. He found a place that could be descended and started down, these few moments when he would be open against the cliff the most perilous.

He landed, in a leap that brought pain shooting through his thigh, almost knee deep in green growth. Before him were bushes, and he believed he was near that spring with the small pool. Looking up to where Jarvas must come in, he saw a hand raised and lowered and signaled back.

Ayyar moved on under the canopy of the trees. He had rounded one trunk when he came across a trail, and the sight of the crushed and broken vegetation stopped him short. Whoever had passed that way had paid no attention to any obstruction less than a tree, plowing ahead to beat and break a road. And Ayyar did not need to sight those footprints deep in the moss to enlighten him as to the identity of the invader.

One of the space suits, probably of the humanoid type since it left clear footprints, had stamped that path down the valley, one set going and then returning, or so the over-trodden prints spelled out—and some time ago, for growth not quite crushed was rising slowly.

Along that trail Ayyar ran, heading for the narrowed point of the valley, already knowing in his heart what he was destined to find. Those stones he had worked with such care to pile had been scattered in all directions. And the hollow wherein Illylle had been left was empty.

Ayyar stood there, not wanting to believe the evidence of his eyes. His the blame! If he had not left her— Perhaps he could have devised some way of getting her out. But, no, he had gone, leaving her to be found by some servant of *That*, taken off in bondage. If indeed she was still alive—

"She was there?" Jarvas joined him.

Ayyar nodded dumbly. How long had it been since they had taken her? Perhaps if the Iftin force had left the bay before nightfall—had he done so—it would have been in time.

Jarvas' hand on his arm tightened, anchoring him solidly to this spot where the earth was scarred by those ponderous beating feet of the space suit.

"Steady!" That was an order, delivered so sharply that the word pierced Ayyar's turmoil. "What is done"— Jarvas' words were slowly spaced, as emphatic as that "steady"—"is done. We go on from here—"

"To the mirrors in the burrows." Ayyar, remembering what he had seen there, twisted in an effort to throw off Jarvas' grip.

"Perhaps. But what good will it do us—or her— Ayyar, if you run headlong without thought? I do not believe that they can do aught with her while she lies in that sleep—"

Ayyar rounded on the other. "What do you know about it!"

"She fell asleep when she gave unto you what the Mirror had placed within her," Jarvas replied quietly. "I may not remember all that Jarvas who was once Mirrormaster knew, but I know this much, one who has been a vessel of that kind of power and emptied herself of it for the use of another is still under the protection of Thanth. Remember, you once saw the force of Thanth in action. And around you now, above this valley, lies the evidence of how it wrought here. The nature of *That* is a mystery. So also is the nature of Thanth, save that we of the Forest know that to call upon it wholeheartedly in peril brings an answer—"

"I am no Mirrormaster," Ayyar flung at him. "And the memories I hold from the mists of time long past are of death and defeat. Where was Thanth then?"

"Who knows? But dare you, having stood and watched the Mirror rise to our call for aid, say that there is not power to challenge *That*? You carried that power within your body, did you not? And could you deny it then? I say to you, there are paths ordained for us, each with a purpose beyond our reckoning. If it is possible, then we shall bring Illylle forth again. Do you want my formal oath on that?"

Ayyar's eyes blinked, but they did not drop. He nursed this new rage in him, drawing from it a kind of strength that cast out all but the shadow of fear.

"At least this thing has left a fresh trail to follow—"

"Which we cannot take now."

It needed an instant or two for those words to register. When they did, Ayyar jerked free from Jarvas' hold.

"*You* may not take it," he cried, "but I shall!"

"No!"

Again so full of authority was that word that Ayyar paused.

"First the door and then—"

"No!" It was Ayyar's turn to cry out in denial.

"Yes!" Overriding his refusal, somehow by its very tone holding him there when he would be gone, came Jarvas' command.

"Show Drangar and the others the rightful door.

Then we shall go for Illylle. Do you doubt me?" There
was an undercurrent of emotion in the other's voice,
enough to hold Ayyar.

In the end Ayyar won. The sun was rising, and its
glare had long since deadened their sight of the beacon, so that they could not know whether that other
party had had any success against the sinister rod of
light.

Every nerve in Ayyar's body urged him on, but in
the broad day, with goggles for only four of their
number, such a journey was impossible. They must wait
for night or be fatally handicapped from the start.

He tried to work out some of his restlessness on
sentry-go at the rim of the valley, keeping a wary eye
on the crushed road that led through the ruined wood.
This time no spacesuit sentries rewarded his vigil,
nothing stirred on the land or in the air. It might almost
be that the forces of *That* were as bound by day as
the Iftin. But there was an expectancy in the air, a
tension such as a man might feel while waiting at a
barrier for the rush of attack, as if the Enemy drew
now upon all stored strength, marshaling forces, moving
out *Its* pieces on the game board that twice in his
dreams Ayyar had faced.

The noontime glare was so great that he had to
retreat into the valley and seek out green shade to rest
his eyes. Lokatath came to him.

"Ayyar, you spoke of the women and the children
drawn out of the garths—"

Ayyar nodded absently. That was all far, very far back
in time, separated from the here and now by the
dragging hours since he had found that niche empty,
the trail down the valley.

"Did you know—from which garth?"

Ayyar shrugged impatiently. What did it matter?
The Settlers were less than nothing to him. Once he

had been a labor slave, then a changeling Ift, and neither looked upon garthmen, with their cruel, harsh religion, their morose ways, with any liking. "I do not know—"

"I suppose not." Lokatath was studying the broken bushes beyond. "It has been many seasons now; I have not tried to keep count. But sometimes I remember that I was once Derek Vessters, and I see old, known faces dimly, hear voices I once knew. It was a harsh, hard life, so narrow that no sun or moon ever lit to the bottom of it, so that no man sang as we Iftin do who know the joys of the Forest, or would know them if we were left alone. Still—one remembers—and then one wonders how matters have chanced with those one knew—"

"You left close kin?" Some note in the other's voice reached Ayyar. He had his own meaningful memories from off-world.

"A father who sent me to the Forest when the Green Sick struck, and a mother who wept. I remember her tears. Perchance both are long since dead. Garth toil does not make for long lives. I do not know if I would recognize their faces if I were to look upon them now. By their standards I was no fit and proper son. Such strangeness to my kin was what brought me to the treasure and set the Ift seal upon me, for it is true that only those who can be so influenced have any desire to take up the bait and change."

"Listen!" Ayyar swung around, facing the rise that led to the glitter of the shards. He had been right; that was no wind through the splinters. Something moved—along the crushed roadway.

He climbed, crept out into the ruins, aware that Lokatath came with him. Together they took cover in a tangle of fallen prisms, broken trunks and branches.

Men, true men, walked with a steady tramp back up

from the valley. They were not garthmen but wore uniforms, work clothes of the port. There were ten of them, and they strode as if with no fear of what lay either behind or ahead of them, rather as if they were moved by a purpose demanding their full attention.

"Are they robots?" whispered Lokatath.

Ayyar could not be sure, but it was very probable. They were armed with stunners and blasters, but those weapons were holstered—*That*'s servants went on some unknown errand.

XVI

"It may be that *That* mans the port with *Its* servants in order to welcome in a ship," Jarvas speculated when he was summoned to watch that squad march northeast.

"Has it occurred to you," Rizak asked, "that the Enemy may not be native to Janus at all? Suppose *It* came here from space, has been in exile, and now would return. That *It* has reached for ships before, to find such efforts fruitless, and now makes another attempt—?"

"Why then the garthmen?" questioned Lokatath.

"Servants to use on this planet. Or, merely, *It* would immobilize a possible opposition to *Its* desires for now. I cannot forget those racked image mirrors. Perhaps those were brought with *It*—"

"But the Larsh," cut in Drangar, "the Larsh were *Its* servants before. Why not use those on the mirrors if they were available?"

"It might have had several kinds of servants," Jarvas cut in. "But this is a thought to hold in mind, Rizak. Iftin memories are only of Janus, and of the nature of *That* we have no idea, nor did those whose personalities we now wear. If *It* came out of space ages ago, then the burrows, like unto space-ship corridors, all the rest—fit! Do you not see how it is so? And being alien to Ift, *It* could well have no common meeting from the beginning, no common thoughts, for the Iftin were always planet bound, they were rooted deep in this earth, even as the Great Crowns, and they did not wish it otherwise. *We* can understand such thoughts, for we were once men who knew the stars beyond the sky."

"Are we then better fitted to deal with such an alien should we uncover him?" asked Myrik, the other Ift from overseas, a quiet, steady-eyed companion.

"That also we should think upon. Utterly alien has *That* always been to the Iftin. A planet-bound race could well be subject to xenophobia. Perhaps our present revulsion to close company with off-worlders and their possessions is not altogether a device set in the Green Sick to keep us apart from our one-time kindred. Perhaps it is just a stronger strain of what the Iftin always felt toward that which was not of Janus. To them—to us now—*That* embodies all evil, but by other standards that judgment might be different."

"But *That* has always been. The survivor of any ancient crash would not live so long. Kymon was of the Blue Leaf, and he knew *It*. Ages have passed since then."

"How long have you been Ift?" Jarvas counter-questioned.

Myrik's lips moved. Ayyar thought he was counting.

"I was Rahuld Urswin, stat-comp reader for the Combine. I came here in the year 4570 ASF. It was the next season that I took the Green Sick while on a hunting party in the sea islands to the south."

"And you"—Jarvas spoke now to Ayyar—"you are the latest come into Iftdom. What year was it when you landed on Janus?"

"The year 4635 ASF."

"And I landed here in 4450 ASF, or thereabouts," Jarvas continued. "Now, have I aged or have you, Myrik?"

Slowly the other shook his head.

"Therefore, we can assume that the Iftin have a life span far longer than the two hundred years granted those of our particular species. And the Zacathans live close to a thousand years. Among those of the galaxy that we know, they are the longest-lived race. But how much of the galaxy do we know even yet, with all our wanderings and exploring just begun as the stars measure time? There may be other species to whom the Zacathans' span would be a quickly passing day."

"What if such a being could have no common meeting ground with another species?" Rizak hazarded. "What if to *It* the first Iftin, and now these off-worlders, were as animals?"

"That could well follow. We shall not know until we meet *It*. But the fact that we are each two and not one may give us greater power against whatever lies behind that sealed door, for we have memories reaching into the dim past here, and also memories fed with lore from beyond the moon and sky of Janus. And if *That* is not native to this world, we can accept that knowledge to build upon."

All this could be true, but it brought them no closer to Illylle. Ayyar watched the squad of off-worlders march out of sight. There might be others sent out by *That*. And what stand could the Iftin make against the weapons they carried? He said as much.

Rizak nodded. "I guess four hours more of sun. If we try to move during that, we are handicapped. We must wait—"

Ayyar wanted to hack the earth before him with his sword— Wait, and continue to wait! But for Illylle there might be no waiting. He put little faith in Jarvas' suggestion that she might be safe because of the sleep in which he had left her. How did they know anything about it? *That* might have merely plunged her more quickly into the fate of the mirror reflections. Ift hatred and fear of *That* and all *Its* powers haunted him. But side by side marched old terrors from his other life. Science, too, had its demons and dark powers. Almost it was easier to accept *That* as Ift saw *It*, a vast, threatening force of evil without concrete form, than to reduce *It* and make *It* more tangible by fitting it with an alien "body."

Jarvas' hand on Ayyar's shoulder drew him back into the green shade of the valley while Rizak took his place on guard.

"Once more," the older Ift said, "tell us of the passages."

He had gone over this not once, but many times. Why again? Surely they knew it all well. But if it must be— Wearily, step by step, once more he marched through the burrows, retelling in detail all he could recall. Twice Jarvas stopped him, once during his description of the chamber wherein he had seen the port officer's body placed in the container, and the second time the area of the space below the false tree where the lines of Ift and Larsh faced each other.

"It would seem that the bodies of those reflected on the mirrors are preserved," Myrik commented. "Does that also mean that the process can be reversed? If so—what of those who made the patterns for the false Ift? Ayyar recognized one as a comrade of the last days. And the girl in the false wood, she was also one he could put name to."

"That line of Larsh," Jarvas mused. "I cannot think but in that lies the key, or perhaps one of the keys that, if we might turn them, would make us free of what we should know. But for the rest, are we now all sure of the ways?"

They gave assent. But still the sun was too high, keeping them prisoners in this valley. And time marched so slowly.

When Jarvas did give the signal to issue forth, in the early evening, Ayyar broke into a run along the rutted road, hardly aware of what he did until Rizak caught up with him and threw out an arm against his chest.

"Do you want to break your neck, brother, before you have a chance to break one of theirs? Give a thought to your footing here and to the saving of strength for what must lie before us."

Prudence was a hard dose, but he swallowed it. And they came at last into the valley of the mounds. Ayyar looked for some sign of the women and the children. But no one, nothing—not even the driver-less machines—wandered here now, though they proceeded with caution along the rows of heaped-up earth. Kelemark paused by one, scraped off a little of that sour-smelling soil, and brought it closer to his nose. Then he flung it from him and stooped to scrub his fingers in the sand.

"That is not of Janus," he said, "or if it is, it has been changed by some process." He spoke with authority. As one-time medico from the port, he had first been drawn into the Forest of Iftcan in search of native herbs for experiment. Though his Iftin memories were different—those of a lord of growing land—yet in part his interests remained the same and had blended into a whole as a healer.

Drangar looked about with a shiver, drawing closer his cloak.

"All the Waste is changed after the coming of *That*. There is naught here that is clean."

Resolutely, because he knew he now must, Ayyar passed the mound that had given him first entrance into the burrows. He made them pause there and pointed out the hold that opened the inner way. There were numerous scuffings and markings in the sand, but the powdery stuff held no clear prints. He guessed there had been much traffic through here recently.

They continued on to the other mound, climbed to its crest. Ayyar dug away the soil he had replaced to cover the entrance. And then they descended the ladder to the first level. Myrik swung off to investigate the other openings, and a moment later he was back.

"Slagged shut—and by more than just a blaster job. Melted tight."

The passages of the second level ran a little farther but ended abruptly in the same destruction. Then they came to the one where the stopper had been so firmly applied to the stairwell itself. Myrik knelt and ran his hands over the congealed mass.

"Same kind of job as that above," he commented. "And this was done a long time ago, I believe. Wonder why they did not close off the top of the stair as well."

"Who can understand any of *That*'s motives?" demanded Drangar. He, too, knelt by the stopper. "This cannot be stirred. You would need such a blast as would topple one of the Great Crowns."

"Or a ship torch," supplied Rizak. "Well"—he tossed back his cloak and set his hands on his hips—"what about this repair door Jeyken spoke of?"

Ayyar brought them into the passage that led to the hall of the stacked mirrors, and Drangar, Myrik, and

Rizak began to search for the opening that might or might not be there, while Ayyar shifted unhappily from foot to foot, eager to be on his way in search of Illylle.

"Right in this much!" Drangar pressed his hands to the wall and outlined an oblong space. "Ayyar, has your sword power returned?"

He drew his sword, but no sparks flew from its tip; he felt none of the answering flow within him. "No."

"Then we try these. It will make a long job, if we can do it at all." Drangar took from his belt a roll of soft bark cloth. He opened this wide on the floor, revealing small tools fashioned of the same metal as the Iftin swords, intended for working in wood. Could any of them serve against metal?

"Do your best." Jarvas turned to Kelemark and Lokatath. "Do we go?"

Their answer was quick. With Ayyar well in the lead, they climbed the ladder and came out again on the top of the mound where the dusk of night had settled. Lokatath's head was up. He sniffed as might a hound.

"Smell that!"

Stink of false Iftin, strong enough to suggest the Enemy was close.

"There—!"

The flitting of a shadow from one mound to another. But that was not the only one out there. Some must be closer, or that warning would not reach their noses so strongly. Ayyar searched the sides of the mound by eye.

Lokatath shared his suspicion, crawling along the small level space on which they had come forth, heading in the opposite direction, while the rest waited, alert for what might come.

There—Ayyar spotted a shape flattened on the wall of the mound, still escaping any eye from above. It was three-quarters of the way up to their perch. That climber would not attempt to use a bow. He must depend upon a sword, did he go armed with Iftin weapons. But the robot Illylle and he had killed in the Waste had been furnished with a hand arm of a new type.

The spidery figure was frozen on the slope, as if it were aware that its presence was known to those above. Ayyar dared to look away, along the rest of the mound wall. Another, he was sure, that was another just there—

"Around us"—Lokatath's whisper was soft—"and moving up—"

"Back"—that was Jarvas—"into the passages—"

Against his wishes Ayyar obeyed, but he was the last to seek the ladder and drop as far as the second level with its sealed-off exits.

"How many of them?"

"Six at least!" Lokatath made answer. "Doubtless more. What do we do?"

"The other way—" Ayyar's thoughts clung to Illylle and his own mission. "Back through the hall of mirrors, the false wood—" He had one foot on the ladder when Kelemark caught him.

"The others must have time to work—"

"Your cloaks," Jarvas ordered. "Off with them!"

Ayyar fumbled with the neck clasp and freed the length of cloth.

"Flat. This way." Jarvas threw his own cloak on the space about the ladder, to be followed by Lokatath, Kelemark, and Ayyar. Together they now covered the floor and encircled the ladder.

"Now, each of you, into a passage!"

Jarvas' plan remained a mystery, but Ayyar found himself obeying the order. The passage was a short one, the fused metal sharp at his back as he swung around to face the ladder area. He was just in time to see

Jarvas toss onto the carpet formed by their cloaks what looked to be some common pebbles. Then he knew what surprise was intended for those who hunted them.

The Forest was not only the Iftin home. It also provided that race, born and bred in its shadow, nourished by its life, with many things. And there were oddities in the vegetable world of Janus that were as dangerous as some of the wild life that roamed the woodland's aisles and glades. Those gray pebbles were not the stones they resembled but seeds that could be used as a weapon. Would they work against false Iftin as they had at times against the true?

Jarvas was in no haste to trigger them. Ayyar watched him across the space by the ladder, down on one knee, a flask of tree sap ready in his hand, his head up as he listened.

Waiting was always hard, but this was the kind that dried the mouth, set one to the need for moving, to break the tension. Ayyar must stay, sword ready, crouched in his small section of safety, listening for the sound of a boot on the ladder, glancing now and then at those small things lying innocently on the cloth, hardly to be seen in the gloom, save by Iftin eyes.

Sounds at last. Ayyar caught a small movement across from him. With one hand, Jarvas was worrying the stopper from the flask of sap.

Light, not as brilliant as a blaster ray yet deadly in promise, caught the cloak fabric, to be followed by a curl of smoke. Jarvas threw. The sap spattered over the pebble-seeds. There was an instant of anxious waiting, then soft plops, loud in the silence, steam rising where the sap touched the scorched cloth.

Wriggling things burst from the seeds, writhed reptile-like around the ladder, clinging to it. Water alone would have brought life from those seeds, but sap made the growth twice as rapid. It seemed as if those stems reached into nothingness, caught emptiness to them, wove substance of it. From finger size they swelled into lengths as thick as Ayyar's wrist, putting forth all the time more and more tribute vines. They seized upon the ladder as a trellis, leaping up its steps at a speed Ayyar could hardly believe, filling it in, winding about it to choke the opening.

From the vines came a thin orange light. This streamed upward, revealing itself as a cloud of dancing motes. Each of the Iftin in the passages snapped up the edges of the cloaks, shielding their own bodies from that cloud. But the motes did not drift much laterally. Following their nature, they rose vertically, drawn by the promise of outer air in the roof opening.

The Iftin heard nothing as they huddled behind the cloaks. Whether the false Iftin had already been attacked by the motes as living flesh would have been, those in hiding could not tell. But they had put an efficient stopper in the passage to form a rear guard. Jarvas motioned. Ayyar saw Kelemark raise his portion of the cloak yet higher, slide under it, creep to the ladder hole and descend, the others holding steady as he moved.

Ayyar went next, finding that way of escape a stifling one, yet he dared not hurry. He tried to hold his breath, fearing some seepage of motes; inhaled, they would root and grow within a body. Then he was through the bolt hole, waiting for Lokatath, and last of all, Jarvas.

"No sound up there," their leader reported as he came. Above him the cloaks heaved, bulging downward under the weight of what grew there. They had made their escape just in time. Lokatath watched with satisfaction.

"It feeds, or it would cease to grow," he murmured.

"It closes the door, whether it does aught else," Jarvas commented. "Well, so now we must go hunting another way."

There was a ripping overhead. A white serpent of root wriggled free, swung in the air, then writhed and curled up to force its tip back through the same hole, seeking the air above rather than that of the burrows below.

Ayyar relaxed. He knew the nature of the thing they had loosed, but the small fear that it might follow them down had been with him after he had witnessed that frenzied growth. As Lokatath said, it must have fed enough to give its spread further impetus. Robot or not, the false Iftin had not been immune to balweed.

They went to where the others worked on the door. A hole now gaped in the wall, but Drangar looked at the mass of wiring so disclosed and shook his head.

"How goes it?" asked Jarvas, after a brief explanation of what had passed overhead.

"Thus—" Drangar displayed four broken tools. "We do not have what is needed here now."

"But elsewhere there is plenty!" Rizak broke in eagerly. "Those machines stored under the false tree. Among them should be maintenance tools."

"Worth trying." Drangar sat back on his heels. "Let us go—"

He would play guide so far, Ayyar decided, but once there, he would keep on, across that ill-omened wood, back to the place of the captives. And Lokatath, at least, might go with him.

They hurried down the passage into the place of racked mirrors. There they paused several times to wipe away the coating to look upon the reflections.

"How many—?" Kelemark looked about. "There must be hundreds!"

"Or a nation," returned Rizak soberly. "Maybe more." He had halted by one Ayyar had earlier uncovered and was looking at what was not human-oid but furred, with a narrow muzzle. "What was this, another species of intelligent being, a pet—?"

"On!" Ayyar urged, and they quickened pace after him.

They came below that opening in the floor of the place of machines. One standing on another's shoulders, a third using them both for ladder, then Ayyar was above, fitting together the lengths of sword baldrics to give them all a way up and out. They swept aside the dust with impatient hands, explored the vehicles, forcing open long closed spaces that might have been intended to hold cargo or passengers or both. The designs were alien to what their off-world memories could recall, and only dire need kept them at their search, since the revulsion operated here also.

But in the end Drangar had a selection of tools, oddly shaped, perhaps intended for work far different from the use they would be put to now, but better than those they had brought with them.

"These—but—" He glanced at Jarvas. "We could do better with one of the blasters the suits carry."

"Yes, if we can find them. Start with these. We shall do what we can."

At least the space suits and Illylle lay in the same direction, Ayyar thought. They would not put him off again!

Rizak, Jarvas, Kelemark, Lokatath, himself—five to face whatever concentration of power there might be in the burrows. Ayyar did not wait to watch the others take the back trail. He was already at the doorway into the place where Iftin and Larsh faced one another for endless time. Between those lines he sped. There was still the false wood and its pitfalls waiting.

He did not linger, if the others did, to look upon those figures. Now he was in the narrow way down which he had fallen on his race to the false tree, hoping he could find again the spot where he had made that unplanned descent.

Lokatath caught up with him as he was forced to cut his pace to search the other rim for some landmark.

"Where now?"

"Up there. But I do not know just where—"

The other was looking back at the rise of the tree.

"That—that is one of the Crowns—" There was an odd note in his voice. Ayyar glanced from the ridge top to his companion.

Lokatath stood staring at the tree, a kind of hunger, even a shadow of rapture on his face. He began to walk back and down the cut toward it. Ayyar caught his arm and held him so as the other three joined them.

"Do not look at it," he ordered. "It is a lure to pull you!"

Involuntarily the others looked up. But Jarvas instantly turned his face away. Like Ayyar with Lokatath, he caught at Kelemark and Rizak.

"He is right. That is a deadly thing for us! Turn!" He pulled and shoved them along. "Do not look at it!"

Yet the temptation worked in them all and had to be fought. Ayyar no longer tried to locate the right place on the opposite earth wall. He merely wanted to get up, anywhere.

Again they stood one upon the shoulders of another and so reached the top. Each aiding the other—so they came into the wood. And there might be other pitfalls than those Ayyar had already encountered.

Single file they worked their way under the canopy of green that was false in its welcome, where they must look upon all as suspect. Following Ayyar's example, when they reached the real trees, they climbed aloft, using every patch of shadow as cover in reaching the distant wall and the entrance to the burrows.

XVII

There was a difference in the wood. Those sounds that had lulled Ayyar's suspicions were now stilled. The Iftin moved in silence, save for the noise made by their passing. Yet it was not a waiting silence, as if a trap beckoned them. Rather it was as if that which had animated this place had been turned off or withdrawn. And Ayyar commented on that to the others.

Jarvas steadied himself on a wide branch before making another leap. "Withdrawn?" he repeated thoughtfully. "As if, perhaps, there were a need for concentration elsewhere. But where?"

"At the door Drangar seeks to force?" suggested Lokatath.

"Perhaps. Yet I am not sure. *That* makes a bid for power, all power now. It is sending *Its* servants out, rather than massing them here for defense."

"All the more reason for us to hurry." Ayyar led the

way up the slope. Already they were skirting the place
where the poison vines hung heavy in the trees. He
found himself listening, watching, for the false Vallylle.
But if she still walked this evil wood, she did not seek
their company. And, somewhat to his surprise, they
reached the wall below the burrow mouth with no
challenge from any creature of the Enemy. The passage down the cliff was still missing. But they did not
hesitate to hack at the trees, trimming their spoil to
make a crude ladder.

As they entered the burrow above, they hesitated,
nostrils wide, eyes alert. Disgusting odors in plenty, or
so they seemed to Ift, came out of the corridor. It was
hard to identify any one smell. Jarvas spoke:

"Machines—"

"Chemicals," added Kelemark, sniffing.

"No false Iftin, I think," Lokatath began.

Rizak put his hand palm flat against the wall of the
passage.

"Power flows here. This place is alive with energy."

Jarvas followed his example, then snatched back his
hand as if the vibration were a searing burn for his
flesh.

"The crystal panels," Ayyar warned. "I think they are
alarms; we must avoid them."

As far as he could see the passage ahead by the
wan light, it was empty. He slipped past Jarvas to
lead again, dropping to his knees to pass the first
pair of crystals.

"This is the room where they store the bodies," he
said a little later, pausing by that door. Kelemark
pushed past him and stood staring at the lines of
containers.

"More—there are many more of them now filled,"
Ayyar whispered. "When I was here before, only four
in this line were occupied—now all are completed!"

"Where do they make the mirrors?" demanded Jarvas.

Kelemark had gone to the nearest cylinder. He put his face very close to its surface, his hands cupped about his eyes. He shook his head. "It cannot be seen—"

"The mirrors—" pressed Jarvas.

Illylle! That sent Ayyar racing down the corridor. He had to force a curb on his reckless need to get her out of this place—if he still could.

"Let me see the place where they grow the robots!" Kelemark ordered as if he were now in command of the party. But Jarvas held up his hand:

"First the mirrors!"

Ayyar was cautious enough to halt before he passed any of the doors, listening, sniffing for trouble. So far there had been nothing, no stir of any space suit in action. Save for the feeling of life in the walls about them, the Iftin invaders might have been walking through halls as deserted as those leading from the false Great Crown.

They came into the place where he had witnessed the making of the reflections. The table there was unoccupied, nor were there now any mirrors on the wall! But there were suits—two of them.

Ayyar signaled caution. The suits were humanoid, yet not of a type he knew. One had an arm twisted and snapped off short a little below the shoulder plate. The ends of that break slagged into a blob of battered metal. The other lacked a helmet.

When neither of the metal cripples moved, Ayyar decided they were harmless. Rizak crossed warily to examine them. Once an astro-navigator on a spacer, his acquaintance with such aids to stellar voyaging was far greater than Ayyar's. But now he shook his head.

"Nothing such as these have I seen before."

Ayyar went to the table, bent his head, and sniffed long and hard. There was odor of garthman, undisguised, and of the port men. But not Ift—at least not so lately that it had not been completely overlaid with the effluvia of the others.

Yet Illylle must have been brought here. From the deserted mirror room Ayyar sped to the laboratory, where he had witnessed the growth of the false creatures. The stench was a blow in the face, but the tables here were also empty. No jelly bubbled on a mirror bed.

Kelemark sniffed deeply, in spite of the torture to his Ift senses.

"Some form of plasta flesh—proto base—" he reported.

There was that third room Ayyar remembered in which he had seen the false Ift body being fitted with wires, up corridor. There he went now, to find it empty.

"Where—?" He knew that Jarvas, the rest, could give him no better answers than his own mind could supply. Maybe—Ayyar's head swung sharply around—maybe not his mind but his nose!

There were other doors along the corridor, and from one of them—it must be from one of them—came that scent, so faint in this place of ugly odors, yet to be traced. Illylle—surely Illylle!

Sniffing, rejecting, sniffing, Ayyar prowled along. Illylle or Ift—but there were other smells, strong, piercing as a pain when he breathed them in. Garthpeople—here—here— Ayyar's head swung from side to side at two closed doors facing one another across the hall.

Illylle—Ift—to the right! His hands went to the door, strove to push it, first inward, and then to either right or left. But it was as immobile under his hands as if it had been sealed by slagging. Lokatath joined him, then the others, all with their nostrils distended as they followed that same faint scent.

"Locked," Jarvas decided.

"Wait!"

As if they could do anything else, Ayyar thought impatiently. Rizak ran back toward the chamber of the mirrors. Ayyar continued to push at that stubborn portal, but it only wore out his strength uselessly. If only that which the Mirror of Thanth had planted in him had not been so exhausted. Thanth!

He stopped his vain fight with the door and glanced at Jarvas. "You are Mirrormaster. What can be summoned now from Thanth to our aid?"

Jarvas stared back, almost as if that demand had come as a shock. Then he looked thoughtfully at the door. "If you no longer hold the power, there is naught Thanth can do—"

"No?" The Mirror had sent him here filled with the substance of its force. And Illylle had given him a double portion when she had sent him to fulfill their mission. He had failed at the fused stairway. Then the power had ebbed with every step of retreat from that failure. But now, cried Ayyar silently, I have returned. I am here to do whatever is needful to free Janus from this burden long laid upon her clean earth. I have not deserted the quest or fled battle. I have returned with fresh forces!

He closed his eyes, trying to visualize the ledge above the Mirror, the great sparkling tongue rising from its surface to touch upon Illylle and then him, choosing them as fit receptacles of whatever force did enter into Janus through Thanth. He did not know that he had drawn his sword, that its point rested on the floor of the corridor between his firmly planted feet, that his two hands were clasped on its hilt.

In those moments when he had stood before the Mirror and watched it in action, he had known awe, belief in something beyond his powers to understand or explain. How much of that was inherited from the

Ayyar who had been he did not know, nor even if that belief itself was so strong in him once he was removed from the Mirror where the united worship of the others had been a part of what he had seen and felt.

The Mirror, that reaching finger or tongue of sparkling water that had risen from it—Ayyar tried to will to life that tingling which had coursed through him.

He was out—no longer in his body—but in a space like unto that where he had sat across the game table from that other presence, he had never seen, save that this space was not the same, nor was the presence he sensed now—in any way.

> "Green the growth, deep the seed.
> Stand high a Tree, to Iftin need.
> Sweet the wind, soft the rain—
> Rich the soil, without bane—"

Green growing about his feet, up and up, he did not have to see those plants. They were a part of him, like his blood, his flesh, and the bones beneath them were a part. As if he, too, put roots into the soil, drew life and nourishment from it? Around him blew a wind as caressing as the dawn winds of summer, and on his cheeks, his lips, was the soft, refreshing touch of gentle rain, satisfying all thirst, all hunger.

> "Straight the sword, sharp the blade.
> Bright the leaf that does not fade.
> Still the Mirror, wide and deep,
> High the Moon that doth keep
> Silver caught within the Mirror.
> Stand here, Ift, without fear.

He could not see Thanth with the eyes of his body. But it was there—deep, dark, yet silver where it caught

and held the moon. That moon's reflection shivered and
broke into a thousand silver motes, free and floating.
They arose and were one with the wind, the soft rain.
So were they borne to him, gathering about his body—
entering—

> "Iftin sword, Iftin hand,
>   Iftin heart, Iftin kind!
>   Forged in the dark,
>   Cooled by the moon—"

That was the Lay of Kymon, Kymon who had walked
the blazing white, searing paths of the Enemy, and
returned therefrom with the Oath for the safety of his
people. Ayyar did not sing that, the chant came from
without and beyond.

> "Borne by warrior who will stand—
>   When tree grows and *That* will fall.
>   Iftin swords, Iftin hands—
>   Come to save and cleanse a land!"

The sparkling silver touch of Thanth was once more
within him. As he had before, he felt that strange life
allied with his own, and he exalted in it. Ayyar opened
his eyes to face Jarvas. And the Ift who had once been
Mirrormaster and so able to call upon the power looked
back with a depth of concentration, a willing. His lips
moved as if he would speak, but at first he did not utter
a sound. Then he said:

"Power has returned to you, brother."

"It has returned." Ayyar raised his sword with confidence and traced the outline of the door. A bright
line followed the touch of that point, easing away the
substance. Ayyar put out his hand, and the door fell
away, back into the locked chamber, just as Rizak

came up with a blaster from one of the suit belts in his hand. Jarvas waved him back, and they stepped into the room.

The occupants lay on the floor as if they had been struck down without warning—women, children, perhaps those Ayyar had seen enter the valley of the mounds—garthpeople all of them, yet his nose told him that among them was an Ift. They found her in a far corner, as if she had been flung there in haste, some broken machine for which *That* no longer had any use.

Jarvas gathered her up and carried her into the corridor, held her while Ayyar took her two limp hands into his. As she had willed her Mirror-born strength into him, so did he now return that with which he had been newly filled to her. And he heard them chanting softly:

> "First the seed, then the seedling.
> From the rooting to the growing.
> Sap of trunk, stir of leaf,
> Ift to Tree, Tree to Ift!"

Kelemark held a flask to her lips, dripping sap drops between them. Then Illylle opened her eyes and looked at them, at first in an unfocused stare, as if she still saw, not them and the burrows, but another place in which she had been long lost and wandering.

"Illylle!" Ayyar called gently, but yet as one arousing a comrade at the first alarm of battle.

Now she saw him, knew him, moved in Jarvas' hold. And her eyes were anxious.

"Do you not feel it?" her voice was strained and hoarse. "*That* knows!"

They glanced about them as if they were suddenly beleaguered by Enemy forces, for she was right. That silence, that lack of watchfulness, that emptiness

through which they had come had vanished. They were
now discovered.

"Come." Jarvas, his arm about Illylle in support, led
them past all the other chambers. Ayyar saw Rizak and
Lokatath drop behind, dart into the doors they passed.
When they returned, they bore not only the blaster
Rizak had already found, but also two more strange
weapons, but clearly designed as arms.

All that time they listened for what might march
upon them, watched for any sign of movement ahead
or behind. But they reached the false wood aware only
that *That* was conscious of them in the midst of *Its*
own place. Ayyar wondered uneasily why the ruler of
these burrows held off from attack, why *It* had not
overwhelmed and crushed them as *It* might have so
easily done, for, Mirror power or not, they could not
stand up to the off-world weapons in *Its* arsenal.

There was a change in the place of the wood. That
unaltering moon that had been such a relief to Ayyar's
eyes on his first journey across that sinister jungle was
gone. The dark was that of a stormy night. But in the
dusk his bared sword gave forth a steady glow, and as
they descended into the wood, the growth drew back
and away from the brand, which it had not done
before.

Illylle put forth her left hand and laid it on Ayyar's
shoulder, saying:

"Link, brothers, link. I do not know why it may be,
but in this hour that which speaks through the Mirror rises in all of us. Perhaps it may in turn draw upon
the very forces here to feed. Link, one to the other,
so that it may flow equally through us all!"

Her touch drew nothing out of Ayyar as he had
thought that it might. Rather did there follow a new
warmth and confidence. They did not take to the
trees but went steadily ahead by the shortest path to

that tree which aped the Great Ones with such evil travesty.

Things fled from their path or perhaps from the light of the brand, and once they heard a moaning call, like unto an Iftin voice, but with no words they could understand. Then did Illylle turn her head to that portion of the underbrush whence came the sound. And she chanted what could be an answer, a counterspell, or a warning. The words were not of the common speech, and Ayyar knew that they came to her out of the far past when Illylle had been a Sower of the Seed, thus one who dealt with the beginning of life and not its ending, while this place in which they walked negated life with counterfeit shadow and so was to be faced only by the real.

They continued without hindrance, though a part of Ayyar's mind continued to wonder and be alert for any sign of trouble, to the tree and into that place where stood the lines of Iftin and Larsh, frozen so for eternity.

As they passed between, Illylle and Jarvas, inspired by something Ayyar did not share, out of the old mysteries of which they had once been a part, turned their heads to certain of the Iftin and greeted them by name in such tones that Ayyar half expected those statues (if statues they were in truth) to step from that company and join theirs.

Next they went through the place of machines and down into the corridor that brought them to the vast room of mirrors. There for the first time Illylle faltered. She dropped her hold upon Ayyar and Jarvas, breaking their linkage, holding up her hands before her eyes as if she dared not look upon the racks, crying out:

"These are the children of *That*! Let them be shattered, and it will come to an end!"

Then, once more, her trembling hands came out to Jarvas and Ayyar, but she would not look upon the mirrors, shutting her eyes tightly, letting them guide her. And she did not cease trembling until they were out of the chamber.

For the first time they heard sounds—from behind and also ahead. They began to run to the place where they had left Drangar and Myrik. What came from there, Ayyar was sure, was the sound of battle. Of a sudden his sword blazed, yet the brightness did not hurt his eyes.

A tangle of wiring twisted and broken had been dragged from the service door into the corridor. And in the midst of that lay Drangar, dead, while, flattened to the floor, among the coils, was Myrik, pinned by beams that laced back and forth. As one, the others threw themselves down behind that tangle that was so poor a shield. Rizak and Jarvas had blasters and began a counter sweep.

Myrik raised his head. "The door—if we can get through—"

They had done well with the tools from the storage place. Ripped out were all the cables and fittings that had once filled the shaft. Ayyar hesitated to descend without knowing what might wait below—yet to remain here, pinned by those ahead, hunted by what moved from behind—

"I go!" Lokatath crawled to the opening, entered feet first, then sank from sight, but slowly, as if there was something in the way of hand and footholds within.

"You—" Ayyar pushed Illylle to that only promise of safety.

She did not protest, but went. And after her, Myrik, and Kelemark followed. Jarvas spoke to Ayyar—

"You!"

He and Rizak still replied to the beams of destruction

with the counter rays from their weapons. And now there were lulls in that exchange of fire.

Sheathing his sword, Ayyar wriggled through the opening. The shaft was not as confining as he had expected, and torn-off projections of metal and wire gave him foot and hand supports. Then his feet touched more wires, and he had to work a passage through this obstruction, crawling on hands and knees into a corridor twin to that above. Those who had preceded him were alert and waiting. That force which enlivened the walls of the other portions of the burrows was here much greater. The whole of the space around them throbbed with it. When Ayyar ventured to touch the wall, energy ran painfully up his arm, so that he cried out. Instinctively his other hand had gone to his sword hilt. Now the scabbard that held the blade smoked until he snatched it forth from that covering.

The length of well-forged metal was blue and green, then both colors together, rippling, dripping sparks that vanished as they hit the floor. Ayyar was no longer sure that it was fed by the energy stored in his body or whether it now fed him. But he was not its master. No, now it was the wielder and he the weapon. Under the compulsion it wrought, he turned away from the rest of them and marched back down the corridor.

He expected to confront danger. He was not surprised nor, oddly enough, alarmed when things moved out of the gloom to intercept him. They came with a steady purpose to match his. And, without his willing it, his sword raised waist high, point outward. The force in it grew so strong that it jerked and quivered, so that the only way Ayyar could continue to hold it was to turn that movement into a swing, right and left.

They were armed, those thundering, stalking machines. There were beams that bit into the walls where they chanced to touch; there were other energies. But that waving, dancing sword set up a barrier of its own force to stop, to suck, to feed— for feed it did, and the backlash of that feeding was in Ayyar. Once he had been man, then Ift; now, thought a small part of him, he was a vessel of energy, alien to the place in which he walked in that he could draw upon the Enemy's strength to give fuel to his own.

The machines continued to attack until the light from the sword touched them. There were blazes of shorting wires, the acrid smell of destruction. He pushed past them, stepped over them, to advance.

How many did he meet in that corridor? Ayyar did not count; there was no need. In him was only the compulsion to move ahead, seek that will which lay behind the machines, behind this plague spot that sickened Janus.

The passage ended, and he stood in a great chamber, near its roof, he thought, with dark below. He was on a platform from which descended a curling stairway. Down that the sword pointed, and he must go. This whole place was charged with force, and Ayyar wondered dimly if he would end as Man or Ift, burned out by the weapon he bore, which yet had not been used as it must be. Round and round the steps he went, down and down. Now his eyes were no longer dazzled by the raying, and he could see what lay below, built up against the walls, clicking, flickering with small lights, filling all the vast place with a moaning hum. Sections of it were dark, dead, perhaps long dead. But others were very much alive, with something inimical to all living flesh and blood. Naill-memory supplied an answer, for Ayyar memory had never seen machines mankind had built to supplement brain power. He was descending into the heart of the largest computer he had ever seen or dreamed might exist.

XVIII

"Computer!" Myrik's voice rose above the hum that filled the place as the murmur of wind in leaves filled the Forest.

Ayyar faced the great banks of flashing lights. The sword and the power had led him here. But what weapon was it against this, no thing which could be put to rout by any attack that he knew. Unless—who had set this giant brain to running? He was the Enemy!

He began to run along the towering wall of machine, came to a corner to front another section at right angles, turned along that to face another, and eventually returned about the square to join the others by the stairway. There was no other exit from this chamber, nothing here but the machine—part of it running, part dark and dead. Baffled, Ayyar came to a halt, still unable to believe there was no Enemy to front.

"Computer"—Jarvas studied the walls—"and programmed."

Myrik walked, not ran, along the same path Ayyar had taken, surveying closely each bank as he passed it.

"It is a computer, yes. But of no type I have ever seen—and it has been programmed, is in operation, part of it. Also, I think that it has once before been interrupted in the task set it. Come here—"

He motioned and they followed, almost timidly, to one of the dark sections. There he pointed to lines burned into the fabric of the machine. There was fusing, signs that repairs had been made—perhaps more successfully—in a neighboring section now working.

"Those machines Ayyar knocked out in the passages," Myrik said, "were servos—for computer repairs. I would say they have been on duty here perhaps longer than we can guess."

"Kymon!" Illylle's voice shrilled. "Kymon was here! But a machine—why—?"

"It was intended"—Jarvas moved out into the open area in the center—"for some great and important task. And it is not Iftin. Once it was half destroyed; now it is partially at work again. And we have seen the results of that work. It was set a task, which it strives to carry out—"

"But who set it?" queried Illylle. "Who or what is *That*?"

Rizak had gone to the nearest wall and was watching the lights in motion there. "I think," he said slowly, "that this is what we seek."

"This is what I was sent to find!" Ayyar broke in, as sure of that now as if someone had spoken in his ear.

"I do not think it was ever programmed on Janus at all!" Jarvas added. "It is not Iftin in any part. And we cannot but believe that Ifts are truly native to this world; they are so one with its nature. Therefore, this is alien—"

Rizak laughed a little wildly. "Did it ever occur to you, brothers, that what we stand in now might be a part of a ship—a long planeted ship?"

"Ship?" echoed Kelemark. "This—this *big?* What kind of ship could be so large?"

It was Lokatath, perhaps because he had once been a garthman, who ventured to answer that.

"A colony ship?"

Jarvas turned sharply, but Rizak spoke first:

"Could just be! A ship, with a computer programmed for colonization duties, perhaps never meant for Janus at all, making a crack-up landing here. Then the computer taking up its duties—not properly, under the circumstances."

Jarvas caught him up, speaking out of the knowledge of Pate Sissions, First-in Scout, one who had been the forerunner of such flights for those of his own species.

"Trying to alter the country to fit the needs of alien colonists. Ready to put down whatever would be inimical to settlement—"

"Such as the Iftin!" broke in Lokatath.

"And Kymon," Illylle added quickly, "coming here, armed with power, perhaps doing this—" She pointed to the bands of ancient destruction. "Then it was repaired after a long time. But why would it come to life again now?"

"Perhaps it has been alive all the time," Ayyar said, "but crippled, and it did not sense an enemy until the Ift changelings went abroad in the land. Why did it not rouse the colonists—or were they all killed in the crash?"

"The mirrors!" Illylle's eyes widened. "The colonists are the people on the mirrors."

"A reasonable assumption," Kelemark agreed. "And now it will be my turn to guess. You were right, Jarvas, when you claimed there was much to be read in those companies at the foot of the false tree. I do not know why the Iftin were set up there—but the Larsh—they were not the beginning but the end!"

It would seem that Jarvas understood, for the one-time Scout nodded. "De-evolution, not evolution. The computer aroused some of the passengers, found that there was that on Janus it could not change, could not alter. Though I imagine that all the resources left it have been turned to that task ever since—"

"What are you talking about?" Lokatath demanded.

"The ones it aroused did not remain the same," Jarvas explained. "They must have slipped back, generation by generation, from men—or what we may term 'men'—into the less-than-men we remember as the Larsh. And finally the Larsh were thrown against us to free Janus from any interference while this machine labored to fashion a new world, one that would safely accommodate its burden. But it was crippled—perhaps actually by Kymon of the legend."

He looked at the ancient sear marks. "We may never know whether those represent the coming of our folk hero or not. But the destruction was certainly deliberate, and it must have taken a long time to repair, even in part."

"But it failed—that destruction—" Myrik mused.

"Because," Rizak broke in, "it was wrought by an Ift, not one who knew the real meaning of this. He may have sprayed some energy back and forth, wrecking widely, but not to the roots—the heart of the machine."

"But the Oath, what then was the Oath?" asked Illylle.

Jarvas shrugged. "What history does not take on embroidery when it becomes heroic legend? I do not think that Kymon, the Ift, could explain, even to himself, what he found here—if this *is* where he fronted *That* in all *Its* might. Now we must have an answer to something else—what do we do? Myrik, Rizak, what do we do?"

"We can cripple it as was done before. But again that might prove to be but temporary, if you reckon centuries as temporary. If this was programmed to do what we guess it was, then it has also been provided with safeguards and repairs. And we do not know what lies in all these burrows. No, we have to find the heart control, wherever that lies, and burn it out for all time!

"Jarvas." Illylle took a step forward and laid her hand on his arm. "What of those it controls, made into mirror patterns and then robots? Can they be restored—saved?"

He did not meet her eyes. "Perhaps no, perhaps yes. But for that we must have both time and knowledge. And with this running, ruling the burrows and the Waste, able to muster an army against us—time we do not have. The machine first—"

They were all agreed upon that. Ayyar lifted the sword. Should he use the energy in that weapon to blast the banks around him? He had taken a step toward the nearest when Rizak thrust out his arm as a barrier before him.

"Not there!" He looked not at Ayyar but at the banks of lighted, clicking relays on the nearest wall.

"Where then?" Ayyar demanded. All he knew of computers was their servicing, not their innermost workings.

"We do not know," Myrik returned. "This thing runs the burrows—it controls ventilation, everything else. Smash it and it could close doors, stop air, bury us— and still we might not finish it off. We cannot move until we are more sure—"

"Look!" Illylle called sharply. She pointed to one of the banks they had thought dead, as it had been dark since they had entered.

Now a zigzag of lights streaked down it, to be as quickly gone. A second pattern flickered into life and vanished while they watched it. So small a thing, sparks of light coming and going swiftly. Yet somehow it was ominous, an alert they did not understand.

"Back—" Jarvas' voice was a whisper, as if he feared words could be picked up, read, understood by the machine that boxed them in. And Ayyar shared that feeling for the moment. An enemy one might see, that came openly, a kalcrok, one of the false Ift or an animated space suit, could be faced with firmness of purpose. But lights on a computer board, meant to awaken some menace, they were certain—that was another matter.

Three times those lights drew a design on the board, and each time the sequence was different, as was the color. For the first time they had been a light blue, the second a darker, and the third time purple. Ayyar knew that the others were as tense, using all their senses for any intimation of present danger.

"Myrik—where do you place the master controls?" Jarvas whispered.

"They can be anyplace. I am not expert on alien computers."

"Ayyar, do you feel any pull from a source of power?" The Mirrormaster rounded on him.

He raised the sword and pointed it to the board that had just come to life. He could feel his own form of force surge through his body, as if it fretted at the bonds of flesh now containing it—would be free to meet, in some flare of incandescence, that other and alien power.

Closing his eyes, he tried to measure that ebb and

flow of energy, turning slowly, blindly, using the sword as a pointer to hunt out the center of *That*. There was a slight change as he turned to the right, so slight that he could not actually be sure he had felt anything. He took another fraction of a turn, *was* aware of a difference, for now he was rent by a rising storm. He might have cried out; he was not sure, but still he turned. Ebb, to be followed again by flow, now ebb—complete quiet. Ayyar opened his eyes. Now he faced a dead portion of the banks, crisscrossed by the old scars, with no signs of repair.

Eyes closed once more—why that was needful he did not know—but self-blinded he was more inwardly aware of that other force. Turn—flow—to a lesser degree, turn, ebb, flow, sharp and strong, lessening—dead. Then, following so quickly on the dead that he swayed and nearly fell, strong, very strong, flow, flow, ebb, flow—

Yes, by so much could he chart the life of the banks, but that also the others could see and hear for themselves. He was about to say this when Illylle spoke.

"Try underfoot."

Why she suggested that Ayyar did not know. He took a step or so along, and the sword dipped in his hold, its tip not now pointing to the banks but to the floor. Again he made that slow swing to face each wall. Ebb and flow again, as above—

Then he was being pulled forward as if the sword were a rope, the end drawn by a port machine. This time Ayyar could not save himself against the urgency but went to his knees, and as the sword point dug into the flooring, Ayyar opened his eyes. He was at the foot of the ladder down which they had come. And from his sword point sparks arose higher and higher, while under the tip the floor began to glow red. He dared not watch; the glow hurt his Ift eyes. The sword sank,

as if the floor were soft sand, to engulf the blade and
finally the arm of its bearer.

"Move it to cut!" Jarvas knelt beyond that fire of
sparks. He put out a hand as if to lay it on the sword
hilt, then flinched back.

Only half understanding, Ayyar tried to move the
blade. It yielded a little so he was cutting through the
substance of the floor, or was that merely melting away
from any contact with the blade? Wider grew the hole.
He thrust right, left, forward, back, enlarging it yet
more. Now he must jerk back himself to escape a puff
of heat coming from the red and glowing edges of that
opening.

Out of him flowed the energy that had been pent
in his body. He could almost watch it going into the
sword, helping to open this door. Now the opening was
large enough for a man, and the smell of molten metal
a fog.

"On the stairs—watch out!" He did not know which
of them shouted that warning. A beam cut down, struck
across the edge of the hole, touched the sparks of the
sword force, flashed up in a great burst of light.

Ayyar cried out, blinded. He could not drop the
sword that moved, pulling him after it. Heat seared
his body, pain such as he had not known could
exist— He fell, blind, the sword a great weight he
could not master or loose. He struck something
below, close below, and lay there writhing in pain. Still
the sword was heavy, inert; he could not even stir the
hand that held it. And again energy flowed out of him.
He could smell burning—acrid—choking—

He sat by the game board, and on that board shone
brightly all those curious lines, squares, and dots he
could not read. *That*, which had been his opponent
there, which he had never seen, only sensed—yes, *It*
was there, but *It* no longer heeded him. *It* had—not

retreated, no—*It* had closed into *Itself*. When he looked down upon the board, all those figures—the space suits, the Larsh, the others—were overturned, rolling. Now and then one rose, only to topple.

On his side, though the trees—the thin line of Iftin—trembled and shook, they did not fall or roll.

And *That* which had played the unknown game so confidently—*It* drew farther and farther in upon *Itself*. Yet *It* was still to be feared, for now *It* was mad—mad!

Arms about him, holding him—the board vanished. He must say it aloud—

"*It*—is—mad—"

They were pulling at him, racking his body with pain. He could not see—

"Let—me—" But they did not listen to his pleas, and he was an empty thing, hollow of all save the energy he had held, so that he could not beg or fight those hands.

"To the air—can you bring him? Look out! Blast that one—now move!"

Words without meaning uttered in high voices. Words did not matter—nothing mattered. He was lost and empty and knew only pain that was sometimes sharp, sometimes dull, but always a part of him. After a space it was in his chest, so he choked and coughed and choked again. And this added to the pain. He longed for the dark to shut it out.

"Look—*It* has gone crazy— Oh—" Shrill that voice, so shrill and high as to pierce his dark. "The trees— Rizak, look out for the trees!"

Ayyar could breathe better now. There was a difference in the air. Hands still on him, holding him tight. Liquid dripped into his mouth, cool on his lips and chin as it dribbled out again. He swallowed. It was cool inside him, too.

Coolness on his eyes, soothing their burning. He drew a breath that was a little broken sigh, relaxed.

Around him was a sickening lurch of earth, a grinding—then a shrill screaming from farther off. He could not move, though in him worked a ferment to be up and running, away from this mad place. The arms that held him tightened, bringing stabbing pains to his chest and shoulder. Ayyar tried to cry out, but any sound he might make was lost in the surrounding tumult. Again the earth heaved, there were crashes—

He blinked, trying to clear his dim sight. Shadows moved against a lighter surface. Something large and black flew past—he heard another cracking—splintering—

"Out! Out of this trap!" That came at his ear. He was raised and carried between two others, his feet helplessly bumping against the ground.

They paused, holding him upright. The ground no longer swung sickeningly underfoot, yet still he waited for that to happen again. They were fumbling about his body, pulling a band tight under his arms. He was hauled aloft, the pressure of that band causing such agony that once more he plunged into a blackness of nothing at all save the blessed ceasing of torment.

"Ayyar—Ayyar—"

He lay in the hold of a ship, frozen, dead. He was Naill Renfro who had sold himself into labor on a distant world. But he had awakened before his time, and now he was dying deep in the emigrant capsule, his lungs denied air, his flesh freezing in the cold of space. He strove to fling out his hands, his arms, break open that coffin for a few moments of life—of—

Dark—but no longer cold. There was moisture in his mouth, soothing, more on his eyes, his face. They had heard him in the ship and had come to save him. Not death between the stars—but life!

He opened his eyes as that cooling substance was withdrawn. He could see—mistily—but still he could see!

No ship's officer, no medico bent over him. An oval face, green of skin, large eyes set slantingly in it. A delicate face, in its way fair. No eyebrows, no lashes, no hair above the wide brow—

"Ayyar—" Those lips shaped a word.

Ayyar? Greeting, inquiry, name? He wanted to ask which, but he could not find the energy to speak.

Another figure behind the one bending over him rose out of the ground. Like unto the first—still different—

"How is he?"

"Awake, I think—" Doubt from that first one, the nearest.

"Ayyar?" The newcomer dropped beside him, a green hand passed before his eyes, and he watched it move.

"He sees!" There was satisfaction in that as the tester straightened. "Ayyar?" More demanding now.

Ayyar? Who, what, was Ayyar? Ayyar of Iftcan! Triumphantly his memory supplied so much. He—was—Ayyar! He was pleased, excited at that discovery.

"He knows—he is Ayyar once again!" The first of the green people—Green People? Iftin! Again his mind sluggishly supplied a name and knew it to be the proper one.

"Ayyar, we must go!"

The taller of the two drew him up and let him lean against his shoulder to look out dizzily on what lay below. The ground swung wildly and then steadied. Red and black, churned earth, stirred together as one might mix the ground if one were a giant and set to work with a paddle or a sword of force—

Sword? His hand went out—seeking. "Sword?" He was not sure he asked that aloud, but perhaps he did, for she who faced him, concern in her eyes, made answer swiftly:

"It is gone—when it met *That*. Kymon's blade did not do as well in its time as that which Ayyar bore—"

"Later will come the weaving of legends," he who supported Ayyar said. "Now let us go, if still we can."

Another man came to aid him who held Ayyar. He looked from one to the other. Memory again gave Ayyar names.

"Jarvas—Kelemark—"

They smiled at him eagerly, as if that naming gave them pleasure. But the smiles did not last, for they must go down into the torn land and make their way through it.

Ayyar thought he dreamed sometimes as they made their slow and painful journey, for it seemed to him that once they hid in a cut in the ground as a hurtling thing, squeaking and groaning, rocketed by. And again they crouched among rocks as green people, like unto the Iftin, yet very different inwardly, struggled blindly, seizing upon one another with fierce tearing, or rushed headlong into rocks, making a wild, mad battlefield of a place where light hurt his eyes so he must close them tight. But none of this was real, nor did he fear what he saw.

The world began with a green covering. Thin was that covering, a small lacing of budding leaves along stem and branch, and through that delicate pattern came the silver of the moon to rest on his face. He breathed in subtle scents, and in him Ayyar awakened fully, so that though his body did not have the strength when he strove to move, yet his mind was clear, and ᵉ could recall the past—some of it.

His struggle to sit up must have summoned her, for Illylle came to him and knelt, carrying in her hand a wooden bottle. She gave him to drink, holding it quickly to his lips a second time when he would have asked questions. Once more the sap revived, and he let it do its work, coursing through his body. Then he braced himself up with his hands. They were in a glade of a forest or wood, and spring was there. Was this a dream—?

"Where are we?" he asked, for somehow it was important to be sure they were free of the burrows.

Illylle sat back upon her heels, smiling at him, one hand tamping the stopper well into the bottle.

"In the wilderness to the north."

"Iftcan!"

"No. Iftcan is not and will not be again." There was a shadow on her face. "It cannot be again, for a new rooting is needed, not a graft upon the old—"

Ayyar did not try to puzzle out her answer. For the time he was content they were in the woods again, Iftcan or no. But that content did not hold long. When the others came through the aisles of budding trees, he wanted to know more.

"We have won the victory against *That*," Jarvas said. "Or rather the power granted by Thanth won it, for your sword—with its energy—ate to the center of the computer, burned it out. But *That* went mad when the controls were cut. And we do not yet know what remains. The false Iftin, the machines *It* took as servants—they, too, went mad and destroyed themselves. How it fares with those it captured, we do not yet know. A party has gone to the port. If they find the false off-worlders there and also uncontrollable, they will do what they can to take over. What has happened, how far the curse set upon Janus has passed—" He shook his head.

"This much is true. We have finished *That* for all

time, for with *Its* heart burnt out *It* can never rebuild *Itself* again. The chaos *It* has left is wide wreckage. If we cannot free those *It* captured, and we may not be able to do so, then we have a second plan. We shall leave a tape at the port stating all that has happened and also beam an off-world distress signal. Our own secret that we are changelings—we shall keep yet awhile. But we can treat with any who come as natives of Janus. Only, until such arrive, we shall retreat overseas—if nothing can be done for the prisoners."

He looked beyond Ayyar as if he sought something, to find it missing, and regretted that, but was willing to put aside his regret.

"Iftcan is gone, not to rise again. We do not know how much of Iftin past lies in the wreckage of the Waste and *That*'s domain. Perhaps with off-world aid we can learn. We shall raise a new nation, and one that will not have the canker of *That* eating at it. But for one day, one task. Seeding, growing cannot be hurried—to try that is to fail."

He fell silent, and Ayyar, who must forget that he was ever Naill, lifted his head to the night wind. It was cool, sweet with all the promise of spring. They rested in the wreckage of a world, yet around them grew strong new life to which they were akin. And in him, just as that energy from the Mirror had risen, so did another renewing begin. Iftcan was dead to them, yes. But the Great Crowns would rise again, and there would be songs sung there of the remembrance of this time down a long, long trail of years, though legend might twist and turn the tale so that false would in time bury true.

> "Iftin sword, Iftin hand,
> Iftin heart, Iftin kind.

Forged in the dark,
Cooled by the moon,
Bane of evil, final doom.
Borne by a warrior who will stand
Before the Enemy, blade in hand—"

Illylle was singing, gaily, almost tenderly, as if her thoughts marched side by side, sword comrade with his. Ayyar shook his head.

"I am not Kymon, and I was not alone. No hero song for me."

Jarvas laughed. "Leave judgment to the future. Now, shall we be about the needs of the present?"

He held out his hand, Ayyar grasped it, and the Mirrormaster's strength drew him to his feet. His other hand went out to Illylle. And they went from that glade singing the song of Kymon, as was fitting on a day of such victory.

BAEN

DAVID WEBER

The Honor Harrington series: *(cont.)*

Field of Dishonor
Honor goes home to Manticore—and fights for her life on a battlefield she never trained for, in a private war that offers just two choices: death—or a "victory" that can end only in dishonor and the loss of all she loves. . . .

Flag in Exile
Hounded into retirement and disgrace by political enemies, Honor Harrington has retreated to planet Grayson, where powerful men plot to reverse the changes she has brought to their world. And for their plans to succeed, Honor Harrington must die!

Honor Among Enemies
Offered a chance to end her exile and again command a ship, Honor Harrington must use a crew drawn from the dregs of the service to stop pirates who are plundering commerce. Her enemies have chosen the mission carefully, thinking that either she will stop the raiders or they will kill her . . . and either way, her enemies will win. . . .

In Enemy Hands
After being ambushed, Honor finds herself aboard an enemy cruiser, bound for her scheduled execution. But one lesson Honor has never learned is how to give up!

Echoes of Honor
"Brilliant! Brilliant! Brilliant!"—*Anne McCaffrey*

continued ☞

DAVID WEBER

The Honor Harrington series: *(cont.)*

Ashes of Victory
Honor has escaped from the prison planet called
Hell and returned to the Manticoran Alliance, to
the heart of a furnace of new weapons, new
strategies, new tactics, spies, diplomacy, and
assassination.

War of Honor
No one wanted another war. Neither the Republic
of Haven, nor Manticore—and certainly not
Honor Harrington. Unfortunately, what they
wanted didn't matter.

AND DON'T MISS—
—the Honor Harrington <u>anthologies</u>, with stories
from David Weber, John Ringo, Eric Flint, Jane
Lindskold, and more!

HONOR HARRINGTON BOOKS by DAVID WEBER

On Basilisk Station	(HC) 57793-X /$18.00	☐
	(PB) 72163-1 / $7.99	☐
The Honor of the Queen	72172-0 / $7.99	☐
The Short Victorious War	87596-5 / $6.99	☐
	7434-3551-6 /$14.00	☐
Field of Dishonor	87624-4 / $6.99	☐

continued ☞

PRAISE FOR
LOIS McMASTER BUJOLD

What the critics say:

The Warrior's Apprentice: "Now here's a fun romp through the spaceways—not so much a space opera as space ballet.... it has all the 'right stuff.' A lot of thought and thoughtfulness stand behind the all-too-human characters. Enjoy this one, and look forward to the next." —Dean Lambe, *SF Reviews*

"The pace is breathless, the characterization thoughtful and emotionally powerful, and the author's narrative technique and command of language compelling. Highly recommended."
—*Booklist*

Brothers in Arms: " ...she gives it a genuine depth of character, while reveling in the wild turnings of her tale.... Bujold is as audacious as her favorite hero, and as brilliantly (if sneakily) successful." —*Locus*

"Miles Vorkosigan is such a great character that I'll read anything Lois wants to write about him.... a book to re-read on cold rainy days." —Robert Coulson, *Comic Buyer's Guide*

Borders of Infinity: "Bujold's series hero Miles Vorkosigan may be a lord by birth and an admiral by rank, but a bone disease that has left him hobbled and in frequent pain has sensitized him to the suffering of outcasts in his very hierarchical era.... Playing off Miles's reserve and cleverness, Bujold draws outrageous and outlandish foils to color her high-minded adventures." —*Publishers Weekly*

Falling Free: "In *Falling Free* Lois McMaster Bujold has written her fourth straight superb novel.... How to break down a talent like Bujold's into analyzable components? Best not to try. Best to say: 'Read, or you will be missing something extraordinary.' " —Roland Green, *Chicago Sun-Times*

The Vor Game: "The chronicles of Miles Vorkosigan are far ⎼oo witty to be literary junk food, but they rouse the kind of ⎼ving that makes popcorn magically vanish during a double ⎼e." —Faren Miller, *Locus*

MORE PRAISE FOR
LOIS McMASTER BUJOLD

What the readers say:

"My copy of *Shards of Honor* is falling apart I've reread it so often. . . . I'll read whatever you write. You've certainly proved yourself a grand storyteller."

—Lisa Kolbe, Colorado Springs, CO

"I experience the stories of Miles Vorkosigan as almost viscerally uplifting. . . . But certainly, even the weightiest theme would have less impact than a cinder on snow were it not for a rousing good story, and good story-telling with it. This is the second thing I want to thank you for. . . . I suppose if you boiled down all I've said to its simplest expression, it would be that I immensely enjoy and admire your work. I submit that, as literature, your work raises the overall level of the science fiction genre, and spiritually, your work cannot avoid positively influencing all who read it."

—Glen Stonebraker, Gaithersburg, MD

" 'The Mountains of Mourning' [in *Borders of Infinity*] was one of the best-crafted, and simply best, works I'd ever read. When I finished it, I immediately turned back to the beginning and read it again, and I can't remember the last time I did that."

—Betsy Bizot, Lisle, IL

"I can only hope that you will continue to write, so that I can continue to read (and of course buy) your books, for they make me laugh and cry and think . . . rare indeed."

—Steven Knott, Major, USAF

What Do You Say?